TIME REVOLUTION
Book 3 of the Marc McKnight Time Travel Adventures

By Kim Megahee

The Kimmer Group

GAINESVILLE, GA

Kimberly Megahee/The Kimmer Group
Gainesville, GA
www.AuthorKimMegahee.com

Publisher's Note: This is a work of fiction. Names, characters, places, and incidents are a product of the author's imagination. Locales and public names are sometimes used for atmospheric purposes. Any resemblance to actual people, living or dead, or to businesses, companies, events, institutions, or locales is completely coincidental.

Book Layout © 2017 BookDesignTemplates.com

Book Title/ Author Name. -- 1st ed.
Paperback ISBN: 978-1-7340190-4-9
eBook   ISBN: 978-1-7340190-5-6

Dedication

"Time Revolution" is dedicated to my amazing wife Martha, who is always in my corner and keeps me on my toes. Life with her is a great adventure every day and I can't wait to see what's next.

Cover Design By
Aleaca / 99Designs.com
Vesna Tišma

*Don't worry about your heart, it will last you
as long as you live.*

—W. C. FIELDS

Acknowledgements

There are always too many people to thank.

First and foremost, I want to thank my amazing wife Martha Rice Megahee, who knows me better than anyone else on the planet. She has been a fountain of ideas and suggestions for this book. We think so much alike, it's pretty scary.

I want to thank my extended family for all the support they've given me over the years.

Thanks to retired Army Rangers Colonel John Cornelson and Major Randall E. Batson for the military protocols and relationships. Any discrepancies from actual military workings are my misunderstandings, not their errors.

Thanks to my beta readers. In alphabetic order, they are Thomas Bing, Mac McDaniel, Ben Meeks, Martha Megahee, Mary Ann Megahee, Renee Propes, and Jerry Sloane. They're a very diverse group of successful individuals with a wide assortment of skills. They found grammar, punctuation, and plot errors I missed, and made some great suggestions that made this book much better than it would have been. Thanks to Aleaca (Vesna Tisma) from 99Designs for the cover design. This is the third cover she has done for me and they have all been stunning.

CHAPTER 1

Thursday, November 16, 1786 — 11:55 am — The Great Smoky
Mountains, Northern Virginia

Hiding under the leaves in a forest was not Major Marc
McKnight's idea of fun. But doing it during a mission in the
Appalachian Mountains of Northern Virginia in 1786 was worse.

He followed normal protocols after time-jumping the 250 years
back to this date. After landing, he stood and did a three-sixty
assessment of this unfamiliar environment.

The mission plan called for him to land at the intersection of two
Indian trails.

One was a wide, much-traveled trail that ascended the mountain
from Harper's Ferry to a Cherokee Indian village. The narrower
crossing trail came from the mountain summit. It was much steeper
and leaped across the wider trail on its way downhill to the Potomac
River.

He'd been in this part of Virginia before, hiking with friends.

Just barely in Virginia, he corrected himself as mission planner
Kathy Wu pointed out.

His position was just south of Harper's Ferry where, one day, the
future states of Virginia, West Virginia, and Maryland would meet.

Most of the season's brilliant leaf colors now lay on the forest
floor. The few leaves still on the trees rattled in a light breeze. The
earthy smell of Virginia mountain forest filled his nostrils.

He could hear sounds in the distance — voices, laughter, and
cooking utensils — from the Indian village up the hill.

Made it. I'm in the right place. Now to head back toward Mount Vernon to scope out the travel routes from there to the Cumberland area.

Before he took ten steps, he heard sounds coming up the trail. The mission plan called for avoidance of interaction with locals, so he left the trail and hid underneath the leaves five yards off the trail. Concealment wasn't his forte, but every Army Ranger has exposure to stealth techniques.

With a little luck, they'll pass by quickly and I can move on.

From his hiding place, McKnight could see the trail sections in front of him. Two Indian families made the sounds he heard, traveling together and making their way up to the Cherokee village. The Indians themselves made surprisingly little sound. Their horses' hooves and their sleds made the noise as they scraped across the rocky ground of the trail.

He decided to wait fifteen minutes after the Indians passed before moving. Another small band walked by ten minutes later. He reset his internal timer. Five minutes later, three braves with long rifles and game bags passed his position.

McKnight chuckled to himself.

This trail is the 1786 version of Interstate 81.

If the foot traffic subsided for a few minutes, he would continue the mission, but with a modified plan. Traveling on this trail wasn't an option. The volume of traffic was too high to avoid significant contact with locals. He didn't speak Cherokee and didn't sound like a colonist or a frontiersman.

McKnight asked himself again why he, the team leader, had given himself this mission. Of course, he knew the answer. He was the best choice for several reasons.

At six feet in stature, he was tall for this era in history. But his dark brown hair and brown eyes came from a full-blooded Cayuse great grandmother on his mother's side.

None of the rest of his team were a fit for this mission. Captain Tyler was on his honeymoon. Lieutenant Wheeler was Hispanic with a Detroit accent. And Lieutenant Hatcher was… gone.

This time-jump was reconnaissance for a future mission. Later this year, retired General George Washington would travel through these woods on the way to the Cumberland region, looking for a viable commerce route.

But now, the recon mission was in jeopardy.

McKnight didn't need his watch to know he had been under the leaves for four hours. The sun had climbed from just over the horizon to directly overhead in the November sky. His legs itched like crazy. There was no telling what kinds of ants or other insects were crawling on him, not to mention other potential vermin. At least he was warm, but otherwise he was uncomfortable.

While lying here in the leaves, he saw his share of animals. A dozen deer, two black bears.

There was a lull of fifteen minutes in the trail traffic. He needed to move. His body was stiff from remaining motionless for so long. His joints and muscles screamed to stretch and be moving.

He hated to do it, but he was ready to call this mission a wash and a failure. For the next try, he'd get Kathy to find another place where it wasn't so damned crowded.

The hair on the back of his neck stood up. He thought he heard something up the hill behind him. It was almost imperceptible, but he felt another presence.

With the excruciating slowness required to sustain his hiding place, he turned his head to the left. There, ten feet away, was a snake. He's seen several today, but this one was much closer and appeared to be staring right at him. He guessed it smelled him and was trying to decide what manner of prey was hiding in the leaves.

It was a large reptile. Or at least its proximity made it seem that way. Its head was rust-colored, and the body was rust and pale pink.

The head was V-shaped. Kathy briefed him on the indigenous poisonous snakes, and this one was most likely a copperhead.

Go away!

He knew the snake couldn't read his mind, but he couldn't help thinking the command.

The snake moved ever so slightly. It gathered its coils beneath it and raised its head, apparently to get a better look.

Oh, shit. Go away!

The snake moved closer, almost imperceptibly. But the move wasn't lost on McKnight.

He had weapons. His pistol was next to his hand, but he didn't want to use it. Without the dampening effect of leaves on the trees, every human within a mile would hear the report and he didn't need that kind of attention.

His knife was at his hip and was the preferred weapon, but he didn't want the snake to be close enough for him to use it.

But the snake didn't agree. It moved closer. It was only five feet away now. It wasn't close enough to strike yet, but it was definitely interested and edged closer to him.

It happened so fast, McKnight flinched. A long knife severed the snake's head from its body. McKnight saw two legs clothed in buckskin land next to him in the same instant.

The danger from the snake was over, but McKnight's instinctive move ensured that his presence was no longer a secret.

He rolled away from the legs and came to his feet.

Before him was a young brave. McKnight knew most people in this era were shorter than present-day humans, but this Indian was an exception.

He was taller than McKnight. He was warmly dressed, but McKnight was sure the man was built like Superman's kid underneath his buckskin and fur. A long rifle and a game bag lay on the ground behind him.

The brave looked McKnight up and down, then shrugged off the robe that covered his shoulders.

That's not good.

McKnight was a stranger here and engaged in stealth. He'd be perceived as an enemy. What else could the young brave believe?

McKnight raced through his options. The large man before him would not know martial art techniques. That was an advantage. But Indian fighting was unconventional and influenced by personal style. Or at least it was in Oregon where he grew up. That was a disadvantage.

They faced off for only a second before the young brave charged. He still had the bloody long knife in his right hand and tried to deliver a slashing stroke as he approached. McKnight stepped toward him, caught his knife hand with both hands, spun and dragged his attacker over his right hip. He stripped the knife from the Indian's hand in the process. His attacker went airborne and landed on his back in the middle of the trail.

McKnight jumped down the slope onto the trail. The Indian had regained his feet and now looked embarrassed and angry.

He smiled at McKnight and let out an articulated whoop.

Calling for help.

He guessed the brave was younger than he looked and inexperienced at fighting.

But not inexperienced enough to be stupid.

From the uphill vicinity of the Indian village, McKnight heard answering whoops. The alarm was raised.

The young brave whooped again and smiled broadly at McKnight.

Help is coming.

He guessed the help was less than 300 yards away. If he wasn't gone in thirty seconds, he'd be captured.

When I press the recall button, it'll take fifteen seconds to fire.

McKnight needed to get away from the brave to initiate travel. He couldn't risk allowing the young man to be hurt or killed by contact with the time bubble.

Not to mention that the Indian was merely protecting his village from a perceived enemy.

This time, as the young brave attacked, McKnight sidestepped and pushed him off the trail and down the hill. His momentum carried the young man ten yards down the slope below the trail. McKnight guessed the young brave would be unable to negotiate the slippery leaves and steep slope before he could time-jump.

He pulled out his travel beacon and clicked it. The welcome bubble of brilliant white swirling air surrounded him.

He looked up the trail toward the village and saw four Indians sprinting down the rocky path toward him. He took a deep breath and expelled it with relief.

I'll be gone before they can get here.

McKnight turned back to check on the young brave, but not quick enough to avoid being knocked to the ground. The kid was faster than he expected and oblivious to the pulsating time bubble.

They rolled on the ground together with the bubble now encasing them both. After a moment, the Indian leaped up and backed up a step.

He's confused by the time bubble.

McKnight did a quick mental calculation.

He's too close. If the time bubble fires now, he's dead.

McKnight took three steps backward to move the bubble away from the young brave.

The Indian hesitated for a second, then leapt forward to attack. He hit McKnight like a linebacker in a pass rush. McKnight had no choice if the brave was to survive.

He grabbed the young man in a bear hug. The Indian tried to bite him, but McKnight head-butted him in the face, breaking his nose. Stunned, the Indian slumped. Blood gushed over his lips and chin.

McKnight glanced at the approaching Indians in time to see one of them stop and raise his long rifle. The others continued running toward him, but slanted to the side to give the other a clear shot. But then the time bubble bulged and dissipated.

McKnight and the young brave fell backward through a field of stars.

****

Sunday, November 16, 2036 — 12:02 pm — HERO Team Lab, Alexandria, Virginia

Trevor George and Doctor Kathy Wu waited in the HERO Team Lab for McKnight to return from 1786. As always, team members took shifts on watch in the Lab while a time travel mission was in progress.

Congress created the Historical Event Research Organization within the U.S. Army, but it required at least one planner to be a civilian. General Drake selected Kathy Wu when the team was first formed because of her eidetic memory, her expertise in history and politics, and her uncanny ability to read people.

Kathy and Army Captain Winston Tyler were the two mission planners for the team.

Kathy stood about 5'4" and her inky hair was nearly always pulled back in a ponytail. She was born in Washington DC in the Chinatown district. In college, she majored in Psychology and minored in Business Computing. Her doctorate was in Politics. She loved to quote lines from old movies whenever she had the chance.

Trevor George was the newest member of the HERO Team. Before he joined, he was a cold case investigator for the Atlanta Police Department. He assisted with the HERO Team's first mission and General Drake invited him to join after he showed superior analytical skills in his support role.

Trevor was curious about everything. Any mystery or puzzle interested him, whether it was scientific, relational, or a clue to a case. Other than that, he was average — 5'9", 175 pounds with curly reddish-brown hair and brown eyes.

Some people believed Trevor accepted the job because of the excitement and challenge associated with time travel. Others believed it was his attraction to Kathy Wu. If you asked Trevor, he would smile and admit both were excellent reasons.

The HERO Team Lab was the size of a small gymnasium. The Lab and the team's offices were in the temporary Defense Logistics Agency facility on Telegraph Road near Alexandria, Virginia.

Dr. Robert Astalos, the inventor of time travel, had an office and conference room in the Lab. He spent half his time on site and the rest on other projects.

Dr. Astalos' office and conference room were in the east end of the Lab. On the north side were the loading dock doors, one primary and operational Time Engine, two backup Engines under construction, and a row of storage lockers. A break and huddle area with tables and chairs dominated the center of the room. On the west side was a kitchen and a staircase with access to the roof. The secure entry to the rest of the team's offices was in the south wall.

Kathy was the first to notice the static electricity increase in the room. The primary Time Engine switched on and hummed with increasing pitch and volume.

"Well, here he comes," she said.

"Yup," Trevor said.

The time bubble formed with two figures inside it.

"Damn," Trevor said. "He's got company with him."

He sprinted to the storage cabinet and brought back two sleep bulbs.

The brilliant white air within the bubble spun furiously, whipping the two men's clothing and hair about them like a violent windstorm.

Through the blinding light of the time bubble, Kathy recognized one figure as McKnight and that the two men were fighting.

The bubble pulsated, then bulged to twice its previous size and winked out. The travel momentum threw the two men to the floor.

The room seemed dark now without the bubble's brilliant light. Trevor bounded onto the travel platform and squeezed the sleep bulb in the Indian's face. The young brave blinked in surprise and collapsed, unconscious.

McKnight untangled himself from the Indian's limp form and stood.

"Thank you," he said.

"No problem. Did you bring him back here on purpose?"

"No, and yes. I didn't plan it, but it was that or let him get killed by the bubble."

Trevor chuckled. "Well, good. Can we send him back now, then?"

"Yes. Perfect."

"Okay, let's get it done before he wakes up so I don't have to dose him again. Give me your beacon so I can get the point of origin."

McKnight handed Trevor the beacon. Trevor took it with him to the Engine Console.

Kathy came to the edge of the platform and stood in front of McKnight.

"Are you okay, Major? No injuries?"

"No," he said. He stepped off the platform and sat at a table. "Just some insect bites and a bruise or two. I'll make it."

Kathy sat next to him. "Good. Do you have all your equipment, Major? Nothing left behind?"

McKnight straightened. "Yes, sorry. I have everything I took with me. And I brought nothing back…" He pointed back over his shoulder at the Time Engine platform. "Except this guy."

When the time bubble appeared on the platform behind them, they turned toward it. The bubble bulged and disappeared with a loud crack. The sleeping Indian was on his way back to 1786.

Trevor came to the table and sat with them. "Mission accomplished?" he asked.

"No. I didn't even get started."

McKnight turned to Kathy. "I landed on the trail we targeted. Your research was perfect. Unfortunately, the traffic on the trail was much more than we expected. We have to find another landing place if we want to avoid contact with locals. I spent the day hiding from them until…" He pointed at the platform. "Junior there showed up. We need to rethink our landing place on this one."

"Bummer," said Kathy, smiling at him. "I guess somebody will have to go back in the next few days to complete it."

"Yes. I think scouting Washington's route is still a good idea. We just need a new starting place."

"Exactly," Trevor said. He sighed and smiled at Kathy.

Kathy thought McKnight looked sad. It occurred to her that McKnight was thinking the same thing she was.

"Too bad Hatcher isn't here," Kathy said. "She would have loved to be a part of this mission."

"Yes, I know," McKnight said.

"I miss her," Kathy said. She patted McKnight's arm.

"I do, too," Trevor said.

McKnight stood. "Me, too. If you guys will excuse me, I need to go get cleaned up. I think I'll take the rest of the day off."

"Good idea," Kathy said. "You've put in more than a day's work and we learned something new."

"I know what I learned," McKnight said. "I learned not to hide under leaves for four hours. I'm afraid to count the insect bites."

"Go wash 1786 off yourself and go home," Kathy said. "And say hello to Megan for me."

CHAPTER 2

Situated just eight miles south of Washington DC, the city of Alexandria has a unique character. It has an Old Town section where the buildings are two centuries old, a modern downtown, government agency complexes, and office parks — all mingled with farms and cornfields.

The sky was gray, and snow was in the forecast for northern Virginia.

McKnight hung up the phone and turned to stare through his transparent office wall at the parking lot and the woods beyond it. As was his habit while thinking, he rested his feet on the credenza and put his hands behind his head.

Calls from the Hatchers were always depressing. His thoughts went back to that day when he lost their daughter. The family was reassuring to him and always reiterated it wasn't his fault. But as her commanding officer and the leader of the HERO Team, he felt a keen sense of responsibility for Karen Hatcher's disappearance.

Four months ago now, that day was as clear to him as if it had happened ten minutes ago.

They were working a case they stumbled upon by accident. A young girl was missing, and she appeared in a 25-year-old docudrama. It was a time travel crime. Someone kidnapped her, traveled her twenty-five years into the past, and murdered her to embarrass a young, up-and-coming politician. The team saved the girl and realized her murder was the tip of the iceberg of a bigger case.

Cindy Ginn was their new receptionist back then. She came to them with a glowing recommendation from her previous boss, a U.S. Senator. She sailed through her security clearances with flying colors. Nothing in her background suggested she could orchestrate the theft of one of their Time Engines. Their investigation proved she was an imposter, a time traveler, and a skilled operative. When the team exposed and confronted Ginn, she produced a knife and attempted to escape. Lieutenant Hatcher grabbed her from behind just before she time-jumped, and she swept Hatcher along with her to an unknown time. Minutes later, a separate attack disabled their only functioning Time Engine to prevent interference with Ginn's escape. The time travel technology she used suggested she was from the future.

Hatcher had been missing since that day. At McKnight's request, General Drake postponed their planned move to the DLA Headquarters building so they could focus on finding her.

In the days after Hatcher's disappearance, they had hopes of using technology to track Ginn's time jump. Time and time again, they thought they had a breakthrough, some idea that would help them locate and rescue Hatcher. But all the ideas and theories yielded no results.

The team's time scientists Robert and Robby Astalos worked an incredible number of hours to find a solution. When the excessive time spent affected their health, McKnight imposed a work schedule on them to prevent them from working themselves into exhaustion or sickness. After weeks without success, General Drake reluctantly reassigned Robby Astalos to the ongoing propulsion project.

Today, Hatcher's parents called and suggested McKnight give up the search and recognize Karen in a memorial service.

McKnight knew where they were coming from. They were a military family. Connie Hatcher was one of the first female Rangers in the U.S. Army and a general today. Richard Hatcher was a retired colonel from Special Forces.

It wasn't that they didn't love Karen. On the contrary, they were proud of her and were a close-knit family. But they had lost all hope of her returning. They were convinced their daughter was dead and they wanted the agony of uncertainty to end.

McKnight understood because he was losing hope, too. There was no way to resolve her status. Every contact with other military teams eventually led to a cautious question about the search for Lieutenant Hatcher. He knew the others were concerned, but the questions were increasingly discouraging and demoralizing for himself and his team.

He could only guess at how hard it was for her parents.

The truth was, he couldn't grant their request. Karen was MIA and her status couldn't change unless they found her body or the military declared her BNR — presumed dead; body not recovered. But there was no evidence to support either the BNR or KIA status, so Karen's status was in limbo. He grimaced at the thought.

Damned bureaucracy! Paralyzed because the situation was unprecedented.

The family wanted closure, and he couldn't offer it to them.

McKnight closed his eyes and let the memories come back again. Karen was a second generation female Ranger. She was intelligent and one of the best warfighters McKnight had ever known.

Hatcher and Mitch Wheeler were his Time Engine technicians. Both excelled in physics at the University of North Georgia and their skills bloomed under the tutelage of Doctor Astalos. When the HERO Team formed, McKnight hand-selected Wheeler and Hatcher.

The two lieutenants loved each other in the way soldiers do when they work, live, and fight together. Despite his name, Wheeler was Hispanic and his personality was outgoing and friendly. Hatcher was quiet but radiated internal resolve and strength. Their personal skills complemented one another and they were so in tune with each other, McKnight grew accustomed to thinking of them as a unit.

And now Hatcher was missing on his watch. If he hadn't selected her, she would still be alive.

Or at least she'd be here in this time.

That was the hard part. Was she a prisoner in some distant future time, locked away somewhere with no hope of rescue? Or was she already dead?

He couldn't think of a fresh way to approach the problem. He rubbed his eyes with the heels of his hands. Though he didn't know what to do next, he resolved to arrange a memorial service for the family. He was about ready to give up hope.

A knock on the door interrupted his thoughts. He kicked off from the credenza and whirled his chair to sit back at his desk. "Come," he said.

The door opened and Wheeler entered the room and came to attention.

"As you were, Lieutenant," McKnight said. "What's on your mind?"

Wheeler shifted his weight. "Permission to speak frankly, sir?"

"Of course. What?"

"I just talked to Colonel Hatcher, sir. I don't think we should do it, sir. Hold a funeral for Hatcher? It's only been a few months. That's crazy. She's still alive out there somewhere."

"It's not a funeral, Lieutenant. But, for the record, I agree with you. So... do you have any suggestions on how we might go on from here?"

Wheeler hesitated. He glanced at the ceiling, his eyes glistening with the tears he was holding back. He started to speak but couldn't.

McKnight stood and walked around the desk to stand at his side.

Wheeler cleared his throat and spoke with a shaky voice. "She was trying to protect me. And she paid the price for it."

McKnight remembered it well. In the confrontation with Ginn, Wheeler was the first to approach her, and she sliced his face with a knife. Hatcher grabbed the woman from behind, Ginn's time aura engulfed her, and they both vanished. That was the last they saw of Hatcher.

Wheeler's reflexes saved him from a deadly knife thrust to the neck. A skilled team of doctors repaired his damaged cheek and chin. But he still bore a thin scar across his chin that was more visible when he was under stress. Like now.

"Lieutenant?" McKnight said.

Wheeler looked away and McKnight continued. "Mitch."

"Sir, I—"

McKnight pointed to one of the side chairs in his office and sat on the edge of his desk. "Sit down, Mitch."

As Wheeler moved to the chair, McKnight continued. "It wasn't your fault. She was doing her job, just like you were."

"Yes, sir. I know that. But we can't just leave her out there." Wheeler turned toward McKnight. "We never leave one of ours behind. There has to be a way to find her."

"I know. Believe me, I know. The service is intended for the family. We haven't given up. But it doesn't look good, Mitch. I can't think of any more options or ideas. You know Doctor Astalos has worked hard, looking in the time frequency logs for something, anything, that might offer a clue. The future is unknown to us so far. You know Kathy and Trevor are plotting out history ideas to guess what timelines might lead to her, but it's all speculative. There's no genuine science behind it. We just don't have any path forward."

"Yes, sir, I know, but I can't... I just can't give up."

"I know you don't want to hear this, but we don't even know if Cindy's time travel plays by the same rules as ours. We can only access times that are a multiple of twenty-five years from the current date. And we think Cindy came from the future. Her technology was different and faster. Remember? We create a time bubble around the traveler. But she just had a thin aura around herself. When Hatcher grabbed her, the aura expanded to include her and took her. And I never saw her click a beacon. Did you? How do we know there aren't other differences? What if they've solved the twenty-five-year multiple problem? Or even trimmed a month off that limit? We just don't know. We have too many variables."

McKnight paused and looked at Wheeler. The lieutenant was staring at his hands in his lap.

McKnight sighed and softened his tone. "I'm not saying it's impossible. We just don't know enough yet. We won't stop, Mitch. But we need a break. Just a small one. Let's keep thinking about it."

Wheeler looked up at him. "Sir, I can't think about anything else."

McKnight came off the desk, walked around it and sat in his chair. "Yes, I know. It's hard for all of us, but especially for you, I know. You and Hatcher go way back to UNG. Working as closely as you have... I can't imagine how tough it is."

Wheeler leaned back in his chair.

"Lisa, my wife. She doesn't understand. She was never jealous of the bond Hatcher and I had. She loved her, too. But she told me she doesn't know how to help me with this and it's like there's another woman, only she can't compete with her because it's not the same thing. It's coming between us and neither of us know how to fix it."

"Yes," McKnight said. "I'm dealing with that, too, but not to the extent you are. Look, you have nothing earthshaking pending right now, do you? Why don't you take the rest of the day off? Go home and spend time with Lisa and little Terry. Go to the movies, go play putt-putt. Just leave this behind for a little while."

"I'll be okay, sir. Thanks for listening. I'll check with Doctor Astalos and see what he's working on."

McKnight stood. "Lieutenant, I don't think I made myself clear. Let me try again. Take the rest of the day off. That's an order."

Wheeler jumped up and came to attention. "Yes, sir."

"Is there anything else?"

"No, sir."

"Good. Get out of here."

"Yes, sir." Wheeler saluted and left McKnight's office.

McKnight walked back to the transparent wall and stared at the parking lot and the trees beyond it.

The tough thing about soldiers bonding is the mess it leaves when one of them is killed or gone missing. There's no fix for this.

His phone rang. He glanced at it, there on his desk. It vibrated across the desktop with each ring, a little song and dance that begged for attention.

It was that familiar sound that tugged at his heart. When he first set up that ring for his live-in girlfriend Megan, it excited him whenever he heard it. It brought a sense of joy to him he had never experienced. Since Hatcher disappeared, that joy slipped into dread. He loved Megan, but felt he was neglecting her since then. It was his fault, he knew, but he couldn't put it behind him. He could tell Wheeler it wasn't his fault, but he couldn't tell himself the same thing.

It is my fault. I chose Hatcher for the team and put her where she was when Cindy time-jumped and took her along.

The phone stopped ringing. He shook his head.

How do I fix this?

The familiar ring started again. He walked to the desk, picked up the phone and pressed the 'Answer' key. He stood by the office window, looking at the pine forest outside.

"Hi, Babe. How's your day been?" he said.

"Good. And yours?"

"Busy. Sorry I missed your call a few minutes ago. Mitch was in here talking to me."

"No problem. How's he doing? How's Lisa?"

"He's still suffering through this thing."

"I'm so sorry. Is there anything we can do?"

"Unfortunately no. I got another call from the Hatchers. They want a memorial service for Karen."

"Oh," she said. "They've given up on her? It's only been four months."

"I don't think they want to, but they're hurting because they just don't know where she is and what happened to her. I think they're trying to find some peace about it."

"Uh-huh. I can see how much it bothers you and Mitch. I can't imagine what it's like for them."

"Me, either. The idea upset Mitch quite a bit. He sees it as giving up on her."

"I can see that, too. I wish… well, you know."

"Yes, I do."

She paused. "Are you coming home early or at the regular time?"

She's asking me if I'm staying late at the office again tonight.

"I'm still taking care of some things. I'm not sure yet."

"Okay. I was hoping we could go out to dinner as we planned last week."

McKnight put his phone on speaker so he could check his calendar.

That wasn't tonight, was it?

He paged through his calendar.

Megan said nothing. He found the entry and sighed.

"Well," he said. "There isn't anything happening today that I can't push off until tomorrow. I'll leave here in the next 30 minutes."

"Okay," she said. "It'll be nice to get out and have a change of scenery."

"Yes, it will." He leaned against the wall and focused on his tone of voice. "Baby, I know it hasn't been easy for you these last few months. I invited you up from Atlanta to live with me, took you away from friends and family, and what do you get? Not enough. I'm sorry."

There was silence on the line for a few seconds. "I know. I just want to spend more time with you. Is that so bad?"

"No, not at all. I'll try to do better. It's just hard to cope with something like this."

"You feel it deeply. These people aren't just your team. They're your extended family. You care about them. I wouldn't love you so much if you didn't. We'll get through this together."

"Thanks, Babe. You don't know what it means to have you here with me... I just can't tell you..."

"Yes, I know. Hurry home. I'm waiting for you. Love you."

"You, too. Bye."

"Bye," she said and disconnected the line.

McKnight looked out the window again but saw nothing beyond his thoughts.

I've got to figure out how to get past this.

****

Tuesday, November 18th, 2036 — 8:32am — DLA Telegraph Road Office Parking Lot, Alexandria, Virginia

McKnight drove his Ford F-150 into the parking lot and saw Trevor and Kathy standing next to his reserved spot. He pulled in and lowered the window as Trevor and Kathy approached the driver side.

"What's up, Trevor?" he said.

"I'm glad you're here," Kathy said. "He wouldn't tell me anything until you were here with us."

Trevor nodded. "That's because I didn't want to have to go over this twice."

"Okay," McKnight said. "Then shall we go inside and talk, or is there a reason you wanted to meet in the parking lot? Can I at least have a cup of coffee?"

"Sure," Trevor said. "We'll get us both one, and a hot tea for Kathy on the way."

"On the way? Where?" McKnight said.

"Yes, where?" Kathy said.

"On the way to the J. Edgar Hoover Building downtown. We'll hit the Starbucks down the street," Trevor said. He looked from

McKnight to Kathy and back. "It's important. I think you'll be glad you came. I checked your calendar first, Marc. You have a meeting this afternoon, but we'll be back before then."

McKnight studied Trevor's face for a moment. "Well, okay then. Jump in," he said, and tapped the door unlock button on the console.

Trevor and Kathy dashed around to the passenger side of the truck and opened the door. Kathy slipped into the back seat and stretched out across it. Trevor sat in the front. McKnight backed out of his parking space and left the building, headed for downtown DC.

Kathy glanced at her watch. "At this time of day, it should take us an hour to get there and find a parking place. And if you plan to be secretive until we get there, I'm taking a nap."

"It's not that," Trevor said. "I think they have evidence of serious time-related crime events, but I don't want to bias you with my opinion."

McKnight pulled into Starbucks and turned to Trevor. "Yet you thought it important enough to go learn more right away."

"Yes."

"Then you buy the coffee and the tea. It's the least you can do."

Kathy laughed. "That's right. Make mine a mint tea. No cream."

Trevor grinned at her. "I know what you want in your tea, smart-ass."

Kathy giggled.

"I'll be right back," he said. Trevor got out and jogged into the store.

McKnight turned so he could see Kathy in the back seat. "You don't know what this meeting is about?"

"No," she said, "but something's bugging him. He talked to them on the phone early this morning and now he can't wait to get there."

"Well, I guess we'll find out soon enough. Damn, I was looking forward to catching up on things today. Whatever it is, I hope it's more informational than actionable. I have enough to do, working on the Washington mission."

"Maybe, but I can't see Trevor pulling you along on this if it wasn't something you'd have to decide on, do you?"

"No, I don't. That's why I didn't pull rank and stay at the office. I guess we'll find out. Maybe a senator lost a dog."

Kathy laughed. "Yes, a big one."

CHAPTER 3

Tuesday, November 18th, 2036 — 9:45am — J. Edgar Hoover
Building, Washington DC

FBI Special Agent-In-Charge David Ritter met them in the J.
Edgar Hoover Building lobby.

"Thank you for coming, Major McKnight," he said, as he shook
McKnight's hand. "Hi, Trevor. And this must be Doctor Wu.
Charmed."

Kathy beamed, and Trevor nodded.

"Let's go up to my conference room," Ritter said. "I have data and
slides to show you."

He turned on his heel, and they followed him to the security desk
for visitor IDs and then to the elevator. Ritter punched the button for
the fourth floor and the elevator began its labored way up.

"First time in the Hoover Building?" he asked.

McKnight nodded.

"Yes," Kathy said.

"I may have been here before. Looks familiar," Trevor said.

Ritter laughed. "Sorry," he said. "Haven't changed, have you,
Trevor?"

Trevor smiled without showing his teeth.

To Kathy and McKnight, Trevor said, "David and I go way back.
About eight years ago, I came up here to help with a cold case. David
was the ASAIC back then. We were able to solve it together."

Trevor stopped and looked at Ritter. "David, could this case be
related to that one?"

"I don't think so," the agent said.

The elevator stopped, and Ritter led them off the elevator and down the hall to a conference room.

They sat around the table, and Ritter picked up a poster board that was leaning against the wall. He turned it around so they could see it was a map of the continental United States. He placed the board on an easel.

McKnight scanned the map. There were ten red pins on the map. Two in Atlanta, two in Dallas, two in Frankfort, Kentucky, and one each in Miami, Columbia, South Carolina, and Charleston, West Virginia.

"Are those event markers?" Kathy asked.

"Yes," Ritter said. "Each of the pins represents one of ten suicides. All the same in MO, with one exception, and all within six weeks."

"What was the exception?" Trevor asked.

"This one," Ritter said, pointing at a pin in Atlanta. He replaced the red pin with a black one. "All the MO's of the suicides are the same, but there's no 'John' with this one."

"No 'John'?" Trevor said.

"Right. We're getting a little ahead of ourselves here. Let me lay it out for you. Beginning on October third and until a week ago, we have been tracking this. There may have been more before we started documenting them. Each of the events played out like this — A guy is found in an apartment with a dead girl. He's married, and he claims the girl seduced him. They met them at a party, a bar, or whatever, went back to the girl's place and had sex. Afterwards, they were disoriented or asleep, but when they pulled themselves together, the girl was dead. The victims all died by the same MO - gunshot wound to the right side of the head."

"Interesting," Kathy said. "Are they related? The victims, I mean?"

"We know little about them. But they were all what you would consider attractive, even pretty. They were young, well-dressed, manicured, no drugs in their systems except a couple had traces of cannabis. All tested positive for having sex with the man found there.

Except for the one exception — no man in that apartment. There were traces and DNA from a man in the exception case, but he had an ironclad alibi. It was his birthday and there was a family and friends celebration at a local watering hole. Dozens of witnesses."

"Has he been interviewed by you guys?" Trevor said.

"Yes. The ASAIC in Atlanta talked to him and passed me the file. His story is that she was a co-worker at the CDC and they worked late together three nights before and had a one-night stand. He also said she got clingy and a little crazy, so he left as soon as he could without a fuss. She was seen at work on subsequent days and made a scene in his office, so we don't doubt that part of the story. It plays like a classic case of coworkers who had a few drinks together and got carried away. There's no reason to doubt his story, but we're keeping an open mind."

"Could the 'John' have left after seeing the body, maybe?" Trevor asked.

"Maybe, but we didn't find any hits in the database for the rest of the DNA found on the scene." Ritter shrugged. "But there was precious little of it. Maybe it isn't related to the other events, except that the gun has the serial number filed off. That's unusual for a suicide case."

"Weird. Okay, let's come back to that later. Is there anything else that sets this event apart from the others?"

Ritter grimaced. "Yeah, there is. She's the only victim we can identify."

"If I remember correctly," Trevor said. "You told me the dead girls' fingerprints and DNA profiles were checked, but you have no hits on them in any of the crime databases. Right?"

"That's correct."

"Even all the international databases?"

"Even them. Nothing. Nada."

McKnight looked at Trevor and Kathy. Trevor turned to face McKnight. "Sound familiar?" he said.

Uh-oh.

McKnight leaned back in his chair and looked at the ceiling.

"Marc?" Kathy said.

McKnight leaned forward again. "Special Agent Ritter? I wonder—"

"Major McKnight, call me David or Ritter. 'Special Agent' has too many syllables."

"Okay. David, then. Do the 'Johns' have anything in common?"

"Yes," he said. "All of them were young — in their late twenties or early thirties — and all of them were running for political office."

McKnight sat still and looked at the table.

Trevor fidgeted. "Now you know why I wanted you to be here, Major."

Ritter looked from face to face. "What do you guys know that I don't? I called Trevor's office in Atlanta and found out he moved up here to DC. I wanted him to consult on this case and he insisted you guys come along." He paused. "Trevor, do you mind catching me up here?"

Trevor looked at McKnight and raised an eyebrow.

He wants permission.

McKnight nodded.

"Sorry, David. It was a case we worked earlier this year where someone changed history. The scenario was very much like this one. The MO was different — that girl allegedly jumped off a building in that case — but otherwise very close to the same scenario. I needed to have Major McKnight and Doctor Wu approve before I shared anything related to it."

"I get it," Ritter said. "What can you share with me or is it classified?"

"Well," Trevor said. "What I can tell you is we learned a local girl was time-jumped into the past and murdered to embarrass Wade Harrison."

"The President-Elect?"

"Yes."

Ritter rolled his eyes. "How come I didn't hear about it?"

Trevor smiled. "Most people haven't. Nobody except our team and a few others. It's a long story, but in short, the perpetrators changed history to influence the election result. Our team found out about it and went back in time to stop it. After all was said and done, we put history right and nobody remembers it because, on this timeline, it never happened."

Ritter looked stunned.

"There's only one instance of this crime—" Trevor said.

"That we know of," Kathy said.

"Right," Trevor said. "That we know of. But it was a big one." He turned back and searched the map with his eyes. "But this has the potential of being bigger. *Much* bigger."

"Wait a second," McKnight said. "Yes, similar scenarios. But let's not get ahead of ourselves. We need to confirm that time travel events happened that match up with the dates and times of these suicide events. It could be a coincidence."

"Are you kidding?" Kathy said.

"No, I'm not," McKnight said. "Granted, it would be the mother of all coincidences. But we can't get involved in this until we prove beyond reasonable doubt someone has committed a time-related crime. Until then, it's still a set of open suicide cases and a matter for law enforcement, not the HERO Team."

"Okay," Trevor said. "But we'll take the case details with us and check, right?"

"Oh, yes," McKnight said. "It could possibly be our case, but let's not start running with the ball until we're sure. No handoff yet — not until we confirm. Fair enough, David?"

Ritter shrugged. "Yeah, no problem. I wasn't expecting to hand it off. I just wanted Trevor's opinion."

Trevor turned back to Ritter. "David, what are you calling these cases?"

"The news media just got hold of it. They're calling them the Suicide Scandals."

"Okay. Can you get someone to pull together the dates, times, and locations for us so we can compare it to the Frequency Log?"

"Better than that," Ritter said. He pulled a thin folder out of his briefcase. "I took the liberty to do that in advance, and I've included everything else we know about the case." He handed it to Trevor. "What's the Frequency Log?"

Trevor waved the folder at Ritter. "Thanks for this," he said. "We have equipment that monitors time. We discovered that time has an oscillation, or a frequency, if you will. If an event changes history, we see a blip in the frequency."

Trevor held up the folder again. "If we find blips that match these dates and times, then we know time travel occurred and someone changed history." He slipped the folder into his briefcase.

"I'm tempted to leave out the one case that's different," McKnight said, "but let's leave it in until we check on the dates. My guess is that, other than the cause of death, it isn't related to the others ."

"Okay," Trevor said. "David, we'll check into the dates and I'll let you know as soon as possible."

Ritter nodded. "How long?"

"Not very. We just need to get the Frequency Log and check it against the date/time stamps for the events. If our Doctor Astalos is available today, I can let you know this afternoon."

"Doctor Astalos? He works with you guys?"

"Yes, he does, when he has time."

Trevor stuck out his hand. "In the meantime, let us get back to our office and get started on this."

They rose together and headed for the door. Ritter led them from the conference room out to the building's lobby.

Kathy claimed the front seat this trip.

No one spoke until they were in McKnight's truck on the way back to Telegraph Road.

"Marc?" she said. "What are you thinking?"

McKnight frowned. "I'm thinking we haven't addressed all the issues related to disaster recovery for the team. Our Time Engine got destroyed by time travelers once before, and we are building several backup Engines to make sure we don't get caught flat-footed again."

She turned toward him. "And?"

"It occurs to me that we're leaving out something. We need to download and archive everything from each machine every night. The software, the configurations, the history of the day, everything. We're not doing that yet. If we set that up and we get our backup Engines built and tested, then destruction of the Time Engine can only delay us by a few hours, tops. That's what I'm thinking about."

"I see. Trevor and I can get that started when we get back to the office, no problem. But I was asking what you think about the meeting we just left."

McKnight shrugged. "We'll run this stuff by Doctor Astalos and go from there. One step at a time, by the book."

Trevor chimed in from the back seat. "Do you really think the suicides aren't time crimes?"

McKnight glanced at Kathy beside him and in the mirror at Trevor. He shook his head.

"Not one chance in a million. We have a new mission and it'll push everything else to the back burner."

CHAPTER 4

McKnight let himself into the apartment he shared with Megan and set his briefcase on the wooden cadenza next to the front door.

It was a simple two-bedroom, two-bath apartment, but it was the perfect size for the two of them.

The dining room and kitchen lay directly ahead of him. As he passed through the dining room, the apartment expanded on the left into a living room. Two doors branched off the living room to the two bedrooms and baths. They shared the master bedroom and turned the other bedroom into a double office, with room for both of them to have a workspace.

McKnight used his workspace frequently, but Megan was still looking for a job in the area.

He had to admit Megan did a bang-up job decorating the place. In the two months since they moved in, the change in the place was dramatic. There were colorful pictures tastefully distributed across the walls, and her choice of furniture was far superior to the "early bachelor" pieces he brought from the Bachelor Officers' Quarters.

"Megan?" he called.

"Here," she called from the bedroom.

She bounced out of the bedroom in shorts and a close fitting top that showed off her figure. Her strawberry blonde hair swung in a ponytail while her bluer than blue eyes sparkled at him. She met him in the middle of the living room for a hug and a quick peck on the lips.

It crossed his mind how glad and lucky he was she agreed to move up to DC and into an apartment together.

"Are you hungry?" she said.

"Yes, I guess I am."

She stepped back with her hands on her hips.

"What? Did you eat something at the office or on the way home?"

"No, it was just really busy today. I hadn't even thought about it until just now. Yes, I *am* hungry."

She nodded and stepped into the tiny kitchen and turned on the gas stove. She dragged a pot of beef stew from the counter to a burner.

"I was too hungry to wait for you, so I've already eaten. But I saved some for you. I just need to heat it up."

McKnight joined her in the kitchen and leaned against the counter.

"Sorry I didn't call to say I'd be late. We have a new mission and we worked on it all afternoon."

"Yeah? What kind of mission? Or can you not talk about it?"

McKnight rubbed his jaw and wished he hadn't mentioned the mission. Megan didn't like to hear about things and then be told he couldn't talk about it.

"Not really," he said. "We just got it today and I don't know what is and isn't classified. Anyway, I apologize for not calling. I'll get better at it."

Megan stirred the stew with a wooden spoon. She turned to him and pointed the spoon at him. "You know it's boring here without you."

"I do. Hey, that smells good."

"Don't sound so surprised. I do have some skills, even if no one wants to hire me."

Oh, the interview!

"I take it your interview today didn't go as well as you hoped? Sorry, I meant to ask as soon as I got here."

"Not really. They're looking for someone to be more of a secretary or admin assistant. I want to be part of a team that's doing important stuff."

"That's important. I know we couldn't survive without our receptionist and the two clerks assigned to us."

She waved the spoon at him again. "Yeah, but that's definitely not what I want to do."

"Okay, okay. I'm sorry. I know we're not yet in a position where you have to settle for a job you don't want."

"That's right." She motioned him out of the kitchen. "Go sit at the table. I'll bring it out to you. Do you want a beer or a glass of wine?"

"A Blue Moon, if you don't mind."

He went back to the dining room and sat with his back to the wall.

She dished up a plate and brought it to the table.

"Thanks," he said.

She left the room, then reappeared with the beer and one for herself. The smell of the stew floated up to him.

"Um, smells good," he said.

"Of course it does." She smiled and sat next to him.

They sat in silence for a moment as he enjoyed the stew.

"Can I ask you something?" she said.

"Sure."

"Do you think it was a mistake for me to come up from Atlanta and move in with you?"

"No, of course not."

Megan looked thoughtful.

McKnight laid down his fork. "Hey, Baby. Look at me. What's bugging you?"

"Nothing."

"No, not nothing. I can tell you're upset about something."

"No, I'm not. Well, not upset per se. It's more that I'm lonesome. I haven't really met any friends here yet, and you're gone all day and part of the night. I came up here to be with you and that's worth leaving everything else behind, but we're not together because you're not here."

"I see."

"I'm sure it would be better if I was working, but until I find something, I'm going a little stir-crazy here."

"And I'm not helping much, because I can't seem to get out of the office earlier."

"Well, that's true, but I know your job is one of those that requires long hours and sometimes you can't avoid working late. It's just that I don't get to see you and when I do, you're usually tired."

"Do you want to go somewhere? We can do it right now, tonight." He put his napkin on the table and stood. She stood with him and put her hands up.

"No. Are you kidding? Not on this short notice. I'd have to change and put on makeup. But it *would* be nice some time for you to call from work and tell me you want to go out. We've only done that once, and it was the first week I was here."

"Okay, I understand. So let's plan to do something tomorrow night. I'll come home at the normal time and we'll go to that new bar and grill in Old Town. Does that sound good?"

"Really? Yes, it sounds great." She threw her arms around his neck and pulled his face down to kiss it. "I can't wait."

"And I'll work on my schedule so I can get home earlier. It's my fault you're so isolated. I promise I'll get better."

"You'd better."

She smiled that pouty little smile that always intrigued and attracted him.

He pulled her to him.

"This will be great," he said. "Tomorrow promises to be a slow day. It shouldn't be hard at all to get away early."

CHAPTER 5

Wednesday, November 19th, 2036 — 5:10am — Cameron Run Park, Alexandria, Virginia

It was the first significant snowfall of the year in Alexandria. A gentle wind spun the heavy flakes around in countless swirling patterns. The first light of morning struggled to penetrate the cloud cover and bring the day.

In the brief stretch of open grass between Eisenhower Avenue and Cameron Run, a deer pawed at a tuft of grass. Like many watercourses in Washington DC, Cameron Run hurried across boulders and flood control barriers on its way to the Potomac River.

The jogging path along Eisenhower Avenue was deserted. Most people didn't run this early, and fewer still ran at this time of year. It's hard to get out of bed to exercise when it's cold outside.

The solitary runner on the path didn't see it that way. It was his time to think and work out problems in his head before work.

Granted, it was harder at this time of year. The falling snow and low light made it hard to see the path. The icy conditions forced his thoughts to the immediate demand for his attention — the risk of slipping on the snow and injuring himself. So he gave up on work thoughts and focused on keeping his feet and completing his three miles.

He had run on this path every day for the last ten months and was surprised to see a bright light appear in the field next to Cameron Run.

It wasn't a flash of light. Instead, it was a continuous bright light where there should be nothing but grass. He estimated it was fifty yards ahead of him.

As he got closer, the light pulsated. At first, he thought the sensation was because of the thick flurries. When he was twenty yards away, the light surged brightly and winked out. After focusing on such a bright light, the morning seemed much darker.

He stared at the place where the light had been. There was something there on the ground.

His divided attention failed him. He slipped on the icy running trail and sprawled face first on the path.

"Dammit!" he said.

It took a moment to collect himself. He had road rash on both palms through his gloves from the ice beneath the fresh snow. He pushed himself up to his knees and pulled off the gloves to examine his injuries. They weren't too bad but burned like fire. He leaned back on his heels and caught his breath.

What the hell was that? He was sure he heard something, but couldn't find the source. He looked to his left where the light had flashed. There was something dark on the grass ten yards away.

The snowfall was heavier now. It hindered visibility and dampened sounds.

He heard the sound again. This time, it sounded more like a moan or a low growl. He jumped to his feet and scrambled toward the source, slipping and sliding as he went.

A woman lay on her back on the ground. She wore army fatigue pants and a t-shirt. She wore her black hair in a ponytail. There was a box next to her, lying on its side. Papers and folders spilled out scattered around her legs. The swirling wind made them flutter as it threatened to carry them away. Even now, the heavy snowfall was covering her.

"Oh, my God!" he said, as he fell to his knees beside her.

Large snowflakes landed on her upturned face, but she didn't react. He slipped his arm under her neck to cradle her head and half-lifted her to a sitting position.

"Can you hear me?" he said. He patted her cheek to revive her. "Are you alive?"

Her eyes fluttered open and searched his face. After a moment, the eyes focused, and she grabbed his neck and pulled his face near hers.

"When am I?" she whispered.

"You're on Eisenhower Avenue."

She shook her head as if frustrated. "No! *When* am I? What's the date?"

"The date? It's November nineteenth. Are you okay? Are you hurt?"

She shivered. "No, what year?" She pulled his face closer and bared her teeth. "What *year*, dammit?"

"What year? Are you kidding? It's 2036."

The woman relaxed and lay back. Her teeth chattered from the bitter cold as she spoke. "Thank God. I made it back."

The runner shook his head. "You need an ambulance." He pulled out his phone and dialed 911.

She sat up. "Tell them I'm here."

"I am. I'm calling right now."

"No, tell them to call Senator Lodge. Tell him Hatcher made it back."

Then she noticed the scattering papers.

"My papers! I need my papers!"

"Lady, don't worry about that. We need to get you to a hospital... Yes, operator! I have a woman out in the cold without enough clothing to stay warm. I think she may have injuries. Please hurry!"

While he completed the call, she struggled up to a sitting position and tried to reach the papers around her legs. The snow was already covering them, and some were becoming damp and limp.

"Oh, no," she said. "Where's the sticky note? It's gone!"

"Okay, okay," he said. "I'll get them together. You relax. You might be injured and I don't want you to move too much."

She ignored him and crawled on her hands and knees to the box and shoved the papers within reach into it. She dug through the papers in the box.

"Argh! It's gone. I can't find my way back without it. Everything else is worthless if I lost it."

The jogger ran after two papers the wind caught and threatened to carry away. He brought them back and put them in the box. The last page he found had a green sticky note stuck to it.

"Is this what you were looking for?"

"Yes, yes, oh, thank God, you found it."

She relaxed, laid back in the snow, and closed her eyes. She shivered and her teeth chattered.

The jogger could hear an ambulance in the distance.

I need to get back to the road to flag them down.

He stripped off his outer sweater and covered her torso. Then he ran to the road.

CHAPTER 6

Wednesday, November 19th, 2036 — 7:00am -- The White House, Washington DC

Retired General Mike Drake was having breakfast at the White House.

His companions for the meal were Senator James Lodge, time scientist Robert Astalos, President-Elect Wade Harrison and Wanda Taylor, the President of the United States. He had dined here before, but this time the meal was also a meeting.

The President was on her way out of office. She has nearly completed her two terms, and her number one choice has been elected as her successor. This meeting was part briefing, part working.

"Wade," President Taylor said, "I know you've met General Drake and Doctor Astalos before, but now you get to see why I and so many others hold them in such high esteem."

Harrison smiled. "They saved my ass last year, Madam President. They're right up there in my book, too."

"Yes, I know. Today I want to talk to you about an idea I had. They've worked on it and are hip-deep in planning and recon, right, Mike?"

Drake nodded. "Yes, Ma'am, we are. The project is workable and we think we have a time window to do it that will avoid any impact on history. And it would be helpful if we could act proactively to respond to history changes by unauthorized entities."

"Good. Now don't get ahead of me, Mike. I'm working on it."

She turned to Harrison. "Wade, what the General is saying is the charter for the HERO Team states that they exist for research only.

They can't go after people who use time travel for illicit purposes without an executive order."

"Yes, I believe I read that," Harrison said. "But we can do *that*, right? You've done it twice already."

"Yes, we have," President Taylor said. "But this really handicaps them if something happens. They can't respond without legal exposure until after they talk to me... And soon, that means you. What if we are attacked through time travel and the HERO Team needs to go after the attackers? Worse, what if the Russians or the Chinese or worse, the Iranians, get the same ability? We won't be able to react fast enough. We'd be off balance and that's deadly if we don't get it fixed."

"I see. Then we need to get a law passed to change their charter so they can be more autonomous."

"More autonomous for the short term. Somewhat like the War Powers Act, maybe. They can respond to an attack but must get a supporting directive or law within 90 days after the event. So what they really need is a change to their charter. We need to get the Legislative Branch to pass a new charter."

"But we'll start with an executive order giving autonomy for 90 days. I'll issue an order and you can continue it after you come into office. First, though, I have to talk to a few members of Congress and the Senate so they see the reasoning and don't fight me on the first executive order."

"Okay," Harrison said. "Madam President, I agree and will support you on this."

"Good." Taylor smiled at her replacement and turned back to Drake.

"Mike, I'll get to those legislators as quickly as I can. I understand the urgency."

"Yes, Ma'am," Drake said. "I can tell. Thank you."

"What about this new project?" Harrison said. "What's it all about?"

President Taylor rested her elbows on the table and leaned forward. "Wade, you know about the train wreck our country is in right now. The partisan politics is about to tear everything apart. You don't have to look any further than your own experience to know how far the people will go to get into and hang onto power."

"To make a long story short, I want to call in a consultant whose credentials are so good that no one would dare question him. My thought is to have him brought in to look at the current state of the government and testify at a House Judiciary Committee hearing. I want him to tell us how to get back on the track our Founding Fathers put us on."

"Sounds great," Harrison said. "When can I meet him?"

Astalos laughed, and Drake couldn't suppress a grin. Even Senator Lodge smiled, though he tried hard to suppress it. President Taylor was setting the stage the way she always did, bringing her keen sense of drama into play.

"Well, it's difficult to get an appointment with him," she said. "You see. he lives in the 18th century."

"Say what?" Harrison said. "Ah, you got me. The presence of Doctor Astalos and General Drake should have given it away." He straightened in his chair. "You're bringing a Founding Father through time to this century?"

President Taylor's expression turned serious. "Not *a* Founding Father. *The* Founding Father."

Harrison was stunned to silence.

President Taylor continued. "General Drake, will you outline the mission as it exists so far?"

Senator Lodge's phone emitted a tone. He looked at it and frowned.

"Yes, Ma'am," Drake said. "We're targeting the year 1787. Our time travel technology can only allow us to travel to a period that is a multiple of twenty-five years from the current date. For example, we can go back or forward twenty-five years, fifty years, seventy-five years or more, but we can't travel to last year. We think time must be 'folded' in the way that makes it easier to hit a multiple rather than just any date. In a month, we'll be at 250 years from 1787, a perfect time to intercept our target in a remote location. We—"

"Excuse me, Madam President," Lodge said, "but this text I just got is important."

"What is it?" she asked.

Lodge turned toward Drake. "Actually, it's for you, Mike." He handed Drake his phone.

Drake read the text and looked up with a smile. "They've found Lieutenant Hatcher. They have her at Walter Reed for observation."

"That's fabulous, Mike," President Taylor said. "Do you want to take a few minutes to alert whoever you need to?"

"Yes, Ma'am. That would be great. Thanks. I'd like to let the HERO Team and her parents know." He stood and walked to the window for privacy.

"Great," she said. "Okay, let's put the new mission on the back burner until we can get a report on Lieutenant Hatcher's experience and see if further action is required there. For now, let's break for about five minutes so Mike can get things rolling."

****

Wednesday, November 19th, 2036 - 7:10am - McKnight Apartment, Alexandria, Virginia

McKnight woke before his alarm at 7:30. He glanced over at Megan. She was still asleep. He loved the way her hair got in such a mess overnight.

He propped himself up on one elbow so he could see her better.

I might be the luckiest man in the world.

His phone chimed to announce a text message. He rolled on his back and sighed.

Megan stirred and mumbled. "Is that my job or yours calling?"

"Mine," he said. "You don't have a job."

"Oh, that's right." She giggled. "Well, you'd better answer it."

He rolled over and grabbed the phone. "It's from Senator Lodge. I wonder why he's texting me?"

McKnight opened the text.

<Marc, this is Drake on Lodge's phone. Hatcher has returned. She is suffering from exposure and is at Walter Reed. See the following text for the details. I will ask for 24-hour protection. Please alert your team and call her parents. Hoorah!>.

"Is everything okay?" Megan asked.

McKnight read through the second text. "It's more than okay," he said. "They found Karen Hatcher. She's at Walter Reed for observation."

He jumped out of bed and headed for the bathroom.

"That's great!" she called after him as she climbed out of bed. "I'll get you some coffee."

Ten minutes later, McKnight emerged from the bedroom in uniform. Still in her nightgown, she handed him his coffee and pressed herself up against him.

"I'm so glad to hear they've found her. Are you headed straight to the hospital?"

"Yes," he said. "I'll call her parents and text the team on the way."

"Good. Now get out of here and come back home to me as soon as possible. Remember, we have a date tonight."

He kissed her and held her close. "I haven't forgotten. I'll keep you posted. Love you."

He gently pushed her away and left the apartment.

****

Wednesday, November 19th, 2036 — 7:25am — Kathy Wu's Apartment

Trevor and Kathy sat together at her breakfast table. They made it a practice to eat together in the morning. Kathy was a stickler for having a healthy breakfast in the morning, and Trevor abandoned his coffee only routine to match her habit.

Both their phones pinged at the same time.

"It's from Marc." Kathy said. "What could be so important to call us before we get to the office. I hope nothing's wrong."

Trevor read the message and chuckled. "Not at all."

"That's fantastic!" she said.

They both started for the bedroom. Kathy stopped in front of him, giggled and wagged her finger at him. "No, no. I get the master shower first. You can wait or use the guest bathroom if you're in a hurry."

Trevor raised his hands in submission. "Whatever you say, Dear. I'll meet you at the front door in fifteen."

"I'll be there first," she said, and pushed him toward the guest room.

He laughed and hurried to the shower.

Wu stripped off her robe and climbed in the shower.

Hatcher is alive. Thank God. I can't wait to hear her story.

****

Wednesday, November 19th, 2036 — 7:25am — DLA Officers' Gym

Wheeler completed the last set of leg lifts of his routine at the DLA gym. He picked up his towel and headed for the locker room.

A text ping interrupted his playlist of 70s Classic Rock. He opened the text and read it.

With an enormous grin, he speed-dialed his wife.

When she answered, he said, "Honey, guess what?... Hatcher's back!... Yes, she is... What?... Oh, I'm still in the gym, but I'm headed to see her as soon as I shower... Yes, love you, too."

He disconnected the call and ran to the locker room.

****

Wednesday, November 19th, 2036 — 7:25am — Fontainebleau Hotel, Miami, Florida

Captain Winston Tyler buttoned his shirt in front of the closet mirror. The honeymoon suite at the Fontainebleau Hotel in Miami was perfect. Outside, the temperature was pushing 80 degrees — Much better than 20 degrees in Alexandria.

Tyler was McKnight's XO and the second mission planner for the HERO Team. He grew up in a prosperous family in Atlanta before attending West Point and rooming with Marc McKnight. Unlike McKnight, Tyler was light-complected, blondish, and five foot ten.

"Winnie?"

Tyler turned to his new wife. Sarah was sitting on the bed, slipping on her shoes. Her royal blue dress set off her blue eyes and shoulder length red hair. Three days in the Florida sun brought out the freckles across her nose and cheeks.

"Well, good morning, Mrs. Tyler," he said.

"And a good morning to you, too, Captain Tyler," she said, then laughed.

"Still trying to get used to the new name, eh?"

"Not at all. I've said to myself over and over for the last few weeks. I've got it now. Now that we have three days under our belt, how does it feel to have a ball and chain?"

Tyler pulled her to her feet and into his arms. "I think I might get used to it. We'll see."

Sarah pushed him away and punched his arm. "You'd better watch it. I've heard the murder rate for obnoxious husbands by new wives is high and rising."

Tyler laughed. "Are you ready for breakfast?"

"Yes, I am. Where do you want to go?"

Tyler's phone pinged to announce a text. He pulled it from his pocket and read the message.

"Outstanding!" he said. "Honey, Karen Hatcher's been found."

"Is she okay?"

"Sounds like she is. Marc is headed to the hospital now."

"She's in the hospital?"

Tyler shook his head. "I don't think there's any problems. Marc says it's for observation."

Sarah assumed a pouty expression and slipped back into his arms.

"Do we have to go back today?" she said.

Tyler laughed and patted her lips gently with his forefinger.

"No, I think they can handle this, don't you?"

She showed him the smile he loved so much. "Yes, I know they can."

He pulled her closer and kissed the top of her shoulder. "After all, Mrs. Tyler, this *is* our honeymoon. I can't think of any reason to cut it short and go back to snowy Virginia, can you?"

"No, Captain Tyler, I can't. Shall we go to breakfast?"

"Absolutely, Mrs. Tyler."

He gently separated himself from her, acknowledged McKnight's text, and slipped his phone back into his pocket.

"We'll leave tomorrow as planned," he said. "We still have one more night in Florida and I intend for us to make the most of it. Let's go. I'm starving."

CHAPTER 7

Wednesday, November 19th, 2036 — 8:30am — Walter Reed Hospital

Hatcher's room was on the third floor at Walter Reed. McKnight had been there before, but rarely enough to know where everything was.

When he found her room, he tapped on the door.

It opened and a large MP sergeant stood before him.

The man saluted, then said, "Sorry, sir. Are you family?"

McKnight returned the salute.

"You might say that. Is there a problem?"

"Access to this patient is restricted to family, except designated individuals. Are you family, sir?"

"I see. I'm not family, but I'm her commanding officer. Major Marc McKnight. Am I on the list, Sergeant?"

"Yes, sir, you are. Please come in."

The MP moved out of his way and came to attention by the door. McKnight slipped inside.

Hatcher was asleep. Only her face showed outside the blankets covering her. An IV line from a hanging bag snaked under the covers. Her raven hair was spread out on the pillow around her face. Her flawless complexion was pale and there was a bluish tint to her left cheek.

To McKnight, she looked like a teenager, napping after a long day of school and soccer practice.

A nurse came to the door, and the MP allowed her inside.

"How is she?" McKnight asked.

"She'll be okay. She was dehydrated, weak and cold when she got here. That makes hypothermia a risk. We're keeping her sedated and warm for the next couple of days."

McKnight nodded and stood over Hatcher. He touched her wrist and pushed a few errant strands of jet black hair out of her eyes.

"What happened to her? Has she spoken to anyone?"

The nurse nodded. "Yes, they couldn't shut her up when she came in. Based on the marks on her wrists and ankles, they confined her to a bed or a chair most of the time. We think she was beat up, too, but no broken bones, thank the good Lord. No permanent physical damage as far as we can tell."

"How about psychological problems?"

"We won't know about that until she's awake and able to talk to us."

"Good," McKnight said.

"Wait a second. There's a note from the admitting physician. Let me get it." She turned and left the room.

McKnight ran the edge of his finger down Hatcher's cheek. "Don't worry, kiddo. We'll figure this out and get Cindy back here to account for what she's done."

The nurse came back in with a clipboard and an EMT came with her. The MP moved to block the EMT.

"No, no," the nurse said. "This is one of the guys who brought her in. He's okay to be here." She looked around and walked to the closet.

The EMT approached McKnight.

"All the way here in the ambulance," he said, "she kept talking about her box and that she needed to get it to Major McKnight."

The nurse approached McKnight and stood, looking at her clipboard. "May I see your ID please? What did you say your name was, sir?"

"I'm Major McKnight. Hatcher is on my team."

"Good deal, sir," the EMT said. "I'm Baker. My partner and I brought her in. She was about frozen, but she wouldn't stop saying that she needed to get this box to you. She didn't calm down until I promised to wait here for you and make sure you and no one else got it."

"Really?" McKnight said. "Let's have a look at it."

The nurse pulled it out of the closet and set it on the visitor chair next to the bed.

McKnight opened the box and peered inside. A sticky note lay on top of the papers inside. The numbers written on the note had the same format as a time travel destination — location and time.

He shifted through the top few documents. One of them was an official-looking letter on "Federal Time Services" stationery. It was dated January 23rd, 2085.

Oh, my God. She brought back intel.

He glanced at the unconscious woman in the bed.

After all she's been through, she escapes and has the presence of mind to gather intel on the way out.

"This is good," he said. "Very good."

The nurse and Baker exchanged a look of relief.

"Where's the rest of her gear? And her clothes?"

"Taken to Security," the MP said. "General Drake's orders. He said all of her clothes, shoes, her phone... everything... is to be examined for harmful substances and, well, anything unusual."

"Ah, I get it," McKnight said. "We've been sabotaged before. The General wants to make sure it didn't happen again."

"What could be in her clothes?" Baker asked. "Poison or something?"

"Or something," McKnight said. "He's just being cautious. They're probably just fine."

"Okay, well, I guess I'll get back to work," Baker said. "I promised her I'd get that box to you. Now that it's done, I need to get moving. Nice to meet you, Major. That's one tough lady you got there."

McKnight smiled. "You have no idea. No one on my team had ever beaten her in combat sparring, except me. And I only beat her once. She's the best warfighter I know."

Baker looked at the figure lying in the bed. "Wow. And nice-looking, too."

"You could say that. Thanks for your help, Baker."

Baker nodded and left the room. The nurse checked Hatcher's IV and blood pressure monitor, smiled at McKnight and left the room.

McKnight moved the box off the chair and sat. He wished she was conscious and able to give a report. He decided to sit with her for a while.

After thirty minutes, the door opened and a mature couple entered. It was Hatcher's parents. The MP saluted. McKnight leaped to his feet and did the same.

The woman smiled at McKnight and said, "As you were, gentlemen."

McKnight saluted and relaxed. "How are you, General? Colonel?"

"Much better now, Major," General Hatcher said.

She walked to the bed and caressed her daughter's face. Her husband approached the other side of the bed. He stood over his daughter, his face like stone.

"Yes, much better now," she said. "How is she? Have you gotten a report from the doctor yet?"

"No, ma'am," McKnight said. "Just from the nurse. She advised that Hatcher... Karen... should be fine. She was very weak when they brought her in, and she needed warming up and hydration."

Her father dragged his eyes from Hatcher's face and looked up at McKnight.

"Major, any idea what happened to her? Do we know anything?"

McKnight turned toward the man on the opposite side of the bed. He knew Colonel Richard Hatcher by reputation. Retired Special Forces.

Give him the straight skinny. No platitudes or false assurances.

"Not much, sir. The nurse says it looks like they restrained her most of the last couple of months — on a bed or in a chair."

The colonel's mouth drew into a tight line. He looked back at his daughter and stroked her cheek with his finger. Without looking at McKnight, he spoke in a tight, measured tone.

"I'm presuming this treatment will not go unanswered?"

"Rich," General Hatcher said, "That isn't for us to—"

He waved her off, and said, "I know, I know…"

Then he looked at McKnight with an unwavering gaze.

"…But the Major understands me, don't you, son?"

"Yes, sir, I do, and I assure you we will make an appropriate response. My first priority is to get Karen healthy and get her story. Then we'll determine the next course of action, sir."

The colonel nodded and turned back to his daughter.

The door opened and Wheeler stuck his head in. As soon as he saw who was in the room, He closed the door from the outside.

General Hatcher stepped to the door and opened it. "Lieutenant Wheeler, come in. Karen would want you here."

Wheeler entered the room and saluted the General. "Thank you, ma'am. How is she?"

"We'll get the doctor in here in a few minutes," she said. "As you were, Lieutenant. There is no rank in this room."

McKnight stepped forward. "General? I'd like to get this box of intel Karen brought back with her to our Doctor Astalos ASAP. If anyone can tell us where she's been, he can."

"Very well. Carry on. And thank you, Major."

McKnight saluted, picked up the box and headed for the door.

General Hatcher said, "Mitch, is anyone else out there in the hall?"

"Yes, ma'am. General Drake, Kathy, and Trevor are out there. We didn't want to bring everyone in at once."

"Okay. We'll step out to talk to them in a few minutes. Thank you, Major McKnight. We'll keep you posted on her condition."

McKnight had his hand on the doorknob. He turned and nodded to Hatcher's parents.

He looked at the MP. The man's body stiffened to attention. "Come with me, Sergeant," he said.

As soon as they were outside the room with the door closed, McKnight turned to the MP.

"What are your orders, Sergeant?"

"Sir, my orders are to guard the Lieutenant and make sure no one harms her."

"Sergeant, do you know what our unit is?"

The MP shook his head. "No, sir."

"We're part of the Historical Event Research Organization. Does that mean anything to you?"

"No, sir. Sorry, sir."

"No problem, Sergeant. We're the time travelers. That means there's a threat that somebody might time-jump into this room to do her harm. Do you understand?"

The MP's eyes widened. "Yes, sir!"

"I'm telling you about this out here because I don't want to alarm her parents. If someone is jumping in, you'll feel a sudden increase in static electricity. If you feel that, draw your weapon and be ready to fight. Start yelling for help. You'll see a white silhouette form in the room. As soon as you see it, don't wait to see what else happens. Empty your clip at the silhouette. Understood?"

"Yes, sir!"

"Thanks. You're dismissed."

The MP saluted and went back into Hatcher's room.

McKnight spoke to the others in the hall and left the hospital. The key to the mystery of where Hatcher has been all this time was most likely in this box. He wanted to get it into Doctor Astalos' hands as soon as possible.

It crossed his mind that, by now, Cindy knew Hatcher was gone and might come looking for her.

CHAPTER 8

Thursday, November 20th, 2036 — 10:00am — Kathy Wu's office at DLA Temporary Offices

McKnight walked from his office to Kathy's. The door was open and Trevor and Kathy sat at her conference table. McKnight knocked on the doorjamb. "Are we meeting? Did you hear anything back from Doctor Astalos?"

"C'mon in, Marc," Kathy said. "We haven't heard from him yet, but we expect him here any time. In the meantime, though…" She looked at Trevor. "We've uncovered a couple of interesting ideas."

"Yes, we have," Trevor said.

McKnight entered, closed the door and sat with them. He set his phone and notepad on the table. "Okay, let's hear it."

"After reading through all the cases and doing a little research, we've learned a few things. The girls have nothing in common that we can find. DNA results show ethnicities all across the board. They are all attractive. If somebody selected them for murder to embarrass someone, that would make sense."

"Okay. What about the men? They were all politicians, right? Did they have anything in common? What party or parties were they associated with?"

"Ah," Trevor said. "You've hit on one of the interesting points. They are both Democrats and Republicans. Seven Republicans, two Democrats. And the Democrats were way over to the moderate side. Some say that they both would be Republicans if their constituencies weren't Blue — Democratic, I mean. What I'm trying to say is, some people think these guys registered as Democrats because most of the voters in their district are Democrats."

McKnight scratched his chin. "I see. You think someone targeted them because they are on the conservative side?"

"Well, that's at least one scenario," Trevor said. "The implications of that are a little scary."

Kathy leaned in across the table. "If I let the conspiracy theory junkie part of my brain run away with me, I might think someone is trying to nudge the average position of Congress to the liberal side. You know, take out the more conservative voices and what's left are more liberal positions."

McKnight shook his head. "Let's not go down that road until we have more information. Have you shared that idea with Ritter at the FBI? What did he say?"

"We haven't discussed it with him yet," Kathy said. "We figured we'd call him after you got in here so we could hit all the points together."

"Well, then, let's get him on the phone," McKnight said.

Trevor placed the call and, a few seconds later, Ritter was on the line.

"This is Ritter. Is that you, Trevor?"

"Yes, it is, Dave. And I have Kathy and Marc here with me. Question for you?"

"Sure."

"We noticed that most of the politicians involved were on the conservative side. Did you guys notice that?"

"Yes, we did," Ritter said. "With the political situation as it is, you know, kinda tense? Yes, we looked at that."

Trevor looked at McKnight and Kathy before speaking again. "And what did you conclude?"

There was a pause on the line before Ritter answered. "Nothing."

"Nothing?"

"Right. It's an interesting idea. But so far, there's no evidence to support that one party is moving against the other. We didn't find any evidence of some big conspiracy theory. All we know are the details of the deaths. So far, they look like suicides. It might be a weird-ass coincidence, but I've seen weirder ones. Without more information or proof... With today's political environment, I can't imagine even saying that out loud."

"Understood," McKnight said. "Might it be a radical political cell trying to push the government their way?"

"Sure, that's logical and all that. But with no proof, I have to stick to the coincidence theory."

"What about the Russians or the Chinese? Or even another foreign player?" Kathy said. "International meddling in the politics of another state happens all the time. Shoot, we interfere with their politics, too, from what I understand. It's normal."

"Yes, that's possible, and we considered that. But there's no convincing evidence of that, either. There's no evidence to tie these cases to any government — ours or foreign. There's no commonality between the cases except the politics of the men involved."

There was a knock at the door.

"Hold on a second, Dave," Kathy said.

She walked to the door and let Doctor Astalos into the room.

Doctor Robert Astalos was the inventor of time travel and still came up with useful innovations to the HERO Team.

He looked and acted like he was in his seventies. In actuality, he was 106 years old and in good health because of the habits he changed after glimpsing himself at an older age.

McKnight got up and offered Astalos his seat at the conference table. Astalos thanked him and sat with the others.

Kathy spoke to the phone again. "Dave? You still there? Doctor Astalos has joined us in the conference room. Doctor Astalos, this is Special Agent-In-Charge David Ritter. He's our liaison with the FBI and the source of the dates and times Trevor gave you."

"Yes, I'm here," Ritter said. "I'm honored to meet you, sir. I think I've read every paper you've published about time travel. It's fascinating."

"The honor is mine, Special Agent," Astalos said. "I think we may have some information for you."

"Call me Dave, please, sir. I'm eager to hear what you've learned. I guess we all are."

"That, we are," McKnight said. "What do you have for us, Doctor?"

"I hope it's useful news," Astalos said. "I checked each of the dates and times you provided me against the Frequency Log. The bottom line is that a time distortion or spike exists at the same date and time as each of your examples."

"Useful, but not good news," Trevor said.

"No, it doesn't sound good from here," Ritter said. "For the record, Doctor Astalos, does that mean someone traveled through time and created these events?"

"No," Astalos said. "What it means is, a time travel event occurred at the approximate same time as each of the events. I can't tell if any connection exists, but if you have ten events and something affected the Time Frequency at the same times? The chances of coincidence drop precipitously."

"I agree," McKnight added. "Enough that I think we have to assume time travel was involved. Since we can't identify the victims, except for one, I… Wait a second…" He turned back to Astalos. "All ten of them coincided with a time event? All ten?"

"Yes," Astalos said.

"So, we have ten suicide victims. Nine we can't identify, but were found with a politician, and one we can identify with no politician."

"Maybe there's a politician, but he panicked and left before we discovered the body?" Kathy said.

"Maybe," Trevor said, "but there's still the fact that the MO is the same, with a weapon with the serial number filed. No, I think we have ten murders by a killer with a certain mode of operation. But he... or she... committed nine crimes for the same reason and one for another reason." He held up his hand. "Hold on for a second." He stood and paced.

He looked out the window as he walked and then stopped to scan the room. "Okay. Another way to approach 'who dun it' is to look at the potential impact. What is this person... or persons... trying to do? That's one approach we used at Atlanta PD."

"I agree," Ritter said.

McKnight held up his hand. "All right. Before we go further with this... Dave, I think it's clear this one belongs to the HERO Team. Let's cut you loose so you don't have to sit through all our brainstorming. We'll take it from here. Trevor can keep you posted about what's going on."

"Okay," Ritter said. "Actually, I'd love to stay and hear all this, but I do have some other stuff on my plate. I'll mark this one as assigned to you people and get out of the way." He laughed. "Better you than me."

"Understood, Dave. Have a great day."

"Same to you. Trevor, I'll look forward to hearing what you people figure out."

"Yes, I'll keep you posted," Trevor said. "See you. Bye."

"Bye," Ritter said, and disconnected the call.

McKnight looked around the room. No one was smiling now.

"First, what's the motive? Where will these events take us?"

Kathy spoke. "Seems to me that someone is trying to influence the general direction of local politics in those areas."

Trevor nodded and smiled. "Okay, Doctor Kathy Wu, with your P-H-D in politics from Princeton... What is it that politicians say about local politics?"

Kathy's eyes shone with enlightenment. "They say all politics are local."

"Um-hmm. And what does that mean?"

"If you eliminate some conservatives from the running, you push the local — and national — politics toward the liberal side."

"I think so, too," Trevor said. "And if the politics drift slowly but surely toward the liberal side, what do you get? What does the country look like?"

"Based on the atmosphere today?" She thought for a second.

"The liberals in power now are pushing for open borders, sanctuary cities, autonomous zones, statue destruction, climate change. Kinder, gentler foreign policy..." She fell silent and looked at the floor.

"And more than a few Alinsky adherents are in play," Astalos added.

McKnight felt the room go silent. He looked at their faces. Everyone was considering the implications.

"I don't like where this is going," he said.

Trevor nodded. "Kathy?"

She looked up at him with a frown.

"What is usually the result?"

"Best case?" she said. "Social unrest. Political segmentation. Divisiveness. Legislative paralysis."

Trevor nodded. "And if they continue with this, ratcheting up the pressure? What's the worst case?"

She stared at him for a long moment.

"Kathy?" Trevor said. "Where does it lead?"

She took a deep breath and sighed heavily.

"Revolution," she said. "That's what you get... Revolution."

"You mean, like a political mandate to change everything?"

"If you're lucky."

"I assume that's the best case," McKnight said. "Right, Kathy?"

"Yes. And before you ask, the worst case is that the country becomes so unstable a shooting war breaks out. The more fear-based politics you have — on both sides — the more you have people at each other's throats. 'I'm right and everyone who disagrees with me is wrong' — that sort of thing."

McKnight leaned back against the conference room door.

"You mean like… civil war?" he asked.

Kathy sighed. "Yes. I mean, like civil war."

McKnight waved his hands at the room.

"Okay, let's not get too excited about this scenario yet. Do we really think someone is trying to push the United States in that direction?"

Kathy spoke again. "I don't want to jump to conclusions either, Marc. But we need to keep this possibility in mind. Countries get involved in other countries' politics all the time for this purpose. I'm sure there are people trying to influence our government, and I'm sure our government does it, too."

"Yes, I know," he said.

"I hate this idea, too," she said. "But based on the evidence and what we already know from experience — Cindy Ginn and her attempt to knock Wade Harrison out of the Presidential race, for example — it's the most likely scenario. Think about it."

McKnight paused. "Lay it out as best as you can, Kathy. Let's get it on the table."

"Okay," she said. She rose, walked to the dry erase board next to the conference table and erased the information on it. McKnight took her seat at the table.

She drew a timeline from left to right. At the left end was 2011, in the middle was 2036, and at the right end was a question mark. Then she drew an arrow from 2036 to 2011 and turned back to the room.

"We know Cindy kidnapped a present day girl, took her back to 2011, and murdered her in a scenario that looks a lot like these cases, right?"

"I see where you're going," Trevor said.

Kathy smiled at him. "I know you do, but let's wait for everyone else to catch up."

McKnight shifted in his seat. "I don't like this at all. Are you saying that someone, perhaps Cindy, is doing the same thing again? Kidnapping more girls and sacrificing them for a political agenda?"

"I think what Cindy did before was a rehearsal, a proof of concept," Kathy said. "Sure, it would have moved the country in that direction. It would have worked, too, had we not interfered. She probably sees it as a failed project, but a successful experiment."

"Then after that experiment, they figured they had a working model, and have implemented it to push us — the United States — to the political climate they want."

"Yes," she said. "And we can't do anything about them, because all the events so far are more than a week old."

"...Which means we can't go back and fix them," Trevor said. "They're out of time travel range for the next twenty-five years. We need a broader solution."

"Right," Kathy said. "And this pushes everything else we're doing to the back burner. We've got to figure out how to stop this interference."

CHAPTER 9

<u>Thursday, November 20th, 2036 - 10:18am - Kathy Wu's office,</u>
<u>Telegraph Road, Alexandria, Virginia</u>

McKnight stood.

We need to get out in front of this. Better take charge now and push it forward.

"Okay, I want a plan for getting after this thing. Kathy, please get with Tyler to put a mission plan in place by day after tomorrow. He should be back in town from Miami tonight."

"Sure," she said. "What's the mission?"

"The only clue we have so far is Cindy. We know she's from the future and isn't above changing our history. And the MOs for these suicides look like a pattern to me. That's where we start."

"Got it," Kathy said. "Where and when are we going?"

"I don't know yet. I'm hoping Doctor Astalos will tell us from the box of intel Hatcher brought back with her. Doctor Astalos?"

"Nothing yet. I was just finishing up with another project. I can start on it as soon as we finish here."

With Tyler and Wu on the job, McKnight felt better. They were the best at planning and organizing missions. And Doctor Astalos had no equal at the technology side. They should be able to come up with an actionable plan.

Better than sitting around with our thumbs up our collective ass.

"Marc," Astalos said. "Where is Mitch... Lieutenant Wheeler? I wanted to share this with him. It was his idea."

"He's at the hospital with Hatcher's parents, waiting for her to wake up. What's up?"

"I see. I hope she'll be okay."

"She will be."

"Good," Astalos said. "About six months ago, Mitch came up with the idea to send status messages through the travel beacon. It was a great idea and, as it turns out, easier to do than I thought. The Engine already pinged all beacons for status periodically, so I piggybacked the message capability on the ping signal. It was mostly a software change, about fifty lines of code and a data structure change on the ping message. We did have to re-engineer the beacon to add a proximity interface. There's an update to your proximities app on your phone, too. I worked it out and tested it. We're ready to implement the changes now."

"Really?" McKnight said.

"I did."

"I'm dumbfounded."

"About what?" Astalos said.

"Well, *you*... When do you find the time? I mean, you have family, you work on other projects. Your energy level is amazing."

"Well, I work from home some at night. I get bored, or I get interested in something, so I just go down to the basement and piddle around."

"Wow," McKnight said and shook his head. "I should be able to piddle like that. But anyway, back to business. How does it work?"

"Well, it's limited, but the functionality is in all our new beacons. The interface is very simple. You can prox from your phone to a beacon nearby and the beacon passes the message on to its Engine. It's as simple as sending a text message."

"What's the practical application?"

"Simple. Have you ever wanted to send a status message during time travel but couldn't? Well, now you can."

"How close to the beacon do you need to be?"

"Within ten feet," Astalos said. "We're assuming you want to prox to your own beacon, but the capability is there to prox to another beacon if it's close."

"Cool," Trevor said. "Does it also work the other way? Can we send out a message from the Engine to the travelers' beacons?"

"Yes, but right now, it's a broadcast message. You can't send it to just one person. It's everybody, or nobody. You can't be selective about who gets the message. It'll be useful if you want to call everyone to return home, or to alert everyone about something."

"That could be useful. Doctor. Thank you. Now, the—"

"There's more," Astalos said. "I've also implemented an arrival and departure alert for the Engine."

"A what? What does that mean, exactly?"

"No more standing around the Engine, waiting for someone to return. The Engine will send subscribers an alert whenever it turns on. You'll know whenever someone jumps in or out. All you have to do is log into the Engine and subscribe to get the alert. That's it."

"Excellent," Trevor said. "That means we can be in our office doing work instead of babysitting the Engine when someone is on a mission."

"Correct," Astalos said. "I thought you guys might appreciate that."

"Thank you, Doctor," McKnight said. "It'll be very helpful and it's much appreciated."

"You're welcome."

"Good. Now, the most important thing I need from you right now is to dive into Lieutenant Hatcher's intel box and figure out where they held her. When we learn that, we'll have a starting place to look for Cindy, or whoever she is."

"I will, Major. There's a sticky note on top of the other documents that looks like a time coordinate. I just need to translate it."

"Good. Can you do that right away, please? And let me know as soon as you have something for me? Anything?"

"Of course."

McKnight glanced around the room at the grim faces there. He walked to the door and turned back toward them.

"We all have our marching orders. Let's get moving before something else happens. My worry is that we're now on borrowed time, waiting for another shoe to drop on our heads. My worst fear is that we'll get a visit from Cindy and a squad of troopers with advanced weaponry that we can't deal with. Is that clear?"

After getting nods from everyone, McKnight left the room.

CHAPTER 10

<u>Thursday, November 20th, 2036 — 11:30pm — Walter Reed Hospital</u>

When she became aware, all Hatcher could see was light. Slowly, things took shape. There were two bars of light overhead. In front of her, a wall with two pictures on it. And a TelExtraVision monitor.

She turned her head to the right, and the images heaved and swirled. She closed her eyes to let it pass, then opened them again.

Better.

There was a door and a side chair. Next to the door was a large MP. She turned the other way and saw a window.

It's dark outside.

A little further to the left was a steel pole with an IV bag on it.

For the first time, she realized she was in a bed. She struggled to move and couldn't. She looked for restraints and there were none. She tried to move again. This time, she could.

God, I'm so tired.

She closed her eyes.

When she opened her eyes again, she didn't know how long she'd been unconscious.

I've got to get out of here. Rachel will be back any moment.

She looked at the MP again.

"What year is it?" she asked.

He smiled, then opened the door and stuck his head outside for a moment. Then he closed the door and resumed his vigil.

Hatcher couldn't figure out if that was good. Now that she was awake again, Rachel might come back sooner.

A doctor with black hair, glasses and kind eyes entered the room and stood by her bed.

"Good Evening, Lieutenant Hatcher. Nice of you to join us. We've been waiting for you."

"Where am I?" she said. "What year is it?" She tried without success to keep the tremor from her voice.

"You might feel a little disoriented for the next few days, Lieutenant. I'm Doctor Epstein. I'm the hospitalist on this floor. You're at Walter Reed."

"Right," she declared. "What year is it, please?"

"Oh, sorry. It's 2036. You made it home."

"Could you show me your phone, please?"

"My what?"

"Your phone. Go to your calendar page."

The doctor smiled and held out his phone for her.

"I see," she said. "Thank you."

"No problem. I don't blame you for being skeptical. I would be."

She nodded and said, "Where's Major McKnight?"

She tried to sit up and looked off the side of the bed. "Where's my box? I need my box."

"It's okay, Lieutenant. Major McKnight was here earlier today, and he took the box with him when he left. The EMT who brought you in made sure the Major got the box, knowing that you wanted him to have it. Your parents and all the Major's team were here. They took turns coming in to see you. We ran them off about a half hour ago because they all looked dead tired."

Hatcher relaxed for the first time since she awakened. She studied the doctor. "Am I going to be all right?"

"Yes, I think so," Epstein said. "You have a few bruises, you're dehydrated and suffering from exposure, but you should be as good as new in a couple of days."

She nodded.

I need to debrief.

"Doctor, I need to talk to Major McKnight. Can you get him to come here? I need to tell him what I've learned."

"Yes, ma'am. He left his cell number with me, and I can call him whenever you are ready."

"I'm ready now. Please call him. It's important."

"I'll do that right away, Lieutenant. Now you close your eyes and get some more rest and I'll wake you when he gets here, okay?"

"Okay," Hatcher said.

She closed her eyes and allowed herself to drift back to sleep.

Someone was shaking her left arm. She tried to pull away, but couldn't move.

"Karen?"

She opened her eyes.

The woman they knew as Cindy stood before her.

Cindy the Imposter. Cindy the Murderer.

Hatcher glanced to both sides. The hospital room was gone. She could only see the walls of her cell.

She tried to punch Cindy, but couldn't move. She glanced at her chest and saw leather straps restraining her.

No, I can't be here! I escaped!

"Hello, Karen," Cindy said.

"This is a dream. You're not here."

"Ha," she said. "You wish. It's time for another little talk."

"Why don't you go screw yourself, Cindy?"

"How can you say that, now that we've become best friends? And Karen? You've been here long enough to figure out my name. See? I even have my name tag on today. Can you call me by my actual name?"

Hatcher tried to look perplexed.

"Oh, please," Cindy said. "Don't insult my intelligence. You're an Army Ranger Lieutenant and I've left you enough clues."

"Rachel Patterson."

"See? That wasn't so hard. We're getting along better and better. Oh, and here's another friend you might be missing."

Rachel beckoned to someone out of Hatcher's range of sight. She heard movement behind her.

Then, right in her face, was Freddie!

"How can *you* be here?" she said.

You're dead. I killed you.

"I know you remember me," Freddie said. "After all the marvelous times we had together."

Unbidden, Hatcher's mind flashed back to the first day of her captivity. The day he beat her for the first of many times.

Hatcher made a show of relaxing, then pushed hard against her restraints and tried to head-butt Freddie. Both Rachel and Freddie recoiled, then laughed.

"You're wrapped up tight, Karen," Rachel said. "I know better than to underestimate you and your strength. Are you ready for today's lesson?"

"Blow it out your ass, bitch!"

"That's my girl. Keep that animosity raging. We'll need it later. First, a little refreshment. Freddie?"

Freddie nodded and produced a squeeze bottle of a red liquid. He pinched Hatcher's nose and shoved the straw into her mouth. Rachel reached over and held Hatcher's jaw closed.

Hatcher swung her head to the side, but it did no good. Freddie squeezed the bottle, and she tasted the cherry flavor of the liquid. They held her nose and jaw until she had to swallow. The sweet liquid and its aroma overflowed her mouth into her nasal passages and down her throat.

She coughed to clear her windpipe of the sweet elixir.

"Honestly, dearie," Rachel said. "Such a big fuss over a little hydration."

"What was that?"

Rachel smiled. "It's my own personal concoction. It contains a drug we discovered years ago. It makes a person more... agreeable."

Hatcher sensed her resistance and her focus slipping away in favor of the warm feeling the liquid produced.

"Ah, I see it's having the desired effect. Your pupils are constricting."

Hatcher shook her head. She wanted to resist, but her mind was losing focus. She landed in a relaxed state. The room dimmed around her.

Rachel pulled away, and Hatcher melted into the chair. She no longer noticed her bonds, but she didn't care.

"Lovely, isn't it? But that isn't the reason for this little visit. I want to ask you a question. Are you ready?"

Rachel's voice was soft, but it filled Hatcher's awareness completely. She knew she should ignore it, but she couldn't.

"Repeat after me, soldier," Rachel said. "I am an officer in the Glorious Kosar Movement."

Hatcher closed her eyes. She tried to focus and shut out Rachel's voice.

"Say it," Rachel repeated.

Hatcher opened her eyes. "I'm an officer in the 75th Ranger Regiment of the United States Army."

Rachel nodded at Freddie and leaned back.

Freddie stood in front of her and smiled. "Naughty girl," he said, and struck her left cheek with his fist.

"Oh, I'm so sorry," Rachel said. "Wrong answer. Let's try again. Say it. I am an officer in the Glorious Kosar Movement."

Her cheek tingling from the blow, Hatcher struggled to offer a smile.

"Okay. Sorry, I misspoke. I'm an officer... in the 75th Ranger Regiment! Eat shit and—"

Freddie struck her again.

"C'mon, Karen," Rachel said. "Freddie and I can do this all day. Get with the program."

Hatcher opened her mouth to speak and Freddie jammed the straw back in her mouth and squeezed the bottle. She tried to spit it out, blowing a fine spray of elixir into the air. But she couldn't avoid swallowing most of it.

A wave of cherry flavor, warmth and peace spread through her body. The sensation of the taste reverberated through her consciousness.

"Mmm, I'll bet that feels good," Freddie said.

"Love that concoction," Rachel said. "Let's start again, Karen. I know you can say it. It's so easy and it will stop the pain. I am an officer in the Glorious Kosar Movement."

Hatcher awoke with a start. She was back in the hospital room.

She glanced at the heart monitor next to the bed. Her pulse was high.

Was that a dream? Or a memory?

CHAPTER 11

Thursday, November 20th, 2036 - 11:30pm - McKnight Apartment, Alexandria, Virginia

McKnight had just nodded off to sleep when his phone pinged.

He rolled over and felt for it on the nightstand. When he found it, he pulled it close to his face and opened the text application.

The text was from Trevor:

<Marc, Ritter called. There's been another death with similar M.O. The victim was the daughter of California's governor. They found her body in the same room with a city councilman in Miami who remembers nothing. They're asking how she got to FL so fast and what is the FBI doing about this rash of suicides? The same M.O. except they identified her. Ours, you think?>

"Oh, shit," McKnight said.

Megan rolled over. "Bad news?"

"Maybe another Suicide Scandal death. Another young girl dead and nobody knows how to stop it."

"What does that have to do with your team?" she said.

"We think it might be a murder carried out with the help of time travel. Hang on a minute," he said, and typed his reply to Trevor:

<I think so. What are the details? Can we launch a mission to intercept/interfere with it?>

Maybe this time, we can do something about it.

"Why would they do that?" Megan asked.

"I don't know."

"Does that mean I Don't Know - You Can't Tell Me... or I Don't Know - You Really Don't Know?"

He glanced at her. "I guess a little of both."

McKnight's phone pinged again. Megan rose from the bed, went into the bathroom and closed the door.

From Trevor again:

<Too late for a mission. She disappeared from Sacramento Tuesday 11/11 night and they found her Wednesday 11/12 morning. Over a week ago. She had no ID on her and it took Miami PD several days to get the DNA results back. They didn't hurry because they assumed it was a routine sex for pay deal that went bad.>

McKnight typed out his response:

<Since we ID'd her, why do we believe it's one of ours?>

After a moment, Trevor responded:

<The politician is the common thread. Don't know why they started kidnapping identifiable women unless they think maybe it will distract us or create political issues.>

McKnight considered the point.

I don't understand. The political pressure should spur us on to get results. What am I missing?

He typed out his response to Trevor:

<I don't see distraction or political issues as barriers to us. What else is different about the M.O.?>

He looked toward the bathroom. He needed to say something to lower the tension between them.

He sighed and called out. "Megan?"

She opened the bathroom door. "Yes?"

"Sorry. I was half asleep when the text came in. I shouldn't have said what I said. It's classified."

She returned to the room and laid on the bed next to him.

"And you can't even talk to your wife about it?"

"No. I can't talk to anybody about it."

"You might as well. I'm awake now, too."

McKnight lay on his back, looking at the ceiling. "You know that's not how it works, Honey."

"I know. It's just that... well, it's hard to watch you worry about something and I can't do anything to help. Makes me feel useless."

He rolled over and laid his arm across her waist. "But you're not. Just being here with me helps, believe me. I can't share the details — most of it is conjecture so far, anyway. Our guesses."

"It's hard for me, you know. Stuff like this pulls us further apart."

"Only if we let it," he said. He pulled himself up on his elbow and kissed her forehead. "Hang in there with me."

"I'll try."

"That's all I ask — that you try not to let it get to you."

He waited, but she said nothing else.

His phone pinged again.

Trevor again:

<Nothing else different, but the interval from disappearance to discovery was only 7 hours. No way she could have flown from Sacramento to Miami — simply not enough time. Had to be a time travel jump of the zero multiple. That trumps all discussion of M.O., right?>

McKnight had to agree. No other explanation fit the facts.

<Yes. It must be ours.>

Trevor texted back:

<Ritter wants to know what we will do. The FBI Director called him.>

Should have seen that one coming... Maybe Trevor's right about the political issues. We can't chase the bad guys while we're explaining to people why we couldn't prevent what they did.
He texted back:

<Tell him we're on it. I'll call him first thing tomorrow to discuss. Later.>

Trevor responded:

<Wilco. GN>

McKnight dreaded the activities of the coming morning.
If they involved the FBI Director, I'll hear from Senator Lodge and General Drake first thing in the morning.
McKnight put his hands behind his head, closed his eyes and tried to relax.
This time, the phone didn't ping.
It rang.

Friday, November 21st, 2036 — 1:07am — McKnight Apartment, Alexandria, Virginia

McKnight answered the phone.

"Major McKnight?"

"Yes?"

"This is Doctor Epstein at Walter Reed. Lieutenant Hatcher asked me to call you."

McKnight threw off the covers and sat on the side of the bed.

"She's awake? How is she?"

"She's a little disoriented, which you might expect. I had to convince her she was in the year 2036… whatever that means. But she's asking to see you."

Megan woke with a start and said, "What are you doing?"

She crawled over and wrapped her arms around his shoulders.

McKnight craned his neck to meet her eyes. "It's the hospital," he whispered.

To the phone, he said, "Is she coherent? Alert? Able to make intelligent conversation?"

Epstein laughed. "Well, yes to the first two questions. You'll have to be the judge about intelligent conversation. She asked where her box was and I told her we gave it to you. She sounded relieved that you have it now, but she wants to make her report. She insisted I call you right away. To be honest, I think she's terrified of not doing her duty."

McKnight smiled. "Well, that sounds normal enough… I'll get there as soon as I can. I'm about 45 minutes away." He pulled the phone away from his face long enough to read the time. "It's about 0110 hours. I'll be there by around 2:00 am. Will I be able to get in the building?"

"Your military ID will get you in. When you get to the desk downstairs, tell them I wanted them to notify me as soon as you got here."

"Great! I'm on my way. And thanks, Doc. Much appreciated."

"You're welcome. See you in an hour."

The line disconnected.

McKnight stood as Megan released her grip on his shoulders.

"Where are you going?" she said.

"I have to go to the hospital to get Hatcher's report."

She climbed out of the bed and put her arms around him. "Of course, you do... but do you have to do it now? Can't it wait until morning?"

McKnight considered her question.

Wait until tomorrow? Probably so.

But it wasn't in his DNA to wait.

I've got to know what she knows before something else happens or someone else gets hurt.

"No, it can't," he said. "We don't know what will happen later and I need to know what she knows."

McKnight saw the disappointment and a trace of anger on her face.

"I'm sorry, but it's my responsibility. It's important."

Megan let go of him. "Okay. Be careful. Can you at least call me later and let me know how she's doing?"

"I will. And I'll tell her you said hello. I love you, Megan. Try to get some sleep. I'll call in a little while."

He stepped into the closet, dressed, and left the apartment.

As he drove his truck out of the parking lot, he called Wheeler to let him know his partner was awake. As he expected, the lieutenant insisted on meeting him there.

It occurred to him that Wheeler lived closer to the hospital and might beat him there.

CHAPTER 13

<u>Friday, November 21st, 2036 — 02:30am — Walter Reed Hospital, Bethesda, Maryland</u>

McKnight arrived at Walter Reed later than he expected and checked in at the front desk. They advised that Doctor Epstein told them to expect him and bring him right up to Hatcher's room. The Marine corporal who escorted him told him Wheeler was already there.

He caught up with Wheeler in the hallway outside her room. Wheeler jumped to his feet and saluted.

"As you were, Mitch," McKnight said. "Have you been in to see her?"

"Yes, sir. We should give her a minute, sir."

"Why?"

"Because I just told her about her fiancé. When I got here, she pinned me to the wall. 'What's up with Richard?' she said. She called his roommate in New York and the wimp-ass lawyer dodged the question. Said Richard was 'out'."

"Oh."

"Yes, sir. And you know Hatcher. She pushed him and he hung up on her. Then I showed up, and she got out of bed and in my face and wanted to know where he was and why he hadn't bothered to come see her. I *had* to tell her." Wheeler hung his head.

"I'm sorry you had to be the one to tell her, Mitch. That would have been my job, my responsibility."

"Sorry, sir, but I don't see why her best friend couldn't tell her about this. Why not? What else am I good for if I can't tell my friend the truth?"

"Understood. You're right, of course... How'd she take it?"

"About as you might expect, sir. She was ripped out of her life and taken God knows where. And now, she comes back to find out someone killed her fiancé in a hit-and-run accident."

"I see."

"Yes, sir, but no one's tougher than Hatcher. She picked up a box of tissues and sat back down on the bed. She told me to show you in as soon as you got here."

McKnight sighed. "I think we can give her about ten minutes, don't you think?"

"Yes, sir. Thank you, sir."

The two men sat together in the hall to allow their comrade-in-arms a few minutes to adjust to the death of her fiancé.

McKnight thought about how he would feel if he was in her shoes — What if Megan was killed? He pushed the thought away. He didn't even want to contemplate that scenario.

"Mitch, do her parents know she's awake?"

"Yes, sir. The doctor already called them, sir. They should be on their way here by now."

"Okay. But you give them a call now. Don't let them agonize over telling her about Richard. Let them know you already told her."

Wheeler nodded. "I'll be happy to, sir."

"Good."

"I *do* have a little good news."

"What's that, Lieutenant?"

"Security came by. They did a heavy duty scan of all Hatcher's stuff. No foreign substances, no clandestine devices, nothing that could harm her or others. Nothing except the lockpick kit in her boot, but we knew about that already."

"Great," McKnight said. "Then we can be pretty confident her escape was not on purpose. She saw an opportunity, assessed it, improvised, and made it happen. Sounds like Hatcher, doesn't it?"

"Yes, sir, it does."

A nurse strode down the hall toward them. "Are either of you Major McKnight?"

The two soldiers stood. "Yes, that's me," McKnight said.

"Good, Lieutenant Hatcher just buzzed the nurse's station and asked if you were here yet. She said she's ready to see you at your convenience."

"Thank you," McKnight said. He turned to Wheeler. "All right. Call the Hatchers."

"Yes, sir," Wheeler said and saluted.

McKnight returned the salute, took a deep breath, and stepped into Hatcher's room.

She was sitting up in the bed with an IV tube in her right arm. The MP sergeant came to attention by the door.

There were two vases of flowers on the dresser. A box of tissues lay on the bed and she clung to one in her hand. Her eyes were closed.

"Lieutenant?" he said.

Her eyes flew open, and she raised herself up in the bed and tried to salute.

"As you were, Lieutenant."

Hatcher lay back down on her bed.

"Thanks for coming, Major."

McKnight turned to the MP sergeant. "Sergeant, could you give us a few minutes? Why don't you take a break and I'll find you when we're done?"

"Yes, sir," he said and left the room.

McKnight turned back to Hatcher. "Lieutenant, I'm happy to see you again. I wasn't sure we'd get to do that. How are you feeling?"

"Not a hundred percent, but functional, sir. I just need to get out of this damned bed."

"Understood. I think we can get that done pretty soon, but for now, I want you to relax and enjoy some well-deserved leave. Can you do that?"

A ghost of a smile crossed her face. "Under protest, sir."

Well, some things haven't changed.

"Megan and I were sorry to hear about Richard."

"Thank you, sir. It was... a bit of a shock." Her voice quivered. "But I'm a little tired, so can we get to my debrief? There's a lot you need to know."

"Okay, Lieutenant, we can do that."

"They told me you got the box I brought back, sir. Is that accurate?"

"Yes, I haven't gone through it in depth, but Doctor Astalos has it and is digging in to see what's there. Is there something in particular I need to be searching for?"

"No, sir. I was in a bit of a hurry and I grabbed what intel I could. I just hope some of it will be helpful."

McKnight nodded. "I'm sure it will be. Where shall we start? Do you know where you were? Can you tell me anything about Cindy? Who is she?"

"Yes, sir," Hatcher said. "She's as good a place as any to start the story. First, her name isn't Cindy. We already knew she was an imposter before we confronted her. Did we ever find the real Cindy Ginn?"

"No, and I doubt we will. So, who is she?"

"I was flabbergasted to learn who she is, sir. She's a major in the U.S. Army. A Ranger. Her name is Rachel... Rachel Patterson."

"What organization was she in? What Regiment?"

"The 75th, sir. Her uniform has all the right markings, although it's a little different from ours. She's in a group called the 'FTS', whatever that is."

"She's a Ranger? Wow. That defies reason."

"Yes, sir. And the place felt like an army facility. They kept me drugged most of the time, but I tried to observe what I could. Whenever I came to, I played possum, hoping to learn something or have an escape opportunity."

"Sorry," McKnight said. "'Played possum'? What does that mean?"

"It's a Southernism, sir. It means I pretended to be unconscious. I hoped it would give me an advantage I could use to escape. Which it did, eventually."

"I see. Go on."

"I'm getting ahead of myself. After Cindy and I jumped from the Telegraph Road office, they must have gassed me, because I don't remember it. The first time I came to, I woke up in my skivvies. They took my uniform and my boots. I saw them in front of a locker and later that's where I found them. Then Rachel and this guy named Freddie came in."

"Okay, Freddie... Was there anyone else around that you remember?"

"I saw several other folks there — all in uniform except Freddie — and they all deferred to Rachel."

"Okay, good to know... Did you get the impression that she was running the show, or did you see anyone else that might be in charge?"

Hatcher thought for a moment.

"There was this one guy," she said. "I think it was like the second time I woke up. Rachel was talking to someone across the room from me. I opened my eyes a little and saw an older guy — maybe around General Drake's age. I got the feeling she was briefing him, or at least she was doing most of the talking. I heard him say something like 'Keep me posted' when he left. Rachel seemed relieved after he was gone."

"You didn't hear a name or anything?"

"No, sir, but I heard her briefing someone on her phone on another day. At least I think it was another day. All the things run together, you know? I was gone about four months, right?"

McKnight nodded.

"Yeah, anyway, she called that guy on the phone Four. You know, like the number? Sounded like a movie villain. 'Yes, Number Four. Whatever you say, Number Four.' Anyway, as she got off the phone, I acted like I just woke up and I asked her if that was her boyfriend on the phone. She didn't say anything, but she looked pissed."

"Okay. Yeah, he sounds like the boss, doesn't he?"

"Yeah," Hatcher said. "And then, there was this other guy. All I know is, he said his name was Freddie." McKnight noted the tone Hatcher used when she said his name. "Asshole."

"Tell me about Freddie."

"I never saw him in uniform. He was always in a suit, or at least suit pants, white shirt and a dark tie pulled loose. Now that I think about it, I don't know if I ever saw a coat. I'm not sure."

"Could you tell me anything about him? What did he look like?"

"Skinny. I could have taken him any time if I hadn't been tied up. He hit me a few times. Okay, quite a few times. Bastard. Well, I took him and killed him. That's how I got away."

"Well, that explains the bruises you came in with. That's good. We'll come back to that. Was he trying to break you?"

"I guess," Hatcher nodded. "Indoctrination."

"Indoctrination? What does that mean?"

"I think he was trying to brainwash me. You know, bring me into their... 'Movement' or whatever... their noble cause."

"Tell me about that."

"He kept going on and on about the 'Movement' and the glorious Kosar brothers. Something about Hungary and their impending arrival in the United States."

"Anything else?"

"Yes. According to Freddie, their coming to the States sounded like Jesus coming on Judgment Day. Like it was prophesied and a hundred years in coming. Wacko. And I mean, way out there." She stared off into space for a moment.

"Karen? Are you still with me?"

She blinked twice and looked back at him.

"What?" she said. "Of course, I am. Why would you think otherwise?"

The thought that nagged McKnight's subconscious slipped unbidden to the surface.

If this place was secure, how the hell did she get out?

"Lieutenant, this is all good intel," he said. "Tell me about how you got away. They kept you tied up and sedated. What changed?"

"I think I got lucky, sir. I told you I pretended to be unconscious for as long as possible each time I woke up. I hoped it would establish an expectation of how the drugs affected me and maybe avoid some beatings."

"Okay. So, what happened?"

"The day I escaped, I came to, but didn't move. I played possum, and I heard Freddie come in. He came over to me and checked my pulse. Then he started feeling me up."

She looked McKnight in the eye. "What a pervert! He did it every time there was no one else around. It was all I could do to pretend I was still out."

McKnight pulled on his chin. "I get the gist. So…"

"Anyway, I think he got some stones this time and decided to do more. I think he wanted to get a look — you know — at my tits. He tried to pull up my shirt, but he couldn't do it very well with all the restraining straps, so he took the strap off my left arm and pulled my arm out of the shirt. Then he could pull my shirt up and see more."

She shivered. "It was all I could do to remain still. With that hand free, I could kill him, but I wouldn't be loose. So I just laid there and pretended not to feel anything. Then he stopped touching me."

"He stopped?"

"Yes, and I heard him walk away. I sneaked a peek, and I saw him over at the door. He was sticking his head out. I guess he was checking to see if there was anyone else around. Anyway, he came back and took the strap off my other arm and pulled my tee shirt up to my neck and moved away. My legs and head were still bound, so I was afraid I couldn't get hold of him. Through my closed eyes, I sensed a flash. The son of a bitch took a damned picture! Then he came back to the rack and started feeling me up. Then I made my move. Bastard."

"What did you do?"

"I felt him lick me and knew he was close enough. I opened my eyes and bashed in his larynx. He grabbed his throat; I threw my arm around his neck and heeled him over into a choke hold. I squeezed until he was dead. Maybe a little longer."

"Good. Then what happened?"

"I got loose from the head strap and freed my legs. All I could think about was to get out of there."

"Yep. Then what?"

"I remembered Freddie stowed my boots in a locker. I needed those boots to get away. I took his ID card and his keys from his pocket and opened it. They were still there and so was my phone. I checked for the lockpick kit in the heel and it was still there, too. So I put them on, grabbed my phone and ran out the door, looking for an exit. Then I realized... what if there was a Time Engine here? If I just ran out the door, I'd be free but God knows what time period I was in. If there was an Engine, I could get to 2036 and make my way home from wherever I was."

"Logical. Then what?"

"I walked down the hall and saw a door with Rachel's name on it and right across the hall there was a door that said FTS personnel only on it... A room that only Rachel and her team could go into, right? I tried it, but it was locked. I wanted to bang on it, I was so frustrated. I thought about picking the lock, but it was a card lock — no way to pick it. I thought of Rachel's office — maybe there was a card in her desk? I turned to her door and used my kit to unlock it. There was a desk, two side chairs, a file cabinet and a small conference table. The desk had a computer screen built into it."

"Okay, so you broke into her desk?"

"No, it was unlocked. I found two key cards right away, so I hoped one of them opened the Engine room, and it did. It was a lab like ours. I saw an Engine on the far wall. Then I started thinking — wait, what about intel? What can I bring back with me that will help us stop these guys?"

"Good thinking. What did you do?"

"I went back to Rachel's office and broke into the file cabinet. I wondered why she would use a file cabinet instead of keeping her stuff online."

"And?" McKnight said.

"Sir, I reasoned it was just like today. If hackers are a problem today, they're still a problem then. Anything that's online has a possibility of getting hacked. Maybe not from your average hacker, but there might be people in the military and in power that she didn't want to see her stuff."

"Makes sense."

"In the top drawer of the cabinet, I found folders behind a tab that read 'Current Projects'. Sounded like a good find to me, so I pulled it out. A set of folders about six inches thick. Fairly heavy. I toted it across the hall to the Engine room and found a box to carry it in. Then I checked the Engine. It was more complex than ours and I was a little surprised there was no login required to get into it. We need to talk to Doctor Astalos about that, sir," she pleaded. "Nobody should be able to access one of our Engines unless they have valid credentials, right?"

"Good idea. We'll pass it on. What else did you do?"

"First, I checked the date. I knew we'd need to know the 'when' of where Rachel was coming from. She's from 2086, sir. Fifty years in the future. It's not proof, but it implies they haven't conquered the twenty-five year limitation yet. Looks like the playing field is a little more level than you might expect."

"Yes, it does, That's good."

"There was a digital clock on the wall. It read 3:30am. I calculated the time and location with the machine and wrote it down on a sticky note."

She looked up at him. "Did you find it, sir? I put it in the box."

"Yes, we did. Doctor Astalos recognized what it was just by glancing at it."

"He would."

"Okay, then what happened?"

"I had no coordinates to get home. I mean, I've entered them so many times, I thought I knew what they were, but I started second-guessing myself and got scared, you know?"

"I do. So, what did you do?"

"I set up a beacon to send me to 2036 at the current location. I thought I would jump then and there, but then thought the better of it. I might jump to 2036 and be stuck in this same building, or worse, be inside another building's foundation. It was a pretty scary thought. I decided to get outside and find a better place — at least I'd be outside with a fighting chance. I grabbed my box and looked for a way out."

She paused. "Then, I found the loading dock. A metal slide bar secured the doors, so I pushed it back, lifted the door and took off."

"How did you decide what to do?"

"I wasn't sure. My priority was to get as far from that building as I could. I hauled ass down a hill, across a pretty big highway and into some woods. It was cold as shit."

"Did you see anyone?"

"No. I could hear some vehicles in the distance, but it was too early in the morning for many people to be out and about. Anyway, I ran for a few miles, through the woods and across a couple of fields."

"You were looking for a place to jump where it might be safe to land in 2036?"

"Yes, sir. But the cold started getting to me. In my hurry to get out, I didn't think to look for a coat or anything. Hell, I didn't even know what season it was. I didn't know how long I'd been there."

"Understood. Go on."

"Well, I came to this wide creek. According to the EMT, it was Cameron Run, just west of town, so I guess it was more than a creek. It wasn't moving fast, but it was hip deep when I waded through it. In hindsight, I should have risked finding a bridge, but I was tired and cold and not thinking clearly."

McKnight nodded. "I'm still with you."

"Anyway, the water crossing did me in. I came out of it frozen to the core. I was shivering and could barely walk. A little park was on the far side. It was just a narrow strip of lawn beside a highway. I remember hoping it wasn't wide enough to have a building on it in 2036. I didn't think I could go much further, and I was losing my train of thought. The last thing I thought about was, I might die here in 2086 and no one would ever know who I was or where I came from. So I thought, screw it, let's jump from here. I put the box down, kneeled and pressed the beacon. The next thing I knew, I was in an ambulance with an EMT talking to me and telling me I was in Cameron Run Park."

"Yes. Anything else?"

"No, sir. I can't think of any more right now. I'll get back with you if I remember anything else."

"Good. Very good and detailed report, Lieutenant."

"Thank you, sir."

"Now I should let you get some more rest."

"Yes, sir. When can I get back to my duties? I feel better and, well, you know... Wheeler is starting to annoy me."

McKnight looked her in the eyes. He hoped he'd find that hint of amusement that said she was glad to be back with her friend and co-worker. It was there.

"I'll see what I can do. For now, your orders are to sleep as much as possible and then we'll get you some physical training to get back in shape."

"Yes, sir."

"Karen, I'm glad you're back and still in one piece. Your parents are on the way."

"Thank you, sir. Could you tell them something for me?"

"Sure."

"Would you tell them I already know about Richard? I don't want them worrying about me all the way over here."

"Already done. Again, we were all so sorry to hear about his death. Now, you get some rest. That's an order, Lieutenant."

"Yes, sir."

McKnight nodded and left the room. He directed the MP sergeant to return to his post.

In the hallway, he ran into Hatcher's parents and Wheeler. He stopped and saluted.

"As you were," General Hatcher said. "Did you finish your debrief, Major?"

"Yes, ma'am."

"Very good. How is she?"

"All things considered, I think she'll be fine. She's already talking about getting back to work."

The General sighed and leaned against her husband. Her expression softened, and she smiled.

"Lieutenant Wheeler was just updating us," Colonel Hatcher said. "Is there any chance that she can take some leave when she gets better? Her mother and I would like to spend some time with her during her convalescence."

"There's every chance, sir," McKnight said. "I'd sign that order with no reservations. But I think the hard part will be getting her to take the leave."

He smiled and glanced at Wheeler.

"Yes, that's what Lieutenant Wheeler was just saying. I think he knows her better than anyone."

"Yes, sir, I agree with that. But if she's willing, I'll sign the order."

"Thank you, Major." He reached out to shake McKnight's hand. "You must be exhausted. We'll let you get home to your wife, so you can get some sleep."

McKnight and Wheeler saluted as the Hatchers passed them and went into Hatcher's room.

McKnight turned to walk down the hall.

Wheeler fell in step with him. "That's a couple of class acts, sir," he said.

"Agreed. And the acorn didn't fall very far from that tree, did it?"

"No, sir. When will Hatcher be fit for duty?"

"In a couple of days, I think," McKnight said.

"It'll be good to have her back."

"Yes, if she doesn't request some leave."

Wheeler chuckled. "And what do you think the chances of that are, sir?"

"Zero, Lieutenant. Absolutely zero. I'll see you in the office in a few hours. Go get some sleep."

CHAPTER 14

Friday, November 21st, 2036 — 8:34am — McKnight Apartment, Alexandria, Virginia

McKnight slipped back into bed without waking Megan but didn't sleep much. There were too many unanswered questions and his mind refused to settle down. He gave up trying and rose before she woke up.

He was brewing coffee when she came out of the bedroom. She wore the blue satin robe he liked and she stretched as she approached him. She slipped into his arms. He felt the heat of her body from sleep. She got on her tiptoes and kissed his neck.

"Mmm, good morning," she mumbled. "How's Hatcher?"

"Better than I expected. She had quite an adventure."

"I'm sure. What happened?"

I opened the door to that question. I shouldn't have.

He looked at his watch. "I need to brief the General. He should be in his office by now."

"Fine," she said, separating herself from him. "I'll go get a shower so you can talk in private." She turned on her heel and walked back to the bedroom. McKnight was sure she wasn't happy with him, but didn't have time to think about it.

As he expected, General Drake was in his office. McKnight gave him a summary of Hatcher's report. Drake asked a few questions related to Hatcher's physical and mental health, and her fitness for duty.

Then McKnight asked about response versus reaction.

"Sir, has there been any progress on getting approval to take strategic action against these people?"

"Actually, there has," Drake said. "The President completed her round of discussion with members of Congress to garner support. Last night, she signed an Executive Order that gives us permission to investigate criminal events that involve time travel as 'clear and present dangers' to the United States. The Order also permits us to act to prevent or reverse any changes to the natural flow of history as needed and to the best of our abilities."

"That's great, sir. Great news."

"There's more."

"Sir?"

"Senator Lodge has submitted a bill to integrate the Executive Order into our charter. That strengthens it and makes it harder for future administrations to reverse without legislation, though I doubt they would, based on what has happened and could happen."

"That's good. We can create some long-term policies and scenario responses without fear of the work being a waste of time."

"Yes. That's the goal," Drake said.

"Seems like Senator Lodge is doing his oversight job."

"He is today, so far. But we expect limited support for the legislation. Many people in Congress still don't like state-sponsored time travel. They argue there's too much temptation to use the technology to shape history. I agree, but if time travel is illegal, even for government..."

"Then only outlaw states and organizations will use it," McKnight said. "And you can't stop or deter it if you don't have the capability."

"Exactly," Drake said. "If we don't watch for and prevent changes to history, who's to say what kind of world we'll have in twenty, thirty, or fifty years?"

"Yes, sir. I agree. Could you please send me a copy of the EO so I can review it and find all the edges?"

"I already sent it to your email. Major, what are you thinking about your first steps here?"

"Good question, sir. I think some recon is in order. I'd like to find out if Rachel Patterson and the FTS have anything to do with the Suicide Scandals. We already know she personally orchestrated illegal changes to the natural path of history and the M.O. is similar. I think it's a good place to start."

"I agree," Drake said. "What do you have in mind?"

McKnight paused.

What other choice might there be?

"I was thinking I would jump to the location where they kept Lieutenant Hatcher. I'd go in the middle of the night and gather intel."

"I think you're half right. We need to jump in, but I don't choose to send you or anyone else in when we don't know what to expect. If it were me on the other side, I'd be expecting someone to come in. It would be a nice little trap, eh?"

"Yes, sir. I guess I would."

"I'm not sending any troops into a dangerous situation without reconnaissance. Do you remember our discussion about equipping drones for jumps into hostile environments? I'll leave it to Doctor Astalos to give you the details, but he advised me last night that he's been talking to the Air Force about their recon drones. He's got some equipped with beacons and armed for the job."

It made sense, but McKnight wasn't crazy about sending a machine to do recon.

"That's good, sir. But don't we want to get a human there... I mean, I realize the danger, but how much recon can a drone do other than pictures and recording sound?"

"I agree recon information gathered by a human would be preferable, but the risk is too great. I can't see sending in Rangers until we have more info about what they might be facing. No, we'll send the drones first. They'll record what they see and hear, and then we'll have more information about what to expect if and when we jump there."

"Then we may or may not jump in after we know and understand the risk?"

"Correct. We don't want this to be an assault on a beachhead. It's gathering intel."

"Understood and agreed, sir," McKnight said. "I'll call Doctor Astalos and find out how soon we can be ready. And I'll have Doctor Wu and Captain Tyler make a plan."

"Good. Let's start that today."

"Yes, sir. I'll get that ball rolling as soon as we get off the phone. I'll make sure the team understands what the Order says we can and cannot do."

"Good," Drake said. "Anything else, Major?"

"No, sir. Thank you and I'll keep you posted."

"Thanks. I'll get back with you later today to get the mission details."

Today. He wants it planned out today.

"Yes, sir."

Drake disconnected the call.

McKnight entered the email program on his phone, scanned the Executive Order, and forwarded it to Kathy and Tyler. He also asked them to pull together a first draft plan by noon.

He poured himself a cup of coffee and leaned against the kitchen counter while he thought about what the drones might find and what the next steps might be.

The HERO Team enters a new phase of their existence today. Starting now, we can take offensive measures instead of reacting. Now, we're cooking.

CHAPTER 15

Friday, November 21st, 2036 — 8:40am — McKnight Apartment, Alexandria, Virginia

Megan came back from the bedroom. She wore her blue robe again and dried her hair with a towel.

"I don't think I like this life that much," she said.

"What?" he said.

"I knew there would be times when we couldn't talk about your job, but I didn't realize it would be all the time and everything. I'm not sure I can take it."

McKnight walked to her and moved to embrace her, but she put up her hands to stop him.

"Just let me get this out, okay?"

He stood still and listened.

"I need to be a substantial part of your life and I want you to be a big part of mine. But there's this huge piece I *can't* know about, and it takes away from my ability to support you and be a rock for you. Does that make sense?"

He nodded.

"You get to know everything about me and everyone I might work with — provided I should ever *find* a job, which frustrates the hell out of me — But anyway, I can't know the same about you. It just feels so… lopsided."

He nodded again.

"Is it all so classified? I don't care about the details, but is there nothing I can know about your work so I understand what you go through every day?"

Yeah, I could tell her things, but they lead to other questions and I'll have to be aware of the boundaries all the time.

"Well?" she said. "Don't you have anything to say?"

"I was listening."

She frowned. "Okay, talk to me now. Isn't there anything you can talk about?"

"Okay, the problem is that unclassified discussions can wander into classified areas. I have to be very careful about that, and I hate to be on guard constantly. I want to relax with you and not worry all the time about revealing classified stuff. Does that make sense?"

"No, it doesn't. Because you still have to be on guard all the time anyway so you don't talk about it."

McKnight rubbed his chin.

She's trying hard to work this out.

"Well, how about if I tell you all the unclassified stuff when our investigation is over? You won't be right up to date, but at least I can satisfy your curiosity after the fact?"

She paused for a moment.

"Okay, that's an improvement," she said. "It isn't very satisfying, but it's a better plan than what we're doing now. Can you tell me what happened to Hatcher then?"

"Most of it, I think. Yes, there *are* some things I can share. Does that help?"

"Yes, it does. I'll be glad when you finish this. I have lots of questions."

"I know." He glanced at his watch. "How about I tell you what I can about Hatcher when I get home tonight? I'm running late and the General gave me some new stuff to do."

"Okay, it's a date. By the way, I have an interview with a law firm this afternoon. Wish me luck."

"I do. You'll be great. I'll see you tonight," he said. "Love you."

"Love you, too. Good luck today."

McKnight left the apartment to drive to work.

CHAPTER 16

<u>Saturday, November 22nd, 2036 — 01:47am — HERO Team Lab at</u>
<u>Telegraph Road, Alexandria, Virginia</u>

It was a long day.

McKnight went home for two hours earlier and fulfilled his promise to tell Megan what he could about Hatcher's experience.

It wasn't as hard as he expected. She was in a much better mood afterward, now that she understood why he devoted so much energy to discover and process the information they had.

Earlier in the day, McKnight, Doctor Astalos, Kathy and Tyler crafted a short mission for the recon drones. The drones were armed, designed to have both whisper-quiet and battle modes, and to capture video with sound in low light.

Since Astalos created arrival and departure alarms for the 2036 Engine, they assumed the 2086 machines would have the same feature. But Rachel's team wouldn't be configured to receive alarms from present-day Engines.

The plan was to get in, recon the area, and get out before local personnel detected them and responded.

McKnight left his office and walked to the HERO Team Lab. He used his key disk to open the double doors and headed for the kitchen.

I need coffee.

Trevor, Tyler and Kathy were together at the break table, populated with coffee cups and snacks. Doctor Astalos tinkered with the two drones.

Tyler came to attention as McKnight entered.

"At ease, Winnie," he said. He and Tyler sat with the others. McKnight looked back over his shoulder toward the Engine platform. "What's the Doc doing? I thought he had everything ready to go?"

"Just a few last-minute adjustments," Tyler said. "Not sure what they are. You know the Doc. There's always room for improvement."

"Where's Wheeler?"

"Last minute detail, sir. He'll be here in a few minutes."

"Okay, when do we start?"

"Soon. General Drake said he wanted to come by, but he might not. Senator Lodge has him tied up with some stuff."

"At two in the morning?" McKnight said.

"You know the Senator, sir."

"Jeez," McKnight said. "Oversight."

"Yes, sir," Tyler said. "Why couldn't we be one of those government agencies that takes forever to do something? I could use a little more sleep."

Kathy laughed out loud.

"What?" Tyler said.

"This from a newlywed," she said, and then giggled. "Work is probably not the reason you're not getting enough sleep."

Tyler's face turned red.

"I can't imagine what you could be talking about," he said.

"Next chance I get," Kathy said, "I will smack you. I owe you one."

"Me?" Tyler replied. "What did I do?"

"Nothing," she said. "But I'm sure you deserve it."

Tyler laughed.

"Anyway," he said, "We'll have another guest."

McKnight eyed his second in command. "What? Who?"

"It's a surprise. You'll see."

"You know I'm not overly fond of surprises."

"This will be okay. Five more minutes. You'll see."

McKnight shook his head. He liked to be in full control, and this sounded like he wasn't.

Time out, asshole. You trained these guys. You delegated this work. Let them take it.

He leaned back in his chair and tried to relax.

Tyler's phone pinged to announce a text. He looked at it as it pinged again in his hand.

"Okay, y'all. The bad news is, General Drake will not be joining us. He wishes us luck."

The team members glanced at each other.

McKnight knew that look.

They're disappointed.

Everyone enjoyed having face time with the General. Despite the fact he was a legend in the Rangers, he was approachable and open to ideas from everyone under his command.

"The good news is," Tyler continued, "our special guest has arrived and will be here any second now."

Smiles from everyone.

They're excited about something... or someone.

The doors opened, and Wheeler walked in with Hatcher.

The team stood and applauded.

Hatcher couldn't hide a shy smile. Wheeler tried to hold her arm, but she shook it off, walked to the table and sat.

"I'm okay," she said. "Just a little weak from laying in that damned hospital bed."

"Yeah, I know," Wheeler said. "But Doctor Epstein said you have to take it easy for a couple of days."

"Blah, blah, blah," she said.

"You checked her out of the hospital?" McKnight said.

Wheeler shrugged. "It was that, or she was going AWOL. Doctor Epstein said she should be fine as long as she doesn't overtax herself. But she wanted to be here, and everyone wanted her here. So there you are."

"I'm fine... really," Hatcher said.

McKnight thought she looked pale.

"Fine," he said. "You can stay for the mission and then go home to rest. When you come back next time, I want you functional and ready to work."

"No problem, sir." Hatcher said.

"Okay," Tyler said. "Doctor Astalos? Are you about ready to go?"

Astalos popped his head up and said, "One more minute."

"Okay, Captain Tyler? Doctor Wu?" McKnight said. "Since we have a couple of minutes, could you give a brief rundown of what will happen here?"

"Yes, sir," Kathy said. "Very short mission. And because of the urgency, we'll dispense with the usual pre-mission formalities. Is that okay?"

"Yes, please continue," McKnight said.

"Yes, sir. In a nutshell, we're sending in two LF-50 drones to do a recon of the place where they held Hatcher. They're going in at this hour, hoping no one is paying attention on the other end. If they are, then we'll just have to deal with that, but we don't think they have any reason to expect us."

"What if someone's there?" Trevor asked.

"We'll get a nice photo of them and good footage of the place to supplement Lieutenant Hatcher's description. So, anyway, the two drones will start out airborne, over the Engine platform. They'll time-jump to Rachel's lab in 2086. As soon as the time bubble disperses, their cameras will turn on, they'll fly to the center of the room, and they'll do a 360-degree turn with video. They're programmed so that, while one is pointing his camera in one direction, the other points in the opposite direction. Their 360-degree turn takes thirty seconds. Then they'll return to their landing point and activate their beacons. Then they jump back here. That's it in a nutshell."

"Okay, all set," Doctor Astalos said. He walked back to the break table. "The drones are ready."

"Good," Kathy said. "Let's get the show on the road. Mr. Wheeler, will you assist me with the launch?"

"How about both of us?" Hatcher asked. "I'd really like to take part in the first shot back at these people."

"Sure," Kathy said. "Mitch, give her a hand over here to the console."

Hatcher stood and nearly lost her balance but recovered quickly. She wouldn't allow Wheeler to help her, so he walked by her side as she approached the Engine console.

The three of them configured the Engine for the jump. At the end the countdown, Hatcher pulled the launch trigger.

The bubble formed, and the air inside glowed and spun.

The drones fired their propellers and went airborne, hovering at four feet in the center of the maelstrom. They constantly altered their attitude to compensate for the violently swirling air within the bubble.

The hum of the Engine grew louder and covered every other sound in the room.

A loud crack punctuated their departure. The bubble dissipated, but the drones didn't disappear.

"Doctor Astalos," Tyler said, "Were the drones programmed to come back to the exact departure time instead of returning when done?"

"No," Astalos said, "they weren't."

Instead of landing, the drones flew to the center of the Lab and rotated in place.

"What's happening?" Trevor asked.

"They're executing their programming," Kathy said. "But they didn't jump."

"You mean they think they're in 2086 and the FTS lab?"

"Correct. If I'm right, they'll stop rotating in a second, return to the platform and land."

As if she had commanded it, the drones stopped turning and whispered over to the platform, paused for ten seconds in the air, and landed.

No one spoke for a moment.

Kathy walked from the Engine console to the table, with Hatcher behind her.

"Did they travel or not?" McKnight asked.

"No, sir," Kathy said.

"Why not?"

"One theory is you can only go back in time, not forward."

"No, I don't think so," Astalos said. "I think they've blocked their lab."

"Blocked?" McKnight said. He glanced at Hatcher. She looked disappointed and angry.

"Yes, I saw a reference to a Time Engine Inhibitor in Hatcher's intel box," Astalos said. "If I understand correctly, they've perfected a way to shield a location from a Time Engine visit. They called it a TEI."

"You mean they can jump here, but we can't jump there?"

"Yes. For now, anyway. I'll see if there is anything else about it in the box. If I can figure out how to do it, I might be able to defeat it."

"Dammit," Wheeler said, and patted Hatcher on the back.

She turned and glared at him for a second. Then her expression softened, and she said, "Take me home, please. I want to rest and get back here ASAP."

"Sure, Hatch. No problem." Wheeler said.

Astalos waved at them. "Mitch, take her home and then come back and help me with this. Two sets of eyes are better than one and there's more stuff in that box, including some storage disks."

"Wilco, sir," Wheeler said, and escorted Hatcher out of the Lab.

McKnight turned to Tyler and Kathy.

"What's our next step?"

They looked at each other and back at him.

"There isn't one, Major," Tyler said.

Kathy nodded. "If we can't jump there, we may be defenseless against Rachel and her people."

"Can't we jump someplace else and go to where they are?"

"I don't know, sir," Tyler said. "Theoretically, we can. Finding the best place will be tricky — you know, sending the drones or one of us to a place we know nothing about. What's space today might be a block of concrete in 2086."

"Right," Kathy said. "We need an alternate plan. Don't worry, we'll come up with something. You know we will."

McKnight met their eyes, taking in their intensity of purpose.

"Yes, I do," he said. "For now, shut the place down, go home, and get some sleep. At least we learned what we can't do. Yet."

CHAPTER 17

<u>Friday, November 22nd, 2086 — 11:47am — FTS Lab, Alexandria,</u>
<u>Virginia</u>

Major Rachel Patterson approached the communications station in the FTS lab.

Her weekly status meetings with Number Four were stressful, but today she had a negative point to deliver. Depending on his mood, it might not go well. But it was time, and he didn't like to wait.

She had no illusions about her relationship with him. She was a talented and valuable resource, and he was loyal and generous to those who served him well. But that support would stop if he believed her goals conflicted with his own.

And Rachel did have her own objectives. But so far, their association took them both where they wanted to go.

Very few people today knew who he was, but he was one of the most influential people in the world.

Influential? Deadly, you mean.

She had no doubts about Number Four and his capabilities. He was cold as a reptile and dangerous to anyone who got in his way.

To the outside world, he appeared to be a friendly, innocuous member of the United States' current administration — an advisor, an expert in politics.

Rachel and a few others knew him to be one of the five senior members of the Movement, with allegiance to the Kosar family. He and the other four were among the Chosen, the elite believers in George Kosar.

But Rachel suspected that Number Four, like herself, was mostly interested in his own power, and association with the Movement was convenient and useful.

She pressed the call button and watched it connect across the city. Number Four's automaton answered and asked her to wait.

She looked at her watch. She was late, which would irritate him.

Too late to avoid that now. I have an excuse.

Number Four's face appeared on the screen. His silver hair, cropped beard, and piercing blue eyes dominated the video screen. As usual, he wore an impeccable tailored navy suit, white shirt and blue tie, the mark of privilege and power.

"Rachel," he said. "How nice to hear from you." His smile was more a baring of teeth than a warm greeting.

"Good morning, Number Four."

"I was expecting your call a little earlier. Is anything wrong?"

"No, sir. There was an event earlier I needed to investigate and I was unavoidably detained. My sincere apologies."

"I see. Is there a problem on your end?"

"Not really. There was an attempt to time-jump into my lab early this morning."

Number Four's eyes narrowed. "From where?" he asked.

"It appears to be from the year 2036, sir."

Number Four said nothing, but stared and waited for her to speak again.

Rachel hated this skill he had. When you answered a question, he waited and watched you, applying subtle pressure to talk more and reveal more than intended.

And today, she wanted to reveal less.

"They didn't get in," she said. "The Time Engine Inhibitor worked perfectly."

Number Four nodded, but said nothing.

Rachel smiled and said, "That's all there is to the event, sir."

"I see," Number Four said. "And what is the next step? What do you expect Major McKnight's next move to be?"

"I expect he will figure out why the jump didn't work. Then he'll jump to another location and approach us from outside the facility in our time."

"That might be a concern. What are his chances of getting into your lab?"

"Near zero, sir. Our security is the best. I reviewed it myself, just last week. We are secure."

Number Four's smile froze into a grimace. "Then, if he gets in, it would be your failure. That's not an option."

"I'm not concerned, Number Four. As you know, I am good at this job and this place is near-impregnable."

"Oh, no reflection on your abilities, my dear. But you said, 'near zero'. I would have expected 'zero'. Is there an open problem or maybe an opportunity for our friend Major McKnight?"

"Only a small opening, sir. Nothing worth your time."

Don't ask. Don't ask. Don't ask.

"Indulge me, Rachel. What is the small opening? What is the risk?"

Rachel felt her breath becoming shallower and faster.

Can he read my mind?

"Well, as you may remember, we conditioned Lieutenant Hatcher as a weapon and allowed her to think she escaped. I argued against the plan."

"And your point is?"

"When she escaped, we expected her to go straight to the Time Engine and travel back to 2036. What we didn't expect was, she had enough presence of mind to take intel with her."

"I see. She pulled information out of the Time Engine and took it with her? There's not much she can use in the Engine, is there?"

"No, but she was more resourceful than we expected. She broke into my office and stole some information from my file cabinet. She escaped with a box of project files."

Number Four stared at her.

How can I get him off this subject?

"Then, she got into the Engine room and programmed a beacon and left the building. We didn't expect that. We thought she would search for the address of her team's lab and jump directly there. But, for some reason, she left the building, ran across the road and into the woods."

"And no one saw all this? No one followed her?"

"But we did, sir. We monitored her escape, start to finish. Stopping her during her escape would have ruined our plan."

"But you didn't attempt to recover the box from her?"

"We thought of that, but she set a grueling pace through the woods. To be honest, none of our troops could keep up with her."

"A miscalculation on your part."

Asshole.

"An unexpected and inconsequential thread," she said.

Number Four showed his teeth again. "Let's go back to the intel she stole from you. Have we done an assessment on the material she took?"

Damn, he came back to it.

"Yes, sir. The material she took has information and references to several projects. Nothing very interesting."

"Rachel," he said softly, "At my age, I tire easily. What specific project records did you lose to her?"

No way around it now.

"She has most of the plans to the Time Engine Inhibitor, and..."

Number Four's expression bordered on anger.

"I said *most* of it, but not all. And there are two reports from Major McKnight."

"Most of it? *Most* of it? And do you think perhaps his Doctor Astalos — the *inventor* of time travel — cannot figure it out? Please, you insult my intelligence."

"Sir, we don't know if the box made it back to 2036. I—"

"Wait," Number Four said, holding up his index finger. He looked thoughtful.

Not good. He's getting pissed.

"It occurs to me that the worse problem is the reports from Major McKnight," he said. "Are they from 2036?"

"No, sir. From 2040."

He frowned.

"I'm sure you thought of this already, haven't you, Rachel?"

"Yes, sir, I have."

"What is your plan, Rachel?"

Push him away from this line of thinking.

"Leave it to me, sir. I'll take McKnight out of the picture."

There has to be a way without killing him…

Number Four shook his head. "I'm afraid I must insist. Will you use the weapon that is Lieutenant Hatcher? Or some other mechanism?"

I need to show logic behind this. Else, he'll think I'm squeamish.

Rachel sighed and said, "Lieutenant Hatcher is my failsafe option, sir, if all else fails."

"If all else *fails*? Why not do it now and move on?"

Careful now. It must make sense.

"I'm trying to preserve our ability to do what we do," she said. "Let's remember the situation McKnight is working under. The HERO Team is only two years old. There are many people in Congress in 2036 who aren't in favor of the project. They view time travel as dangerous, which it is. If McKnight or a member of his team dies as a result of the project? The future of the HERO Team might be in jeopardy. If Congress cancels the HERO Project as a result, then it moves to private industry, and McKnight's team no longer has an impact."

"I see your logic," Number Four said. "Then the projects McKnight and his team execute never happen, they don't win the approval of Congress, and we don't own the technology today."

"Yes, sir. That's what I'm thinking."

And I never hear of Marc McKnight and vow to follow in his footsteps.

Number Four nodded. "I approve of this track… for now. You can use Hatcher if all else fails. That was the purpose of her programming, was it not?"

"It was, sir. Trust me, McKnight will not interfere with our plans."

"Make it so," he said. "Don't fail me, Rachel. I so enjoy our time together and I would hate for it to end."

Bastard.

"Yes, sir. I feel the same way."

"Very good. Keep me posted, Rachel. Don't make me worry about this."

"I won't, sir. Thanks for your time."

Number Four smiled and broke the connection.

Rachel let out a sigh of relief.

I survived another status report.

A voice came from behind the video screen. "That sounded like fun."

Freddie eavesdropping again. I have to watch this guy.

"How long have you been here?" she said.

"Long enough. Do you think you can pull it off?"

"What? Use Hatcher as a weapon? Of course, we can. Why not?"

"Well, you might recall I said she wasn't ready yet. I had her for four months. It takes longer than that to guarantee the results. And she's a strong-willed bitch."

"I don't remember you saying that. Are you saying your programming will fail?"

Freddie glared at Rachel.

"My programming *never* fails. But you interrupted it before completion. I cannot guarantee the results."

Already trying to defer the blame.

"Well, we'll see then, won't we? For now, be ready, because I may want to pull the trigger on this soon."

Unless I can think of another way.

"You mean the ringtone?" he asked.

Rachel stared at him.

Freddie studied the floor. "Yes, ma'am, we'll be ready."

"And Freddie?" she said. "Don't let me find out you're talking to Number Four about my business without me being there. I would not appreciate that."

"I would never consider something like that," he said. "How could you say such a thing? We're a team."

Liar. I'll cut your nuts off if you sabotage me.

"See that you don't. I'm not a patient person, and you don't want me angry with you."

CHAPTER 18

<u>Sunday, November 23rd, 2036 — 01:47pm — McKnight's office,</u>
<u>Telegraph Road, Alexandria Virginia</u>

McKnight sat in his office chair, looking out through the transparent wall into the trees and the parking lot.

He thought of Megan and their time together yesterday. Last night, they went out to dinner in Old Town Alexandria and had a superb dinner.

It was a perfect evening.

He was glad for the time off, but his work situation frustrated him. He wanted to apprehend Rachel and bring her back for questioning, but he couldn't get the effort moving.

A knock on his door interrupted his thoughts.

Someone else is here today?

"Come," he said.

The door opened and Doctor Astalos entered. He was grinning from ear to ear.

McKnight jumped to his feet. "How are you, sir? I didn't know you were here. What can I help with?"

Astalos slowly moved across the room to McKnight's side chair. "May I sit down? I may have over-exerted myself in my excitement walking here."

McKnight moved to his side and helped the elderly man into the chair.

"Can I get you anything? Some water or something?"

"No, no," Astalos said. "I'm fine. Just need to catch my breath for a second."

McKnight watched as the old man took deep breaths to normalize his breathing.

After a few moments, he smiled at McKnight. "I forget my age sometimes. Very inconvenient."

"Are you sure you're all right, sir?"

"Yes, yes, more than all right. I've made a discovery from Lieutenant Hatcher's intel prize. A very important discovery."

McKnight was more than ready for good news.

"What did you find?"

"This," Astalos said, and pulled a small data disk from his coat pocket.

"What is it?"

"I almost overlooked it. It was at the very bottom of the box in an envelope. It's the plans for the TEI."

"TEI? What's that?"

"Exactly my reaction when I found the envelope. It had TEI written in big letters on it. TEI stands for Time Engine Inhibitor. What does that make you think of?"

"Something that prevents the Time Engine from working?"

"Exactly. It is my belief that a TEI was in place and working in Rachel's lab in 2086 when we tried to jump drones there yesterday morning."

"Oh, so that's why the drones acted so weird," McKnight said. "They couldn't jump in, but they had no way to know they hadn't, so they carried out their programming where they were."

"That's my theory, but I'm certain it's what prevented our mission."

"Okay. What are our options? Can we get it implemented here? Can we figure out how to defeat it — the TEI, I mean?"

Astalos nodded. "That's my thought. We should be able to, if the plans are correct."

McKnight rubbed his chin. "Is there a reason to doubt the plans?"

"Perhaps. The disk may contain a very early version. Someone might have created this disk as a backup during development to prevent the loss of work. I do that all the time. Anyway, I need to study it and ensure it works and is safe."

"How will you proceed?"

"First, I'll see if I can make it work in our lab."

"That would be great, Doctor Astalos. These people — at least we think it's these people — are kidnapping young women, traveling them here to our time, and killing them. We need to stop that. But before we do that, we have to ensure they can't jump a team into our lab and take us out of the fight. They haven't done it so far and I don't know why, but we need a TEI online to protect us as soon as possible."

"Yes, I agree," Astalos said. "And I'll start on that right away. Step two would be to learn how to defeat it. I don't know if you can, but we should learn how if it's possible."

"Yes, sir."

"And I'm sure this has occurred to you, but TEI defeat capability would be essential for an offensive attack on our part."

"You're a mind reader, Doc. What's next?"

"I'll start on this. I could work faster if I had Lieutenants Wheeler and Hatcher working with me. They're both quick studies, and it'd be great to have their military savvy there to pull the most potential out of this device."

"You can have Wheeler first thing tomorrow. I'll most likely see him in the gym tomorrow morning. We'll wait a little longer for Hatcher. I scheduled a psyche exam for her. I want to make sure she's okay before putting her back to work."

"Would it be okay to give her some light work, like looking over the rest of the intel she brought back? That way, she'd feel productive, and you could observe and decide what's next for her."

McKnight considered this.

"You know, that might be just the right thing for her. She's determined to get back to work, but likely to push herself too hard. Her dedication to duty exceeds her ability to perform, at least until she gets a little more rest."

"Yes, I worried about that."

"Doc, the more I think about it, the better I like the idea," McKnight said. "I'll set it up tomorrow. We can give her a conference room where she can focus and feel productive."

"Wonderful. Well, now I'll start piecing the TEI plans together. Is there anything else I can help with?"

"No, sir," McKnight said as he stood. "Let me walk with you."

He helped Astalos to his feet and walked with him to his office. He couldn't help but notice how frail the old man was.

When he got Astalos in his chair at his desk, he said, "I hope you know how much we appreciate you around here, sir."

Astalos looked up at him. "Thank you, Marc. I do, but it's always nice to hear it."

McKnight excused himself and returned to his office.

Finally, a break to help us move forward.

CHAPTER 19

Monday, November 24th, 2036 — 07:30am — Officer's Gym at DLA HQ, Alexandria, Virginia

As he expected, McKnight found Wheeler and Hatcher at the Officers' Gym at DLA Headquarters.

He finished up his workout and walked over to where they were standing and cooling down from their run.

"Good morning," he said. The two officers came to attention and saluted.

"As you were," he said. "Hatcher, how are you feeling?"

"One hundred percent, sir," she said. "Ready to get back to work."

McKnight turned to Wheeler. "What do you say about her, Mitch?"

"She's good, sir. She just smoked my ass in the run. Not her best time, but she beat me as usual."

"That's not so hard," she said, and turned to McKnight. "But I *am* ready for duty, sir."

McKnight looked at her face.

No emotion there, but that's normal for her. She's stone-faced, even when they're kidding around.

Wheeler chuckled. "I was holding back so you wouldn't exert yourself too much. I should have thrown it in high gear and led you a merry chase."

"Not on your best day, pal," she said.

This time, a hint of a smile crinkled her flawless lips.

"Okay," McKnight said. "Are you ready for some light duty, Lieutenant Hatcher?"

"Only if I can't have full duties."

"That's the best I can do for now. Doctor Astalos needs some help from both of you with the intel you brought back from the future."

"Yes, sir," they said in unison.

"We're on it, sir," Wheeler said.

"Good. Lieutenant Hatcher... because you were there, you may have picked up on something that'll make sense to you now. Doctor Astalos has already found the designs for a TEI — a time engine inhibitor — in the box. I need you to sift through the contents of that box and see if you can find anything else valuable."

"Yes, sir," she said.

"Lieutenant Wheeler, I want you to help Doctor Astalos go through those TEI plans and get it working so nobody can jump into our Lab without our permission."

"Yes, sir."

"You start today. Report to Doctor Astalos this morning. Keep me posted on what you find."

"Yes, sir."

"Lieutenant Hatcher, you're dismissed. I have some questions for Lieutenant Wheeler. He'll catch up with you."

"Yes, sir." To Wheeler, she said, "I'll grab a shower and get over to the lab. See you there."

"Not if I see you first."

She made a rude gesture and strode away from the two men.

McKnight watched her leave. "So... what do you think, Lieutenant?"

"She's good, sir. She beat my ass yesterday in boxing. It's amazing how fast she's recovering."

"And her mental state? How does that seem to you?"

"Ah, good, sir. Good. She's coming along."

He's not as confident on that one.

"How so, Lieutenant? Is there anything wrong?"

Wheeler paused. McKnight sensed there was something bothering him.

"Permission to speak confidentially, sir?"

"Not in this case, Lieutenant. She'll assume I discussed her readiness with you."

"I see." Wheeler said. "Okay, here's what I'm willing to say. She seems like she's ninety-nine point nine together. Like her old self.

"But?"

"But every once in a while, I get the sense that she isn't with me — that she's somewhere else."

"You mean, like a seizure or something?"

"No, sir. It's like her attention is elsewhere. I speak to her and she's right back with me, no problem. She seems a little more introspective."

"Hasn't she always been that way? She's never talked all that much."

"Yes, sir, but this seems different. I can't put my finger on it, but… sir, they kidnapped and beat her for four months. You can't expect her to be completely unchanged by that."

"I see. Here's the bottom line. Would you be sure she had your back in a combat situation? Do you have any doubts about her ability to perform as expected?"

Wheeler didn't hesitate. "No, sir. She'd have my back and I would have no problem putting my life or anyone else's in her hands."

McKnight nodded.

"Okay, that's what I needed to hear. You think she's ready to get back to work now."

"Sure seems that way to me, sir."

"Okay, Mitch." He smiled at Wheeler. "You guys keep me posted on what you learn and on your progress at developing a TEI. You're dismissed."

"Yes, sir." Wheeler saluted, turned on his heel and walked away.

McKnight's smile faded.

Just to err on the side of caution, we need a psyche evaluation. Just in case.

****

<u>Tuesday, November 25th, 2036 — 2:30pm — Military Psychiatric Office, Silver Springs, Maryland</u>

Hatcher sat across from the psychiatrist. She assumed the session was nearly over, because it was the Wednesday before Thanksgiving and, like everyone else, the doctor wanted to get out of the office early today.

This is taking too long.

Hatcher was not looking forward to the drive home to her place in Alexandria. Driving across DC during rush hour before a holiday weekend was not her idea of fun.

She pulled her mind back to the doctor, who was rambling on about her own childhood.

Hatcher sighed and nodded as if she had paid full attention to the shrink in front of her.

Why am I here? This is a complete waste of time. But orders are orders.

"Karen, I think we're just about done here," Doctor Johnson said. "How are you feeling? Do you have anything you'd like to say?"

"Not really," she said. "I'm eager to get back to work."

"I'm sure you are. Do you have any plans for the weekend?"

Hatcher's mind jumped to her fiancé Richard's face, but then reality returned.

He's gone.

She shook her head.

I'm not talking to her about that.

She forced a smile to her face.

"Not really," Hatcher said. "I'm spending the day tomorrow with my parents. Then Friday my work partner and his wife invited me over for a few beers and a football game."

"To watch? Who's playing?"

"No, to play. We challenged some Air Force guys to a six on six game. It'll be touch football that becomes tackle by the end of the game."

This time, Hatcher's smile was genuine.

"That sounds like fun, Karen," Doctor Johnson said.

She doesn't sound like she thinks it's fun.

"Yes, it will be. Okay, Doc, is there anything else?"

"Yes, there is. Karen, have you had any strange dreams?"

Unbidden, a stream of images rushed into her mind.

The room was spinning, but it gradually slowed down and became clearer. It was black, but there was a color video playing in front of her on an enormous screen — large enough that it wrapped around her. The music was loud, and she realized someone fitted headphones over her ears. It faded and a pleasant voice talked about our Flawless Leader, the Anointed One. The Baron George Kosar. The film showed him speaking and his voice was like honey and the Devotees swooned.

Her eyes were dry. She tried to blink but couldn't. Something restrained her eyelids.

The event came to its conclusion, and she couldn't help but be excited and inspired by The Baron's words. The film stopped, and the room went black.

She didn't know how long she sat there in the dark, but then bright lights assaulted her eyes. Too bright to look at, but she couldn't blink or turn her head.

A silhouette approached her. She could only see the outline of a man, a black space between her and the lights. She struggled to see a face, but shadow obscured it. Only the man's flattop haircut, his white shirt and his loosened tie were visible. She smelled tobacco.

She recognized who it was, but something impeded her thoughts. She knew she should be able to think faster, but her senses wouldn't cooperate.

The silhouette spoke. "Hello, Karen. I'm so proud of you. You've come a long way."

Hatcher tried to speak, but no words came.

The man came to her, stood over her, and kissed her on the lips. A soft, lingering kiss.

He withdrew a step. "Now tell me, Karen. Who are you?"

Hatcher knew the right answer, but it wouldn't come out.

"I... I'm a soldier of the Movement. I am loyal to my Baron and his family. I would do anything for him."

"Good," he said. "And what will you do?"

Hatcher tried to stay silent, but her lips and throat and lungs refused to obey her silent commands.

"Anything. I'd do anything."

"Good. And now I will give you a new command. Are you listening? Are you ready to serve the Baron?"

"Yes, I am ready to serve."

He held up a small device. "Listen."

Music played. It was a light, tinny sound, but she recognized the tune. It was a classical piece. She couldn't remember the composer, but it was soothing and soft.

"Do you know this melody?" he asked.

"Yes," Hatcher said.

"Here is your command. When you hear this music again, you will drop everything you're doing, find Major Marc McKnight and kill him. Do you understand me?"

Her voice trembled as she responded. "Yes."

"Repeat back to me."

Hatcher struggled to deny the suggestion. She knew it was wrong, forbidden. But she couldn't stop herself. She repeated the command.

"You will let no one or anything stop you from this task."

"No, I won't."

"And after you kill Major Marc McKnight, you will feel bliss and be free forever, for you have carried out the Baron's plan for you. Do you feel joy at this?"

"Yes."

"You know my voice and Rachel's voice better than anything else. When we command you again, you will carry out the order we give without hesitation. Do you understand? Repeat it to me."

Hatcher resisted, but repeated the command.

"Good. Now, one last thing."

Hatcher tried to sit up straight in her chair to give respect to the command. But she was bound to it and couldn't move.

"You'll remember my commands, but no one may know. You'll tell no one about it. It will be as a dream, you'll feel like it's a dream, but you'll know it isn't. You are incapable of describing or telling anyone about these instructions. Do you understand?"

Hatcher tried to shake her head, but couldn't. She knew deep in her soul that she could and would do anything to please the Baron.

She heard another voice. Female and distant.

"Is it reliable? Will it work?"

The man spoke again, so softly she could barely hear it.

"It will be enough."

"Karen?" Doctor Johnson said. "Are you still with me?"

"What? Oh, sorry. What was the question?"

"I asked you if you were having any strange dreams?"

Hatcher shook her head.

"No… No dreams."

CHAPTER 20

Thursday, November 27th, 2036 — 08:20am — McKnight Apartment, Alexandria, Virginia

McKnight sat with Megan at the little breakfast table next to their apartment's bay window. They finished breakfast and lapsed into their normal morning routine — McKnight checking email on his phone and Megan checking job ads on hers.

"Well, here's some great news," he said.

Megan looked up from her job search. "What? Did you win the lottery?"

McKnight laughed. "Maybe if I bought a ticket. No, it's Doctor Johnson's psyche report on Hatcher. She says Hatcher's ready for duty."

"And that's good, right?"

"Absolutely. She's been waiting for this. She's not the type to sit around and do nothing. I think I'll call and give her the news."

Megan looked incredulous.

"Now? On Thanksgiving? Won't she be busy with family or something?"

"Maybe, but she'll want to hear this. I know she's going crazy."

"Well, you know your people better than I do."

"Yeah, but I always like your input. Sometimes you think of something I didn't."

Megan grinned at him. "Yeah, yeah. Shut up and call her. I'm taking a shower. Clean up the kitchen, will you?"

"Sure," he said, and punched the speed dial for Hatcher.

The call rang twice before she answered.

"Hatcher," she said.

"Lieutenant, this is McKnight. Good morning."

"Good morning, sir."

"Sorry to disturb you so early."

"Not at all, sir. I'm at the gym, whipping Wheeler's ass in hand-to-hand. What can I help with?"

McKnight chuckled.

Of course she is. Where else would she be?

"I have good news for you, Lieutenant. Doctor Johnson expedited your psyche exam. You're cleared for duty."

"That's outstanding, sir. Thanks. When can I start? I have a few things to do before lunch, but I can report early afternoon."

"Hatcher, it's Thanksgiving. Take the day off. I plan to be in the office tomorrow for a little while. But please, take the rest of the week to have some fun, some R and R, and report on Monday."

"Excellent, sir. I'll see you tomorrow. And please say hello to Megan for me."

"I will, Lieutenant. And you *did* hear the part where I said to take the rest of the *week* off?"

"Yes, sir, I did. I'll see you tomorrow."

"Very well, Lieutenant. Don't beat Wheeler up too bad."

"It's his own damn fault, sir. But I'll see what I can do."

McKnight couldn't help but smile. "Very good, Lieutenant. As you were."

"Thank you again, sir."

"You're welcome, Lieutenant. Have a great day."

"You, too, sir."

They disconnected the call.

He typed in a quick text to Drake and the HERO Team.

<Based on doctor recommendations, Lieutenant Karen Hatcher will return to active duty effective today. Glad to have you back, Lieutenant.>

McKnight slipped his phone into his pocket.

Okay. The team is back at full strength now, so we can get after these Suicide Scandal events. Time to rock-and-roll.

****

<u>Friday, November 28th, 2036 — 4:30pm — McKnight's office, Telegraph Road, Alexandria, Virginia</u>

At 4:00 in the afternoon, McKnight completed his high-level plan for the next step in the Suicide Scandals investigation.

There were no clues except their experience with Rachel and the case he investigated earlier this year. As far as he could tell, he only had two options.

The first option was to wait for another event and hope he had time to go back and prevent it, or at least learn from it.

Nope. That option is defensive and will likely cost another innocent life.

Option two was to find Rachel and find out what she knows. He was certain she was behind the Suicide Scandal events. If she was behind it, he might get his hands on her plans and find the purpose of the deaths. If she wasn't, she would know who was.

Better option. It's proactive, and maybe we can prevent another death.

He spun around in his chair, set his feet up on the credenza, and gazed through the transparent wall to the trees outside.

It was raining today, and he heard the soothing rhythm of raindrops falling through branches from leaf to leaf. He listened and watched the heavy clouds move as he turned his plan over in his mind.

The motive had to be political. There was no other reason he could think of. When McKnight called him earlier, General Drake agreed.

The next step was to pick the personnel, and he needed Tyler and Kathy to craft the plan for a two-stage mission — a recon, followed by a kidnapping.

The recon was not optional. They had no idea what to expect in 2086. No one in this era had traveled to the future, except Hatcher. But her experience was limited.

Hell, she never even got outside the building until she escaped.

He thought of Hatcher's behavior this morning. She came by his office to touch base before starting work. He tried to talk her into going home, but she was adamant that she stay and get some work done.

She wasn't happy with the idea of searching through the intel box again, because it was her light duty job and she was ready to get back to a full load of work.

But McKnight wasn't ready for her to do that, so she resigned herself to attacking the box in a closed evidence room.

Wheeler and Tyler would be the best selection for the recon stage of this mission. Both strong, seasoned time travelers.

A knock at the door interrupted his thoughts. He swiveled around in his chair and said, "Come."

Hatcher came in, smiling. She saluted and McKnight returned it.

"As you were," he said, and pointed to a side chair. "Have a seat."

"Thank you, sir. I found something."

"Great, we can use all the intel we can find. What is it?"

She handed him a piece of paper. He glanced over it. It was a memo from himself to the HERO Team to describe a new mission. The investigation was on their calendar for 2040. He didn't get the significance.

"Okay, it's a memo from me to the team. So what?"

Hatcher grinned. "Yes, sir, it is. Did you notice the date?"

McKnight looked back at the paper. The date was March 23rd, 2040.

I haven't written this yet. What the hell?

"Why is there a memo from me in Rachel's file cabinet fifty years from now?"

Hatcher held up her index finger. "Exactly the question I asked myself."

"All of our records are classified. How could she get it?"

"Second question I asked," she said, still grinning.

She's enjoying this too much.

"Okay, I give up. What am I missing?"

"Don't feel bad, sir. I asked Doctor Astalos, and he missed it, too. But now he agrees with me on the significance."

"I don't get it. It's a notification to the team about the schedule. What's so special about that?"

"It isn't the content of the memo, sir," Hatcher said. "It's the *existence* of the memo. Or rather, that she had it in her possession."

McKnight's face went blank.

I still don't get it.

"Sir, she has all our records. Don't you get it? She has this because she's the commander of the HERO Team. She's your counterpart in 2086. They renamed the organization to FTS, whatever that stands for. But it's our team."

The light dawned on McKnight. "Oh, no. If she has all our records…"

Hatcher finished his sentence. "… Then she knows what we're doing. Every note, every plan, *everything*. Whatever we put on paper or in our computers, she has access to. Any plans we make… If we don't want her to know about them… We have to keep them off the record."

McKnight rolled his eyes. "We're screwed."

"Maybe not, sir. This presents opportunities that we didn't have before."

"Like what?"

Hatcher grinned from ear to ear.

"We have to take our plan offline so she won't have a record of it. She's got to know we'll figure this out eventually, but in the short-term, we can build a false plan, a red herring, for her to follow. Let her think we're going one way, but go the other. It won't work for long, but maybe long enough for us to get out in front of her."

McKnight considered this.

"I think you might have something there. We get off the electronics and alert everyone not to make any records. No phone calls unless we have to — we don't know what might be recorded and converted to text for posterity."

"Yes, sir," she said. "We use our computers like typewriters. Write and print everything, but don't save it. Keep the copies in our briefcases or whatever, but don't save it on the computer and don't put it in a file cabinet. We don't throw anything away... we shred it instead."

"Okay. I'll set up a meeting for first thing Monday to take the team off campus and brief them on the plan. What else?"

"That's it, sir," she said. "What else can I do for you today?"

McKnight smiled.

"Nothing." He glanced at his watch. "Go home or go hang out with Wheeler and Lisa. You're back on duty, but I want you to take the weekend to rest and relax. The next few weeks will be tough, and I'll need you and everyone else to be in tiptop condition."

He stabbed a finger at the document on his desk.

"This was excellent work, Karen," he said. "You can be proud of what you've done for us today."

The lieutenant's face lit up. "Thank you, sir."

He handed the memo back to her. "Put this and the rest of the box back in the security closet. That, at least, Rachel would expect us to do."

Hatcher slipped the memo under her arm, came to attention, and saluted McKnight. He stood and returned it.

She turned and left his office without another word. He watched her leave and listened as her footsteps receded down the hall. His reservations about her recovery vanished.

Her mind is sharp again. I might have come to the same revelation with that memo, but not nearly as fast. She's back.

McKnight turned to his computer. He printed six copies of the high-level mission plan, then deleted it from his computer.

Our investigative procedures just took one giant step backward in time.

He gathered up the copies and put them in his briefcase, then called Megan.

"I'm on my way home, Babe. See you soon."

CHAPTER 21

Monday, December 1st, 2036 — 10:10am — Holiday Inn Conference Room, Alexandria, Virginia

The first stage of the mission was recon.

Know the field of battle before you step onto it.

McKnight rented a hotel conference room for their recon planning meeting. He met each team member as they arrived at the Telegraph Road parking lot and re-directed them to the hotel. By 10:00 am, they were all there and McKnight was ready to get started.

First, he warned them about staying off the computers and credited Hatcher for finding out about Rachel and the FTS team.

It wasn't easy for the team to give up their computers at work, but it was especially hard on Kathy and Trevor. They regularly interacted with their peers around the country and gathered ideas and clues from sources on the internet. But they acknowledged that, since the mission was going into the future, their contacts and other resources wouldn't be much help.

The high-level plan for the recon was to have a two-week mission conducted by Wheeler and Tyler.

The Engine worked most efficiently — using the least amount of power — by traveling to times that were exact multiples of twenty-five years from the current moment. The more time before or after an exact multiple and when you jumped, the more power was required. If you tried to access a time more than a week before or after that anniversary, the power requirement spiked to the point of melting the power cables. Earlier in the year, Doctor Astalos improved that time slightly, but the working limit of the technology was still approximately a week on either side of the anniversary.

McKnight proposed to save time by having Tyler and Wheeler time-jump to approximately a week before the anniversary and return approximately a week after it. This would give them nearly two weeks for recon and a safe return to the exact moment they left.

"Okay, let me get this straight," Tyler said. "Let's say we leave tomorrow at noon. Today is December first. We'll jump to, let's see, November 24th in 2086 and return early on December 8th?"

"That's the idea," McKnight said.

"Oh-kaay…" he said.

Doctor Astalos laughed. "Major McKnight, you must excuse Captain Tyler. He's a new husband and cannot be away for long."

A few chuckles broke out in the room.

Tyler's face turned red.

"Not at all. I just need to know if I should tell Sarah I'll be home for dinner or not."

"Exactly," Astalos said.

"Tell her you'll be home for dinner," McKnight said. "In local time, you and Wheeler won't be gone over five minutes."

"Good to know," Tyler said.

McKnight began again. "In a nutshell, you'll be doing a recon in 2086 to see what we'll be dealing with when we go after Rachel. That's the impetus for this."

"Are we sure going after Rachel is the best thing to do?" Tyler asked. "We don't have proof she's behind this, do we?"

Kathy put up her hand. "Major, do you mind if I answer that question?"

"Not at all, Kathy."

Kathy stood and faced the team. "Trevor and I have been discussing this. We don't have any proof of Rachel's involvement, but there is plenty of circumstantial evidence. As you all know, earlier this year, a girl was kidnapped from the present and murdered twenty-five years ago to ruin the career of Wade Harrison, the future governor of Illinois and now President-Elect. We interfered with that plan and prevented the murder, but we're sure Rachel was involved at some level — and maybe was the instigator. While that isn't conclusive evidence, it makes her worthy of investigation."

While Kathy sat, McKnight continued. "And she's the only lead we have. I don't believe we have any other approach to the Suicide Scandals. Have we beat this dead horse enough that we can accept the premise and move on?"

No one disagreed.

"Okay, let's continue. You'll go out dressed in your Greens, because army uniforms will change styles less often than casual fashions. You'll collect some pictures or samples of clothing for stage two of the operation. Also, you'll be trying to find out as much as you can about the political situation in 2086. Hatcher mentioned some groups in her debrief that should concern all of us. The Devotees, the Faithful, the Kosar family and this Baron character."

"What do you expect, sir?" Wheeler asked.

"In today's world, if I were like Rachel, I would need help to get into a leadership position. And I don't think it would be much different in the future. This means she has connected friends, or maybe worse. Maybe the entire government is corrupt and Rachel is just another cog in the wheel, trying to get ahead."

"Well, that's encouraging," Tyler said.

"Just be careful," McKnight said. "And stay sharp. I'd hate for you to get locked up with no way back."

McKnight saw General Drake slip into the back of the room.

"Ten-HUT," he said.

The military team members leaped to their feet and came to attention. The others stood.

"As you were," General Drake said. "Please continue." He took a chair in the back of the room.

The team dropped back into their seats.

"What's our mission, sir?" Wheeler said.

McKnight shrugged and said, "A lot of it will be at your discretion. We don't know what's there, so we don't know what to look for. Here's where I would start... Find out about the political climate. Compared to today, is it more liberal or conservative? Is it the rosy future we would like it to be, or is it dystopian? Is it a scary place to be? Do we need weapons when we go back to get Rachel? Is it a place of law and order or the law of the jungle? Who's the President? What's the biggest problem the government has? Who's the biggest enemy of the United States?"

"Wow," Tyler said. "That's a lot of change possibilities."

"Well, we don't know what to expect. Remember, the United States was in two World Wars in the 20th century. And they took place between 1900 and 1950 — less than fifty years. Hell yeah, a lot can change. Am I right, Kathy?"

"Yes, sir. World War I started in 1914 and World War II ended in 1945. There's only 31 years. Much less than a lifetime."

"Okay," McKnight said. "Take lots of pictures. Get the lay of the field. Find out more about Rachel. Where is she and what would be the best time and place to intercept her? When we go, we do it fast and with as little muss and fuss as possible. Understood?"

"Yes, sir," Tyler said.

"When and where do we go?" Wheeler said.

"Good question. You go tomorrow at noon. In local time, you'll jump out and come right back. From your point of view, you'll be gone two weeks. As far as where is concerned, we'll put you down on the Manassas battlefield west of here. It's a safe bet it'll still be clear of structures in the future. You'll make your way back to civilization from there. All set? Questions?"

"What about money and weapons, sir?" Wheeler asked.

"Kathy?" McKnight asked. "What do you think?"

"First, I don't think they go without weapons, but just handguns. There might be restrictions on what a citizen can carry. And I'll sign you out with a hundred grand, just in case."

Tyler and Wheeler glanced at each other.

Kathy said, "Don't start planning your shopping spree. Currencies *do* fluctuate, and that sum might not buy you dinner in 2086."

"Okay," McKnight said. "I agree. Handguns and a hundred grand. Anything else?"

No one moved.

"Okay, I'll leave it to you all to get ready to go. Remember, no computer records, no phone messages, and no notes you can't carry with you at all times. That includes the money they check out, Kathy. Let's not leave any clues. Dismissed."

The military members of the HERO Team filtered out of the conference room, each saluting General Drake as they left.

Kathy and Trevor approached McKnight. "What can we do, sir? Anything else we can help with?"

McKnight leaned back against the lectern and crossed his arms. "Nothing I can think of, except I haven't heard from Ritter in a few days. Trevor, would you reach out to him to see if there have been any more developments or, God forbid, another death?"

"Sure, Marc. I can do that," Trevor said.

Kathy touched McKnight's forearm. "In the meantime, I'll try to think of anything else we might want to know or any other precaution we might take. See you tomorrow."

"Right. Thanks."

Trevor and Kathy left the room. Only then did McKnight notice General Drake and Doctor Astalos were still sitting in the back. They were engaged in quiet conversation together. He walked to where they were sitting and stood, waiting for them to finish their discussion.

They noticed his presence, and Drake pointed at a chair.

As he sat, McKnight noticed Drake looked unhappy.

"Is there an issue I need to know about, sir?" McKnight said.

"Yes, Major. The President called me. She's getting pressure from the governor of California… The one whose daughter was found in Florida? Anyway, the President wants a status report for herself and the President-Elect. I think I can give her enough to satisfy her without saying too much. We don't want a whiff of this to get out. If I tell her what you're doing and she passes that on to the governor, there's no way it won't get out into the public record and somewhere Rachel is likely to see it."

"Yes, sir."

"Much as I hate it, the best approach is to stonewall the governor. The President won't like that, but it's the best course of action for now. Do you agree?"

"Yes, sir. Or maybe she can tell him we expect more information after Thursday. By then, we should have more to share and won't be concerned about people reading our reports and learning our every move before we make it."

"Okay," Drake said. "I'll take care of it." He and Doctor Astalos stood.

"Good luck, Major. I look forward to your report."

McKnight saluted the General and shook hands with Astalos before they left.

He strode back to the front of the conference room to gather his notes. As he approached, he scanned the lectern for them.

They're gone!

CHAPTER 22

Sunday, December 1st, 2086 — 11:42am — FTS Time Engine Lab

Rachel landed in the FTS Lab. When the time jump aura winked out, she fell backward and lost her grip on McKnight's notes. They fluttered to the platform around her.

She laid there for a moment, staring at the ceiling. Her stomach reeled and her head pounded.

Freddie ran to her side. "Are you all right? Did the shield work?"

Rachel rolled over and raised herself on her hands and knees.

"Oh, my God," she said, and coughed.

She unbuckled the personal shield belt and slung it across the room.

"Yes, it worked well enough to get the job done. I stole McKnight's notes without him seeing me. Get me an anti-nausea packet and a painkiller."

"Sure," he said, and dashed to the meds locker. He retrieved the items and brought them to her.

"You took it off the lectern, right in front of him?"

She swallowed both drugs and closed her eyes as they moved into her bloodstream. Her breathing slowed as she recovered.

Then she opened her eyes and looked at Freddie.

"No, of course not. He was distracted and talking to his people in the back of the room. The personal shield isn't perfect. I couldn't have done it if he was right there. If he had looked toward the lectern, he'd have seen the shield's shimmer and known something was happening."

"Excellent. We now have a tool that allows us to be practically invisible," Freddie said.

"We can use it in an emergency," she said. "But it's not ready in its present form."

"Why?"

She started gathering McKnight's notes.

"Because I used it for less than five minutes and I'm nauseated and I have a nasty headache. I feel like someone hit me with a lethal dose of radiation. I'd be afraid to use it for an extended period. In fact, I won't use it again until they fix that."

She stood and staggered. Freddie moved to take her elbow, but she pulled away from him. She straightened and carried the notes to the break area, spread them out on the table, and sat. Freddie stood beside her, looking over her shoulder.

She glanced at him and said, "Sit down, please. You're distracting me."

When he didn't move right away, she turned and glared at him.

"Sit. down."

He did as instructed.

Rachel remained silent for ten minutes, reading and rc-reading McKnight's notes.

"Okay," she said, "it looks like they were planning to do a recon here, and then attempt to capture me."

"What do we do?" he said. "Do we wait and set a trap?"

Rachel glared at him again.

Idiot.

"No, you fool. Do you think I want to give him the initiative? Stupid. No, we go after them."

"You mean take him out?"

Rachel glanced at Freddie, then returned her attention to the documents before her. "That's one option. We have the means to take out their capability."

"Or," Freddie said. "We could activate Hatcher."

No!

"That's an option," she said.

Freddie stood and leered at her. "You don't really want to take him out, do you? What is this, a crush on the legend from the past?"

Rachel rolled her eyes. "Oh, please. You gotta be kidding me," she said. "Haven't you heard of history preservation? McKnight still has a lot of things to accomplish. Things that protect our history. Taking him out without a detailed plan could have catastrophic consequences."

"We can get around those things. We know what they are. We can send a surrogate to carry out his missions."

"No, we can't. If he's taken out, Congress defunds their team, and we lose all access to fulfill those missions. Use your head."

Freddie snorted. "We can do the missions first — before him. Taking McKnight out is our first and easiest option."

I need to stop this talk right now.

Rachel stood and moved into Freddie's personal space, nose to nose.

"Please tell me you're not forgetting whose call this is. This is *my* team and *my* project. You're just a contractor here. *I* make the priorities and the decisions. Are you getting my drift here?"

Freddie raised his hands in defense and smiled. "Hey, I'm only here to serve. I like this job and want to keep it. Only..."

"Only what?" She stood before him, hands on her hips and her nose scant inches from his face.

"Only I was just trying to put ourselves in Number Four's shoes. I can't help but think he would want us to take the quickest, most crippling action against these bumbling fools."

"Isn't that smart?" she said, and laughed. "The minute you underestimate these guys is when we lose. Just because they're living in a culture that's outdated by fifty years doesn't mean they are stupid. They might be ignorant of our technology, but they aren't dumb and they certainly don't lack courage. Make one mistake and it's over."

Freddie listened in silence until she finished.

"Or," he said, "you take them out before they figure out how to beat you."

"Jeez, it's like talking to a wall. Think about it this way. *You* did the research on them. How many Time Engines do they have?"

Freddie checked the date in the notes on his phone. "One operational. Two others in pieces — under construction. Time to operational status for them is estimated at five to six weeks. Best case would be four weeks. That would put their response time at January first. *If* they are working on that and nothing else."

"Then you know what to do. Set in motion the drone attack plan we discussed."

"Yes, ma'am." Freddie said.

Rachel walked to her locker.

"I'll tell you what," she said. "I'll set up for triggering Hatcher. If we don't manage to take out their capability, I'll trigger her."

From the locker, she took an ancient phone and a small programming box. She set them both on the table, connected the phone to the box, and typed in a few commands. Then she touched a button on the box. A quiet, soothing classical melody floated into the air. Rachel smiled and completed the phone's programming.

"What if they detected the trigger app you put on Hatcher's phone?" Freddie said.

"Makes no difference," Rachel said. "They might, but I doubt it. But even if they do, I installed the melody as a ringtone on her phone and associated it with a dummy contact. If the app is missing, I'll jump to their time and call as the contact. The effect will be the same."

"Brilliant," Freddie said. "You're amazing."

"Don't be a suck up, Freddie. It isn't becoming."

She put the phone and the programming box back in her locker. She picked up the papers.

"I'm going back to my office to file these and I have some other things to do. I'll be back in about an hour."

"Yes, ma'am," he said.

She stopped. "Find something productive to do. Start programming the battle drone and be sure to activate the self-destruct."

Without waiting for an answer, she turned and walked out of the lab.

CHAPTER 23

Freddie watched Rachel as she left the Lab.

He stood still for a few moments.

She's lost her mind! Can't she see it's the only winning strategy?

He stared at Rachel's locker. The danger and risk of disobeying a direct order and the potential rewards paraded through his consciousness.

If Number Four finds out Rachel has personal feelings for McKnight, he'll be looking for a new FTS leader. I'd be a candidate. Why not?

He clenched his right fist and drove it into his left palm. The decision made, Freddie pulled the phone from Rachel's locker, glanced at the doors leading to Rachel's office, and strode to the Time Engine.

****

Monday, December 1st, 2036 — 1:02pm — McKnight's office, Telegraph Road, Alexandria, Virginia

Hatcher and Wheeler were waiting for McKnight when he got back to Telegraph Road.

"Let's go to my office," he said.

They fell in step and followed him there. He unlocked it and they filed into the room. He pointed at the two side chairs in front of his desk and sat behind it.

"Look," he said. "The mission has been compromised."

"How?" Wheeler said.

"Do either of you remember the set of notes I brought to our meeting this morning?"

The two lieutenants looked at each other and nodded.

"Yes, sir," Hatcher said. "You had four or five pages."

"After you left, someone stole those notes. When I went to collect them, they were gone."

Wheeler shifted in his chair.

"No disrespect intended, sir, but... are you sure? Could someone have cleaned the room and taken the notes while you weren't there?"

"No, I was still there. I never left, and no one came in. The only conclusion I can draw is that our friends from the future were there and got them somehow."

"I find it hard to believe, sir," Hatcher said.

"You called it this morning, Lieutenant. They figured out we were having an offsite meeting and showed up to see what we were up to. I can't think of another explanation. Can you?"

"No, sir."

"Right. I can't imagine how they could reach back to this time and take something from right under my nose," he said. "But we're not taking any chances. Just in case, I'm changing the plan. Rather than wait until tomorrow, Hatcher and I are going out on recon today. We'll have two teams."

He pointed at Hatcher. "You and I go today — in two hours. And Tyler and Wheeler go tomorrow as planned."

"Yes, sir!" Hatcher said.

"Except..." McKnight glanced at them both. "We forget about reconnoitering for two weeks and manipulating time. Let's keep it simple. Get there, learn what we need to learn, and get back here. I'll brief Tyler before we leave."

"I think that's a good idea, Major," Wheeler said.

He raised his hand to add more. "Also, I'm thinking we can expect an attack on our Engine. Do you agree?"

"Yes, I do. What do you suggest?"

"Let's get some firepower in the Lab, sir," he said. "Let's be ready to fight them off."

"Agreed. Let's arrange for armed support for your launch tomorrow, but we'd better get that security team in the lab today. I'm not sure how much good it'll do, but we have to try."

"Do you think their weapons will be that much better than ours?" Hatcher asked.

"With fifty more years of innovation? If they decide they want to destroy our machines, I doubt we can stop them."

"What can we do, sir?" Wheeler asked.

"We can try to defend the Lab, but we have to assume we can't, so we focus on recovery. The first thing is to execute a full software backup of the primary Engine and ask the assembly to speed up the work on the back up Engines."

"Yes, sir."

"And check with Doctor Astalos to see if he's figured out how to block an incoming time-jump yet. What's the status on our TEI? We need it yesterday. Mitch, check on that first. Can you do that right now?"

Wheeler rose. "Yes, sir. I'm on it." He saluted and left the room.

Hatcher fidgeted in her chair.

"Sir, I want to thank you for letting me come along," Hatcher said. "I'm good to travel and I'm at a hundred percent. You can count on me."

"I *am* counting on you, Lieutenant. Do you have questions about the mission, now that you're going along?"

"Yes, sir. Do we split the objectives between the two teams or will each team have the same objectives? I think both teams should have the same objectives, just in case something happens."

"Agreed, Lieutenant. Both teams will have the same mission — Reconnoiter so we have a sense of what they are doing and capture Rachel to get their plans. We need to understand what's going on before we try to pull their plans out of her. Otherwise, we won't have any idea if she's telling the truth."

"Yes, sir."

McKnight looked at the papers on his desk. There were a few to-do items he'd have to postpone until after the mission.

He heard a slight tinkling sound.

What's that? A ring tone?

He looked at Hatcher. She was staring out into space.

"Is that your cell phone?" he asked.

Hatcher shifted and looked at him. He saw no recognition in her eyes.

She doesn't recognize me.

McKnight jumped to his feet, as Hatcher launched herself at him across the desk.

McKnight deflected her to his right. She fell to the floor, but scrambled to her feet and launched herself at him again.

This time, McKnight tried to grab her arms and hold her at bay. He caught one, but the other punched him in the neck. It was aimed at his larynx, but his reflexes saved him.

She struck at his groin with her knee, but the blow landed on his upper thigh. He caught her free wrist when she tried to punch him again, but she turned and used his grip to carry him over her hip and to the floor.

McKnight hung onto her wrists for dear life, knowing she was trying to kill him. Once on the floor, he dragged her down to him.

As long as she's loose, I can't beat her.

If he could get his arms and legs around hers, his larger mass and strength could hold her until help came.

But getting control of her legs was a problem. Though he got his arms around her, she kicked and powered him across the floor, knocking over chairs and plants. No matter what he tried, he couldn't maneuver her into a position to pin her legs.

She head-butted him in the face, square on the nose. Blood gushed from it and he almost blacked out from the pain.

He was losing his grip on her as she squirmed back and forth, biting, kicking and scratching. McKnight had never seen her so fierce and overpowering.

God, she's strong! If I don't get control, I'm dead.

Hatcher broke free and rolled away from him. She leaped to her feet and opened his desk drawer.

My service weapon!

He kicked as hard as he could and swept her legs from under her. She landed heavily on her side, but bounded up again. McKnight tried to get up, but she aimed a kick at his head and struck him a glancing blow.

The kick stunned him. He tried to rise, but his body wouldn't respond. Hatcher reached into the drawer and withdrew McKnight's pistol. She held it up, and chambered a round.

McKnight had no place to hide and no strength to resist.

I'm dead.

"Hatcher!"

Wheeler stood in the doorway. She whirled and aimed the weapon at him. Her facial expression changed from anger to confusion. Then she turned back to McKnight.

Wheeler leaped toward her.

McKnight instinctively curled into a ball, trying to be as small a target as possible.

Wheeler crashed into Hatcher full force, pushing her arms aside as she fired two rounds in rapid succession, the detonations intensified by the closeness of the room.

The first round whistled past McKnight's ear. The second slammed into the credenza behind him.

Hatcher roared in frustration.

Wheeler slammed Hatcher into the transparent wall next to the credenza. He jammed her arms up against her chest and pinned her to the wall.

Hatcher struggled furiously. She couldn't get enough leverage to free her gun hand. Wheeler used his legs and all his strength to keep her pressed against the wall. His arms were like a vise — he wrapped around her and constricted her breath.

McKnight pulled himself to his feet. Hatcher glared at him as he pulled the weapon out of her hand.

Trevor, Kathy, and Tyler appeared at the door.

Hatcher roared again, but Wheeler's constriction of her chest dampened the sound.

Wheeler talked softly to her.

"Karen. Do you hear me?"

She continued wriggling and squirming. She grunted with the effort of pushing against his arms and trying to move away from the wall.

"Karen, it's me, Wheeler. What are you doing?"

More grunting.

"You tried to kill your commanding officer. What were you thinking?"

She continued to squirm, more in desperation now.

"It's me... Mitch. Look at me, Karen."

Tears rolled down her cheeks. She swung her shoulders back and forth, but couldn't break Wheeler's grip.

Kathy moved to stand next to them and put her arms around Wheeler and Hatcher. "Karen, it's us. What's wrong?"

Hatcher looked at Kathy, and her expression softened. She slowly turned her face to look at Wheeler.

"Stand down, Hatcher," he said softly. "Stand down, it's over. There's no more danger."

Hatcher's eyes fluttered and rolled back in her head. She went limp, and Wheeler laid her on the floor, face down.

He set his knee in the small of her back and pulled her hands up behind her and held them together with one hand. Without taking his eyes off her, he extended the other hand toward McKnight.

"Restraints," he said.

"I'll get them," Tyler said and sprinted away.

Trevor pulled tissues from a box on the desk and handed them to McKnight.

"What just happened?" he said. "Did she attack you out of the blue?"

McKnight wiped most of the blood off his face. He grabbed another tissue and grimaced as he blew his nose. He threw the tissues at the trash can.

"Are you okay?" Kathy asked.

He nodded and knelt by Hatcher. He reached into her pocket and withdrew her phone. It was locked.

He looked at Wheeler. "Do you know her code?"

"Yes, it's 1023."

McKnight entered the code and checked the last call. It came in less than two minutes earlier. The name on the caller ID was Cindy Ginn, and the number was from the local exchange. He played the ringtone from the directory entry. It was the same melody he heard earlier.

Tyler returned with the plastic restraints. Wheeler slipped them on Hatcher.

"Is that really necessary?" Kathy said.

"It's just in case," Wheeler said. "When she comes to, we can't allow her to come up fighting. Can we get someone to call an ambulance?"

"I've got it," Trevor said and turned to go to his office.

Wheeler called after him. "Tell them to bring restraints."

McKnight waved Hatcher's cell phone.

"She got a call from someone named Cindy — I guess we know who that was. As soon as it rang, her face went blank, and she came after me."

"They triggered her," Kathy said. "Somebody called her and the sound of the ringtone set her off."

She looked up at McKnight. "Rachel. Rachel did this."

"Yes," McKnight said.

"During the time she had Hatcher, she programmed her to kill us."

"Not us," Wheeler said. "Just the Major. When she trained her weapon on me, I thought I was dead. But she looked at me like, you know, 'not my mission'. Then she turned to the Major and tried to shoot him."

"Thanks, by the way," McKnight said. "I'd be dead now if you hadn't showed up."

"It's lucky I came back when I did, sir. Hatcher wouldn't have missed. You know how good a shot she is."

"I do. Lucky is the right word."

She needs expert help," Kathy said. "We need someone to probe into that conditioning and counteract it somehow."

McKnight nodded. He was already thinking about how to get the mission back on track.

Kathy stared at her friend, bound up on the floor.

"This might be it for her," she said.

"What do you mean?" McKnight asked.

Kathy sighed. "Her career might be over now, thanks to Rachel."

He shook his head.

"Let's not wash her out so quickly. Let's get an expert on the job and see what's what, okay?"

"You're willing to keep her after this?"

"If we can get her well. She's the best warfighter I know, except for General Drake, and she fits into the team. And she has two years of experience in the technology."

He smiled at Kathy.

"And she's part of our family. I'm not letting her go if there's a chance she'll recover."

He looked around at the group. "This ramps up the urgency of the mission. Let's get Hatcher taken care of and discuss the next steps."

"It just got harder, sir, but we're up for it," Wheeler said.

"I hope we are, Lieutenant," McKnight said. "I hope we are."

The ambulance came faster than expected.

Within fifteen minutes, Hatcher was on a stretcher and restrained. The EMTs wheeled her out.

"We're going with her," Kathy said. "Trevor and me. We want to make sure she's okay and the doctors understand what's going on. She needs to be restrained, but I don't want them throwing her in a hole for attacking her commanding officer."

"Okay," McKnight said. "Contact General Drake. Ask him if he can get us a super expert to probe into her programming and remove it. Without that, she's done on our team. He'll understand that, but you might remind him if you think it's necessary. C'mon now, I'll walk you out."

They reached the ambulance and lifted Hatcher's stretcher into it. Trevor and Kathy piled in beside her. The door closed, and the ambulance pulled away.

CHAPTER 24

Monday, December 1st, 2036 — 1:34pm — Loading Dock of the office at Telegraph Road, Alexandria, Virginia

McKnight, Wheeler and Tyler watched the ambulance until it moved out of sight. With an exchange of glances, they turned and went back to McKnight's office without a word.

McKnight stopped them at the office door.

"Guys, I need a few minutes."

"Yes, sir. No problem, sir," Wheeler said.

"Do you have a change of uniform here, sir?" Tyler said. He pointed at the blood on McKnight's Greens.

"Yes, I do. Thanks," McKnight said.

Tyler nodded. Both men saluted McKnight and walked down the hall.

McKnight entered his office and walked over to the window. Outside, the wind was blowing and the trees were swaying gently. He stood there for a long minute, his mind racing.

Thoughts and images flew through his consciousness. The close brush with death he just experienced. The mission in jeopardy. Losing Hatcher. The danger from an irresistible attack from the future. The murders of those young women.

The last thought lingered. An image of people using time travel and murder to forward their agenda.

He realized he was trembling.

Stress release?

He went to his desk and sat. He swung his chair around and set his feet up on the credenza. His hand shook as he pulled out his phone. He hesitated, then put it back in his pocket and closed his eyes. He focused on relaxing.

He realized it was not stress release.

It's anger.

McKnight opened his eyes and stared out at the trees.

They reached into my command and tried to kill me and one of my people. And they killed those girls with no remorse or even any guilt. If they can do that, there's no limit to what they might do to stop us. If they can't keep us from traveling, they'll kill us. We're living on borrowed time.

McKnight stood and took deep breaths. He desperately wanted to put his fist through the wall.

If I'm going to fix this, I have to calm down. I can't let my anger overcome my judgment.

After a few minutes, the deep breaths had an effect. Logical thought returned and so did his resolve.

From this point forward, I'm dedicating everything I think and do to stopping Rachel and......whoever's orchestrating this.

He removed his feet from the credenza and pushed back to his desk. He pulled his phone out again and held it to his lips.

"Call Tyler," he said, and waited while the phone rang.

A click.

"Yes, sir?" Tyler said.

"Captain, find Lieutenant Wheeler and come back to my office. We have a job to finish."

****

Monday, December 1st, 2036 — 2:13 pm — McKnight's office at Telegraph Road

McKnight, Wheeler, and Tyler sat at McKnight's conference table next to the window.

"More than ever before, I want to bring Rachel back to face justice," McKnight said.

"Yes, sir," Tyler and Wheeler said together.

"We have to do something she isn't expecting and we need to do it now. Any time now, she will try to take out our machine — I'm sure of it. We need a distraction. Captain Tyler, you and I jump in fifteen minutes."

"Yes, sir," Tyler said.

"Lieutenant Wheeler, you'll operate the Engine to send us. Then you jump tomorrow as scheduled if we don't come back before then. Kathy can man the Engine for your jump."

"Why don't we all go now, sir?" Wheeler asked. "Doctor Astalos can operate the Engine."

"No. Understand this. I half-expect them to find out about this jump and maybe have a reception committee waiting for us. If we're lucky, they'll focus on us and not bother with you tomorrow. So, you'll be in 2086 on your own when you jump. You know what needs to be done for the reconnaissance."

McKnight put his hand on Wheeler's shoulder. "I'm counting on you, Mitch. I know you'll do us proud."

"Yes, sir."

"As far as Doctor Astalos operating the machine goes... As long as he is the only person in the country who can fix it, I don't want him near the Engine while we believe it to be in danger. If he gets hurt, there's no one on this continent that can help us."

"Understood, sir," Wheeler said. "There's still Hatcher, who can work on it—"

Tyler shook his head. "Not now. We need to consider her MIA for the time being."

"She can still work on the machine, sir. Respectfully, she's injured, but not out of action."

"No," McKnight said. "Tyler is right. We assume she is out of action until they assess her and she undergoes treatment. It might take weeks. She may never get over it."

Wheeler was crestfallen. "Yes, sir. Understood."

"Lieutenant Wheeler, you're a Ranger officer. I expect you to follow my orders as long as they make sense. Circumstances change. We improvise, adapt, and overcome. You do what you have to do if you think it's necessary."

Wheeler stiffened to attention. "Yes, sir!"

"Now, you'll run the Engine to send Captain Tyler and me to 2086. We'll both have the same mission. Recon. We'll still go to the Manassas battlefield outside Washington to avoid any structures. When you arrive tomorrow, visit the park restaurant and look for us. One of us will be there to brief you and we'll go from there. If we're not there, you proceed to carry out the mission and assume we are no longer active."

"Yes, sir," Wheeler said.

"Mitch, you need to be here today. I have other things that need doing here, that Kathy and Trevor can't do. Make sure we do the Engine configuration backup and they step up the work on the second and third machines so we have backup hardware."

McKnight held up his hand.

"But first, move the hardware components for the two backup Engines out of the Lab. If they jump in to damage the primary Engine, I don't want the backups taken out at the same time. We can at least make it difficult for them. I don't want to get stuck in 2086."

"Me, neither," Tyler said.

McKnight continued. "If you can, have someone move the primary Engine someplace else after you jump, just in case."

"Understood, sir," Wheeler said.

"Tyler, call your wife and let her know you're going on a mission, but will be back tomorrow."

"Yes, sir."

"We leave in about fifteen, then."

"Yes, sir."

Tyler and Wheeler stood and saluted.

McKnight returned their salute, and the two officers left the room.

He pulled out his phone and said, "Call Megan."

She answered after two rings.

"Hi, there," she said.

"Hi, how's your day been?"

"Good, actually. I have another interview day after tomorrow."

"That's great!" he said.

"And how has *your* day been? Everything going as you hoped?"

"Not exactly. There's been a slight change in plans for the mission."

"Oh? What does that mean? Are you traveling?"

"Well, yes. We had a little wrinkle and now have to approach things another way. I'll be traveling out today, but I should be home tomorrow for dinner."

"Okay," she said. "Are you all right?"

"Yes, why wouldn't I be?"

"I don't know," she said. "I thought I caught something in your voice. You're not in any danger, are you?"

Wow, I've got to work on my delivery.

"No, no, everything's fine. Hey, I gotta go. How about we plan to go out to dinner tomorrow night after I get back?"

"Sure, that sounds lovely. I'll wear that black dress you like."

McKnight knew what dress she meant.

"I'll look forward to that. Love you."

"I love you too, Marc."

He disconnected the call.

It crossed his mind to caution Kathy not to tell Megan what happened today, but the thought slipped away as the mission requirements pushed their way in.

McKnight walked to his locker in the Lab and pulled out his travel satchel. He kept it fully stocked in case he traveled on short notice.

He confirmed it contained two changes of clothes, a shaving kit, sleep bulbs, motion sensor, and a first aid kit. He changed into a clean set of Greens and walked to the primary Engine. As an afterthought, he returned to the locker and picked out a light jacket.

Tyler met him there after two minutes. He carried his satchel, too.

After another minute, Wheeler ran in from the hall. "Everything is in motion. Priority is to move the backup hardware, and then the Main Engine's software backup. Are you ready to travel?"

Tyler and McKnight both nodded.

"Be sure to erase the configuration from the Engine after we leave, Mitch. I don't want our destination going into the data backup tonight."

"No problem, sir. I've already prepared a cleanup program to save it to my personal thumb drive and erase the official record."

"Good," McKnight said.

He glanced at Tyler.

"Got your anti-nausea med?"

Tyler rolled his eyes and dashed to his locker, pulled out a small bottle and returned to the Engine platform.

"By the book," Wheeler said. "Here are your beacons. I programmed them to take you to 2086 and return to this machine."

Tyler and McKnight took the beacons with their chains and draped them around their necks. Then they knelt on the platform.

"Target date is December 1st, 1900 hours, 2086. Location is hilltop #16 in the Manassas Battlefield National Park."

"Roger," McKnight said. Tyler nodded.

"Do you have your beacons? By the book, sirs."

"We do," Tyler said.

"Location and date configured and activated." He picked up the trigger with its curly cord and plugged it into the console.

"Travelers ready?" he asked.

Both officers nodded.

Wheeler flipped up the safety cover on the trigger.

"Travelers are ready," Wheeler said. "Jump in 5... 4... 3... 2... 1... ZERO!" He pressed the button.

The hum of the machine cycled up in volume and pitch. The time bubble formed around McKnight and Tyler, and the air inside glowed and spun. Their hair and uniforms rippled and flapped as if they were standing outside in the middle of a windstorm.

Wheeler smiled.

From inside the bubble, the two officers gave him a thumbs up.

Then the bubble bulged to double its normal size and dissipated with a loud crack.

McKnight and Tyler felt a tug, then they fell backward into a field of stars.

CHAPTER 25

Monday, December 1st, 2036 — 6:45 pm — HERO Team Lab

"It's about time," Wheeler mumbled to himself.

He had the backup Time Engines crated and ready two hours after McKnight and Tyler jumped out. But it took another two hours for the moving team to arrive to take them to the backup lab in Foggy Bottom.

He directed the men to start with the 'B' Engine. They had just brought in the forklift when he felt the telltale signature of time travel — an abundance of static electricity.

He glanced at his watch.

McKnight and Tyler shouldn't be coming back now. They—

Wheeler ran to the work team.

"Clear the room!" he shouted. The team looked at him, dumbfounded. "Clear the room NOW! Incoming!"

The men and women ran to the loading dock door and disappeared through it.

Wheeler sprinted to the armaments locker and dug into his pocket for his keys. With his back to the Lab, he saw the bright light of a time aura bounce off the wall before him. He glanced over his shoulder. Something big was coming in.

He got the locker open and looked for the heaviest weapon he could find.

There!

He pulled a McMillian Tac-50 rifle from the rack, then rummaged in the ammunition shelf for the rounds. It was a bolt action, single-shot rifle used by snipers.

It'll have to do.

He found the shells and ran with the rifle to the cover of the rooftop access stair. It was made of heavy steel and offered the best cover, though it might not be enough.

An LF-50 attack drone appeared inside the time aura. It was six feet across and three feet high. Four high-speed fans provided the lift, mounted on four sturdy aluminum arms set at ninety degrees apart. The body itself looked like a small flying saucer, with a high-res camera and a 25 caliber gun muzzle between the front fan arms. When the aura disappeared, the drone flew to the middle of the Lab and spun to photograph the room.

Wheeler slid down, his back against the stair, and began loading the rifle. He tried to remember the drone's configuration.

How many rounds does it carry? 40? 50? The most vulnerable spot would be the control unit, mounted on the front between the camera and the weapon.

Wheeler rolled his eyes. To have a shot at the control unit, the drone has to be pointed at you. Which means the camera can see you. And so can the weapon.

He chanced another look at it. It appeared to have completed the recon phase.

If its programmer was smart, the first target will be the primary Engine.

As expected, it floated toward the primary Engine.

Wheeler turned with the weapon and aimed it at the drone.

I can't see the control unit! What do I shoot at?

Some action is better than no action.

For lack of a better target, he fired at the body.

BOOM!

The report of the McMillian sounded like an explosion. His bullet hit the drone, pushing it off equilibrium hover. The 50-caliber round made an impressive dent in the saucer. The pitch of the fans dropped, then recovered, and the drone regained its stability.

It spun counter-clockwise and pointed its gun in his direction. He slipped back down behind the staircase to reload.

Finding no immediate target, the drone returned to the primary Engine, and began firing. It fired in bursts of five rounds, pausing between bursts to re-evaluate its target. The noise from the weapon was deafening and echoed mercilessly in the open Lab space.

Now reloaded, Wheeler chanced another look over the edge of the staircase. The five-shot bursts from the drone's weapon were leaving impressive damage on the primary Engine.

Not enough to bring it down. Try the fan arms.

Wheeler fired at one of the front fans facing the Engine.

BOOM!

This time, the McMillian bullet blew the fan off. The drone dipped, compensated for the lost fan and swung back in his direction, but he was already moving to his right as fast as he could. The drone paused for a second, pointed at the staircase, then focused on the 'A' Engine and began firing.

"Dammit!" Wheeler said.

He ran to the 'B' Engine and set up to shoot. To hit the control panel, he'd have to be in front of the flying killer, exposed to its weapon. It was a risk, but he couldn't think of any other way to approach it. He reloaded and aimed at the right front fan.

BOOM!

Wheeler dropped behind the 'B' Engine to reload. This time, the McMillian broke the fan arm, but the blades continued turning — the wiring to the fan engine was still intact. The untethered fan flapped around, intermittently hitting the drone's body and changing its lift profile. It spun toward him, but the front dipped precipitously as the rear fans tried to compensate. The flying killer lost stability, and tracked across the room toward him, the weapon firing into the floor.

Now that it pointed down, the control panel was no longer visible to him. With no other choice, he shouldered the rifle and aimed at a rear fan.

168 · KIM MEGAHEE

BOOM!

He missed the shot, but it didn't matter. The loose fan collided with a rear fan and the drone lost flight capability. It crashed in front of the 'B' Engine. The gun broke off and skittered across the concrete floor.

Wheeler ran to the side of the crashed drone, careful to stay away from the blades of the single functioning fan.

The drone caught fire. Wheeler debated whether to put out the fire and salvage the drone.

Wait! If I were Rachel, what would I do to ensure destruction of the Engines?

He already knew the answer.

Blow it!

He ran from the drone and took cover behind the staircase again. Five seconds later, it self-destructed. Pieces of hot, shredded metal bounced off the Lab walls. The remaining ammunition blew in a small, secondary explosion.

"Why do I have to be so smart?" he said.

Wheeler turned and sat down with his back to the staircase. He laid the McMillian on the floor next to him.

We're screwed. I can't get to the future and the Major and Captain can't get back.

He stood and walked over to the heap of twisted metal that was the primary Engine.

The next step would be a monumental task. Sorting through the wreckage to find enough whole components to construct one working Engine from the three destroyed units would not be easy. He was glad Doctor Astalos was not here when the drone attacked.

The work team filtered back into the Lab. A few left because of the attack, but most stayed to help. Wheeler directed them to separate the pieces of the Engines that weren't damaged from the rest.

Once the team began the task, Wheeler called Doctor Astalos.

"Hello?" the familiar voice said.

"Doctor Astalos, this is Wheeler—"

"Well, hello, Mitch. I trust this evening finds you well."

"Not at all, sir. There's been an attack on the Lab. As the Major warned, it looks like Rachel sent a drone to attack our time jump capability. I neutralized the drone, but not before it damaged all three Engines — the primary Engine and Engines A and B."

"Oh, dear," the old man said. "And what is going on right now?"

"I have a team sorting out the debris — trying to salvage anything that wasn't destroyed."

"I see. Good. Any idea of the level of damage?"

"Sir, I'm certain the primary Engine is a total loss. Engines A and B were in crates, but there was an explosion, so I'm not sure about them."

"Okay. Please notify Doctor Wu and Trevor about the event. Now, is anyone out on a mission?"

"Yes, sir. Major McKnight and Captain Tyler jumped earlier today. When the attack came, I thought it was them coming back. Instead, it was a battle drone."

"I see. When do you expect them to need to return, Mitch?"

"I was thinking it would be a couple of days, but we don't really know. It's a recon mission. Those are always unpredictable."

"Okay, did you check to see if the MAC-ID module is intact? Their beacons are associated with that unit in the Engine. If it's destroyed, we can't point their beacons at a new Engine. We'll have to send someone after them."

"I'll check, sir," Wheeler said. "Are you coming in tonight?"

"Is it an emergency situation? I can come in now. If not, I'll be in the office in the morning and we'll start salvaging what we can."

Are you kidding?

Wheeler paused. "I can't imagine why it wouldn't be an emergency, sir."

"Is anyone dead?" Astalos asked. "Is anyone in danger right now and needs to jump back to the present?"

Wheeler was stunned.

"Well, no, sir. By those criteria, I guess it's not an emergency, but I would have thought you'd want to come in now anyway, to assess the damage."

"Mitch, the problem will still be there tomorrow morning."

"Yes, sir. But Major McKnight and Captain Tyler are traveling with no way to get back."

"Yes, I know. But tomorrow will be a long day and you weren't expecting them to come back right away, correct?"

"Yes, sir."

"And I will need my sleep to function well. It'll all be fine, you'll see. Thanks for letting me know. I'll see you there first thing tomorrow."

The scientist disconnected the line.

Wheeler held the phone out in front of his face and stared at it.

I can't believe he was so calm and collected. It's a disaster.

Wheeler called Trevor and Kathy to report the event. They told him Hatcher was resting easy and General Drake escalated her medical need. Her psychiatric care should start tomorrow.

The news and Doctor Astalos' response dismayed them.

Trevor reminded Wheeler that he should update General Drake since he was the highest ranking officer still able to report.

Wheeler decided he needed to check on the MAC-ID unit before reporting status.

After ten minutes of tearing broken and warped pieces off the Engine, he found the unit. It looked scorched, but not twisted out of shape. It took another ten minutes to extract it from the Engine and run diagnostics on it. When they completed, he sighed with relief — the unit was undamaged. He looked back at the pile of scrap metal that had been the Engine.

I must be living right. It's a miracle.

He called Drake, who listened for a while, then said, "What type of drone was it, Lieutenant?"

"It was an LF-50, sir."

"Hmm. They're using old drones. Well, old for *them*. Very interesting. Did you bring Doctor Astalos into the loop?"

"Yes, sir," Wheeler said. He wasn't sure what to say next.

"Lieutenant, what did the Doctor say?"

"He said he'd be here in the morning, sir."

"Okay, good. I'll be there, too. Are you wounded or injured in any way?"

"No, sir. Nobody was hurt. But the Lab is a mess. I've confirmed that the MAC-ID unit is undamaged, but I think our primary Engine is a total loss and the backup Engines may be. I tried to save them, sir, but I failed."

"Lieutenant, Major McKnight told me that, if someone jumped in to destroy the machines, there wasn't much we could do to stop it. Are you disagreeing with that report? Are you saying the Major was wrong?"

"No, sir. I just — well, I thought… I guess I'm just very frustrated, sir."

"Me, too, Lieutenant. Okay, find someone to stay with the work team to ensure they complete the cleanup, then go home. Get a good night's sleep and be there first thing in the morning to help with the next step."

"Yes, sir."

"Tomorrow, I want you to put in an order for three LF-50 drones. On second thought, make it ten. I want ten of them. Put my name on it and I'll get it approved."

"Yes, sir."

"Anything else to report, Lieutenant?"

"No, sir."

"Very good. I'll see you in the morning."

The General disconnected.

He sure doesn't act concerned. What am I missing?

CHAPTER 26

Sunday, December 1st, 2086 — 7:00pm — Manassas Civil War
Battlefield, Manassas, Virginia

A cold mist hung over the Manassas Battlefield Park. It was damp
enough to make one miserable, but not enough to snow.

A flash of light appeared in the middle of the field next to the
Stone House. Their time bubble formed and the light and air inside
spun furiously. McKnight and Tyler appeared. The bubble bulged and
went out. They fell backward on the grass.

"Damn, it *would* be cold here," Tyler said as he rose and began a
three-sixty assessment of the terrain. "I can't see a damned thing."

"Let your eyes readjust after the time bubble. Should take a few
minutes." McKnight said.

They stood in silence for thirty seconds with their eyes closed.

Tyler looked again. His night vision wasn't good yet, but was
returning.

"See anything, sir?"

"No. I think we're all alone here."

Tyler drew out his compass.

"I see some lights to the south. That should be the camping ground
I read about. Probably not a bad place to start."

"Agreed."

McKnight stood and drew an anti-nausea packet from his satchel.
He handed it to Tyler.

"What? No, thanks." Tyler said.

Throw up one time and everyone thinks time travel makes you sick.

"Hey, no problem. I'll just put it away."

"Okay, okay. Give it to me." Tyler tore open the packet, upended it to his mouth and crumpled it.

"Better?" McKnight said. "It's not a fun thing to be ill on a mission."

"Yes, sir."

"You and Wheeler planned this recon and I'm afraid the situation didn't give me time to bone up on it. What's next?"

Tyler pointed to the lights in the distance.

"We make our way to the campground over there and pretend to be locals whose truck broke down. We ask directions and try to get a sense of what the government is like by eavesdropping on campers. Then reassess and determine the next move. Probably move toward DC."

"Okay, let's get going. How far would you say it is to that camp there? I'd say 1000 meters."

"Yes, sir. Should be about right."

They looked around to make sure they left nothing on the grassy meadow, then struck out for the lights of the camping ground.

The walk lasted a quarter hour, which included fording a narrow stream.

They passed a modest monument before they got near the campground. Tyler stopped to read it. In the low light, he could barely make out the carved legend.

"Major? Can you see this?"

"What?" McKnight backtracked to where Tyler was standing.

Tyler read it aloud.

"*The purpose of the U.S. Civil War was to bring the Southern States back into alignment with the United States plan to move toward Eastern European values and life principles - Freedom, Liberty, and Respect for the Goals of our Glorious Movement.*"

He turned to McKnight.

"What the hell? That's not right, is it? I mean, it can't be right."

"No, it isn't," McKnight said. "Let's get closer."

They stopped in a stand of trees and surveyed the campground.

To Tyler, it looked like a present day campground.

Shouldn't there be innovation in the camping industry by now?

The mere presence of RVs there told him it wasn't a primitive campsite, so he wondered why he saw nothing new.

"Are you sure we made it to 2086?" McKnight whispered.

Tyler shrugged.

He's right. We should see signs of innovation. That monument sure didn't sound like progress.

There were five campfires enclosed by a ring of RVs. The RVs were old, and two looked ancient. The nearest campfire featured a man, a young boy, and a Jack Russell terrier. In the center of the ring was a larger fire, where an elderly man was talking to two women and what appeared to be their children. Tyler counted two small boys and an older girl. The elderly man seemed agitated.

The other three campfires were scattered within the circle. Elderly couples sat at each campfire, each in various stages of preparing or eating a meal.

"Hey, there's something different," McKnight said, and pointed to the other side of the RV circle.

There stood two men with automatic weapons, dressed in uniforms with an abundance of braids.

"Pretty, aren't they?" McKnight said.

Tyler squinted at the two men. Over-dressed by American Army standards, they looked like third world generals. They appeared to be on guard duty, but they leaned against an RV and smoked cigarettes.

"Who do you think they are?" Tyler asked. "Surely they don't have armed guards at national parks in 2086?"

"I don't know," McKnight said. "They look more like militia, or..."

"Brown Shirts," Tyler finished for him. "They look like Brown Shirts."

"I was going to say National Guard, but you may be closer to the mark. National Guard troops are well trained. These guys don't look the part. They're soldiers all right, but not well trained. They look more like thugs."

The ancient man at the center campfire let out a whoop. Tyler could see a half-pint bottle in his hand. He was getting drunk or already was.

"In my day," he began, "we didn't have all this bullshit going on—"

"Daddy, the kids…" one woman said.

"Sorry, honey. All this bull crap going on. We had more freedom." His voice trailed off into a mumble.

McKnight leaned in toward Tyler. "I'm going to get closer."

He drew an air circle around to his right to show he was moving to that side of the camp.

Tyler nodded. "I'll watch from here," he whispered.

McKnight soundlessly crept off to the right.

Tyler heard the young boy near him ask about the men on the far side of the camp. He pointed at them, and his father gently but firmly pushed his son's arm down.

"They are Devotees, son. They believe in the Movement and they make sure everyone else pays respect to it." The man lowered his voice and said something unintelligible.

Devotees?

Tyler crept closer to them.

The old man's voice rose again. "The kids need to understand that we are *not* hearing real news. It's all propaganda. Everyone knows it's all a lie."

"Hush, Dad," the woman said. "This isn't the time or place to talk about this."

"I won't be silenced. I'm a veteran. There are still patriots among us." He pounded his chest with the hand holding the bottle. Liquid from it splashed out and wet his chin and shirt collar.

Tyler moved closer.

The dog next to the boy stood and looked right at Tyler. He growled.

Uh-oh.

The dog took two steps toward Tyler and barked twice.

Better not look suspicious.

Tyler stepped from behind the tree and walked into the light. The dog started barking. Across the RV circle, he saw the two men pick up their rifles. One moved toward the RV near Tyler. The other went to the old man and his family.

Not good.

The man with the boy stood to face Tyler and pulled the boy close. He reached down and scooped up the dog.

"Hi, folks," Tyler said. "Sorry to spook your puppy there. My truck broke down back over there." He pointed his thumb over his shoulder. "Can you point me to the Ranger station?"

The soldier approaching the old man spoke in a loud voice. "Old man, who is our Anchor?" He looked enormous next to the elderly man. The women gathered their children closer.

The ancient man's eyes darted around, as if he were looking for an escape route. Or maybe a weapon.

The other man continued toward Tyler. He glanced back over his shoulder to his partner and smiled, then continued his approach.

He doesn't see me as a threat. Lack of training. That's an advantage.

When he reached Tyler and the boy, he said, "Who is our Anchor?"

"Our Blessed Baron," the father said, pulling his son closer. "God rest his soul."

"And who is our hope?"

The other soldier kicked the old man's lawn chair, spilling him out on the ground.

The man near Tyler said, "Our hope is his beloved great-grandsons, Joseph and Robert."

"Please," one woman cried, "he's an old man who had too much to drink—"

The soldier near Tyler turned to smile at his partner again, then turned back to the man in front of him. "And when will they come to rescue us?"

The man rattled off the response as if it was long practiced. "Soon, my friend. Soon."

"Thank you, Citizen," the soldier said. Then he noticed Tyler approaching and beckoned him forward.

At the other campfire, the soldier stood over the elderly man on the ground. "I will ask you again, old man. Who is our Anchor?"

Tyler noticed the people at the other campfires had vanished. *Probably inside their RVs.*

The aged man looked up at his tormentor and said, "Up yours, DEE-VOH-TEE".

The soldier raised his rifle to strike him, but the blow never fell. Before he could do so, McKnight was there in front of him. He tore the rifle from the man's grasp and shoved him to the ground.

The soldier near Tyler turned to support his partner, but Tyler was on him before he could raise his weapon. He swung his left arm around the soldier's neck from behind, jerked the weapon from his hands with his right, and pulled the man's right arm behind his back.

"Move again and I'll tear your head off," Tyler whispered in the man's ear.

McKnight glanced at Tyler. Satisfied the other soldier was not a threat, he turned to the man on the ground.

"Where I come from, we don't treat old men like this. Especially veterans."

"He's a Hamilton," the soldier said, and spat.

"A what?"

"A traitor to the Movement."

"I see."

McKnight turned the rifle over and ejected the clip into his hand. He turned and threw it outside the circle of light into the field beyond. He checked and found a round in the chamber. "It's not smart to keep a round chambered," he said. "You might shoot your damned foot off." He ejected it and threw it after the clip.

McKnight dropped the weapon at his feet.

"Now, get the hell out of here before I lose my temper."

The man scrambled to his feet and ran off into the night.

Tyler released the other soldier, who twisted away and glared at him.

The man with Tyler said to the soldier, "Protect yourself from this Hamilton, Citizen. Don't risk your life."

The soldier glanced at him, then back at Tyler. Then he turned and ran after his partner.

The man turned to Tyler and pointed back over his own shoulder. "There's a group of his unit about 200 yards over that way. You and your friend should leave now. They'll be here any second."

Tyler looked over the man's shoulder. McKnight was kneeling next to the old man and was helping him to his feet.

"Who were they and why are they armed here at the park?" Tyler asked.

A shout from beyond the camp circle rang out. Tyler watched McKnight whirl in that direction.

"It's too late. They're already here. Quick! Hide under my camper!"

Tyler saw multiple flashlights outside the circle. Five men entered the lighted area and rushed McKnight.

"Better move, Mister," the man said to Tyler. "They'll be here in a second."

Despite his urge to fight, Tyler thought the better of it and dove under the RV. The man picked up a lawn chair, set it against the RV and sat in it.

He pulled his son next to him and said, "Ricky, get inside the camper and hunker down like I taught you. Go!" he whispered. The boy ran to the RV door and disappeared inside.

The soldiers restrained McKnight, two on each arm. The soldier disarmed by McKnight searched him and found his service weapon in the small of his back.

He held it up and shouted, "Well, lookie here. We have us an armed Citizen. That's sufficient for arrest. Take him, Boys!"

They pressed his hands together, tied them behind his back with cord, and pulled him away from the encircled RVs.

Tyler watched from beneath the camper.

This might be a bad idea. If this guy gives me away, I'm powerless here.

Four men broke away from the group around McKnight and ran to the man and boy. The leader spoke. "And who is our Anchor?"

The man in the lawn chair responded. "Our Blessed Baron, God rest his Soul."

"There was another man," the leader said. "Where is he?"

"As soon as you appeared, sir, he ran off that-a-way." He pointed across the field behind him.

The leader directed his men toward the field. They ran in that direction, but the leader remained.

"You talked with him for a minute. What did he say?"

"Nothing of consequence, sir."

"I asked you, what did he say? Are you refusing to answer me?"

"Of course not, sir. I meant no disrespect. He just apologized for scaring our dog when he approached. Then he said his truck broke down back over there." He pointed in the same direction as before.

The leader looked in that direction, then back at the man.

"I think he was with the Citizen we just arrested. What do you think?"

"You couldn't tell it by me," the man said. "I didn't see the Citizen until the ruckus started. For all I know, he'd been in that camper over there all day. The only stranger I saw was the one who walked in here." He gestured at the edge of the circle next to him.

Tyler lay on the wet earth behind the man in the lawn chair. He chanced a look at the leader from the dark underneath the camper.

The leader looked confused and irritated. After a moment, he spoke.

"Okay. Thank you, Citizen." He ran off after his team.

After fifteen seconds, the man in the lawn chair said, "Do not move, friend. They'll come back this way and may yet search the camp again."

Crap. Stuck here and Marc is being carried off somewhere.

Tyler took stock of his situation. He had his satchel and could survive on his own once he got away from here. No way to tell where McKnight was, unless they took him to another camp just out of sight now. He could check that soon.

If these assholes got hold of his satchel, they might guess he was a time traveler.

They already have Marc and his satchel.

As a precaution, he slipped it up on top of the RV's tire in the wheel well. With luck, they might overlook his gear if they discovered him.

What was it the old man called the soldiers? DEE-VOH-TEE? Devotee? What does that mean?

The soldiers came back. The leader stopped before the man in the lawn chair and handed him a card. "If you see that man again or you remember anything else he said to you, call me at that number."

"I will certainly do that, sir. I want to help the Glorious Movement in any way I can."

"Thank you, Citizen." The man turned and jogged off in the same direction as the others.

They waited twenty minutes before the man stood and called for Tyler to come out of his hiding place.

Tyler retrieved his satchel and crawled out from under the RV.

The man said, "It's a good thing they haven't been trained. I would have looked there first thing. You're military?"

Tyler shrugged. "You might say that. I owe you my freedom, Mister…"

The man smiled. "Alarcon. Richard Alarcon. Everybody calls me Rick."

"I'm Tyler." He extended his hand, and the man shook it.

Alarcon seemed startled by his name.

"Where did they take him?" Tyler asked. "Do you have any idea?"

"Probably to their barracks. And then? I'm not sure. People disappear forever, sometimes."

Gone. Maybe dead.

Without warning, Alarcon raised his phone and snapped a picture of Tyler.

"What did you do that for?" Tyler said.

Alarcon tapped away at his phone. "Don't worry, I'm not turning you in to anyone. Before I tell you much about me, I need to make sure you aren't a spy or something."

"What, you have a database of those guys?" Tyler gestured toward the Devotee camp.

"Sort of," Alarcon said. "Just bear with me a second."

Tyler glanced around, mapping his escape routes from here. He wasn't sure he could believe the man. Despite his reservations, he decided to try to gather intel.

"Who were those men?" he asked. "What are Devotees?"

The man straightened. "You don't know about the Devotees?"

"I've been out of the country for a while," Tyler said.

"Quite a while, I'd say," Alarcon said. "They've been around for about ten years. Where are you from?"

"I grew up in Georgia, but I haven't been back for a while."

Alarcon stared at him for a long moment. "You know, I haven't heard about Georgia in a long time. You *have* been gone for a while."

He looked Tyler up and down. "You need some more up-to-date clothes."

Uh-oh. He's sharp and I haven't been careful enough.

In his eyes, Tyler could see the man's mental wheels turning.

Alarcon's phone chirped, and he looked at it. Then he stood up straight and looked Tyler in the eye.

"I don't believe it. How could I be so stupid?"

"What? Sorry, but I don't—"

"Are you Winston Churchill Tyler?"

Tyler was stunned and couldn't keep it from his face.

"You *are*," Alarcon said. "Good God! Right here in front of my nose."

Tyler couldn't speak and was glad he couldn't. Anything he said might get him in worse trouble.

"Sorry, I can give you more information, now that I know who you are. I'm Major Richard Alarcon - retired, Army Rangers, 75th Regiment. Your team is legendary in the Rangers... well, pretty much everywhere. The number of issues and problems the HERO Team fixed is a matter of record bordering on legend, and I'm pleased to meet you. The stories I've heard about you and Colonel McKnight are..." He stopped, his wheels turning again.

Tyler couldn't decide what to say.

Could he be talking about us? About things we haven't done yet? We're famous in the Regiment? Nobody's supposed to know much about what we do. How does he know any of this?

Alarcon straightened and looked Tyler in the eye again.

"That other man... Was he?... Oh my God... Was he Colonel Marcus McKnight?"

Alarcon was excited. Tyler identified the source as a severe case of hero worship.

Tyler decided to confide in him. The benefit might be worth it. He might get an honest take and report on what the world was like in 2086.

"Well, he's not a colonel yet," he said.

Alarcon looked surprised and then recovered. "Of course not." He sat back in his lawn chair. "You've come here from... the late thirties? Most of what you're known for hasn't happened yet."

Tyler remained silent. As outgoing and charming as he knew he could be, this hero worship was something brand new.

Alarcon looked up at him. "How can I help? Is there anything I can do? Why are you here?"

"Recon," was all Tyler could think of to say. "This is our first time to go forward. Before today, we've only gone back in time. We're investigating some deaths in 2036 and think the Federal Time Services team are behind them."

Alarcon spat. "Those pukes? I wouldn't put anything past them."

"Who are they? That's probably a good question to answer."

"You're going to hate this, Tyler," he said. "Their team was around when you were. They were called the HERO Team until that witch Rachel Patterson took over command."

CHAPTER 27

Sunday, December 1st, 2086 — 10:00pm — In a truck in Virginia

McKnight rolled over on his side and his left cheek screamed in pain. Now he was fully awake.

The vibration beneath him signaled movement. His hands were manacled behind his back.

He opened his eyes. He was lying on the floor of a truck on the way to… somewhere.

The vehicle wall was equipped with a bench. A large, very attentive guard sat on it and glared at McKnight. Everything about the man signaled a willingness to punish McKnight for any infraction, including breathing too loudly.

McKnight resigned himself to saving his energy and wait for a chance to escape.

As an exercise in sanity and to keep himself alert, he tried to recall every detail about his capture and treatment up to this point.

The Devotees who captured him hustled him across 200 yards of country meadow to a large encampment. All around him, he saw lax discipline, but far superior numbers. His chances of escape dwindled by the moment.

The HERO Team standard protocol if captured was silence. But that protocol applied to travel in the past. No one knew about time travel before 2034, so talking about it guaranteed getting locked up. But these guys in 2086 *knew* about time travel, so maybe the protocol doesn't apply?

Better to stick to it if possible.

They took him to a trailer and stood him up in front of a man who appeared to be in charge.

He was a slovenly, overweight man who didn't appear to be the brightest bulb in the bunch. McKnight decided silence was the best course.

"I'm Captain Wilson," the man said. "What's your name?"

McKnight ignored him and counted the men he could see in the trailer.

Too many. Way too many.

"Did you hear me?" Wilson said.

McKnight resigned himself to getting pounded. He assumed these people would resort to beatings quickly. He decided he wouldn't speak unless death was imminent. Then he'd have to improvise.

"A stylish dresser," Wilson said to the room.

The men laughed.

The squad leader approached Wilson and laid McKnight's satchel on his desk.

Wilson opened the satchel and poured the contents out. He sorted through the clothes and found the sleep bulbs. He held one up.

"Antiques," he said.

More laughter from the men.

"What do you have to say for yourself, Major?"

McKnight tried not to react. Wilson was at least smart enough to recognize the rank markings on his uniform.

"You're not in friendly territory, pal. One word from me and you'll be fertilizer in the woods."

He turned to the man on his right. "Bobby, loosen him up a bit."

A chair appeared from somewhere and the men restraining him slammed him into it. His hands were secured to the back of the chair and a rope was looped across his chest and tied behind him. His feet were left untied. A man stood behind McKnight and held his chair in place.

Bobby came from his right and struck him hard on the right cheek.

That's why my cheek hurts.

Bobby stood in front of McKnight and aimed a left hook at the other cheek.

McKnight kicked hard against the floor and against the man behind him. It was just enough for Bobby's swing to miss his cheek. Then he kicked Bobby in the nuts with all his strength.

Bobby went down in a heap, groaning in pain. Wilson and the men roared with laughter as Bobby lay on the floor swearing.

I'm probably dead, now.

Another man next to Wilson leaned over and whispered in his ear. He said something about unauthorized time travel and nodded once. Wilson listened intently, then nodded.

"Sorry, Bobby," he said, "but I'm gonna have to cut your fun short. What there was of it."

He laughed, and the other men laughed with him.

Wilson pointed at another man and then McKnight. Then he rose from his desk and came around to McKnight's left side, stepping over Bobby and being careful not to stand in front of McKnight.

The other man approached McKnight from the right and started rolling up his sleeve. He stuck a syringe in McKnight's forearm and injected something.

Wilson smiled and said, "Well, Major whoever you are, some people want to talk to you. And they won't be as nice as me."

McKnight looked at Wilson, and his image faded into nothingness.

That was all he remembered. There was no telling how long he'd been out.

Now, being on the floor of a truck made more sense. It smelled of sweat and was covered with mud and grass.

A troop carrier.

The truck slowed, and he heard a turn signal blinking. He heard cars going by. Then the vehicle turned left and went up an inclined driveway. It swayed backward and forth as it navigated and finally came to a stop.

The truck's rear door opened, and his captors helped him out.

They pushed him through a stand of trees, and a building came into view.

He was disoriented when he first left the truck, but not anymore.

I know this place.

It was the HERO Team office on Telegraph Road. They escorted him down a short sidewalk and into the loading dock. They entered a room the size of a small gymnasium.

Doctor Astalos' lab.

No one had cleaned the Lab for years. Canvas tarps covered most of the contents of the room, but there were a few new crates here and there. Astalos's old office was on the left as they hustled him across the room. The door was open, but the office was dark.

I wonder if one of the Time Engines is still here?

He craned his neck to look to the right, where the Engines stood fifty years ago. There were piles of… something… under canvas. There was no way to see if the Engine was still there or not.

The guards pushed him through the double doors into the office hallway.

Could this be a coincidence — coming to this place? Not likely.

He guessed the destination, not even aware of how it came to him.

They dragged him into an office. This room was clean and scrubbed. The pictures on the wall weren't his, but he recognized it.

It was his own office.

The guards set him down in a side chair and secured him to it. This time, they tied his legs to the chair.

McKnight's mind raced. He tried, but couldn't think of any reason to be here.

After fifteen minutes, the door opened behind him and someone entered. An attractive brunette woman appeared before him, so close he had trouble focusing on her face.

"Hello, Marc," she said. "Welcome home."

She retreated a step, pulled the other side chair around in front of him, and sat.

He must have looked confused, because she pulled a strand of her hair forward and said, "I went back to my original color. Do you like it?"

Then he knew.

It was Cindy Ginn with black hair.

Not Cindy, he corrected himself.

Cindy's dead.

It's Rachel Patterson.

CHAPTER 28

<u>Sunday, December 1st, 2086 — 10:00pm — Manassas Battlefield
Campground</u>

"You look tired, Captain," Alarcon said. "I think the best way to
bring you up to date on everything that's happened over the past fifty
years is to plug you into the Resistance TEV network."

Tyler decided to trust Alarcon. If the man wanted to betray him,
there was no reason to hide him at the campground.

"How do we do that?" Tyler said. "Won't that bring those
Brownshirts back here?" He swung his hands to indicate the
campground. "Are they smart enough to monitor communications? Or
do they even care?"

"Brownshirts, eh?" Alarcon chuckled. "That's an excellent name
for our friends over there." He pointed toward the armed camp. "Yes,
it would, but we'll be mobile. We should leave. They might extract
information from Major McKnight and come back looking for you."

"Not in a million years," Tyler said. "But it makes sense to get out
of here. What do you have in mind?"

Alarcon considered this. "Well, we need an hour to download the
TEV files. There's a perfect place to hide for a while in Reston, so
we'll head north from here for an hour while downloading the
Resistance files, then we'll double back to Reston."

Tyler trusted the man, but was uncomfortable with being in the
dark about everything.

"What kind of place is it? The place in Reston, I mean?"

"Oh, it's friendly. And I've already received an invitation to take
you there."

"Pardon me if I sound skeptical, and I *do* appreciate all you've done for me, but who would invite me to their place knowing nothing about me?"

"Captain, I can't tell you much yet, just in case we don't make it there. The less you know, the better."

"I see—"

"—But this one thing I can promise you. With these folks, your reputation proceeds you. I don't know how to set you at ease, but you are safe with me and with them."

What choice do I have? I can wait a little longer.

"Okay," he said. "What do we do next?"

Alarcon stepped over to the RV and pounded on the side of it. "Ricky," he called. "We're leaving. Secure the cabin."

"Yes, sir, Dad," the boy said from inside the RV.

Alarcon nodded to Tyler and began disconnecting the RV from the campground's power and sanitation.

"What can I do?" Tyler asked.

"You can put out our campfire and collect the chairs and gear."

Tyler walked around the campsite, picking up gear and stowing it in the RV's undercarriage storage.

Within thirty minutes, the ancient camper turned out of the National Battlefield and headed north on U.S. 29, the Lee Highway.

Alarcon drove, with his son in the passenger seat and Tyler in a seat behind Ricky. Once they were underway, Alarcon asked Ricky to download the Resistance files. Tyler watched as the boy deftly operated the RV's internet access console.

"We're connected, Dad," he said.

"Roger. And what happens next?"

"We download the TEV updates and end the connection."

"Sorry," Alarcon said. "What was that last part?"

The boy laughed. "We end the connection."

"And why do we do that?"

"So they cannot trace us, sir."

"Correct," Alarcon said, glancing back at Tyler and smiling. "And when do we need to do that, Ricky?"

"Every time, sir."

"Correct. And why do we always have this discussion?"

"Because the first time we forget, we'll get caught. We do this so we never forget to disconnect."

"And why is it important to not get caught?"

"Because our lives depend on it."

"You are so right, my son. Make it so."

The boy said, "I'm setting an alarm on my watch to let us know when the download has completed. Then we can disconnect."

"Very good."

Alarcon looked back at Tyler and grinned.

"I like the way you and Ricky work together," Tyler said.

"We're a team," Alarcon said.

Tyler paused and considered whether to ask the next question. It was uncomfortable, but he wanted to know more about the man he had entrusted his life to.

"Where's Ricky's Mom?"

Alarcon didn't speak for a second. Tyler thought at first he didn't hear the question, but then he responded.

"She's no longer with us," he said. "The Devotees took her when Ricky was only six months old."

"I'm sorry to hear that," Tyler said. "I didn't mean to be nosy."

"It's okay… we've been alone for a good while and we've still got each other," He looked at Ricky. "Right, Sport?"

Ricky didn't answer. He was already asleep.

Alarcon smiled and continued. "Alice, my wife, said the wrong thing at the wrong time to a Devotee. Until then, we didn't believe they would dare violate any of the Bill of Rights."

Tyler said nothing.

Things have really changed in fifty years.

"That was about eight years ago. Since then, things have gone from bad to worse. There used to be a lot of vocal Americans who spoke out against the Kosar Movement. Then, they started rounding up all the leaders of these groups."

Alarcon paused.

Tyler couldn't tell if he was gathering his thoughts or trying to hide his emotions.

"I'm sorry," Tyler said.

"It's okay. I was in California when it happened. She spoke out, and they took her. They came looking for me, but I was gone. So they went to her parents. Mom and Dad saw all this coming. When the Devotees came, they said something like 'thank God that bitch is gone, she's been trying to persuade our son-in-law to go against our Beloved Baron.'"

He glanced back at Tyler.

"To save Ricky and me, they said the vilest things about their own daughter. They knew she was already dead, so they put aside their grief to protect us."

"And did the Devotees come after you then?"

"They might have. I wanted to get her freed, but Mom and Dad knew there was no hope. They convinced me to be proactive. So I walked into Devotee headquarters in California and tried to turn her in. I pretended I didn't know they already had her. I told them I left her and came out west because she was a dangerous radical. It was the hardest thing I ever did, but it worked."

"I can't imagine. I'm so sorry."

"I pretended the love of my life was a criminal to save my own damned skin." He pointed at the boy. "And Ricky's. I even offered to testify against her, but they told me it wouldn't be necessary. That's when I knew she was dead."

Alarcon looked at Tyler. His eyes were cold. "It was all I could do not to shoot up the place. If it weren't for Ricky, I might have done it, anyway."

"I'm sorry, Rick," Tyler said. "And I apologize if I offended you with my skepticism. I didn't know what you've given up."

Alarcon shrugged, but kept his eyes on the road. "How could you know? Besides, we have to keep on moving from where we find ourselves to be. Alice would have understood and chastised me for feeling guilty."

"Sounds like she was quite a woman."

Alarcon stole a look back at Tyler. His angry expression had given way to one of sadness.

"She was. That she was."

Tyler wasn't sure what to say next.

"Why don't you try to get some sleep?" Alarcon said. "We'll head north another forty-five minutes until we complete the download, then we'll turn back for Reston."

"Well, maybe I'll just rest my eyes for a few minutes," Tyler said. He leaned his head against the side of the RV cabin and closed his eyes.

He awoke with a start when the ancient camper turned onto a bumpy dirt road. He looked forward and saw Alarcon driving and Ricky still asleep in his seat.

"Where are we?" Tyler said.

Alarcon glanced at him, then turned back to the highway. "Welcome back. We're almost there. Another five minutes."

Tyler shifted his weight and tried to will himself awake. He could use some coffee. He glanced at his watch. It was nearly 3:00 am on Sunday.

"Are we in Reston?" he asked.

"Near enough," Alarcon said. "About 20 minutes south of the city center."

"Whose place are we going to?"

"One of the most influential members of the resistance. She's the one who identified you for me."

"What?"

The RV rounded a bend in the dirt road and their headlights illuminated a small bungalow. There was a carriage house behind it.

"We're here," Alarcon announced.

He pulled the RV around the building and parked it between the carriage house and the bungalow. He reached over and shook Ricky gently. "We're here, son."

The boy moved slowly at first, blinking and yawning. Then he jumped out of the vehicle and ran toward the house.

Alarcon got up from the driver's seat and make his way to the RV's door. Tyler followed him.

Alarcon opened the door, and Tyler saw a small Asian woman standing on the bungalow's back porch, hugging Ricky. She kissed him on top of his head and waved him into the house.

She appeared ancient and delicate. Her age was indeterminate because her face was smooth as sculpted alabaster.

Tyler looked at Alarcon, who smiled and waved him out of the RV. He approached the woman, and her face lit up with a smile. When she spoke, her voice was full of strength and humor.

"Welcome, Winnie," she said, "To a place to rest before your next adventure. It's been a long time."

He searched her face and tried to understand how she knew him.

She smiled knowingly and looked past him to Alarcon.

"Hey, Rick," she called. "He hasn't changed a bit. He's just like the Sundance Kid. 'Just naturally blabby, I guess.'"

The old movie reference shook him and recognition dawned.

It was Kathy Wu.

CHAPTER 29

Sunday, December 1st, 2086 — 11:21pm — McKnight's office on Telegraph Road

McKnight was out of context. He struggled to get his head around this situation. Being at the mercy of Rachel Patterson was a dangerous place to be.

What do I already know about her? She murdered Cindy Ginn to impersonate her. She tried to kill Wheeler when he approached her. She kidnapped Hatcher and programmed her to kill me.

Rachel smiled at him. "Well, I'm glad we're finally able to meet in a more straightforward situation. It was about time, I think."

McKnight raced through his memories of her, trying to remember their conversations when she worked in their office, before they learned she was a traitor. And a murderer.

Rachel leaned back in her chair and put her feet in McKnight's lap. She gave him a coquettish smile and studied her fingernails. Satisfied with them, she met his gaze again.

She was wearing a Ranger uniform with a major's oak leaves. Her name tag said "Federal Time Services".

She's a Ranger? How is that possible? Is this another deception?

Following his eyes, she glanced down at her name tag.

"You're wondering, I see, and you're understanding you don't really know who I am."

She got up and walked past the desk to the transparent wall and the credenza. She dialed the wall to 'opaque' and the outside night disappeared - replaced by a beige wall with images of paintings on it.

"I'm you," she said. "Or at least, I have your job. You know, I first read about you when I was a kid. I read about your work in 2040 — yours and Captain Tyler's. I grew up wanting to be like you. I set my sights for the job you had. And I made it."

"Congratulations," McKnight said. "…Who is the F-T-S?"

"I understand your confusion. My team is called Federal Time Services. We used to be the HERO Team until about five years ago, when I convinced leadership to change our charter and allow us to use time travel proactively."

"Proactively? What does that mean?" he said.

She left the wall and returned to stand before him.

"Things change over the years. As the political climate changed, there was a need to… ensure that events lined up as needed. That's my job."

"I see. Instead of protecting history from those who want to manipulate it, you now use the team's capabilities to shape history to be what the current administration wants it to be."

"No, we change it for the greater good."

"By whose standard?" McKnight said. "Yours?"

Rachel stood still for a second. "No, but I am in close agreement with those in power here. And I follow my orders."

"I see," he said. "Were you following orders when you tried to kill Lieutenant Wheeler? And when you kidnapped Lieutenant Hatcher? And when you triggered her to come after me?"

She shook her head.

"Not at all. First, I didn't trigger Hatcher — Freddie did — And against my orders."

Her facial expression went icy, and she stared at the wall behind him. "And I'll deal with him at my convenience."

After an awkward moment of silence, she looked back at McKnight.

"As for Wheeler and Hatcher, *you* pushed that on me. Wheeler got too close to me and paid for that mistake. I swung a blade at him to keep him back, not kill him. He was quicker than I expected. But I know he's recovered well. He's got a nice scar to show the ladies, too."

"And Hatcher?" she continued, "She jumped me from behind and I couldn't avoid bringing her with me when I jumped out. Do you remember when we first met?"

"Here in this building, you mean?"

"No. I mean in the NewT Center Tower in Atlanta. About two years ago, your time. Don't tell me you've forgotten?"

An old puzzle piece fell into place. He remembered her. In his first mission with the HERO Team, he traveled back to witness a cold case murder. While he was looking for a place to watch the event, he came face-to-face with an unidentified security guard. Later he would learn there was no guard on the tower's security staff that met her description.

And she called me Marc.

"I wondered if that was you," he said. "How did you come to be there?"

She laughed and threw one leg over his and sat on his lap facing him. "I guess you don't yet realize what resources I have because of my position."

She pointed to the file cabinet in the corner. "I have a copy of all your mission records right here. I read that mission… maybe thirty times."

She rose and went to the file cabinet and removed a folder. She came back and straddled him again.

"Get off me," he said.

She laughed, opened the folder, and flipped through the pages.

"You probably think I'm old-fashioned, but I guess I'm a retro-girl."

"Get off me, I said."

She laughed again and pulled a page from the folder. She held the page up like a trophy.

"I like to hold your missions in my hand and read them. It's like I'm holding the paper you wrote on. But of course, it's just a paper copy of what you wrote on the computer. But I like to let my imagination run wild every once in a while. So anyway, I was reading about this mission and I decided, hey, I know where he'll be and I have a Time Engine and the hundredth anniversary of the mission is coming up. Why not go there and see him in action?"

"Are you kidding?" he said. "You took a sight-seeing tour through time?"

Rachel showed him a pouting face. "Well, more like a fact-finding mission. I thought it was important to go see you for myself... the great Marc McKnight, time traveler, righter of wrongs, defender of the weak, and so forth."

She leaned forward until her nose was two inches from his. She took a deep breath. "When I was a teenager, I dreamed of the day I would meet you," she whispered.

"You've already met me," he said.

"Yes, but not as myself. I was playing a role before. I was a security guard in 1985 and Cindy Ginn in 2036. I was acting. But now I'm here as myself. Major Rachel Patterson, Army Ranger and head of Federal Time Services."

She brushed her cheek gently across his and breathed deeply.

"I want to remember this moment," she whispered.

"Get off me," he said. "Please."

She smiled, rose and stepped away from him. She stood there, her back to him.

"Anyway, I didn't interfere, did I? I let you proceed with your mission and I did nothing to change history. I just wanted to see you in action. And you were magnificent. Being there was much better than reading your report."

She's not playing with a full deck. She's a Ranger officer with all that implies — brains, balls, and killing skills. And she's infatuated with me. That makes her more dangerous.

She turned back toward McKnight.

"You know, they ordered me to kill you. Well, more specifically, I was ordered to take you out. I mean, they wanted me to execute you, but it seemed like a waste to me. But you showing up here in 2086 shows me they were right. You're a danger to us and it pains me that I'll probably have to kill you before this is over."

She walked around the desk behind him, and he heard her open a drawer. When she appeared again, she was holding an old 9mm pistol.

"I probably should do it now. Before I come up with reasons not to. Before you convince me I shouldn't."

Uh-oh. Start talking. Get her to put her weapon away.

"I'm glad I finally got to see you as yourself," he said. "We didn't have much time to get to know each other when we worked together."

She pulled the slide back on the weapon to cock it.

She shrugged. "It wasn't *my* fault we didn't connect."

"But we're here now," he said.

"We are, aren't we?"

"Did I mention that I have a thing for brunettes?" he said. Internally, he cringed.

Was that too obvious?

He tried again. *"*Would it be possible for us to start over fresh?"

She smiled, crossed her arms and looked off into the distance.

"Well, maybe… it depends on how respectful you are to me."

McKnight was never good at flirting. He was getting through somehow, but he was teetering on a knife edge.

She sat on his lap again and draped her arms around his neck. Still holding the gun in her hand behind his head.

She shook her head and brought the gun back into view, placing the muzzle against his temple.

"Jeez, I don't know," she said. "If I let you up, we might have fun. Then again, you might be teasing me and…. I'd really hate for that to be the case."

McKnight couldn't think of any way to respond.

In the movies, the hero can always think of something clever to say. I got nothing. Say something, fool!

"I *really* don't want to say anything to make you kill me," he said. "How can I convince you?"

"Mmm," she said, but she moved the gun away from his temple.

She looked thoughtful, then kissed him hard.

If I want to stay alive, I'd better respond.

He returned her kiss with as much passion as he could muster.

Then her phone buzzed.

She swore and got off his lap. She read something on her phone, then smiled at him.

"Just when it was getting interesting," she said. She walked again to the desk behind him and reappeared with a syringe.

She put her arms around his neck again and held the syringe up in front of his face.

"I'm sorry about this," she said softly. "And I really hate that they've interrupted us."

She sighed and kissed him again. He responded in kind.

After the kiss, she lingered close, her lips brushing his. Then she withdrew and rolled up his sleeve.

"It's mission time. I'm giving your buddies a little something to worry about rather than where you are. I'll tell them you said hello."

She plunged the syringe into his arm and injected a burning liquid. He felt drowsy and slid down toward unconsciousness.

Her voice was the last sensation he had.

"I'll be back to continue this," she said. "Don't go anywhere."

CHAPTER 30

<u>Tuesday, December 2nd, 2036 — 7:00am — HERO Team Lab,</u>
<u>Telegraph Road, Alexandria, Virginia</u>

When Wheeler pulled up into the parking lot the next morning, he saw General Drake arriving with his aide Tom Clary.

He saluted and fell in step with the General to walk through building security. Drake said nothing until they were walking in the hall outside the Lab.

"Did you leave someone in charge to complete the salvage operation?" he said.

"No, sir. I stayed and supervised myself. No one but Doctor Astalos knows more about the Engine than me and Hatcher. I wanted to make sure nothing was lost or overlooked."

"Did you get any sleep?" Drake asked.

"Oh, yes, sir. It didn't take long since I was there. I got out at 2100 hours, sir. Not too late at all."

"Good," Drake said. "Have you talked to Doctor Astalos this morning?"

"No, sir, I have not."

They reached Drake's part-time office. Wheeler continued down the hall, but Drake said, "Hold on, Lieutenant. I'm coming with you."

He set his briefcase down behind his desk, gave Clary a few instructions, and turned back to Wheeler.

"Okay, Lieutenant. Let's go see what's going on in the Lab."

When they entered the Lab, they found Kathy with her clipboard and Doctor Astalos standing over the pile of recovered components.

Astalos pointed at components and Kathy made notes and check marks.

As they approached, the General greeted Astalos. "Good morning, Robert... and you, too, Doctor Wu."

Kathy nodded at him.

"How are we doing?" Drake asked.

"Better than expected, sir," Astalos said. "The primary Engine was a total loss, but Engines A and B were less damaged than first believed. Their shredded crates made them appear destroyed. They aren't operational, but Engines A and B are repairable."

"That's great news, Doctor. How long before we have capability back?"

"Three or four days. Maybe less."

This estimate astounded Wheeler.

No way.

He didn't see how it was possible.

Drake noticed the look on Wheeler's face. "What's the problem, Lieutenant?"

Wheeler looked back and forth between the General and Astalos. "Nothing, sir. It's all good."

"Out with it, Lieutenant. Do you have something to say or not?"

"No, I... Well, yes, sir, I do." He turned to Astalos. "Sir, with everything you've taught me and Hatcher... I just don't see it. I don't know how we can recover from the amount of damage we have in that time frame. These parts we recovered... what's to say they will work again? They've all been stressed beyond tolerance, and the odds of them working are not very good."

Astalos smiled at Wheeler.

"I'm sorry, sir," Wheeler said. "I know I'm the student here, but I just don't see it."

"And you'd be right," Astalos said, "if all we had was the stuff in front of you."

The General held up his hand and said, "I'll be in my office if you gentlemen need me." He turned and left the room.

Astalos put his arm around Wheeler's shoulder and guided him to the break table in the Lab. When they were out of the earshot of the others, he stopped.

"Lieutenant... Mitch... I feel I owe you an apology. Last night, when you called me... I forgot you were the ranking officer on site and would have to report to the General. I could have set your mind at ease and I failed to do so. Do you remember when Major McKnight asked me about the beacon innovations and how did I have time to work on them?"

"Yes, sir?"

"Since we started the project, I, with General Drake's permission, set up a Time Engine Lab in my basement at home. I have a spare of every single part we use here at home. That's where I developed the new gadgets and capabilities for the Engines. The General knew we'd require this capability, so he keeps signing the requisitions for the parts. We're only a few days from operational. It's just a matter of assembling a new Engine from the spares."

"Oh, my God, sir. That's great!"

"Yes, but please, please accept my apology. I should have told you last night before you called the General to report."

"That's okay, sir. No problem. I'm just relieved we can solve the problem and the Major and Captain Tyler won't be stranded for long."

"That's right, Mitch. You did an outstanding job and I'll make sure the Major knows it when he gets back."

"Thanks, Doctor. Hope springs eternal... And from strange places. This time, it was from your basement. I'm encouraged."

"Good," Astalos said. "Are you ready to get back to work?"

"Yes, sir. Let's get this thing up and running so the Major and the Captain can make it home."

****

<u>Tuesday, December 2nd, 2036 — 7:21pm - HERO Team Lab</u>

Wheeler walked the General to the loading dock door.

"Good status," Drake said. "Can you think of anything else I need to know?"

"No, sir," Wheeler said. "We're well on our way to getting a functional Time Engine by end of day Thursday. Doctor Astalos had a spare in his basement for all the crucial components."

"Good. Ping me when we are operational. Any word from Major McKnight or Captain Tyler?"

"No, sir. Without the Engine being available, they can't get a message through."

"Oh, right. Of course." Drake shook his head. "Too many details about issues in progress."

"Yes, sir."

"Just so you are aware... the President is all over my ass about these killings. We've got to get them stopped. If we have another one... I want to say 'if'... but I'll bet I should say 'when'... Anyway, when another one happens, we'll all be in a world of shit. The Administration will come down on this program like a hammer."

"Yes, sir."

"Just get it done as fast as you can, Lieutenant. We're counting on you. Make it happen."

"Yes, sir."

With that, Wheeler came to attention and saluted. Drake returned it and left the building.

Wheeler turned and watched Doctor Astalos, Kathy, and Trevor working on the Engine. Astalos was cross-training Kathy on the machine assembly and Trevor was acting as their arms, legs, and heavy lifter.

Wheeler himself was trained on every aspect of the Engine's operation, maintenance and assembly. He didn't understand the theory of how it worked, but he knew how to run the Engine, how to put it together, and how to test it.

It'll be nice to have someone other than Hatcher and I trained on it.

He saw Trevor struggling with a panel and dashed over to help with it. They moved it into place and prepared to bolt it on.

"Hold on a second," Astalos said. He went to his office and brought back a small circuit board and plugged it into one of the Engine's auxiliary ports.

"Okay. *Now* you can bolt on that side panel."

Wheeler had never seen the component before.

"Doctor Astalos," he asked. "What was that you just connected? I don't remember seeing it before."

"That's because it's new," Astalos said. "I figured out how the Time Engine Inhibitor works. That's one of the components we need to make it work."

"Seriously?" Wheeler said. "That little module?"

"Well... that and others. In a way, the attack on the Engine was helpful."

"What?" Trevor said. "I can't see how that's possible."

"Well, not helpful," Astalos admitted. "More like convenient. Before the attack, we would need to shut down the machine and take it apart to add all the TEI components. Since we're rebuilding the Engine, it's much easier to install the components as we go along."

"Oh, I see," Wheeler said. "All things considered, I'd rather have taken it apart."

"Exactly," Trevor said. He laid a finger on the side of his nose, then pointed it at Wheeler.

Wheeler thought about McKnight and Tyler.

"Doctor Astalos," he said, "how soon do you think we'll be able to get a signal from our travelers?"

"I was just thinking the same thing, Mitch," Astalos said. "Not until we complete the Engine reconstruction, I'm afraid. We need everything functioning before we can catch a signal."

Wheeler nodded. He focused on bolting the side panel on, avoiding any contact with the electrical components of the Engine.

"I know this is frustrating to everyone," Astalos announced to the team. "But when we get the Engine running again, nobody will jump in and destroy it again. Next, we'll start working on how to defeat the Inhibitor so we can jump into their space."

Wheeler stopped and looked at Astalos. "I've gotta say, I'll be glad when we get there. I'm tired of being on the defensive. We'd like to take the battle to them for a change."

"I understand your anxiety and feelings about this," Astalos said. "It was a blow to have them come in and wreck our Engine — To destroy what we've accomplished in just a few seconds. It makes me more determined to stop them."

"We all take it personal, sir," Kathy said. "We want those people to pay for what they've done."

"Doctor Astalos, it seems like we are making excellent progress," Wheeler said. "Do you have an idea when we'll be ready?"

"Yes, I do," he said. "We still have three components of the Inhibiter out with the fabricator. When we get them back, it should take two hours to install them. With a day of testing, we should have everything up and running in about forty-eight hours, give or take a couple of hours."

"Sounds good," Wheeler said. "I'm ready to get back in action."

"Me, too," Trevor said. "I wonder how Marc and Tyler are doing?"

CHAPTER 31

Monday, December 2nd, 2086 — The Safe House, Reston, Virginia

Tyler was surprised he didn't recognize Kathy at first. He decided it was because he wasn't expecting her. Now that he knew who she was, it was obvious. He saw his friend in the old face.

"Kathy!" he said. He embraced her gently.

"Winnie, it's great to see you. You remind me so much of... the old days."

"I can't tell you how glad I am to see you," he said. "I know I can trust you, no matter how many years have passed." He extended his arms and grasped her shoulders so he could get a better look at her. "You look great."

"And you're still a flirt and a very sweet liar," she said, and giggled into her hand.

He glanced around.

Could Trevor be here, too?

Part of Kathy's smile vanished. "You're looking for Trevor... I know you guys were great friends."

Tyler looked back at her.

"We lost him about three years ago."

"How? The Movement?"

"No," she said. "Heart attack. You know he always had a thing for Southern cooking — fried this and fried that. I tried to get him to eat healthier and exercise more, but he was always busy and wouldn't take the time. He gained some weight and... well, you can guess the rest."

"I'm sorry," he said. "What about the rest of the team?"

She reached up and stroked his cheek. "I don't think it's good to know too much about the future, do you? Let's just broach that subject as needed, okay?"

Classic Kathy. She knows I'd worry about it.

"Okay," he said.

He looked back at the RV and saw Alarcon and Ricky there, watching them. Rick's hand rested on Ricky's shoulder.

He turned back to his friend. "How do you know Rick here?"

She smiled again. "A blessed event. He's my son-in-law — he married my daughter. Ricky is my grandson."

Tyler glanced back over his shoulder at the man, and the boy besides him.

"He seems like a good man. I like him."

"He is."

He remembered the story Alarcon had told him.

"And Alice was your daughter? I'm so sorry, Kathy."

"Thank you. And now you know why I left government service."

Tyler nodded.

Of all the things he knew about Kathy, he was most aware of the passion and sense of justice that ran through her soul. It was likely what attracted Trevor to her. Tyler himself admired that aspect of the woman before him.

Kathy looked at the sky and shivered.

"Let's go inside, shall we? There's more rain in the forecast and I feel it coming. It's not good for these old bones to get cold and wet."

"Of course," he said. "Let me help Rick get the RV and his gear squared away—"

"No, he's got it. There's a barn back in the trees where we stow away extra stuff. Come in and chat with me for a minute."

Together they entered the bungalow through the kitchen. It was small but comfortable. The kitchen opened to a den with a large TEV and two sofas. A door in the den apparently led to the rest of the home.

"Let me take your coat. Are you sleepy?" she asked.

"Not really," he said. He shrugged off his jacket and handed it to her. "I got a catnap in the RV on the way over."

"I thought as much."

She hung his coat on a hook by the door and pointed at the kitchen counter.

"There's the coffeemaker." She pulled out a drawer. "And here's the coffee and sweetener. There's creamer in the fridge. Just help yourself."

"Thanks. I'd like to review some of those files Rick downloaded."

"I thought you would. But this old body needs a lot of sleep. I'm going to bed. Learn what you can from the videos. I'm sure Rick will watch with you and help you come up to speed. When I wake up, I'll fill in the blanks, okay?"

"I couldn't ask for better," he said. "Thanks."

She reached up and stroked his cheek. "It's great to see you again, Winnie." She turned to walk away, then stopped.

She turned back toward him and punched his arm hard. "I told you I owed you one."

Tyler burst out laughing.

She smiled and left the room.

He rummaged around in the counter drawer for a coffee pod for the machine.

Alarcon and Ricky came in through the outside door.

"Ricky, it's way past your bedtime. Do you need me to tuck you in?"

"Dad. I'm too big for that now. I can do it myself."

"Okay, you know where your bed is here at Gramma's. Don't forget to brush your teeth. You know the routine. Discipline is how we win."

"Yes, sir." The boy walked through the same door Kathy used.

"Can you make that two coffees?" Alarcon said to Tyler.

"Sure thing."

"Let me go stow my gear." Alarcon said.

"Cream and sugar?" Tyler asked.

"No, just black," he said and followed Kathy and Ricky to the bungalow's bedrooms.

While Tyler made the coffee, his mind was already working overtime.

Dancing around in the future is more unsettling than I expected.

He thought about McKnight and wondered where he was. And if he was alive or dead.

He thought of his wife Sarah and hoped he'd make it back home to her.

The second cup of coffee gurgled out of the machine as Alarcon returned to the room.

Tyler handed it to him and they made their way around the sofas to watch the video files on the TEV. Tyler settled into the large sofa in front of it, while Alarcon plugged the thumb drive from the RV into its auxiliary port.

He sipped his coffee and Alarcon returned to sit next to him, TEV remote in his hand.

"So, it wasn't by accident that you and Ricky were there at the Battlefield last night," Tyler said.

Alarcon chuckled. "Mom was right — you *are* quick. No, it wasn't an accident."

"Based on what we know so far, Major McKnight and I are likely to change history if we ever get back home. So how could you be sure we would be there?"

"We weren't. But Mom knew where and when you were traveling to. We hoped *that*, at least, wouldn't change. Yeah, there are many history deviations that were possible. But this guess paid off."

"Well, I for one am glad you were there. So tell me — where do you think they took Major McKnight?"

"I don't know, but I can guess. They'd interrogate him and maybe send him to Rachel Patterson."

"Why do you say that?"

"Because it's been all over the news media. 'There are unauthorized time travelers in the Northern Virginia area. If you see them, call 800-whatever. There's a big reward.' Anyone who picked him up is likely to remember that."

"And it reinforced the probability that we would show up there."

"Correct," Alarcon said. "Want to talk about these videos, Captain?"

"Yes, I do. Call me Winnie, by the way."

"Okay. Well, here's the story behind them. Over time, we all realized that the news and social media were slanting the truth about events — pushing an agenda and skewing facts their way, editing interview clips to distort them, and not reporting on things that don't support their views."

"That was going on in 2036. Even before that."

"Yes, it was. But then we learned why. I'll save that for the video, but in short, we started making these videos to have a record of the truth, as far as we could figure it out. At first, we were doing it out in the open. But when the Devotees got hyperactive, we took it underground. We put it up on the net so everyone could find it. We designed them as documentaries to help people understand what's happened to our country."

"How do you keep the Devotees from finding your servers?"

"There are some sharp software and communications people with us. They keep the files on redundant servers and move them around. We also hack the internet routing so it's impossible to locate them." He paused. "So far, anyway. If they ever capture one of the technical team and learn how we do it, it'll be a problem."

"I see," Tyler said. "And you're one of them."

Alarcon shrugged. "I have a minor part to play. So... Ready to watch them?"

"Yes, let's do it."

Alarcon pointed the remote at the TEV and started the first video.

It took four hours to get through the six videos. Professionals produced the first few. The last three were of poorer quality. Alarcon explained that they no longer had access to the best talent or the best equipment. The quality of the videos suffered as a result.

After Tyler saw the videos, it amazed him how simple it was and how believable it was. Before he watched them, he wondered how the country he loved could fall so far in only fifty years. Now it appeared inevitable if not stopped.

Not long after Tyler and McKnight left 2036, there was an effort in the Executive branch to implement time limits on all government services, including the non-elected bureaucracy. The legislation failed because the members of Congress didn't want it.

Since 2036, there were 25 elections of the House of Representatives and the Senate. Each had the effect of bending the political will of the country away from constitutional government and toward rule by majority.

The Far Left, supported and financed largely by George Kosar, got seventy-five percent control of both houses of Congress and amended the Constitution to eliminate the electoral college. This development offset the balance between the states with small populations and those with large populations.

The net result was, whatever the more populous states wanted became law and the less populous states couldn't prevent it.

The coastal states dominated the fly-over states. The industrial states dictated policy to the breadbasket states.

The two factions of states lined up against each other at every turn. Large population centers — like New York, Chicago, San Francisco, and Los Angeles — were pivotal in every decision.

It was inevitable that they would clash. And clash they did.

Around 2065, most of the fly-over states banded together and announced their intention to secede from the Union. The coastal states declared that secession was illegal. Thereafter, advocates of secession were called 'Hamiltons'.

The fly-over states stopped short of secession, but remained defiant and refused to support laws passed by the coastal-dominated Congress.

When tensions were at their worst, the Devotees appeared. One theory with many supporters claimed they had roots in the Antifa ranks in the early twenty-first century.

At first they were preaching on street corners and running for positions in local government. Then they won seats in the House and the Senate. As they took power, they talked of a new direction, a fundamental transformation of the country. A revolution was needed, they said. And they started talking about the Baron.

George Kosar was an oligarch from Eastern Europe who had dabbled in politics since the early 1980s. The title of Baron didn't stem from any royal connection. It was a title he took for himself to lend legitimacy to his activities and personal entitlement.

That Kosar funded candidates and agendas around the world for many years was well-documented. He taught his sons, his grandsons, and his great-grandsons to carry on his legacy.

The Baron passed away and so did his sons, but his grandsons and great-grandsons continued to promote the Baron's global agenda. The Devotees spoke reverently of the Baron, and their zeal for his ideas and personal charisma bordered on worship.

They pushed the governments of the world to turn control over to his heirs in the interest of world peace. The Kosar Family would rule over a new era of peace, prosperity, and tranquility. The peoples of Ecuador, Peru, France, and Sweden had already invited the Kosar Family to take control.

While the Devotees denied it, the Resistance believed there was a subset of the Movement who infiltrated the highest levels of the U.S. government. People referred to them as 'the Faithful'. According to the videos, the Faithful dedicated themselves to enabling the Kosar Family to come to the United States and assume control.

The fly-over states bitterly opposed this, but many in the coastal states were open to accept the leadership of the Kosar Family.

The last video focused on the near future. The Resistance believed the Devotees were planning a major strike against the U.S. Government, and would blame the Resistance and the fly-over states for it. This strike would cause the U.S. government to beg the Kosar Family to come to America and re-establish peace and order to a desperate war-torn countryside.

As Rick turned off the TEV and pulled his thumb drive from the auxiliary port, Tyler leaned back and stared at the ceiling.

It's the end of the United States as we know it. I never thought I'd see the day.

It occurred to Tyler he now had a unique perspective. No one else from 2036 knew what he knew. When he returned to his own time, that perspective would be a danger to Kosar's plans.

It was too fantastic to believe. Except that each succeeding event was believable and possible.

"That's where we are," Alarcon said. "What do you think, Winnie? Any questions?"

"I do have one. At the campground, you called me a 'Hamilton'. Is that a reference to the Resistance?"

"Sort of. The people who fought against the elimination of the Electoral College were called that because Alexander Hamilton was a proponent. Today, it pretty much means the Resistance. The Devotees are afraid of us, so I thought it might be an easy way to get that asshole to back off. I'd say It worked pretty well."

"Yes, it did."

Tyler felt nauseated.

"Are you okay," Alarcon asked. "You look a little green."

"You know, I think I might throw up. I want to say, how could this happen? But since I've seen it, it seems inevitable."

"I know. It drains the soul and the heart."

"I couldn't articulate it, but you're right. Exactly right."

"We have to fight it, you know," Alarcon said.

"Yes, but it's hard to see how we as individuals could do anything about it. I need to think about this."

"It's a lot to digest in a short time." Alarcon said, and looked at his watch. "Mom should be awake soon. I'm sure she can fill in the details on the earlier events."

Tyler rose, walked to the kitchen, and looked out the window over the sink. While they were watching videos, the sun had come up. The rain cleared off, leaving fluffy clouds and a pale blue sky. It was a beautiful winter morning in Virginia.

Through the window, he saw a small wooden deck with Adirondack chairs.

"Rick, if you don't mind, I think I'll go out on the deck and get a little light to drive out this darkness."

"I don't blame you. Sure, go on out. I'm going to crash for a little while. Then I have some work to do."

Tyler slipped his coat on, walked out the door and around the corner of the house to the deck. It was a cool but clear, fresh-smelling morning. He pulled his coat tighter around himself, sat in a chair, and put his feet up on the railing.

With effort, he pushed the videos out of his mind. He closed his eyes and fell asleep.

CHAPTER 32

Monday, December 2nd, 2086 — 10:00am — The Safe House in Reston

A touch on his shoulder startled Tyler from sleep.

"Sorry," Kathy said. "Good morning, Handsome." She pushed a cup of coffee into his hands.

"Good morning," he said. His voice was still rough from sleep, so he cleared his throat. "How long was I out?"

"Only about three hours. I wanted to fill in some details for you."

He sat up.

"Is there a place where I can grab a quick shower? I'll be more awake if I can."

"Sure," she said. "Follow me."

She led him around to the kitchen door, through the TEV room and back to the living quarters of the house. She pointed him at a bathroom.

"Your satchel is inside. There are towels and washcloths in the closet. Oh, and there's a shaving kit in there, too. You might also check in the closet for some more stylish clothes."

He stepped in, started the shower and stripped off his clothes. The hot water on his back and shoulders soothed his anxiety.

As he grew more awake, he thought of the videos and how quickly the country lost its founding principles. He remembered the words of a brilliant statesman: We're only one generation away from losing our Republic.

Very astute.

Refreshed by the shower and dressed in up-to-date clothes, he returned to the kitchen for more coffee. Kathy was waiting for him at the table. A tray of boiled eggs, fruit, and coffee were laid out for him.

"Ready to talk some?" she said.

"Yes," he said, pulling out a chair.

Before he could sit, Kathy said, "Can we go back outside? It looks like a pretty morning. We can carry this food out there."

Tyler said, "Are you sure it's not too cold out?"

She stood and grinned at him. "If you're too wimpy for it, I guess we can stay inside."

"No, ma'am," he said, and gestured toward the door. "After you."

She picked up the tray and backed out the screen door. He pulled his coat from the hanger and followed her outside. They went back around to the deck.

Kathy set the tray on a card table. Tyler sat next to it and made short work of the eggs.

One hundred feet away, Alarcon and his son were tossing a football together. It was a moment of peace and calm, compared to what was happening across the country. It was a glimmer of hope that some things haven't changed. That maybe the country could be normal again.

"You heard a lot of this in the video," Kathy said. "Forgive me if I talk about things you already know."

"No problem, Kathy. It'll help reinforce what I learned."

"Good. Have some fruit while I talk. Remember the Suicide Scandals case we were looking at back in 2036?"

"Of course. It was yesterday for me."

"Yes, yes. I guess you do. Believe it or not, those events accelerated all this. The politicians were low-level officials, to be sure, but it was part of a long-range plan. Many of them might have become influential Congressmen and Senators later. Do you recall that they were more conservative than their peers?"

"I do," he said. "We thought at the time the extreme left somehow orchestrated the events, but there was no proof. Even the FBI agent Ritter was quick to discount that as an option."

"That's correct. Well, it turns out we were right, but it was the radical left of today — of 2086 — that plotted it. I'm sure you saw the discussions about the Baron in the video."

Tyler nodded.

"More on him in a minute. Let me finish my thought." She smiled. "The older I get, the more irritated I am with my inability to focus as well as I used to. But I *do* still think too fast for my mouth to keep up."

Tyler smiled.

Maybe one day I'll be as quick as she is.

"Remember when we first met Cindy? Or Rachel, as we know her now? I can't tell you how upset Trevor and I were when we first saw her on the TEV. It was when they promoted her to lead the HERO Team. I remember how Trevor jumped up and dashed to the TEV and pointed her out. 'Kathy, that's *Cindy*,' he said. A lot of things came together that day."

She paused, and Tyler waited for her. He didn't want to interrupt her train of thought.

"Winnie," she said. "Would you do me a favor?"

"Sure. Anything."

"If you make it back to 2036, don't tell Trevor and me anything about when he dies. We've had a happy life and I don't want that foreknowledge to influence what we do. No matter how hard we might press you, okay?"

Tyler nodded and said, "No matter what, Kathy, I'll respect your wishes. I doubt you'll ask, but if you do, I'll just say you made me promise not to say anything."

"Good. Thanks, Winnie."

She sighed heavily. "That's a load off my mind. Now, what was I saying?"

"You were talking about Rachel."

"Right. Anyway, before we learned she was a traitor, we were working a case much like the Suicide Scandals. Remember?"

"I do. The similarity is why the FBI referred the cases to us."

"Right. In hindsight, that first incident must have been a test case. They — they, meaning Cindy and whoever she works for — were testing the theory that they could change the past and benefit from it. And they almost succeeded. If we hadn't interrupted them or never found out about it, your President-Elect Wade Harrison would never be more than a city council member in Deerfield, Illinois."

"Yes," he said. "But we stopped it."

"Correct. We didn't prevent it. We corrected it after the fact."

"You're saying that their test proved in the concept?"

"Yes. The Suicide Scandal cases began less than three months after we found Cindy out and she escaped."

Tyler thought for a minute. "Do you think they targeted all these guys because one of them might be on track to be President today in 2086?"

"Well, not exactly. Maybe one or two of them would have been contenders, but all were conservative — more oriented toward the Constitution being interpreted as is, not as a working document."

Tyler scratched his head.

"I think I see. Take a few conservative guys out of the business and the local, state, and Federal governments all lean more to the Left. Toward open borders, bigger government, the so-called Nanny State stuff. Maybe not a lot… but enough to abolish the Electoral College. They tweaked history just enough to swing it their way."

"By George, I think he's got it," she said, assuming a thick English accent.

Tyler chuckled to himself. Kathy still loved to pull lines from old movies to make a point.

Some things never change.

He loved Kathy and Trevor like family. And now Trevor was gone.

"Yes, it makes sense. I'm still not sure I understand why things deteriorated so fast."

"Ah, that's where the Baron comes in."

"Okay, that's good. How did he get to be such a cult figure here?"

"We don't have a full record of it all, but we've been able to piece some of it together."

"We? Do you mean you and Trevor, before he passed?"

"No, I mean Senator Myers and me."

"Senator Myers? Who's he?"

"She, actually. Colleen Myers, the junior Senator from Virginia. We've been working on this for a while."

"Who is she?"

"A distant cousin of yours," she said with a smile. "I'll put you in touch with her and let her share the lineage with you."

He must have looked puzzled, because she pulled him back.

"Stay with me, Captain. This is important. The Baron's actual name is George Kosar. He's Hungarian. He made his money in real estate and currency manipulation in Europe."

Tyler held up his hand. "Where do I know that name from? I'm sure I heard it before."

"I'll bet you have," she said. "It was in the videos, but he was all over the news in 2036. Every time there was an insurrection or socialist revolution in the world back then, Kosar's name came up in association. Sometimes he funded it or helped it along through his influence."

"Okay, that makes sense."

Kathy nodded. "But It's incongruous to me. I've never understood why a man who benefited so much from capitalism would use his resources to destroy the system that created his wealth."

"Wow, it does seem crazy when you put it like that."

"Yes, it does. And all the causes he backed... well, that's not fair... appeared to back... used Saul Alinsky tactics to succeed. You know, things like class warfare, gun control, chiseling away at the Bill of Rights — that stuff."

"There was a lot of that going around in 2036," he said.

"Say, I think you need some water. And so do I," she said. "Drinking this much tea and coffee makes you dehydrated. I'll get us some."

She rose and Tyler moved to do the same, but she held up her hand. "Nope, I got this. You're my guest and it does my old heart good to see you again. I'll be right back."

Tyler leaned back and took in his surroundings. Now that it was light, he saw that woods surrounded Kathy's place. Behind the carriage house and two hundred feet back into the woods, he saw a microwave and cell tower disguised as a tree. He guessed Kathy and her family were more than observant members of the Resistance.

More likely they are high in the organization. This is a good hideout, I bet.

He thought for a moment of Senator Myers, but Kathy's return distracted him. She handed him a plastic bottle of water.

He opened it and took a sip.

"Okay, so tell me more about Kosar."

"Sure."

She set her water bottle on the table between them.

"What we believe is that George Kosar had a long-term plan. One that would continue after he died. He hated the United States and fought it wherever he could.

"But then his approach changed. Instead of fomenting revolution within, he worked on weakening the country's founding principles and substituted other ideas. Things like our rights coming from the government rather than being rights because we are humans and all humans are valuable—"

"—Meaning that the rights are not sacred, but only what the government says they are."

"Correct. And this weakens the strength of the Constitution to manage the three branches of the government and the balances the branches have on each other."

Tyler thought about this for a moment.

"You called it back in 2036," he said.

"What?"

"Marc or somebody — I don't remember who — asked you what the result was likely to be. You said revolution. And now we have it."

Kathy smiled. "I forgot I said that. It sucks to get old. But I'm not dead yet."

"Your grasp on politics was something I always admired," he said.

"Thanks," she said. "And to finish the answer to your question — Near the end of his life, Kosar referred to himself as if he were Hungarian royalty. He called himself a Baron and his sons princes. His extensive resources helped to give that image. Just as the ancient kings of Europe claimed that Divine blood flowed through their veins, the Baron used the same playbook."

She laughed. "I'm saying, he must have had one *hell* of a publicist. His name and regal image appeared everywhere."

"That seems almost too crazy to believe. He wanted to convince folks he was descended from God?"

"It seems to have worked. No doubt you've heard the greetings the Devotees use. You know, the stuff about the Baron coming to rescue us?"

"Oh, that's what that was. It confused me."

"Yup. If you don't talk the talk, you draw immediate suspicion to yourself."

"Wow. I don't know what to say."

"Better learn it. Talk to Rick. He's good at it. Anyway, Colleen and I researched Kosar and his family. We believe this entire thing has been a plan to put his great-grandsons — there are two, Joseph and Robert — at the head of the U.S. government before the end of this century."

"No way."

"Oh, yeah. There are already representatives of our government who are not only Devotees, but members of the Faithful."

"The Faithful? Who are they?"

"They are fanatical Devotees. They consider it their religious mission in life to put Joseph and Robert Kosar at the head of the U.S. government."

"That sounds crazy. You mean, like President?"

"Maybe. Or King or Emperor. Or the Leader."

"Leader?"

"In German, it translates to 'Der Fuehrer'."

Tyler shook his head. "This all seems too fantastic to believe."

"I understand that better than you know," Kathy said. "But you don't have to believe it for it to be true. There are about twenty million Devotees in the United States. We don't know the numbers of the Faithful — most Devotees won't admit they exist. I put the number between five and ten thousand."

"That many?"

"Yes. Here's where we are now. No bull. Many Devotees are calling for the Kosar brothers to come and take over now. Many people in the coastal states favor it. Most of the people in the fly-over states are opposed."

Tyler stretched and shook his head. "Civil War. Sounds like we are getting close."

Kathy nodded. "I think we're one violent act away from it."

"As bad as that?" Tyler said.

"Worse. The word is, the Devotees are planning something big. An attack on the Resistance. And soon."

"If it happens, what will you guys do?" Tyler pointed at Alarcon and Ricky in the yard.

"*When* it happens, we'll make our way to the fly-over states. Saint Louis is the unofficial capital of the Resistance. We have friends in the Midwest who'll take us in. It's a big country and they can't cover every county road. As long as we have fifteen minutes warning, we'll get out without problems."

"Good to hear. Now, what should I do? Rick says Rachel may have Marc and I can't leave him there."

"I know." Kathy looked thoughtful.

"I remember getting intelligence that suggested Rachel commandeered our old office on Telegraph Road. Someone saw her there last year. I don't know why or what she might use it for. One of our folks did a drive-by to see what was going on there. There were two cars in the parking area, but the facility is locked down tight and no reception or even guards. All we know is that someone is using the building and they aren't open to visitors."

"Could Marc be there, you think?"

"It's a long shot. No way to know without a lengthy surveillance," she said. "And we don't have the resources or the time to do it. I want to find him as much as you do, but without knowing for sure he's there, it's a high risk, zero-yield proposition. You understand, right?"

Tyler grunted.

She's right. As usual, her thought process is right on the mark.

"Yes," he said. "I don't like it, but I understand it."

Kathy reached out to touch him but hesitated and withdrew her hand.

"Winnie, I know how you feel. I can't bear that we might lose him. But we must assume he's out of action, unable to join the fight. It's up to you — and us — to carry on."

"You're right. What's the strategy, then?"

"Well, I think now we're ready for the next move. Colleen is the best person to figure out how to use you in the fight. Or at least to tell you how to prevent this back in 2036."

"Okay, when can we meet with her?"

"She's asked to see you already. She has formal offices in Washington, but I'm not letting you go near there."

"Okay, what do we do?"

"She has a home and office about sixty miles south of here. We'll go there day after tomorrow. Rick and I need a couple of days to prepare this place for self-destruction. You know, just in case they come for us sooner than expected. Get some rest and be ready."

"I'm already ready," he said.

She smiled. "I know you are. And you'll like Colleen. I suspect you and she will hit it off right away."

CHAPTER 33

<u>Monday, December 2nd, 2086 — 10:00am — McKnight's office on Telegraph Road, Alexandria Virginia</u>

The first thing McKnight saw was a blur. It moved and purred. Slowly, his vision cleared. Rachel's face was in front of his as she leaned over him.

"Welcome back, Marc," she said. She set a hypodermic needle down on the desk behind him. "Sorry to leave you out like that, but I had an errand to run." She gestured toward the needle. "I brought you back just now."

"What day is it?" he asked.

"Today," she answered. "All day. Why? Do you have someplace you need to be?"

I have to get on her side somehow.

"Well," he replied, "no place you'd care about."

She smiled at him. "You're right."

She pulled up a side chair and put her feet up on the desk next to his left arm.

"Let's chat for a while," she said.

"What would you like to talk about?"

"I don't know." She leaned back, scrutinized the ceiling, then looked back at him.

"You haven't asked me about what I've accomplished with your team."

"That's right, I haven't. What have you accomplished with it?"

"I'm so glad you asked." She giggled. "Your original team numbered five, not counting Doctor Astalos and your new receptionist. Oh, is she as good at it as I was?"

"As a receptionist? She's better. Sorry."

Rachel poked out her lower lip and pouted.

Then she brightened.

"Well, I suppose my other projects distracted me. You understand, don't you? Anyway, I've expanded the team to twenty. I also convinced leadership to restructure the team's responsibilities so we could play a bigger part in aligning history properly."

"Aligning history *properly*? You said something about that earlier. What does that mean?" he asked.

"I also renamed the team from the HERO team to the Federal Time Services, or FTS. Because, *oh my God*, Marc. The *HERO* Team? Historical Events Research Organization? What an awful name! Surely you didn't come up with that?"

"At least on this point, we agree. It's a dorky name. It wasn't my choice."

"Who came up with that name?"

"Congress did. They named the team before I got the job. I already had enough battles to fight, so I didn't start one over the team's name."

"Well, I'm glad to hear that, at least," she said.

"Good. So you have twenty people because you expanded your responsibilities to 'align history properly'. What does that mean?"

"We still research, as your team did. But we don't do it out of curiosity or to solve mysteries. We do it with purpose. There are things we do to smooth the way for our leadership."

"For example?"

"For example, an executive may have an encounter earlier in their career that they regret and they wish didn't happen. We go back in time and warn them off or create a distraction that avoids the situation. We align history to the track it should have taken."

"How nice of you," he said. "You help the executives follow a more chaste path so they don't have any embarrassing stories from their youth that come back to haunt them. So where were you when I was young?"

Rachel laughed. "You don't have any skeletons in your closet, Marc. You're too much of a goody-two-shoes."

"How do you know? I might surprise you."

"No, you won't. I checked."

"You what?"

"I told you. I followed your career. Don't you remember? Since I was a child, you were my idol. There's isn't anything about you I don't know. You're the reason I joined the Rangers and why I asked for this job."

"I'm flattered," he said. "Hey, would you consider letting me out of this chair? I feel like I'm losing circulation in my legs and hands."

"Sorry, you'll just have to deal with it for a while. You understand, don't you?"

"No," he said, "but I guess that doesn't matter." He looked around the room. "You fix things for all politicians in the government?"

"Heavens, no," she said. "Only the ones aligned with our cause."

"Your cause?"

"No, our cause. To be honest, I don't care much about politics. I just want to be on the side that gets to make the rules. Make sense to you?"

"In a way," he said. "Is that why you were in my time a few months ago? You were on a project to fix something or to 'align' something?"

Rachel shrugged. "I was hoping you'd be proud of me for what I've accomplished with your team. But to your question, no. It was an experiment to see if we could do an alignment."

"An experiment?" McKnight's thoughts went back to the previous summer, when a former girlfriend was a casualty of the experiment.

His anger boiled up to the surface.

"You killed one person and tried to kill another as an experiment?"

"Ah, correction. Your friend — Barbara, was it? — was already dead when I arrived in your time. Congressman Phillips killed her. It was an accident, I believe. I leveraged his action."

"And who suggested he kill the other girl to cover it up? You?"

"I did. He had already kidnapped her and would kill her, eventually. Again, I suggested an alternative way to handle it and turn it to his advantage. And ours. I'm guilty of being an opportunist. I took advantage of his position to forward our goals."

"I see. And Congressman Phillips died under mysterious circumstances. They say someone poisoned him, but our experts had never seen a poison like this before. You wouldn't know anything about that, would you?"

"Me? Of course not. I suspect he was about to become an embarrassment to someone. I'm sure there were others who didn't like him, don't you think?"

"Undoubtedly," McKnight said. "What was the experiment?"

"Isn't it obvious, Marc? We wanted to see if we could give a candidate a troubling event in their past and take them out of the running for an election. And it worked very well. At least, until your team stumbled over it by accident. I read your report. It's a miracle you were able to stop it. You are a lucky man, Marc."

"In more ways than you know," he said.

"I'm sure."

"Fill in some blanks for me. You ran this project with Mike Smith and the two of you tested out the ability to change history."

"Close. I never met Smith, but I handled him over the phone. Let's say he was a dupe, but a willing one. I put a considerable amount of money into his bank account. Enough so he was willing when I asked for his help."

"You're saying it was a successful experiment. Did you take what you learned and kill ten girls, just to get some politicians out of the way?"

"No."

"No?"

"No. Nine girls."

"We had ten cases in the Suicide Scandals, not nine."

"Only nine were part of the project," she said.

"The last one was part of something else?"

"Yes. The tenth one was altogether different. Important as well, but we can talk about that another time."

"Okay. Is that why you needed a bigger team? To kill more people?"

Rachel's face flushed, and she stood.

"Marc, you're starting to bore me. I'm a good soldier. As good as you. I follow my orders."

"Even when it means killing innocent kids?"

"It's a sacrifice for the better good. To usher in the new order here in the States."

"What was wrong with the old order?"

"It's outlived its usefulness. Now it's time to change it up for better leadership and smarter laws."

"How do you know it will be better?"

She stared at him for a moment, then turned and walked to the door.

As she opened it, she stopped, stole a look at him, then stared out through the open door.

"I have an assault to plan," she said. "Something to remove the resistance to our plan. Going forward, I'd choose my words carefully if I were you. I thought maybe we'd have more common ground to bind us together. But maybe I was wrong."

Then she looked back at him and smiled sweetly, almost adoringly.

"But be assured," she said, "I'll decide what to do with you soon. I was ordered to take you out of the way, which I have done. I'll let you rest for a while and then we'll talk. But have no illusions, Major Marc McKnight... You're mine and that will not change."

She left the room, closing and locking the door behind her.

CHAPTER 34

Tuesday, December 2nd, 2036 — 9:41pm — Kathy's Apartment, Alexandria, Virginia

Kathy Wu was on her way to bed early when the phone rang.

The caller ID showed a name she knew but didn't talk to often.

Why is she calling me?

She sat on the bed and picked up her phone. "Hello?"

"Hi, Kathy. This is Megan McAllister, Major McKnight's girlfriend...? I hope I didn't call too late."

"Not at all, Megan. How are you?"

"I'm fine. I was just wondering if you know where Marc is. He didn't come home from work yesterday and he isn't answering his phone."

Realization of Megan's perspective came to her in a rush.

Marc didn't tell her he was going out on a mission.

"I'm sorry, Megan," she said. "I'm not supposed to talk about government business."

"Oh, but do you know where he is? He's okay, isn't he?"

I've got to give her something. She's suffering.

"I'm sure he is, Megan. Look, I can't say, but let me assure you. He's out on a mission and he'll be back soon."

"He's traveling?"

Kathy could sense Megan's fear through the connection.

"Megan, everything is fine. He'll be back in a matter of hours. I can't check with him, but I know he wasn't going into anything dangerous."

I hope that isn't a lie.

There was an uncomfortable pause on the line. Kathy sensed Megan wanted to ask more questions.

"Megan? As soon as I can, I'll make sure he knows you're worried about him. I promise."

"Will you please ask him to call me as soon as he gets back?"

She's not convinced, but she is coping.

"I'm sure he'll be back any time now. And I'll make sure he gets word you were asking about him."

"Thanks, Kathy."

"It's my pleasure, Megan. I wish I could tell you more."

"I appreciate it, I really do. Goodbye."

Kathy disconnected the call and set her phone down.

Then she picked it up again.

Maybe I'd better call Wheeler and see where we are.

****

Wednesday, December 3rd, 2036 — 9:28am — Kathy's office, Telegraph Road, Alexandria Virginia

Trevor walked down the hallway to Kathy's office. The door was open and he stuck his head inside.

"Hi, Kiddo."

"Hi, yourself," she said. She was wearing the smile that made him fall in love with her.

"I just talked to Doctor Astalos. The last Engine part we had out being fabricated is on its way here. Turns out the Engine will be ready before we thought."

"That's good news," she said, leaning back in her chair. "I'm getting worried about Marc and Winnie."

"I'm sure they're fine. I wouldn't want to tangle with them if I was one of the bad guys."

She leaned forward again. "I don't know. These are pretty vicious people." She smiled again. "You're right, though. They're big boys with the best training."

"Yup," Trevor said, leaning against the doorjamb. "I—"

A phone started chirping.

"You or me?" Kathy asked.

"Me, I think," he said. He patted his back pocket and pulled out his phone.

"It's Dave at the FBI," he said as he accepted the call.

"Trevor here. Hi, Dave. How y'all doing?"

"We're fine, Trevor. How's Kathy?"

"Awesome, as usual. What's up?"

"We have a new development in the Suicide Scandal cases. I tried to call your Major McKnight, but it keeps going to voicemail."

"Yeah, you'd have trouble getting him right now. I believe he's out of signal range. Say, I'm here in Kathy's office. Just the two of us. Mind if I put you on speaker?"

"Not at all."

Trevor shut the door, sat in one of her side chairs and set the phone on her desk. He tapped the speaker icon.

"Can you hear us, Dave?"

"Loud and clear," he said.

"Hi, Dave," Kathy said. "How are you?"

"Good, Kathy. I'm glad you're on. As I was telling Trevor, we have a recent development in the Suicide Scandal case. There's been another incident. They found a young girl dead yesterday morning — found in an apartment with a young Congressman. He doesn't remember anything."

"Oh, no," Kathy said. "Do we know who she is?"

"Unfortunately, we do," Ritter said.

There was a pause.

"Dave, are you still there?" Trevor said.

"Yes, I was just flipping through my notes to find the right page. The victim was Angela Rosario. Does that name mean anything to you?"

"Sounds familiar," Trevor said. "But I can't place it."

"There's a senator from New York with the same last name," Kathy said. "I hope there's no connection there."

"Good guess, Kathy. Angela Rosario was the youngest daughter of Pete Rosario, the senior senator from New York."

"Oh, dear," Kathy said.

"Oh, no," Trevor whispered.

"She was only sixteen. She went to visit a friend and help with a babysitting job, but never made it there. Poor thing," Ritter said. "The Congressman is only twenty-seven — he's in his first term. He claims he doesn't remember even meeting Angela, much less spending the night with her."

"God save her. Can you send us the file on the incident?" Trevor said.

"Already have. Ah, but I sent it to Major McKnight. I'll resend it to you, Trevor, and you can take it from there. And I need to give you a heads-up."

"What's that?" Trevor asked.

"My boss has already briefed me. Senator Rosario is a real fireball. As soon as he stops thinking about his loss and his family, he'll want answers and he'll be calling everyone he knows that he thinks can help. That includes the President and everyone else down the chain."

"Okay, we get it. Consider us notified. I'll update our leadership so they don't get blindsided — if they haven't already gotten a call."

"Sorry to lay this on you guys," Ritter said, "but I thought you'd want to know ASAP."

"No, thank you very much," Kathy said. "We appreciate it."

"Okay. I'd better let you go so you can respond to the shit that's sliding downhill toward you."

"Thanks, Dave," Trevor said. "Much appreciated."

He disconnected the call.

"That's odd," he said. "In all but one case, the victims were unidentified. Sounds like a change in pattern. The one that was identified? the CDC woman? Was that the last case before this one?"

"No, it wasn't. If I remember correctly, we weren't sure that case was even connected."

"You always remember correctly, Kathy," he said. He stood and paced back and forth in front of her desk.

"What are you thinking?" she said.

Trevor shook his head and continued to pace. He held up one finger, but said nothing.

After a moment, he sat again and rested his elbows on her desk and caught her eyes.

"A change in M.O. usually means something. Maybe anonymity of the victims is no longer required."

"I guess so," she said. "But when we don't know who the victims are, we have fewer leads."

"Okay. Maybe they're getting overconfident. Maybe a little sloppy."

"I could buy that if we were talking about a psycho or a sociopath or something. But we think it's Rachel, operating to achieve an agenda. Overconfidence or sloppiness would be out of character."

Trevor leaned back in his seat. "You're probably right," he said.

"What if it's a diversion?" Kathy said.

"A diversion? What do you mean?"

"I wish Tyler were here," she said. "He'd have ideas about this. The victim was the daughter of an influential Senator who *will* rattle cages all over Washington, if he isn't already. The result of which is…"

Trevor hurried to finish her sentence.

"… Is that we'll be tied up, dealing with the politics and shit storm created by a distraught and angry father."

"Yes," she said. "And while we're doing that, we have less time to correct their history modifications."

"That, too," he said.

"That, too? What do you mean?"

"It could also be a warning. From Rachel."

"What? You mean like 'lay off or we'll make your life hell on earth'?"

"Something like that," he said.

Their eyes met across the desk.

Kathy shook her head. "She doesn't know us very well, does she?"

"No. And we still have time to stop this one."

There was no further need for speech.

"You go find Wheeler and let him know," she said. "I'll try to find General Drake and Senator Lodge." She picked up the phone and speed-dialed Drake.

"Okay," he said, and left the room.

CHAPTER 35

<u>Tuesday, December 2nd, 2036 — 4:21pm — Warrensburg Junior/Senior High School, Warrensburg, New York</u>

Mitch Wheeler stood still in the trees east of the practice football field behind the high school. Through his pocket binoculars, he searched through the line of fifteen girls and one teacher on the sidelines. Behind them, the varsity football team ran drills in two groups, passing and blocking.

Dozens of activities filled his day this morning.

Actually, tomorrow morning, he reminded himself.

The activities focused on one thing — preventing the kidnapping and death of Angela Rosario.

Wheeler picked their vantage point as the most likely route Angela would take after practice. The school's property was carved out of thick woods, with the practice football field farthest from Schroon River Road, the parking lot the closest, and the school in between. The woods surrounding the school provided excellent cover for surveillance and escape routes.

To leave the practice field, students had to walk around the school to get to the parking lot. Wheeler watched from the side with the shortest path.

Their research determined Angela was last seen at this cheerleader practice and never showed up at her friend's house. Somewhere between here and there, Rachel's men would kidnap her, time-jump to DC and kill her.

Not while I can do something about it.

Aided by the photos on his phone, he thought he recognized Angela in the line of girls.

He checked his watch. The security detail they alerted through the Senator's office would be on site within twenty minutes.

To his left, he saw Trevor George forty yards away, looking in the opposite direction for anyone that looked out of place.

Trevor was excited, but not nervous. Normally, Trevor's job as mission planner and cold case analyst didn't require him to time travel, but no one else was available. Wheeler trusted that Trevor's years with the Atlanta Police Department were enough training for what was to come.

Trevor looked back at Wheeler and shook his head. Wheeler motioned for Trevor to join him. In a few moments, Trevor stood next to him.

"No sign of the opposition, Mitch," he said. "I located Angela's car. It's parked in the last row, closest to the road." He glanced around, taking in the entire scene. "This is the most logical place for them to grab her."

"Agreed," Wheeler said, then pointed at the line of girls. "What do you think?"

Trevor raised his binoculars and searched the young faces.

"I think she's the third girl from the right in the line. What about you?"

Wheeler looked again. She was a pretty girl — fifteen years old, 5'4", with black hair and eyes. She wore a stylish blue and gold sweatsuit and athletic shoes.

"Yeah, that's the one I picked out. She's wearing what her mother said she was." He lowered his binoculars. "Any doubt in your mind that's her?"

"None," Trevor said. "The right clothes and she looks just like the photos we have. None of the others are even close."

With luck, we'll get Angela and skate out of here with no trouble.

Daylight was fading, and the girls broke out of line and gathered around the teacher. Behind them, the football coach dismissed the players.

"Practice is breaking up," Wheeler said. "It's showtime."

The plan was to approach Angela as she left practice, give her the family code word to gain her confidence, and keep her safe until the security detail arrived to take her to her friend's home. This would minimize the impact on the timeline and save her from harm.

Angela stood with the other girls until a tall football player joined the group. After some conversation, Angela and the young man left the group and moved toward Wheeler's position.

"Boyfriend, I guess," Wheeler mumbled.

Potential complication.

"Let me go first," Trevor said.

The teens were moving from right to left as they approached them. Wheeler walked behind Trevor and to his left.

As they got close, Trevor pulled out his ID and said, "Miss Rosario? Angela?"

The teens halted, and the boy stepped in front of Angela. "Who wants to know?" he asked.

"Good question, sir," Trevor said. "It's good you asked. I'm Agent George, U.S. Army." He waved at Wheeler. "This is Lieutenant Wheeler."

He extended his hands, palms up. "We're here to protect you, Angela. We have good reason to believe you're in danger, and we are here to prevent that—"

A look of fear covered Angela's face, and the young man's face reddened.

"How do we know you aren't the danger?" he demanded.

"I understand your concern," Trevor said. "You can come along with us. Angela, your father gave us the code word—"

244 · KIM MEGAHEE

"Go, Angela!" the young man shouted and sprang at Trevor. Angela dropped everything and sprinted toward the parking lot. Wheeler cursed and ran to cut off her escape.

The young man tackled Trevor, and they went down together.

The girl was much faster than Wheeler expected. He missed her by a yard and gave chase. Wheeler was not a slow runner, but Angela pulled away from him. He lost ground with every step.

Wheeler redoubled his efforts to catch the girl. Her car was seventy-five yards away. He should be able to overtake her before she could get inside it.

Angela reached the parking lot and sprinted past the long row of vehicles. Wheeler was three car lengths behind her and losing ground.

The code words!

Now she was only twenty feet from her car, running between parked cars.

With ragged breath, Wheeler shouted, "Flossie McNasty, Angela! Stinky May Flossie!"

Angela stopped and turned back toward him.

Good. She recognized the code words.

A man in a green sweatsuit leaped from behind a car and grabbed Angela.

Oh, no!

A man in a blue sweatsuit crashed into Wheeler from the side, knocking him off balance, but he dragged the man down with him. Wheeler got in the first two punches as they rolled together on the ground.

Wheeler heard Green Sweatsuit shouting for his teammate to disengage from the fight so he could shoot. A quick glance at the man confirmed his fears. Green Sweatsuit held onto the struggling Angela with his left arm and pointed a handgun at them.

Blue Sweatsuit pushed Wheeler away from him and Green Sweatsuit adjusted his aim to fire, but Angela lunged at his gun arm and threw off his aim when the weapon discharged. She wriggled to get free as he struggled to hang onto her.

Blue Sweatsuit and Wheeler both pulled out their weapons. Wheeler was slower to draw, but the man sprawled to the pavement before he could fire. A gunshot echoed in the trees.

Trevor had arrived.

Wheeler leapt to his feet and turned to Green Sweatsuit. Wheeler and Trevor pointed their weapons at him and the writhing Angela.

They separated to make it harder to cover them both. He compensated by swinging his weapon back and forth between them.

Green Sweatsuit used his gun hand to squeeze his other forearm. A white aura surrounded him and Angela. Then he pointed his gun at her head.

"He's jumping out," Wheeler yelled.

Two things happened at once.

The security detail arrived with a squeal of tires, and Angela tried to drop to the pavement, putting all her weight on the man's arm. These two things combined to expose Green Sweatsuit's head and torso.

Wheeler and Trevor both fired their weapons. One bullet missed, but the other hit the man in the face.

Green Sweatsuit went down, pulling Angela with him. When they landed on the pavement, she rolled away from him.

Green Sweatsuit vanished. Wheeler looked around for the other man. His body was gone, too.

The security detail team was out of the car, guns drawn and yelling for them to put down their weapons.

Trevor and Wheeler laid their guns on the ground and raised their hands.

"We're the ones who called you," Wheeler shouted out.

Angela sat on the pavement, and the lead of the security team approached her.

"Are you all right, Miss Rosario?"

"Yes, I'm fine." She pointed at Wheeler. "My dad sent him. He knows the family code words."

"Where are the other men? The ones who tried to kidnap you?"

She looked around in surprise. "They're gone! Where did they go?"

"They're gone," Wheeler said. "They've failed and their handlers recalled them."

CHAPTER 36

Wednesday, December 3rd, 2036 - 11:30pm - Walter Reed Hospital

Wheeler sat in the waiting room at Walter Reed, waiting to learn the latest on Hatcher's condition.

He checked his watch for the third time in twenty minutes. He exhausted his supply of distractions. After going through his private and work emails, the games on his phone, and updating his notes on the Time Engine reconstruction, he was out of ideas on how to amuse himself while waiting for the doctor.

He should be home sleeping. The Engine reconstruction hit a snag, thanks to a badly formed part. It had to be recreated, putting them on hold and reducing the effort to a mind-numbing review of the steps and cross-checks on Doctor Astalos' checklist.

Wheeler knew he needed sleep, but he wanted to check on Hatcher.

When he called Lisa, she was supportive. Sometimes he forgot Lisa loved Hatcher, too. Lisa told him to do what he needed to do and nap when he could. When he ended the call, he said a silent prayer of thanks for such an unselfish and loving wife.

He leaned his head back against the wall and tried to doze. For the first hour, his frustration kept sleep away. Now, he was finally relaxing and dozing off.

Someone called his name.

He jerked awake and glanced around in disorientation before he remembered where he was.

"Sorry to wake you, Lieutenant," Doctor Johnson said. "I understand you want an update on Lieutenant Hatcher's condition?"

Wheeler gathered himself together and stood. It took a moment for him to focus. "No problem, Doctor. How is she?"

"I think she'll be fine. She needs more rest and therapy. But she's strong. She'll pull through okay."

"That's great, Doc. But what happened to her? What caused her to attack Major McKnight? Was she programmed or something? Can that be fixed?"

Doctor Johnson held up her hands. "Slow down, Lieutenant. One thing at a time. Let's sit down."

Wheeler dropped into the chair he had occupied and she sat next to him.

"First," she said. "Yes, they programmed her. It was a deep-seated suggestion. They used torture and drugs to drive it home."

"Huh?"

"They used the drugs to keep her disoriented and her mind susceptible to suggestion. And they beat her when she didn't respond as expected."

Wheeler found he couldn't speak.

Bastards.

"Anyway, they pumped her full of drugs and kept after her day and night, until she cracked. She's a very fragile person right now."

"What does that mean, Doc?"

Johnson smiled. "Would I be wrong if I said that Lieutenant Hatcher was very confident and strong?"

"No, ma'am. She's the strongest person I know."

"Okay. They broke that strength down and made her believe her only reason for existence was to follow the Baron and his teachings. They convinced her she should follow his commandments and the guidance of his followers, and she would suffer eternal damnation if she deviated from that path."

"But I thought she fought off the conditioning, killed one of their people and escaped. She even picked up some valuable intel on the way out."

"Yes, that's what she reported. It took a while, but I got her into a deep state of hypnosis and penetrated a shell built around the core suggestion. They designed part of the programming to make her think she had thrown it off."

"Then she didn't throw it off?"

"No. At least not to the point she thought she did. What happened was more complex. They conditioned her to kill Major McKnight, but they had to fake her escape so she could go do it. They let her go, but somehow created a memory of escape. They made her believe she overcame this guy Freddie, killed him, and escaped. I also found memories of Freddie telling her to get up and run away. Whoever did this knew their stuff."

"She was completely under their influence?"

"Well, it's not as bad as you might think. I didn't find any trace of programming that led her to search for intel on the way out. She did that on her own. The conditioning, while very strong, wasn't as total as I thought. Your Lieutenant Hatcher is one tough cookie. But she's still in severe turmoil."

"Okay. But she will recover?"

"I think so. I don't know if I got to the bottom of it. I'm pretty sure I did, but I can't tell. She's strong and smart. With therapy, and if she accepts the treatment... well, I think she has an excellent chance of full recovery."

"Can I see her?"

"Yes. I haven't told her all the details, but I had to tell her something to keep her in the bed. You probably know better than anyone she isn't the type to lie around. I told her about the attack to convince her to stay here. I figured the only way was to make her understand she might be a danger to others. Otherwise, I'd have to restrain her. I thought that would be more hurtful to her emotional condition than telling her about what happened."

"For what it's worth, Doc, I think you're right. When can I see her?"

"Now. I gave her a sedative, so she should fall asleep on you, but she'll be able to talk for a few minutes. Come on, I'll take you to her."

They rose together and walked in silence to Hatcher's room.

At the door, Johnson paused and said, "Let her know you guys are there for her and she needs more rest. Good luck, Lieutenant."

Then she pointed to the door and strode away.

Wheeler took a deep breath and pushed the door open.

Hatcher was sitting up in the bed, and her head jerked in his direction when she heard him enter.

"At last!" she said. "Somebody other than a damned doctor or nurse. Wheeler, can you get me the hell out of here? I'm going *berserk* in this place."

"'Sup, Hatcher?" he said, and approached the bed.

"Nothing I can't handle. But I need to get back to work. This place is driving me crazy."

"I'll bet. And we need you back at work. But you gotta get well first. You still need rest."

"Ah, that's a bunch of crap. I'm fine. I don't need more rest. I need exercise and work. I can feel my brain rotting by the minute with all this nothing to do."

She pointed to a stack of fashion and do-it-yourself magazines on her bedside table.

"See that stuff? Talk about rotting your brain. I need work."

"I'll see what I can do. We need you shipshape first. But I'll bring you some mission stuff from the office so you can do productive work."

She stopped and stared at him.

"It's not true, is it?" she said.

"What?" he said, but he knew where she was going.

"They said I attacked the Major. That can't be true. You know me—there's no way I could do that."

I can't dodge this. She needs the truth.

"It's true, Hatch. I was there."

The look on her face broke his heart. Never had he seen Hatcher in such misery. She collapsed from her sitting position and stared at the ceiling.

"You weren't yourself, Hatch. Doc tells me you were under deep hypnotic suggestion. There was no way you could have prevented it."

Tears welled in her eyes, and she trembled.

"The Major knows what happened and understands. He isn't angry with you."

She glared at him. "He hasn't been here to tell me that. When I asked about him, they said he was probably busy and unable to come by. That doesn't say he understands."

Wheeler stepped over and sat on the side of the bed. He touched her hand, and she brushed it away.

"Don't treat me like a kid. I can still reason this through. He's not coming by."

Wheeler shook his head.

"He hasn't been here because he isn't in this time period. He jumped forward to 2086 to do recon. We're going to grab Rachel and sort this out. But he told me he understood what they did to you, and he's determined to make them pay for it."

Hatcher squeezed tears out of her eyes and said, "When is he coming back?"

Wheeler wasn't sure what to say. Knowing McKnight has few options to return would not make her happy, and she'll want to help repair the Engine.

But she needed the truth.

"He can't get back. Yet."

Her head whipped around. "What?"

"After he jumped out, somebody… probably Rachel… sent a battle drone through time to attack us. No casualties, but they destroyed the Engine."

Hatcher's eyes drooped.

The sedative is working.

"We have to get it repaired," she said. Her voice was little more than a mumble.

"We will," he said. "Doctor Astalos is full of surprises. He had everything we needed in his damned basement. We're almost finished. As soon as that's done, the Major will be able to return."

Hatcher looked at him. He thought he saw a flicker of hope in her eyes before she closed them. She didn't open them again.

Wheeler stood and stared at her. He gently touched her cheek.

Hatcher was more than a coworker. She was a twin sister, a best friend, and a brother at arms. He had never met anyone so strong and confident.

And now, the pain of seeing her so helpless and in such misery was more than he could bear. He shook his head and fought back tears.

She'd hate to see herself this way.

He turned and walked out of her room.

Fifty feet down the hall, Wheeler resolved that Rachel and her bosses would pay for this.

CHAPTER 37

<u>Wednesday, December 4th, 2086 - 3:00pm - Senator Colleen Myers'
Home Office</u>

Tyler watched the little cottage recede in the distance as the RV
negotiated the dirt road, leaving Kathy's bungalow. He and Ricky sat
in the back seats of the RV while Kathy and Alarcon sat up front.

It was much to comprehend, and he struggled to absorb it. All the
wonderful things about America were draining away in this future
world.

He learned Senator Myers lived in Pine Knolls, Maryland, a small
suburb of Washington. The town was only twelve miles from Reston,
but there was no bridge across the Potomac River nearby, so the drive
was sixty miles. Tyler spent the drive considering what questions to
ask and wondering why Kathy was so eager for him to meet Myers.
For her part, Kathy was unusually tight-lipped about it.

He enjoyed the drive to Pine Knolls. Like much of the outlying
suburbs of Washington DC, there were far more woods and streams
than homes and offices.

They arrived while it was still light outside and the small size of
the house surprised Tyler, considering it was the home of a U.S.
Senator. It was a small three bedroom, two bath home. He asked
Kathy about the place, and she said it was Myers' country office.

A man met them in the driveway and Kathy introduced him as
John. An adolescent girl came out of the house at a run and engaged
Ricky. The two of them ran off around the side of the house, while
John led Tyler, Kathy, and Alarcon in through the front door.

The inside of the residence was tastefully decorated. Tyler saw that the formal living room was converted into an office. John led them there and seated them on a sofa.

"Senator Myers will be here in a moment," John said. "May I get you some coffee or something?"

Kathy and Alarcon declined, but Tyler requested coffee. As John exited the room, Tyler could see a kitchen through a swinging door. An enormous desk and a shelving unit dominated the office. Flanking the door into the living room were two file credenzas.

The swinging door flew open, and the Senator breezed in. Kathy and Alarcon stood at once, and Tyler followed their lead.

Senator Myers was a trim, attractive brunette in her late thirties. She wore navy slacks with a white blouse and modest costume jewelry. Her brown eyes sparkled, and she had an engaging smile.

"Kathy," she said, as she embraced her. "How good to see you! And Rick, you devil. How are you?"

"We're fine, Colleen," Kathy said. "May I present to you Captain Winston Tyler, an old friend and colleague."

Tyler bowed. He didn't want to extend his hand to a lady unless she did it first.

Which she did. As he shook her hand, she clasped his with both of hers. She smiled at him with shining eyes.

Do I see tears in her eyes?

"It's my great pleasure, sir… er, Captain."

"The pleasure is mine, Senator."

"Well, sit down, all of you," she said, as she walked around her desk to the executive chair behind it. "I'm glad you're all here."

Kathy and Rick looked at one another, and Kathy said, "Colleen, Rick and I need to be going. We have some details to check and we think our time in Virginia is getting short. I'm sure you and Winnie will have plenty to discuss."

This unexpected announcement left Tyler off balance. Being left alone with a Senator wasn't his idea of fun, and he was unsure what to expect.

"Well, okay, I was hoping you could stay for a while," Myers said.

Tyler noticed she was addressing Alarcon.

"Me, too," Alarcon said. "But Ma has a bee in her bonnet to refresh our plans and make sure all is in order. Once a mission planner, always a mission planner."

"I understand. Duty calls."

"But we'll see you soon," Kathy said. "It's the start of a new chapter."

"Yes," Myers said, "Let's hope it's the best one."

Kathy nodded and Alarcon approached Myers, laid his hands on her waist, and kissed her on the cheek. As he did so, she laid her hands on his shoulders. It was almost, but not quite, an embrace.

Like two lovers who haven't come to grips with their feelings yet.

They slowly separated, and Kathy and Alarcon left the room.

"Well, Captain, I guess it's just you and me."

John came back in with a coffee service and a small table. He placed it by Tyler and poured a cup.

"How do you like your coffee, sir?" John asked.

"No need to bother, John," Tyler said. "I've got it."

"Very well, sir," John said, and turned to the Senator. "Do you need anything else, Ma'am?"

"No, John, thank you," she replied, and John left the room.

"Captain, I didn't get all the details. What year did you come from?"

"2036, Ma'am. Around December first."

"Oh, I see. That explains a lot."

"Ma'am? I don't understand."

She dismissed his words with a wave. "No matter. I need to give you some information that might be useful."

"Yes, Ma'am?"

She smiled again, then her expression turned serious and Tyler felt her mood shift.

"This is a pivotal time in our history. The country has changed for the worst in the last few years and we were late to recognize the danger. Well, Kathy saw it, but the rest of us just couldn't believe it was happening. I presume Rick told you about the Kosar family, their Devotees, and the Faithful?"

"Yes, Ma'am. It's a little hard to take. But I see why Kathy is concerned. I am, too."

"There's more," she said. "It's about to get much worse."

"Worse? How? It seems like the country is falling apart, the rule of law is failing, and there's a chance the Kosar brothers — unelected non-citizens — will take charge soon. That's bad. How could it get worse?"

"Civil war," she said.

"Civil war? You mean the Resistance is fighting back?"

"I hope so, but that's only a part of it. No, the war will break out between the current government and the Devotees. I'm hoping that we in the Resistance will take advantage of their fight."

"I don't understand. I thought the Devotees were in control of the government."

"Many believe that, but it's less true than they think. The Devotees *do* expect to take charge soon, but, in my opinion, they've miscalculated."

"What do you mean?"

"Yes, they've funded people in positions of influence today. They used time travel technology to steer the government to the anarchy side of politics. And yes, they plan to have the Kosar brothers swoop in and save us from ourselves. What they don't appreciate is the people they supported might not let go of the power."

"Oh," Tyler said.

"Our intel is sketchy, but we know there's a star chamber of sorts. A small committee of influencers in the U.S. government. These people are members of the Faithful, but we believe they just used the Devotee tide to ride into power."

"Who are they? Like the President and some of his people?"

"No. As far as we can tell, there are six, maybe seven of them. At least two of them are senior advisors to people in positions of power. Two are elected officials."

"Then how can these people turn the government over to the Kosars? Surely, the President would have a problem with that? And he has the full force of the U.S. Military to back him up."

"The government has diminished the U.S. Military since your time, Captain, but it *is* still formidable. But it isn't the star chamber's power that affords them the ability to give away control. It's their access."

Tyler didn't get it. Politics didn't interest him, and the gravity of her remark escaped him.

"What does that mean?" he asked.

"Think of it this way," Myers said. "We have a national crisis and everyone is depending on the administration to fix it. But what if... right at the most critical time... a series of assassinations occurred? What if they took out the President, the Vice President, the Speaker of the House, and others in the line of succession? Access to these people by trusted but treacherous advisors creates that opportunity."

"Oh, no."

"If that happens, all bets are off. Total confusion. Now everyone in the administration has to decide what to do next with no playbook and dozens of voices yammering about their solution... which, of course, is the best."

"Isn't there still a succession plan or playbook for that sort of thing?"

"Sure. But we're talking about human nature here. The government is full of people focused on their own self-interest. In the chaos that follows, they'll forget the chain of command."

"How do we know that will happen?" Tyler said. "We've survived Presidential assassinations before. Why wouldn't they follow the succession plan?"

"They won't, because we have centuries of history and hundreds of government failures as an example. Cut off the top level of a government to the point where average people don't know who's next in line and whether they can pull it together, and it all goes to Hell. People abandon loyalties and focus on survival. They'll line up with people, based on principle, or who they think will win. If the star chamber people play it right, they can step in and assume leadership. Or they can do as planned and pass the power to the Kosars."

"I never thought about it that way," he said.

"You're not alone. It took me a while to come around to the idea."

"Okay, let's assume you're right. What next?"

"We believe your friend Rachel Patterson reports to a confirmed member of the star chamber, a man named Oliver Stagne. He's one of the worst, and some think he's the leader. He's a political advisor to the President. Anyway, we think Stagne in particular will balk when the time comes to hand power over to the Kosar brothers. When that happens, the Devotees will take up arms and everyone will line up on one side or the other."

Tyler saw where she was going. "And where would the Resistance line up?"

"We're constitutionalists, so we don't find either side appealing. Both mean living in a dictatorship where the average man and woman get the dregs of life and the elite live like royalty. Both lead to totalitarianism — not an American idea."

Tyler thought for a moment.

"Kathy is getting ready to run."

"Yes. At least at the beginning, the fighting will be on the two coasts, where the Devotees have the most sway among citizens. The fly-over states are still resistant to the whole idea and welcome those of us who hate what's happening. So, when war breaks out, we'll head west. But the fight will move out there, too, before it's over."

"Then it's the end of the United States as we know it. Destroyed from within. It's not a pretty picture."

Tyler searched her face for hope. He found it.

"Now you know," she said. "We can't stop it. We can only win it. *You*, on the other hand…" She held his eyes with hers. "*You* can do something about it back in 2036."

"We can sure try," Tyler replied. "What should I take back to 2036? Where can we get the most bang for the buck to stop this?"

"I'm so glad you asked. Back in your time, Kosar is already funding various organizations to create trouble and promote anarchy wherever he can. And it's working. You need to stop the flow of cash from Kosar to those radical groups, the rising tide of Devotees in the mainstream media, and the politicians he bought. There are a ton of other problems, but that's a good start. I believe that's your best option."

"Okay," he said. "That makes sense."

"Good," she said. Then she added, "You know this is pretty weird for me?"

"What? What do you mean?" he said.

"Me, explaining something to you. I don't believe anyone told you, but we're distant cousins. I grew up around you and Sarah."

"Cousins? How?"

"Yes, I cut my teeth on the stories about Daddy and my cousin. You're from the year 2036? You guys haven't lived it yet, but you are famous for solving so many problems and stopping several terrible actors."

"Daddy?" he said, and a prickly feeling rose on the back of his neck. "Who's your father?"

Myers smiled, leaned forward at her desk and turned a picture around so he could see it. There before him, looking so different and yet so familiar, was a photo of Marc, Megan, and an adolescent girl. A glance up at Myers confirmed she was the girl, and he saw Megan's face in hers. It was so striking a resemblance; he was amazed he didn't see it before. The look on his face must have been priceless, because Myers laughed.

Tyler recovered enough to speak. "You're Marc and Megan's daughter?"

"Yes, and while you're Mom's cousin, you've always been more like an uncle to me. I remember sitting on your knee when I was five years old."

She laughed, rose, and came around the desk. "Give me a hug, Cousin. It's been a while."

Tyler stood and embraced her.

CHAPTER 38

<u>Wednesday, December 4th, 2086 - 5:23pm - Senator Myers' Home Office</u>

Tyler sat and listened to Senator Myers talk about her dad. It was incredible to comprehend. Here he was, talking to a woman older than himself, and knowing she was the 'as yet unconceived' child of his best friend.

How do you report on something like this?

Myers continued. "I think the best thing to do is to send you back with a list of people… People we believe funneled money from George Kosar to the people who helped the Devotees get power."

"Sounds good," Tyler said, snapping out of his thoughts to focus on the problem at hand.

"It's problematic, you know," she said.

"How so?"

She leaned back in her leather desk chair.

"Well," she said. "There's a pesky thing called the Constitution of the United States. It's not as if these people were invaders. They were or are citizens of the United States. They have rights and they exercised those rights to run for office. Many of them were pursuing their beliefs. If it's okay for someone who believes in Jesus or Mohammed or anyone else to be elected to office, why isn't it okay for them to believe in the Baron? And the Constitution is designed to be flexible, changed, or even replaced. Just because we don't like the direction the country takes, are they wrong to do what they think is right? I have trouble with that."

"I see what you mean," Tyler said. "Hindsight is always twenty-twenty. So where does that leave us?"

"Well, we do know foreign instigators influenced our predecessors, with George Kosar being the biggest donor. Kosar started meddling in U.S. politics in the 1990s. There are many trails of influence, funding of radical groups, promotion of anti-American ideas, et cetera. I think we can pull together some of that for you — stuff that wasn't apparent then, but we've been able to tease out over the years. Kosar isn't innocent here, not by a long shot. We think he cooked up a long-term plan to get control of our government. It's like the frog in the boiling water."

"The what?"

"You know, throw a frog in boiling water and he jumps right out. But if you put him in cool water and gradually jack up the temperature, you can ratchet it up to boiling and cook him, but he won't jump out because he doesn't relate the pain to the water."

"I think I've got it, but let me see if I can paraphrase it. The American people would react violently to someone trying to invade or execute a political coup, but they'd probably watch it happen if a radical group gradually took power."

"Yes."

"They might sit by and watch the government take away a Constitutional right and grumble about it, but not get angry enough to fight because it's just one thing."

"Yes, you get it," she said, looking at the papers on her desk. "I'll get with my staff and get some details documented for you, and you can take it back."

"Okay," he said. "When can I go back?"

She looked at her calendar.

"Let's see," she said, but her head jerked back up at once. "Do you hear that?"

"What?" he said.

She sat listening for a second. "Must be my imagination. The longer all this goes on, the more my imagination plays tricks on me." She looked back at her calendar again. "I can get it all put together by—"

This time, Tyler heard it.

It was unmistakable.

Automatic weapon fire.

He jumped out of his seat. "Do you have a panic room?"

She shook her head. "Under construction, but not ready. We were expecting a big move, but not this soon."

More machine-gun fire. Closer now.

"Do you have any weapons in this room?" he asked as he started for the door.

"Yes," she said. "I have Dad's old service pistol here."

"Get it out. Is it loaded?"

He pulled his own weapon from his satchel and checked the clip.

Myers' assistant John appeared at her office door. "We're under attack. I—"

Blood flew from his chest as bullets passed through him and splintered Myer's bookcase on the far wall.

"Get out," Myers yelled. "Use your beacon and go back! Do it now!"

Another machine-gun burst outside the room. Very close now.

Tyler drew out his beacon, squeezed it, and ran around the desk to grab Myers. The time bubble formed around them.

"No," she shouted over the din. "My daughter!"

"Sorry, there's no time," Tyler shouted.

He pointed his weapon at the door as the windstorm in the bubble buffeted them. Her hair mingled with his as the wind intensified and the light grew brighter.

Tyler killed the first attacker who showed himself at the doorway. A second stepped through and met the same fate.

The bubble bulged out, absorbing part of the desk and Myer's credenza. Tyler saw her picture of Marc and Megan get caught up in the windstorm and fly off her desk.

A pair of hands and a machine gun appeared at the door and sprayed bullets across the room. One of them hit Tyler's arm, and he lost his grip on his weapon. It dropped to the floor at his feet.

Myers flinched twice.

She's hit, too.

The bubble surged, and Tyler fell through a field of stars with Myers in his arms.

****

Thursday, December 4th, 2036 - 5:35pm - HERO Team Lab

The HERO Team was now into the third day since the drone attack.

McKnight and Tyler couldn't return to the present yet. Doctor Astalos' concern for them and the unexpected delays in part fabrication threatened to overcome his calm demeanor and patience. Except for Hatcher, everyone on the team was on duty, striving to make the Engine operational again.

Wheeler and Astalos arrived early this morning and made dozens of adjustments and configurations. Exhaustion threatened them, but the job was nearly complete.

They settled into a rhythm of work with Astalos and Kathy driving the assembly checklist, while Wheeler and Trevor performed the individual tasks of the effort.

"Okay," Astalos said. "Just three more adjustments, and we'll be able to test. Am I missing anything, Kathy?"

"No, sir," she said. "How long have we been down?"

"Almost seventy-two hours," he said. "I hate being down that long, but we could receive Major McKnight and Captain Tyler in a few minutes — if we didn't need to test it first."

"Don't we always have to test first?" Trevor asked.

"Yes," Wheeler jumped in, "but most of the time, since we followed Doctor Astalos' excellent checklist, everything checks out the first time."

Astalos blushed and tried to hide his smile at the compliment. "I appreciate the confidence, Mitch. But a good scientist *always* tests his assembly. If he makes a tiny mistake, but it still works, he may learn later the lack of testing was the first step down the path to disaster."

Trevor and Kathy glanced at each other. She suppressed a giggle. They had heard this speech before.

"Therefore, we test," Wheeler said. "Every time."

"That's right," Doctor Astalos said with a laugh. "You have learned well, Grasshopper."

Wheeler grinned. "Okay, we've completed step number 38. What's next, Kathy?"

Kathy looked up from her checklist. "We're almost there. We need one round of tightening the fasteners on the edge of the Engine, then power it up."

"Good," Astalos said. "I think we can apply power now. It'll take a minute or two to get to optimum level, so why don't you plug it in, Mitch, so it'll warm up while we finish the fasteners?"

"I'm on it, Doc," Wheeler said.

He stepped behind the massive power cabinet and plugged it into the wall. It would take a second for the power to pass through the conditioner in the cabinet. He came back around the Engine and busied himself with the clamps underneath the console. Astalos walked to Trevor and Kathy to review the checklist once again.

The Engine clicked loudly, and a bubble formed.

"No, No!" Astalos said. "Don't switch it to travel mode. We aren't ready for that yet!"

The Engine hum increased in volume, and Wheeler shouted to make himself heard.

"I didn't!"

The brilliant white light from the bubble threw long, dancing shadows against the walls and ceiling.

"There's someone arriving," Kathy yelled.

"Or some*thing*," Trevor said.

Wheeler ran for the gun locker.

Not again!

He wouldn't face this unexpected jump unarmed. He returned to the room with a submachine gun and tossed a shotgun to Trevor.

"Doctor Astalos! Please go back to your office, just in case," Wheeler commanded.

Astalos didn't move. "No need," he said. "Look!"

"It looks like two people in the bubble," Trevor said, and set his weapon on the floor. "One is holding up the other. That doesn't look threatening."

"No, it doesn't," Wheeler said, pointing his weapon away from the time bubble. He stared at it, straining to identify the figures within.

CHAPTER 39

<u>Thursday, December 4th, 2036 — 5:41pm — HERO Team Lab</u>

Wheeler stared at the time bubble.

"Definitely two people," he said.

"Tyler and McKnight, you think?" Kathy asked.

Trevor studied the bubble. "No, I don't think so. Too short."

"It's Captain Tyler and… a woman," Wheeler said, and set his weapon on the concrete floor.

The bubble bulged to twice its size and went out. The two figures collapsed.

Wheeler and Trevor rushed the Engine platform.

"Kathy, call an ambulance," Trevor said. "They both have… *gunshot wounds*? What the hell?"

"On it," Kathy said, and speed-dialed security.

Tyler clutched at his left arm. He looked at Myers. "Is she alive?"

"Yes," Wheeler said. "But she has two, maybe three wounds. She's in pretty bad shape. Her pulse is weak."

"Captain, what happened? And who is she?" Trevor asked.

"Long story. In short, she's Major McKnight's daughter and a U.S. Senator in 2086."

"She's whose daughter?"

"You heard me. The Major's. She's an ally against Rachel. Where's that ambulance? I'd hate to be the reason Marc's daughter dies."

"It's in progress," Kathy said. "You haven't been here sixty seconds yet."

Tyler laid on the platform and stared upwards. "Things are likely to go south now. The Devotees are confident enough to attack the Resistance. If that's the case, then they believe they're strong enough to take and hold power. It won't be long after that before they try to prevent us taking action to stop their coup. We've got to be prepared."

"For now," Trevor said, "the only thing you're going to do is warm a hospital bed. Looks like the bullet passed through your arm. Bleeding is minimal, so it missed the primary artery. But you need attention. How about her, Mitch?"

"Bleeding isn't too bad, but the wounds are in the torso and there are too many for it to be simple. I'd hate to guess her survival chances. I don't think they're good."

A security team and a DLA medic came running into the Lab.

The lead security agent spoke. "Is there still a threat? What happened?"

"Negative," Wheeler said. "They time-jumped here in this condition. There is no current threat. We just need transport to the hospital."

A security guard spoke into his radio, then announced, "Ambulance is five minutes out."

The doctor assessed the damage and took over Myers from Wheeler. She sent one of the security team for a pair of stretchers.

Myers opened her eyes and flinched in pain. She tried to see past the doctor.

"Is my Dad here?" she said. Then her eyes fluttered and closed.

Tyler sat up, despite Trevor and Wheeler's protests.

"Did Marc beat me here? Is he okay?"

"No," Trevor said. "He isn't here. He wasn't with you?"

"No, we got separated. Have you heard anything? Did he transmit a status or anything?"

"No, sir."

"That's bad. It means he doesn't have access to his beacon. We weren't in 2086 a whole hour before we got separated. Devotee forces captured him, but I was lucky enough to find Resistance people. Pure dumb luck that I found them and the Major didn't."

"Yes, sir."

"If we did a recall, we wouldn't get him, anyway. Last time I saw him, he was a prisoner. If *I* had him captive, I wouldn't let him keep the beacon. We'd bring it back and remove any chance of him coming back on his own."

"Yes, sir."

"But, we'll hang on to that option as a last resort. I have some ideas, though. A member of the Resistance told me Rachel may have commandeered this building for personal purposes."

"*This* building?" Wheeler said.

"Yes. There's a possibility the Major might be here, but the Senator's resources couldn't verify it. But if we want to go looking for him, here is the place to start. We might get lucky, and maybe we'll get some intel we can use."

"Yes, sir. I'd better update the General and arrange for him to debrief you."

"We can do that, but let's make sure the Senator is taken care of first. She doesn't have much time."

The doctor with Myers stood and glanced around the Lab.

"What do you need, Doctor?" Kathy asked.

"She's not likely to make it to the hospital unless we get her there fast. She needs to be airlifted. If we don't, I don't think she'll make it. I'll call it in."

"No matter what else happens, she has to be saved," Tyler said. "Please, let's make it happen."

"Wait, can we time-jump her there?" Trevor asked. "Zero multiple time to another location?"

"Too risky," Kathy said. "We don't have a vector for a clear space in the hospital and it might take too long to get one. Let's do it the old-fashioned way — by helicopter."

"Roger," Trevor said.

The security officer returned with two stretchers. At the doctor's direction, they put Myers on one of them.

The doctor pointed at Tyler. "He can go by ambulance. But let's get her up on the roof right now. Lieutenant Wheeler, I'll leave you with Captain Tyler and you make sure he gets into the ambulance when it gets here."

The security team picked up Myers' stretcher and carried her up the stairs to the roof. The doctor followed them.

Tyler looked at Kathy.

After a moment, he said, "Call Sarah and Megan for me? Let them know about this and send them to the hospital?"

Kathy's eyes widened.

"Yes, for Sarah. Why Megan?" she said. "Are you certain?"

"Do you want to tell her later that her daughter was here, and she died before she could see and talk to her?"

Kathy hesitated. "Okay, I like the idea, but it violates policy. Are you sure?"

"Yes, dammit," Tyler said. "The Major isn't here to decide, so I will. She could die and I know, when Megan understands what's going on, she'll want to be there. Tell them both that it's me in the hospital and Marc is okay, and I'll *be* okay. But Megan needs to go to the hospital as soon as possible. I'll tell her what's what."

"Are you sure?" Trevor asked. "I mean, I like the idea too, but we'll probably get our asses handed to us."

Tyler nodded. "Yes, let's go for it. It's on my responsibility."

"Okay, I'm on it," Kathy said, and stepped away to call.

Tyler called after her. "Tell her to look for me first."

Within a minute, the EMTs arrived and loaded Tyler onto a stretcher. He motioned Wheeler to approach him. When he got close, Tyler whispered to him.

"Why were you all so surprised when we jumped in? And how come everyone is here?"

"We've been busy," Wheeler said. "Right after you left, someone sent in an attack drone that shot up the place. We just now got the Engine up and running. We haven't even tested it. As soon as we turned it on, you guys came back through."

"Jeez," Tyler said. "I'm damn glad you got it working. It would have been awkward to stay there any longer."

"I'll bet, sir."

"What else?"

"Oh, Doctor Astalos told me this morning that he figured out how the Time Engine Inhibitor works. We made the modifications as we rebuilt the Engine. We'll test the Inhibitor after we test the Engine. Shouldn't take more than a couple of hours, sir."

"Good to know. I think we'll need it."

"What are your orders, sir?"

"What you just said sounds like a plan. Expedite the testing. Make sure everything is five by five. Install and test the Inhibitor. Then decide our approach to track down the Major. I hate to say it, but he might be dead."

"I hope not," Wheeler said. "We'll test the Engine and discuss with the General. He'll want your perspective, sir."

The EMTs pulled Tyler's stretcher toward the loading dock door.

"I'm sure he will," Tyler said. "You know where to find me. Let me know as soon as you have status on the Major."

"Yes, sir."

"Nice job, getting the Engine back together, Mitch."

"I wish I could take credit for it, but Doctor Astalos was brilliant and Trevor and Kathy pulled out all the stops to help get it done."

"No doubt. As you were, Lieutenant."

"Yes, sir."

The EMTs wheeled Tyler out the loading dock door to the ambulance. As they loaded him into the vehicle, Wheeler could hear the heavy thumping of the Medevac helicopter approaching. He turned and watched as it landed on the roof of the Lab.

Two on the way to the hospital, and one still in the future.
Wheeler pulled out his phone and speed-dialed General Drake.

CHAPTER 40

<u>Thursday, December 4th, 2036 — 8:27pm — Walter Reed Hospital</u>

Tyler struggled to sit up in his hospital bed. It felt weird to move with his right arm in a sling.

The triage staff sent him one way and Myers in another. She was in much worse shape than he, and he hoped she'd survive.

He waited for Megan to arrive. It was awkward to explain military operations to the spouse of a soldier under your command. It was harder to explain things to your commanding officer's girlfriend. Add in that your commanding officer is your best friend and his girlfriend is your cousin and you have an unpredictable situation.

He hoped Megan was on her way, but he didn't relish the scene that would soon unfold. Megan might be upset and emotional. That would be uncomfortable.

Or she might be pissed.

Is this really a good idea? How do I introduce her to the daughter she hasn't conceived yet? How do you explain this to someone who isn't accustomed to thinking outside normal chronological thinking?

He didn't have to wait long.

Megan McAllister knocked once on Tyler's hospital door and entered. She stepped in and approached his bed. She didn't look happy.

"Well, come on in," he said, then ventured a smile.

"I did," she said. "Where's Marc?"

Damn. She isn't going to make this easy.

"I'm not sure. What did he tell you when you saw him last?"

"He said he'd be home for dinner. I've heard nothing else from him. Do you know where he is?"

"No. But I know *when* he is."

"When? Kathy said he was on a mission and not able to return. Has that changed? And why didn't he call me before he left?"

"Yes. It was urgent and unexpected. We had to jump out to... Well, to where we needed to go."

"And all he had to do was pick up the phone. Why didn't he?"

"Well, he didn't expect to be gone this long. We expected to return before dinnertime, but a change in circumstances forced us to pivot and leave right away. I didn't know he didn't call you, or I would have reminded him."

"Why couldn't someone else call me?"

"Because things changed fast on us, and then we lost the Engine because of..."

I've said too much. Any more information will only make it worse.

"Because of what? What do you mean?"

"It's not important," he said and held up his hand as she started to speak. "We'll get him back here as soon as possible."

Her face flushed with anger.

"I'm so tired of this. I don't know when or even *if* my man is coming home. And I don't know what's happening. Can't you tell me anything? I'm tired of being kept in the dark. I'm starting to think maybe I don't belong here. Maybe I should go home to Atlanta."

"No, Megan, you *have* to be here."

"Why? Why do I have to be here? Because he needs me? You couldn't tell that from my side. I can't be the poor girlfriend who never knows what's going on, but stays calm and provides moral support for my house husband, who can't even tell me what he does? Sorry, Winnie, but this isn't a life I'm willing to live. I need a man who will be present and not preoccupied with stuff in a different era."

Tyler nodded. "I get it," he said. "I do."

She glared at him and didn't respond. Tears rolled down her cheeks.

"What if... What if I can give you a reason?"

"How can you do that? I'm sure it's all classified, and you know Marc would be irritated if you did."

"Bear with me," he said. "Megan, would you please go out to the Nurses' Station and ask for a wheelchair for me? I know I'm not supposed to walk around, but you can wheel me there."

"Where are we going?" she said.

"Just go get the chair. It's important."

Tyler could feel her anger beneath the surface, but she nodded and left the room. Five minutes later, they were rolling down the hall to the elevators and headed up to the ICU.

"Why are we going to the ICU?" she asked. "They weren't lying to me about Marc being okay, were they?"

"No, they weren't lying. We don't know where Marc is right now. He'll return soon, I'm sure of it." He pointed ahead. "Stop at that window there."

Megan pushed his chair to the window. The name on the door was Colleen Myers.

She glanced at Tyler. He was staring through the glass at the *woman*. She couldn't read his expression.

"Who is she?" Megan asked.

"She's your reason," he said. "Or will be soon."

"I don't get it. Colleen Myers. Who is she?"

"She returned with me from 2086. She's a U.S. Senator then. They attacked us when I was in her office. We time-jumped out fast, but not fast enough. Colleen got the worst of it. She might not make it. The prognosis isn't good."

As he spoke, Megan stared at Myers through the glass.

Tyler and Megan grew up together in Atlanta. He knew his cousin well. Megan's heart melted for little lost birds and chipmunks her dog chased. And that heart was breaking for the woman on the other side of the window.

Several machines kept Myers alive. They beeped and displayed waves for her blood pressure, respiration, and oxygen saturation. The sign on the door emphasized no visitors were allowed.

"I met her in the year 2086, Megan. She hasn't been born yet. But her parents are. And that's why she's important."

His tone pulled her attention away from the woman in the bed twenty feet away.

"What are you saying, Winnie? That I will know her?"

"Yes, you will. You and Marc will be her parents in two years."

Megan swayed and might have fallen had she not been holding onto the windowsill.

Her voice cracked as she spoke. "Her... Her name is Colleen?"

"Yes."

Her face grew red with anger.

"He should have told me. Y'all have been working with her and *he didn't tell me.* What's wrong with him? Didn't he think I'd want to know about that?"

"Yes, but—"

She didn't let him finish.

"Sometimes I just don't understand him. Why wouldn't a man tell the woman he loves that he's in contact with their daughter in the future? Where's his heart? Hell, where's his common sense?"

"Megan, I—"

"This is too much. He isn't holding up his part of the bargain. He's supposed to share stuff like this with me."

"Megan, shut up for a second."

"And you, too," she said. "You should have told me before now. What were *you* thinking?"

"Stop talking."

Megan went silent, her sullen expression telling him everything he wanted to know about her thoughts.

"Thank you. Now, first of all, Marc doesn't know about her."

"What?"

"Right. I just met her myself today, or rather a few hours ago."

"He doesn't?"

"No, he's still there. Without giving out classified information, I can tell you we got separated at the beginning of the mission and I haven't seen him since. I'm worried about him, but I also know how resourceful he is. One way or another, he'll get back to us."

She stood there motionless. For a moment, Tyler thought she had stopped listening.

After a moment, she said, "Our daughter."

"Yes," he said.

"Can I talk to her?"

"No, not until she improves. But I wanted you to see her and learn who she is. I knew you'd never forgive me if you found out about her and I kept her from you."

More tears appeared in her eyes and threatened to spill over.

"I owe you an apology," she said. "I can't believe how ugly I was to you and didn't let you explain."

"Under the circumstances? Please," he said. "Don't worry about it."

"And I beat Marc up and imagined all sorts of things without giving him a chance to explain."

"That's why I brought you here."

Tyler's arm began to throb.

"Megan? I'm getting a little fatigued. Could you please take me back to my room?"

"Yes, of course," she said, and stepped behind the wheelchair and pushed him down the hallway. She glanced back over her shoulder at the double doors that led to the ICU.

"Can I come back to see her?"

"I thought you might ask that. The doctor says you can come stand outside the door as much as you want, but you have to stay out until she improves."

"Okay," she said. "After I drop you off, I think I'll come back here for a while."

"I think that's a good plan. I'll let you know as soon as I hear anything at all related to Marc."

"You'll call me?"

"Yes. As soon as I know something. I promise."

She nodded.

Tyler couldn't leave it there. "You know, Marc doesn't want to tell you stuff that worries you."

"I know. But I worry anyway, so what difference does it make?"

"Okay. Point taken... But I want you to understand. Colleen isn't the reason for you to be here. She's a big reason, but not the only one. Marc loves you more than anything. Give him time... He'll figure out how to balance things. I know he will, because he loves you so much. And you know it, too."

She was silent for a moment. "I hope so," she whispered.

They arrived at his room, and she helped him back into his bed. As soon as he was comfortable, she kissed his cheek and left.

Tyler was glad he told Megan about Colleen. But now his thoughts drifted to 2086.

He looked at the window. A hard, cool rain now pelted the windowpanes.

Marc, where the hell are you?

CHAPTER 41

<u>Thursday, December 5th, 2086 — 6:45am — McKnight's old office at Telegraph Road, Alexandria Virginia</u>

McKnight woke to the sound of footsteps. He didn't realize he dozed off or how much time had passed.

The door lock clicked, and it opened.

Rachel stood in the doorway. She traded her uniform for a flattering light print dress and wore tastefully applied makeup and lipstick.

She dragged a chair over to McKnight, and sat in it, leaning forward with her hands on her knees.

"It's time I told you what I'm thinking and where I want to go." A hint of a smile appeared on her lips and in her eyes, then vanished.

Now what?

"A few months ago, I met with Joseph Kosar in Paris. Do you know who he is?"

"I know the name," McKnight said. "Any relation to George Kosar, the billionaire socialist?"

"Grandson. Good. You're aware of the Movement that worships him here in the United States?"

"Joseph?"

"No, George, the grandfather."

"I heard people talking about the Movement earlier tonight. Is that what you mean?"

"Yes. There are millions of people who believe the democracy experiment here has failed, and it's time to think out of the box. They want to bring in new leadership — a faith-based leadership descended from Baron Kosar."

"I see," McKnight said. "You met with his grandson in Paris. Business or social?"

"Yes," she said. The twinkle and smile came back, then disappeared again. "I report up the Army chain of command, but I work special projects for Oliver Stagne."

"Who's he?"

"He's a senior advisor to the President of the United States. His specialty is international policy."

"Then your team reports indirectly to the President through this guy Stagne? You carry out operations for the President that he doesn't want made public?"

"No," she said.

No?

"No, the President is probably unaware of many of Stagne's projects."

"I don't understand," McKnight said.

"Most people don't. In fact, almost no one understands how our country operates. A small group of men and women control the country. Call it a star chamber or the Deep State or whatever. Insightful people have suspected it for a hundred years. I've heard them called 'The Five', but I don't know if that indicates their number. The members of The Five have changed over the years, but their control of the country hasn't."

"Are you saying that this guy Stagne is one of that group?"

"He's usually referred to as Number Four, but yes."

"Number Four?" McKnight said. He couldn't suppress a chuckle. "Sounds like a villain from a low-budget movie."

Rachel put her hands toward him, palms forward. "Don't make fun of what you don't understand. It could be fatal. He isn't what you would call a friendly person. All the moves I've made that you take offense to? He ordered them. I'm not your enemy, Marc."

Yeah, right. She's afraid of this guy.

"Okay," he said. 'Do you know who Number One is? Or Number Two or Three?"

"No, and I don't know how many people are in the group. I know Number Four is one of the leaders… maybe *the* leader."

She stopped talking. Her eyes were questioning, imploring.

She wants me to understand something. What?

"What does Number Four have to do with you meeting Joseph Kosar in Paris? Did he set up the meeting?"

"No, he just found out about it and wants me to entice Joseph to come to the United States."

"Why?"

"I'm not a hundred percent sure. With the Movement and the state of the country now, he might want Joseph and his brother to join him and take over."

"What? A coup?"

"More like a revolution. There are twenty million Devotees in the United States who would welcome the Kosars with open arms."

"What about the rest of the 400-plus million citizens?"

"There are many who will probably resist. We call them Hamiltons. But there are millions who are unhappy and undecided. The rule of law has been slipping for decades and most people just want change. And I think there's a very real chance that change will come."

Collapse from within. Political scientists and conspiracy nuts have talked about this since the 1960s.

"Why would the President not do something about this? He wouldn't just sit around and let it happen, would he?"

"The President is an old man, dependent on his advisors. And the Executive Branch's power has been siphoned away since your time — and the Legislative Branch has increased theirs. Not to mention the fact there are a disproportionate number of Devotees in Congress."

"Then Number Four is a Devotee?" McKnight asked.

"He says he is. I have my doubts. Oliver's a political animal and does what's best for him."

"What do you think he has in mind?"

"Hard to say. He seems to be keeping his options open. He says he's a Devotee, but he might want Joey here close enough to kill him, blame the Hamiltons, and assume control in the Movement's name. Or he might want to solidify his position and power by supporting the new regime."

Why is she telling me this?

"What about you? Won't you be able to ride his coattails to power? Are you a Devotee?"

"I tell everyone I'm a Devotee, but I'm hedging my bets. It's a useful position since they seem to be winning over the people. I'd rather keep things the way they are, but Number Four and Joey will collide sooner or later."

Joey? Not Joseph? There's more here.

"But you didn't just meet Joseph in Paris, right?" he said. "You already knew him?"

She sighed and looked away from McKnight.

"I've known Joey for over ten years. I met him during my senior year at the Academy. Some friends and I went to New York City for a party weekend. I was getting over a relationship and less discerning than I should have been. But Joey was a bright spot for me. He drew me in like a moth to a flame. I guess he saw something in me, too, because he pledged himself to me, told me his dreams, and swore me to secrecy. 'No one can know about us,' he said. If anyone found out about us, my life would be in danger. I've kept that vow until now. Over the years, we've met in secret every six months."

She went silent and didn't look at him.

Maybe he is attracted to her. But a secret, intimate relationship with a West Point officer candidate with potential? Joe Kosar is not a stupid man.

"He believes his destiny is to come here and rule. He's convinced of it. And he told me he wants me to be there with him."

"I think I understand now. You have conflicting loyalties and they're about to collide."

"That's part of it. For a long time, Joey and Number Four had a lot of the same priorities. But as the time grows near, I find myself in the middle and will have to commit to one of them, sooner or later." she said.

"I see."

She looked at him.

"No," she said. "That's most of it, but there's more you need to know."

"What's that?"

"Since I was a teenager — all my life, really — I've looked up to you as a role model. I read about you and Winston Churchill Tyler and the problems you solved with time travel and decided I wanted to be like you. That's why I went to the Academy and became a Ranger. It's been the hardest and most rewarding thing I've done. And you — you were my motivation for doing it."

A switch flipped in the back of McKnight's mind.

Here's leverage. How do I use it?

"I'm honored," he said.

"There's more."

She put a hand on his thigh and the other on his shoulder. She stood and kissed him gently on the lips. Then she sat again.

"Remember that mission where I showed up as a security guard and you didn't know who I was? I did it because I wanted to see the man — the legend — in action. I wanted to reach out and be a part of it somehow. What I didn't count on was the possibility of a relationship. When I was there... right next to you... the desire to connect somehow overcame me. Did you feel it, too?"

Play along. Go with the flow.

"I know I felt something," he said. "I was so focused on the mission, I dismissed it. But I think I know what you mean."

She held his eyes for a moment, then reached out to caress his cheek.

"Here's the problem," she said. "Joe and Number Four have conflicting purposes, but they do still have one thing in common."

"What's that?"

"They both know who you are and want you dead."

CHAPTER 42

McKnight tried to laugh it off.

"They both want me dead? That's inconvenient for me."

"Don't laugh. That's my problem. I don't want you dead, but I let them both think I killed you. In fact, I told them both as much. As far as they know, you disappeared from the past. I brought you here to this time, eliminated you and therefore you are no longer a problem."

"I see. So, no matter which side you pick and no matter which one of them wins their battle for power and control, you've lied to them and they'll find out. They always do."

"Exactly. The smartest and easiest thing to do now would be to kill you. But I don't want to."

Here's a chance. Careful, don't get yourself killed.

"What's your solution, Rachel? What have you come up with?"

"I see you're starting to understand me," she said. "I always have a plan or an idea."

She kissed him again and stood. She walked to the window and stared out of it. McKnight couldn't ignore the shapely silhouette of her body where the morning light passed through the thin dress.

He waited for a full minute before speaking.

"Rachel?"

Her dress flared out as she turned back toward him.

"Yes?"

Try not to appear too eager.

He cleared his throat. "Are you thinking of a solution where you and I are together?"

"It occurred to me."

"I prefer that to dead."

He followed up with a smile he hoped was charming and cavalier.

The slight smile she gave in response encouraged him.

"Where could we go?" he asked.

Her eyes were bright and shining as she strode back to his side.

"Your time," she said. "Back to your time. Then disappear out west. To the Rockies, maybe. Where people don't care about politics or government. It'd be easy."

She laid a hand on his chest and caressed his brow with the other.

"Is that what you want?" he said.

"Yes, if you want it, too."

He heard the excitement building in her voice. "It would be easy to start over. Knowing what I know about the last fifty years would allow us to invest wisely and have a decent lifestyle."

She's interested, but she wouldn't expect me to abandon my mission so easily.

"I like the idea," he said. "But I need to complete my mission. You understand that, right?"

"What? To kidnap me?"

"That was the original mission because I didn't know much about what was going on. Now that I know about Number Four and the Kosar Movement, the actual mission would be to protect our Constitution and the country for future generations. That's the oath we swore at the Academy, remember?"

"I do."

"Then, when we return to my time, can we create some documentation for the HERO Team? You know, some facts they can use to prevent these guys from taking power?"

She looked thoughtful for a few seconds.

"We could do that, if it would make you feel better about leaving."

I think she's with me. This might work.

"Then It sounds good to me, too," he said. "I always wanted to live in Wyoming, near the Grand Tetons. Would that be okay with you?"

"Yes," she said breathlessly, and kissed him hard on the lips.

McKnight returned her kiss with all the passion he could summon. When it ended, they were both out of breath. Despite himself, he was aroused by it. Rachel pressed her cheek against his while they recovered.

He struggled to regain his composure.

What would Megan think?

He felt he violated her trust in him, but he was trying to stay alive. He couldn't think about it now.

"Rachel?" he whispered.

She pulled back and gave him a light, brief kiss on the lips. She lingered there for a moment, then stood over him.

"Yes?"

"Can we go? Let's get out of here."

"You mean, leave now?"

"I do, though I'm not sure I can walk very well yet. I've been tied up for too long."

"Okay."

She gripped the buckle of the main restraint across his chest as if to loosen it, then stopped.

"Marc?" she said.

"Yes?"

"What about Megan?"

He wasn't expecting the question, and he wasn't prepared to respond to it. He said the first thing that occurred to him.

"Megan who?" he said.

"Don't insult my intelligence. The woman you live with."

I forgot she's been surveilling us.

"Oh, don't worry," he said. "That relationship has been on the rocks for a while. We called it off the night before I left to come here."

Even as he spoke, his heart sank. He didn't recover well enough and his response was lame. Rachel stood over him with fists clenched. Her face contorted into a mixture of hurt pride and anger, then went cold as ice.

"Liar," she said softly. "I should have known better."

She walked around the desk and retrieved the pistol from the drawer. She pulled the slide back to cock it and waved it at him. "I should have listened to my first instinct."

"Rachel, I—"

"It's too late, Marc. You had your chance."

She raised the pistol and pointed it at him.

Someone knocked on the door.

Rachel jumped at the sound. She lowered the weapon and walked to the door.

That was close.

She held the weapon behind her, hidden in the folds of her dress. She took a deep breath, then jerked the door open.

Freddie stood in the doorway.

"What?" she said.

"My apologies," he said. "You left the office so quickly, I didn't get to ask you about the project. Did you track down Captain Tyler? We're sure he arrived with McKnight."

He shifted his weight, but she mirrored his movement to impede his view of the room.

"Not yet," she said. "Why are you here? How did you know I would be here?"

"Ha!" he said. "I make it my business to know where everyone is. Besides, Oliver asked me to find you. Can we have a talk?"

He moved to enter, but she blocked his way again.

"No, I'm having some quiet time here and I don't want interruptions. You're intruding. I'll call Number Four in a few minutes."

"I'm so sorry," he said.

McKnight didn't believe Freddie was sorry at all.

"I just need to tell you—"

Freddie feinted to one side, then stepped past her.

When he saw McKnight, he gasped.

"He's alive? So you disobeyed orders so you could have him. How wonderful for you! Are we keeping Rangers for pets, now? In that case, I want Lieutenant Hatcher for mine."

His effort at humor fell flat.

"Get out," she said. "This isn't your business."

"Ah," he said, turning toward McKnight. "I'll bet Number Four would be interested to know he's still alive. And here with you."

When he turned back toward Rachel, he froze. She pointed her gun at him, inches from his face.

"You're intruding," she said.

Her face was scarlet and her chest heaved with anger.

"Yes," he said. "but I'm ready to leave now. Number Four asked me to look for you… but I haven't found you, so I think I'll go home."

"A wise course of action. Don't you have someplace else to be?"

When Freddie moved, she shifted to face him, her arm extended, the gun still pointed at his head.

"Yes, I do," he said. "May I go?"

"Yes, and without further delay?"

Freddie smiled feebly. "I'm doing that right now. Just let me walk past you to the door."

"Go then," she said. She watched as Freddie ran for the door and left, closing it behind him.

Her breathing continued to come in great gasps.

What can I do to drain off the adrenalin?

"I'm glad he left," McKnight said.

Rachel spun and leveled the gun at him again.

"Don't speak," she said.

She walked toward him.

McKnight tried to smile. He focused on the muzzle of the pistol and hoped he set the right tone of respect and subservience to her.

She stood there in front of him; her face a mask of anger. The weapon in her hand remained steady.

He worked to slow his own breathing. It wasn't easy.

"I'm sorry," he said. "What can I do to help you? I can still provide some value for you. Please let me try."

Rachel glared at him for a moment, then her face softened, as if she just now recognized him. She lowered the gun and stood there for another moment.

"This changes everything. Freddie isn't loyal to me unless he wants something I can give, or it benefits him."

She laid the pistol on the desk behind him.

"He'll go straight to Number Four, you know," she said, then laughed. "He might even get in trouble by blabbing to him. Number Four won't want to hear it. He'd rather believe I'd killed you."

"I can help. Let me try," McKnight said.

She grasped his chin and lifted his face to hers. "Is that true? It doesn't sync up with the evidence. I don't believe I can trust you."

"I hope I'll be able to prove it to you somehow."

"I'd like that to be true," she said. "As long as it doesn't interfere with my plans."

"Still..." she raised a finger and waved it in the air. "If Freddie catches Number Four in a bad mood, he might react emotionally rather than strategically. That could be bad. I think I'll go talk to him and make sure he receives Freddie's story in the right light."

She turned and trotted to the door, opened it, and left.

McKnight slowed his breathing and tried to calm his heart rate. He let out a sigh. He couldn't see any way out of this.

When she comes back, I'm most likely dead.

He thought of Tyler.

I hope he got away. I wonder where he is?

For an instant, he let his imagination tell him Tyler would mount a rescue mission. But Tyler didn't know where he was and he had no forces to mount an assault.

Not a possibility. Useless exercise. Move on.

He tried again to push against his bonds. Without getting out of the restraints, there would be no escape for him.

He heard a sound at the door. He closed his eyes until they were slits — enough to see, but not enough to betray that he was awake.

It opened, and a man entered.

It was Wheeler.

CHAPTER 43

<u>Thursday, December 5th, 2086 — 7:15am — McKnight's old office,</u>
<u>Telegraph Road, Alexandria VA</u>

Wheeler laughed out loud as he dashed forward to free McKnight.

"How did you locate me? What are you doing here?"

"I'm glad to see you, Major," Wheeler said. "Are you okay?"

"Better now, Lieutenant. How did you find me?"

Wheeler shrugged. "Pure, dumb luck, sir. I didn't know you'd be here. Captain Tyler returned with intel that Rachel might use this facility for something. I came here hoping to find a clue about where you might be. Who knew?"

"Well, you're a welcome sight, no matter the reason. Could you get me out of this wrap job? My entire body is cramping up."

"No problem, sir," he said. He locked the door and walked over to McKnight.

Wheeler removed half of the restraints before a key rattled in the door. He dashed to position himself behind the door and drew his weapon.

The door opened, and a man entered with a pistol in his hand. He saw Wheeler as he turned to close the door. Before he could raise his pistol, Wheeler sprang forward and stopped with his weapon six inches from the man's face.

"Who are you?" Wheeler asked.

"It's Freddie," McKnight said. Piece by piece, he worked to remove the rest of the restraints.

"Freddie, eh?" Wheeler said.

He moved closer to Freddie and pressed the muzzle of his weapon against his head.

"Hi, Freddie," he said. "I'm Wheeler. Lieutenant Hatcher is a mutual friend of ours."

Freddie trembled uncontrollably.

Wheeler glanced down at the pistol in Freddie's hand.

"Please, Freddie. Move your gun just a little and I'll blow your head off. Hatcher is my partner and friend. You tortured and violated her. I'd like nothing more than to splatter your brains all over this office."

Freddie's mouth worked, but no words came out.

"Lieutenant—" McKnight said.

"Oh, don't worry, sir," he said. "I'm cool. I'd rather take him back with us and let Hatcher have him. But he needs to know I'd enjoy killing him myself if he so much as twitches."

Freddie found his voice.

"No problem, sir. May I drop my weapon? I don't want to give you any reason to pull that trigger."

"Smart choice. Hand it to me. By the barrel, two fingers."

Freddie relaxed his grip on the gun, and it rolled in his hand. It came to rest and dangled from his trigger finger. With his other hand, he grasped it by the barrel and handed it to Wheeler.

McKnight pushed off the last restraints. He grabbed Freddie by the front of his shirt and pushed him into the chair he himself vacated.

"As I recall," he said, "Rachel kicked you out of here a few minutes ago. Why are you still here?"

"I came to get your beacon. We tried to send a drone to your Lab here in the past, but it failed. I'm impressed you could implement the Inhibitor. But I figure it wouldn't stop a traveler coming into the site with your beacon."

McKnight glanced at Wheeler, then said, "I see. So... why the gun?"

Freddie hesitated, then continued.

"Just being cautious. Just in case you got loose. Seems like you did, anyway."

McKnight smiled. "Forgive me for being skeptical, but I think you came here to carry out Number Four's request. To kill me."

"Me?" Freddie said, his voice slipping into a higher range. "No, of course not."

McKnight walked around the desk and returned with a sleep bulb in his hand.

"I like you better unconscious. Then we'll decide whether to kill you."

"No, don't kill me, please," Freddie said, and McKnight sprayed him in the face with the sleep bulb.

He tried to jump up, but slumped in the chair.

Wheeler checked Freddie's pulse at the neck and nodded.

"We aren't going to kill him, are we, sir? Hatcher would love to have a conversation with him."

McKnight shook his head. "No, we're not. I'll bet he knows a bit about Number Four's plans and maybe things Rachel doesn't know. We'll take him with us and let Number Four worry about where he is and what he's revealed."

"Who's Number Four, sir?"

"Rachel's boss. I'd like to capture him, but Freddie and Rachel are easier to grab and, between them, we should get an understanding of what he's planning. Besides, Rachel already told me a lot. I'm surprised you didn't run into her. She left here right before you showed up."

"I don't think so, sir. Unless she's a brunette now—"

"And she *is*. What did you see?"

"Well, I jumped into the Lab, sir. Up the roof access stairs. I was coming down them when this brunette came running through the Lab in a big hurry. I was afraid she'd see me, but she went by fast and didn't even look up."

"I'll bet," McKnight said. "This guy really pissed her off. Come on, let's tie him up and put him behind the desk."

"Excuse me, sir, but don't you want to go home? You've been away a few days."

"I want to go home, but I expect Rachel to come back soon. I think it's worth a delay if we can grab her, too." He glanced at his wrist, but they had taken his watch away. "What time is it?"

"About 7:30am, Major."

"Okay, how about this? We wait for Rachel until about 3 pm and then jump if she hasn't shown up yet?"

"Sounds good to me, sir."

"In the meantime, let's keep sedating Freddie here and try to read through the stuff in her file cabinet. Maybe we can find something useful."

"Yes, sir."

McKnight walked around to the desk and started pulling out drawers. "Seems like Rachel came around here every time she dosed me to knock me out.... Oh, hello."

From the lap drawer, he pulled out a syringe and bottle. "Looks like a bottle of Dilaudid. Probably extra strength. It worked on me, so it'll work on Freddie."

He drew a dose from the bottle into the syringe and injected it into Freddie.

"That should keep him quiet for a while."

He prepared another dose of Dilaudid and set it on the desk. Then the two men carried Freddie around the desk and pushed him under it.

"Let's get to those files," McKnight said. "But first…"

A quick search through the credenza produced his clothing, boots and socks. He dressed and sat at the table with Wheeler and the files.

"What else has happened since I left?" he asked.

"Oh, excellent news, sir. The psychiatrist put Hatcher through deep hypnosis therapy, assisted by a new drug. They got to the bottom of her programming and countermanded it. She's out of the hospital and assigned light duty at work. She's much better, sir."

"Are you convinced that she is okay?"

"Is anybody really okay, sir?"

"All right, not a fair question. What do you really think, Mitch?"

"It *was* a fair question, sir. If she came after me, I'd be uneasy with her around. All I can say is, she seems like her old self. She's a little humbler, if you will."

"What does that mean?"

Wheeler paused for a moment. "I guess... no, I know I would be humbler if I found out someone programmed me and made me attack my commanding officer against my will. The humility — if that's what it is — comes from the knowledge she wasn't able to prevent it, if you know what I mean."

"I do. Okay, we'll see what we shall see. Anything else?"

"No, sir."

"Okay, let's get through those files."

The files from the cabinet contained Rachel's mission logs. They found ten missions that appeared to be part of the Suicide Scandal cases. There was no mention of the one victim they identified, but there was another case in rural Nevada the FBI never heard about.

They found other cases that made little sense. Records of time travel to times and places over 300 years old. These would need more study, and McKnight decided they were better suited for review by Kathy Wu.

It was a long day, and they spent the early afternoon resting and waiting.

At 2:30pm, he heard a rattling at the door. Wheeler jumped up and stood behind the door. McKnight sat in the chair.

It was Rachel, now dressed in fatigues again. She still held the doorknob in her right hand when she realized McKnight was no longer restrained. She reached behind her for the weapon in her waistband, but Wheeler grabbed her hand with an iron grip and put his weapon against her temple.

"Don't make me kill you, *Cindy*," he whispered.

She stiffened in surprise, then raised both her hands.

"Last time I was this close to you, I got a nice scar," he said. "I hope you'll try again."

"No," she said. "I'm yours to command, thank you."

Wheeler pulled the gun from her waistband and set it on the floor. Then he pulled her right wrist behind her and pushed it up between her shoulder blades. She grunted but said nothing.

In her left hand, Rachel held a hypodermic needle and sterile wipes. McKnight walked over and took them from her hand.

"For me?" he asked. He wondered if the syringe contained a lethal dose of poison this time, or just another sedative.

She shrugged and pouted like a teenager whose father wouldn't let her use the car.

"You disappoint me, Marc. I thought we had something special."

"Did you? You have a strange way of showing it."

"Circumstances change sometimes. Now what?" she asked.

He paused for a moment.

"You're coming with me back to 2036 and we'll talk more about what happens next. But understand this — you've hurt a lot of people, some of which I really care about. It wouldn't take much to push me over the edge from doing my job to giving you the justice you deserve. So believe me. I'd rather kill you and be done with it. It's your choice."

"Well, now that I understand the choices, I'd be happy to come along with you. When do we leave?"

McKnight went to the desk and retrieved the second dose of Dilaudid. "In about three minutes," he said.

When she saw it, Rachel struggled to get away and tried to butt Wheeler with the back of her head. She wriggled to get away, but Wheeler was far too strong.

McKnight took her left arm and pinned it with his arm and body. Then he plunged the syringe needle into her upper arm.

"Damn you," she said.

She struggled for a few seconds, then went limp.

"Lieutenant, you take Rachel, and I'll bring Freddie and the files. Are you ready?"

"Yes, *sir!*"

McKnight pulled Freddie out from under the desk and threw him over his shoulder. "You go, Lieutenant. Clear the platform as soon as you arrive. I'll be one minute behind you."

Wheeler carried Rachel to the center of the room and knelt. At the click of his beacon, the time globe formed and Rachel's hair blew in all directions, alternately covering and revealing Wheeler's face. Then the globe bulged outward, and they were gone.

McKnight waited a minute, then waited yet another minute, just in case. He chuckled over his abundance of caution. Then he carried Freddie and the box to the center of the room, knelt, and triggered his return jump to 2036.

CHAPTER 44

<u>Friday, December 5th, 2036 — 2:45pm — HERO Team Lab</u>

While falling through the star field of time travel, McKnight struggled to keep Freddie close.

Every time he traveled, he wondered about the stars.

Surely they aren't stars. I wonder what they are and why they fly by so fast?

Then they were on the floor of the Lab. It was hard to see outside the bubble, but he saw two human forms near the Engine platform.

One was Trevor. And the other? *Hatcher?*

The bubble bulged and dissipated. He glanced around the Lab. Wheeler and Rachel were on the floor to the left of the platform. The people he saw through the globe were definitely Trevor and Hatcher.

They rushed the platform.

"You okay, Major?" Trevor asked.

Hatcher busied herself with slipping plastic bonds around Rachel's wrists. Then she ran to Wheeler and slipped bonds on Freddie. She was none too gentle with Freddie. "Asshole," she muttered.

She held her cell phone against Rachel's arm, studied the display, and tapped in a command. Then she did the same with Freddie.

McKnight looked from Trevor to Hatcher and back, the question on his face.

Trevor saw the look.

"Her?" He pointed to Hatcher. "She's fine. The doc gave her a clean bill of health and released her for light work. Today is her first day back."

"What did she just do?" McKnight asked.

Trevor chuckled. "Another of Doctor Astalos's toys. She just deactivated the beacons they have implanted in their arms. Works on the same principle as the status message app."

"Good. How long was I gone?"

"Just under four days, sir," he said. "We're damned glad you're back."

"Tyler? What about Captain Tyler?"

"He's back, too, sir. He was slightly wounded, but nothing debilitating or dangerous. And he had a guest with him. But you brought back the prize. You guys went for recon to figure out how to grab Rachel, and you got arrested, escaped and captured her back. Is that about it?"

McKnight smiled. "A bit of an understatement, but yes. You said Captain Tyler had a guest with him?"

"Yes, sir, but I'll let him brief you on it. We're glad you're here, sir," he said.

"Glad to be back, Trevor."

McKnight glanced at Hatcher. "How about you, Lieutenant?"

She looked ill.

"I'm fine, sir. I can't tell you how sorry I am for what I did."

McKnight nodded. "You weren't yourself, Lieutenant. Do you even remember it?"

"No, sir. But, well… sometimes I think I remember it, but maybe that's because I was told what happened so many times that my brain manufactured a memory."

He looked at Trevor, who nodded.

"That's what the doc said, sir," he added. "She thinks they programmed Hatcher to forget everything that happened after the fact."

"I see."

"But the doc assured me she dug deep and removed all the hypnotic suggestions with the use of some handy drugs. Hatcher is good as new."

"I hope so," he said.

Hatcher socked Trevor in the arm. "Stop talking about me like I'm not here."

She turned to McKnight. "I'm fine, sir. Once she found the thread of the suggestions, I remembered almost all of it. I told her I couldn't go back to work unless she was certain I was deprogrammed. It scared the shit out of me, sir."

Freddie moaned, and Rachel stirred. McKnight didn't want to fight them again.

"Do you have any sleep bulbs? I ran out while trying to manage these two."

"We do, sir. Would you rather we take them to the lockup for now?"

"Yes, please. I'd rather we do that until we figure out what to do with them. Don't give the guys in the brig any names and tell them not to talk to the prisoners. We don't want any record created that Rachel's people can find and try to rescue them."

"No problems with that, sir. Doctor Astalos got the Time Engine Inhibitor installed, and we tested it. It works like a charm. They can't even jump into this building. The range of the Inhibitor is about a mile wide."

"Good."

"Oh, there's *better* news, sir. He learned how to break through the Inhibitor. We can drop in on Rachel's people and they can't stop us."

"That *is* good news. Is it implemented yet?"

"It's scheduled for tonight, sir. Should take about twenty minutes."

Rachel spoke for the first time.

"You can't beat our Inhibitor. We tried to do that for months and none of our physicists could do it. You're blowing smoke up my ass."

"Hi, *Cindy*," Trevor said. "Talk it up. You'll be in a small cell by yourself for a long time, I hope. Let's go."

Wheeler and Hatcher helped the two up and marched them out of the Lab.

McKnight dragged himself to his feet and shuffled over to the kitchen. He washed his hands and face, then pulled a bottle of water out of the fridge and took a long drink. Trevor came over to stand with him.

Wheeler and Hatcher returned and they all found seats at the debriefing table.

"Those two are quite a pair," Wheeler said. "Rachel won't stop talking and we couldn't get a word out of Freddie."

"Oh, I can explain that," Hatcher said. "Before they let me escape, I promised to cut his nuts off if he ever spoke to me again. He might be taking me seriously."

"What's Rachel saying?" McKnight said.

"She's trying to get information out of us," Hatcher said. "She can't stand not being in control. It couldn't happen to a nicer person."

McKnight smiled. It was like a dream to be home again.

Megan! How could I forget her?

He committed the worst possible relationship sin. He was gone for four days without an explanation or even a goodbye.

"Have you heard from Megan?" he asked.

Hatcher and Trevor looked at one another.

"Yes," Trevor said. "You should call her right away. She talked to Kathy the other day."

"What did Kathy tell her?"

"Nothing. Begging your pardon, sir, but she didn't think it was her place to do that."

McKnight frowned.

"I wish she had," he said, "but you're right. I should have told her what was going on."

What if I wasn't able to come back?

"Okay, I'll take care of that. Let's get out of here for the night and get some rest. Tomorrow, we'll interview Rachel and Freddie and get to the bottom of all this stuff. Then we'll plan our next steps."

"Yes, sir," Hatcher said. "Wheeler, I'll shut the machine down and you go brief the stockade about our prisoners and let them know we want to talk to them tomorrow."

"Wilco," Wheeler said.

"Sounds like a plan," McKnight said. "Make it happen."

They saluted McKnight and set about their assignments.

McKnight speed-dialed Megan and prepared himself for a battle. He was at fault and deserved whatever she dished out. At the moment, he didn't care. He was excited at the prospect of hearing her voice.

It was odd she didn't answer. He disconnected and dialed the number again.

She must be really upset if she isn't answering.

No answer.

He dialed Tyler, who answered right away.

"Hi, Major. We're glad you're back. Are you okay, sir?"

"I'm fine, Winnie. How about you?"

"Well, I got shot at and got a little crease, but I'm okay."

"Good. Are you able to work?"

"Oh, yes, sir. I'm ready for the next step. I have a lot of information to share with you as soon as you're ready. I presume you are going home to rest now?"

"Yes, but I was looking for Megan. Have you guys seen or talked to her?"

"Let me check," he said.

McKnight could hear him talking to Sarah in the background.

Tyler came back on the line.

"No, sir. We haven't. Have you been home yet?"

"No, I haven't."

"Uh, Marc... I talked to her the other day. She was worried and angry that she hadn't seen or heard from you in days. She's probably too angry to talk to you. I hope you have a good story for her."

"I have to tell her the truth. I let her down, and she deserves to know where I've been and why."

He heard Tyler sigh at the other end of the line.

"That's the right thing to do," he said. "Old habits and artificial barriers die hard, Marc. You need to get to where you and Megan are a unit, not two halves of a partnership. Does that make sense?"

"More and more every day, Winnie. That's my plan for tonight... Get it all out in the open and beg her forgiveness."

"Good luck. It'll take some serious groveling."

"I'm up for it. She's worth it. Thanks."

"Good. Back to work items... Can we debrief at oh-nine hundred tomorrow, sir?"

"Yes, that's fine," McKnight said. "My office. I'll see you then."

McKnight disconnected the line and left the office for home.

CHAPTER 45

Friday, December 5th, 2036 — 3:56pm — McKnight Apartment, Alexandria, Virginia

The ride home from the office only took twenty minutes, but McKnight was full of apprehension. The more he thought about it, the more he realized he committed an unforgivable sin. He left his love at home to go fight a dragon without even a word. He'd be lucky if Megan let him in the apartment.

If she's still here.

He pulled into their apartment complex. The apartment they shared was in the building farthest from the entrance. He and Megan had reserved parking spaces in front.

He spotted her ancient BMW in her space.

She's here.

He felt an odd sense of relief. He bounded up the stairs to their landing and pulled out his key. The door gave slightly when he touched the knob.

The door is open?

With a sinking feeling, he pushed the door open. Little of the winter afternoon light filtered into the apartment. The lights were off.

We never turn off all the lights — not when we sleep, nor when we leave.

"Megan?" he called.

No answer.

He entered and flipped on the overhead light. Everything looked in order.

He dashed through the apartment's rooms. She wasn't there, but there was no sign of a struggle or any violence.

Could she be at the apartment gym?

Then he saw the note and a video cube on the kitchen counter.

He read the note. It said only, *"Watch me - 4."*

McKnight carried the video cube to the TEV station in the living room and plugged it into the auxiliary input. The TEV powered up and started a video.

An older man appeared. In the background was a bookcase with unfamiliar titles, some in foreign languages. The man was somewhere near General Drake's age and had intense blue eyes, stylish gray hair, and a goatee. The video showed him from the chest up, revealing an expensive navy suit with a red tie. He looked dressed for a formal event.

The man smiled, then spoke.

"Good evening, Major McKnight. You have something I want, and now I have something you want — the stunning Miss McAllister. She is a lovely and charming young lady, as I am sure you know. If you would like her back... undamaged... you will follow my instructions exactly. I propose that we meet on neutral ground. In the Sandia Mountains of New Mexico. You know the place. Meet me on the mountaintop where you did your testing exactly twenty-five years from tomorrow afternoon at 2:00 pm Mountain Time. That would be December 5th in the year 2061. Bring with you Rachel and my assistant Freddie. Come without weapons. Bring no one else. I will bring Miss McAllister with me. We will execute the trade and all go home happy."

The man paused in his delivery.

"Do not disappoint me, Major," he said. "I do not wish any harm to come to Miss McAllister, but I will have no choice if you deviate from the schedule. If there is anyone there with you, other than Rachel and Freddie, the deal is off. I will not negotiate, and I am not open to any other options. If there is any sign of betrayal, I will take Miss

McAllister back to 2086 and turn her over to... other interested parties. I hope I have made myself clear. I will see you tomorrow."

The man looked off camera and nodded. The video froze on his image.

McKnight stood still, his brain refusing to process the message. Nausea overcame him. He ran into the bathroom, dropped to his knees, and vomited into the toilet. He continued to heave, though there was nothing left in his stomach.

It took several minutes for his brain to stop reeling and register a cognizant thought.

He stood and looked in the mirror. He barely recognized the haggard soul looking back at him — unshaven, unwashed, and ashen. He washed his face and hands, went back to the living room, and stood in the middle, staring at the image of Number Four.

I can't deal with this alone. I need help.

McKnight pulled out his phone and sent a team text.

<Emergency team meeting at 0700 tomorrow. No discussion of this outside the team. Kathy, call me ASAP for mission planning details.>

It took less than ten seconds for Kathy Wu to call.

"What's up?" she asked when he answered. "I'm on speaker. Trevor is here, too, if that's okay."

"It is. I just got home and found a video message in my kitchen. They've kidnapped Megan and they want to trade her for Rachel and Freddie."

"They who?" Kathy asked.

"The person on the video was an older man. Number Four from Hatcher's description. Plus, he signed it with the number 4."

"Oh, Jeez," Trevor said.

"Marc," Kathy said. "You know they have no intention of letting you and Megan walk away from this meeting."

"That crossed my mind. But what choice do I have?"

"None, of course. We have to respond and at least act like we will comply."

"Kathy's right," Trevor added. "This is a no-win situation. We need to expand our thinking. Marc, can we get a copy of that video cube? I want to see his posture and look for nonverbal clues."

"Yes, I'll send it to you right away."

"Good. How long do we have?"

"He said to meet him in 2061 in the Sandia Mountains twenty-five years from tomorrow at 2:00 pm Mountain Time — that's 4:00 pm our time."

"Not much time for planning," Kathy said.

"… but we'll get a plan together, Marc," Trevor said. "Do you think you can rest between now and then? We'll come up with something. We'll call Captain Tyler in, too."

"Go ahead," McKnight said. "I'll see you at the office at seven."

"Try not to worry, Marc," Kathy said. "We'll get her back. See you in the morning."

McKnight disconnected the call. He used his phone to photograph the note and saved the video cube contents to disk. Then he transmitted both to Trevor.

He sat on the sofa in silence for a few minutes, then called General Drake.

Drake was sympathetic, but underscored what Kathy said about Number Four's intentions. He was compassionate, but objective.

After Drake hung up, McKnight felt a little better. He tried to think of something else he could do to advance their investigation.

Investigation?

Even the word was insufficient. In twenty-four hours, Megan would be dead unless they came up with a workable solution.

The emotional side of his mind overcame the logical side. He couldn't keep the ugly images of Megan being violated, tortured, and killed from streaming through his consciousness. Tears came to his eyes and spilled down his cheeks.

After ten minutes, his logical brain penetrated the grisly parade of images.

This is what he wanted. He's using my fear to cloud my judgment. Focus on the problem, not the threat!

McKnight pushed the emotional images away and tried to assess the problem. He began to identify his assets and the risks.

After ten minutes with little progress, he realized his priorities were wrong.

I need sleep more than anything else. I won't be any good to anyone until I get some rest.

He showered and stretched out on the bed.

Sleep didn't come for a long time.

CHAPTER 46

Saturday, December 6th, 2036 — 6:30am - HERO Team Conference
Room at Telegraph Road, Alexandria Virginia

McKnight didn't remember how long it took to get to sleep, but it
was a long time.

When the alarm sounded, he jumped up, dressed, and brewed a cup
of coffee for the twenty minute drive.

He pulled into the office parking lot at 6:30 am, and by the cars he
recognized, the entire team was there, including Doctor Astalos. He
smiled grimly and hurried to the security check and upstairs to the
HERO Team offices.

Kathy had assembled everyone in the large conference room. They
were talking before he entered, but fell silent when they saw him.
Hatcher, Tyler, and Wheeler rose and came to attention.

"As you were, everyone," he said. "Let's get to it. Kathy, is
everyone up to speed?"

"Yes, Major. They've all seen the note and the video. Can we
watch it together?"

"Yes, here it is." He handed it to her.

She plugged it into a receptacle on the table that interfaced with the
large screen on the wall.

The face of Number Four appeared. Like the others, McKnight
paid close attention to see if he missed any clues earlier.

When the video finished, Kathy turned it off.

"Any comments?" she asked. No one spoke at first.

After a moment, Kathy asked, "Trap?"

"Yes," Tyler said. Everyone agreed.

McKnight looked around the table. "That's what the General said when I called him last night. It couldn't be anything else."

"Respectfully, Major," Trevor said, "we don't even have any proof she's still alive. And if he intends to trap or kill you, he doesn't need her. I'm sorry, sir, but it needed to be said."

McKnight shook his head. "I can't let myself think that. I understand your logic and your sensitivity, but I just can't do it."

"Here's what I see," Kathy said. She looked at Tyler. "Winnie, let me know if you agree or disagree or see any other course."

"Sure," Tyler said.

"First, this guy they call Number Four is ruthless and ambitious. From his point of view, he can't let Rachel go because of her access to Joe Kosar. I'm not sure about this Freddie guy, but there must be a reason he wants him back. God knows what it might be. Agree so far, Winnie?"

"I do."

"But the number one thing is this. It's not acceptable to him for anyone to escape. If he has his way, you and Megan will be irrelevant, and we already know he prefers you dead. And he wants Rachel and Freddie, for reasons we can guess, but don't fully understand yet. All this adds up to double-cross. If you show up at the rendezvous point as he requests, he'll be prepared to take home all the marbles. That's who he is."

Kathy looked at Tyler, who nodded.

"Couldn't have said it better myself," Tyler said. "Our only option is to assume double-cross and make our plans from there."

"Yep," Kathy said with a nod.

She looked at McKnight. "Major, what did General Drake say?"

McKnight leaned back in his chair. "Pretty much the same thing."

"Okay, so let's decide what we are and are *not* willing to do."

She rose, pulled forward a whiteboard, and wrote on it.

"First, we *must* respond. We can't leave Megan in his hands."

"Are we willing to let them have Rachel or Freddie?" Trevor asked.

Wheeler spoke. "If we do, and we get Megan back, it's a draw. We all live to fight again, but…"

"But they'll be back," McKnight said. "Sooner or later, they'll be back. The bottom line is, we've proved ourselves to be a thorn in their side they can't ignore."

Trevor leaned forward. "And the only reason they haven't struck at us already is because…?"

"We *do* have an advantage," Kathy said. "We have Rachel, and he probably isn't willing to risk losing her. But we also have our TEI in place. They couldn't break through it to attack us. Once she is safe, we're targets again."

McKnight leaned forward again. "I'm willing to give up Rachel and Freddie for Megan. But the goal should be to get Megan back and keep Rachel and Freddie in custody."

There was general agreement.

"First, we need to even the odds," Kathy said. "Meeting them on that mountaintop in New Mexico is out. They'll be there in force. On the other hand, if they're there and we don't show, they'll go right back home and be in protective mode on their own turf. Somebody has to engage them so they stay and don't jump back right away. It's reasonable to assume that Number Four and Megan won't show up there. Too dangerous. He will probably still be at his HQ, overseeing the operation. And maybe without troops."

"Oh, he'll have troops there, but maybe not as many as he would otherwise," Tyler said, and turned to Doctor Astalos. "Doc, are you sure your capability to defeat their Time Engine Inhibitor will work?"

Astalos nodded.

"I've tested it in several scenarios, but not against their device. I did test it against ours, which I extrapolated from their plans. I exploited a software design flaw to get it to work, so if they've found and fixed that flaw, then all bets are off. But I'm ninety-nine percent sure it'll work. I'm looking forward to a chance to test it in action."

Tyler frowned. "I'd like it better if you were a hundred percent sure. Our chance to use the element of speed to catch them off guard will evaporate if we can't break through."

"Okay," Kathy said. "Our contingency plan will have to assume we couldn't break through. Let's assume we can for the moment."

"Okay, here's a straw man to consider," Tyler said. "Let's jump into the meeting ready to fight. Some of us shoot up the place while others break into Rachel's lab and hope Megan is there. We take Rachel and Freddie there and demand to trade them for Megan, except we double-cross at the end and keep everyone, then jump back out."

"All right, let's start with that," McKnight said. "Who's fit and ready to go?" He looked at Tyler. "Are you fit enough to go on a mission that might degrade into combat?"

Tyler looked indignant. "You're kidding, right? I mean, sir, *yes*, sir. I'm five by five. One hundred percent."

"Lieutenant Wheeler? How about you?"

"No issues, sir. And Hatcher is ready, too."

McKnight frowned. "Let's let her respond for herself, Lieutenant."

"Yes, sir," Wheeler said.

"Well, Lieutenant Hatcher? How about it? You've been through a lot in the last few weeks. Are you up for a mission?"

Hatcher looked McKnight in the eyes.

"Yes, sir, I am. It's true I've had a few challenges lately. But, sir, that's all the more reason I need to go along. Their programming made me violate my sacred oath to the Army and to you, my commanding officer. Do you believe it possible I would shy away from rescuing Megan, your girlfriend and a woman who's been so kind to me?"

Her eyes flared. "No, not one chance in hell, sir. I'm in, and you'll have to put me in the stockade to keep me from coming along."

McKnight considered this. He was skittish about sending her into a combat situation, but her passion moved him.

"You're in, Lieutenant."

"What about the rest of us, Major?" Trevor said. "I'm certified on all our handguns and could learn the automatic ones. Why not include me?"

"No," McKnight said. "I need you here for Kathy to bounce things off. You're good at that."

"How about me?" asked Astalos. "I'm certified, too."

"No, Doctor. I can't imagine what General Drake would say to me if anything happened to you. No, sorry, but you're here to advise Kathy on technical issues, if any."

Astalos frowned, but nodded.

"No, we'll use four resources. Two to go to New Mexico and two to take Rachel and Freddie to FTS headquarters."

"It has to be you and Hatcher there, sir," Kathy said.

"Yes, you're right, Kathy. So that means Captain Tyler and Lieutenant Wheeler to New Mexico."

"Begging your pardon, sir," Wheeler said. "But why not send me and Hatcher to New Mexico? No offense to Captain Tyler, but Hatcher and I have always been a team, just as you and Captain Tyler have an extensive history of working together. Besides, as soon as we show up, they'll know we plan to fight, not negotiate."

"I disagree, Lieutenant," Kathy said. "In New Mexico, there'll be a battle — that I'll give you. But in the FTS lab, having Hatcher present will give Number Four hope that he can work things out and get Rachel, because he may believe Hatcher is still controllable. If Hatcher isn't there, he'll be less optimistic. We want to make him think he has an opportunity. I mean, he probably wouldn't hesitate to kill any of us, but he'd rather not start a fight if he thinks he can get Rachel, and maybe Hatcher, too."

McKnight stood and paced the room.

He touched his finger to the side of his head and said, "I think you have something there, Kathy. Okay. Tyler and Wheeler to New Mexico, Hatcher and me to FTS headquarters with Rachel and Freddie."

He turned to Tyler. "If it were your battle to plan, what would you do?"

"Well, first, I wouldn't want to time-jump in at the appointed time. That's like parachuting into the enemy's front line. They'll see us coming a mile away. I'd much rather go in early and recon the battleground in advance. Maybe Wheeler and I can go in advance and then have Kathy push some attack drones in at meeting time. Depending on the size of their force, the drones could be a superior force."

"How many would you want?"

"Ten."

Kathy objected. "The time bubble isn't big enough to send ten drones at once. We could only send two smaller ones or one large drone at a time."

"Right," Tyler said. "Keep sending them as fast as you can. Two smaller ones at a time would be fine."

"Why not one big drone?" Trevor asked.

"Because, if you send one drone, all their firepower can concentrate on the one drone. If it goes down, you're at square zero again. No, send two and split their fire. They shoot down one, but you still have one, and soon you have three. That's the better plan."

"Okay, you go in as recon and attack at the appointed meet time. Now they have to split their fire in three directions."

"Correct," Tyler said. "If Wheeler and I split up there, they might think we have an entire squad of men and might even surrender."

"How do you keep the drones from shooting you or Wheeler?" Trevor said.

"The drones are smart these days," Astalos said. "Their facial recognition is pretty darned good. If one takes an interest in you, look straight at it and try to be still. They're about ninety-nine percent accurate at identifying friendly resources."

"Hmm. I hope their programmer wasn't drunk the day he tested this code," Wheeler said.

Hatcher laughed. "It would serve you right to get your ass shot off," she said.

"See," Wheeler said. "I told you she was back to normal."

"Shut up," she said. "Pay attention to the briefing, so you know what to do."

"Okay," Kathy said. "I can do that — send two drones out in rapid succession until I send all ten or hear otherwise. What if there's no people there to attack? What if Captain Tyler and Lieutenant Wheeler are there and there's no attack?"

"Oh, there will be." Tyler said.

"Yes, but what if there isn't?"

"Excellent point, Kathy," McKnight said. "Mr. Tyler, as soon as you know what to expect, you'll send a status to Kathy so she can alert us to any changes in plans?"

"Yes, sir," Tyler said.

"Okay," Kathy said. "Now, what about the Major and Lieutenant Hatcher at FTS? Do we send them armed to the teeth?"

Tyler shrugged, but then said, "We don't send them without weapons. They must be able to get and keep leverage. If they have a weapon, they can at least hold it to Rachel's head and make their demands. Otherwise, they're just pissing in the wind."

Hatcher spoke. "Agreed, sir. Let's say the Major wears his sidearm holstered and another pistol in his belt in the back. I'll carry my sidearm in the holster and an HK MP5. If we need relief, a burst will send everyone for cover. Three extra clips and three magazines for each sidearm. We'll keep Rachel and Freddie in front of us at all times. By the way, while we're getting ready to go, no chatter about the mission in their presence. We don't want them to have any insight into our plan."

"Right," McKnight said. "Excellent, Lieutenant. Anything else?"

There was no further response.

"Okay, one more thing, just for sanity's sake," he said. "Captain Tyler, why don't you go in as early as possible? By that, I mean let's stretch the limits of the Time Engine. The meeting time is at 4:00 pm our time, 2:00 pm Mountain time. Why not leave as soon as possible and land on the hill next to the target a week early and watch for activity on the target hill? If you do that, you can send a message back to Kathy and revise the attack plan. Make sense?"

"Yes, sir, it does. Let's get after it. Mr. Wheeler? We leave in two hours. Get your equipment together and let's meet here in one hour and work out the details of the plan."

"Yes, sir." Wheeler saluted McKnight and left the conference room.

"While we're here, Lieutenant," McKnight said to Hatcher, "let's work through some details and ideas. Then please get Rachel and Freddie brought back here. Then we'll try to get a nap before we launch. Understood?"

"Yes, sir," Hatcher said. "Thanks for allowing me to come along."

"I wouldn't have it any other way, Lieutenant."

CHAPTER 47

<u>Saturday, December 6th, 2036 — 12:30pm — McKnight's Office,</u>
<u>Telegraph Road, Alexandria, Virginia</u>

McKnight and Hatcher debated the details of the plan for an hour. It was an imperfect plan because there were too many variables, but at least they covered all the contingencies they could think of.

When they finished, Hatcher left to arrange for security to bring Rachel and Freddie to the Lab. McKnight walked down the hall to his office and closed the door.

Once inside, he leaned back against the door and banged his head against it twice.

Get a grip, asshole!

Then he sat at his desk, turned toward the window, and put his feet up on the credenza.

His stress points were way up, he knew. He could hear his pulse pounding in his ears.

A playlist of what could go wrong repeated itself again and again in his mind. Before he could slow the parade and mitigate a risk, two more flooded into his consciousness and started the cycle again. He closed his eyes and tried to relax, but it did no good.

Am I doing the right thing? Megan's life is on the line.

All his thoughts swirled around that one idea. If he was wrong, she would pay for his error with her life.

His logical side took a beating from his emotional side. He wanted nothing more than to give Rachel back to Number Four and beg for Megan's release.

There was a knock on his door.

I don't want to talk to anyone right now.

He continued the 'what if' game he started earlier with Hatcher.

Be logical!

But the emotional outcry in his brain wouldn't permit it. His subconscious presented him with an image of Megan, lying on the floor of the FTS lab. She wasn't moving.

God help me! If she's dead because of me...

There was another, more insistent knock on the door.

McKnight didn't want any words of encouragement or sage advice. He just wanted it to be over. He wished he could die and not have to do this mission. But then, he wouldn't trust it to anyone else.

I've trained for this kind of mission. But most of the time, the hostages end up as victims. Dead.

Another knock on the door.

It's not going away.

He threw an invitation over his shoulder.

"Come in."

He didn't look to see who it was.

"Marc, are you okay?"

It's Tyler.

He turned. His friend stood in the doorway.

"May I come in?" Tyler said.

"Sure."

McKnight pulled his feet off the credenza and wheeled his chair around, then pointed to the side chairs in front of his desk.

Tyler sat and put his feet up on McKnight's desk.

"Permission to speak freely, sir?"

Tyler wasn't asking for permission. Chain of command be damned, he was going to speak his mind to his friend.

"Megan's my cousin," Tyler said. His eyes drifted up to the ceiling. "I don't think there's anyone in my family I love more."

"I know."

Tyler looked at McKnight.

"Yes, I know you do. But I wanted to repeat it so you understand where I'm coming from."

"Okay."

"This is painful — her being at risk like this. I fear the worst."

McKnight nodded. "Me, too."

"I was talking to Trevor. You know he got involved in a lot of hostage situations down in Atlanta before he joined us."

"Yes, and *none* of them turned out well."

Tyler paused. "I was going to say that they *rarely* turn out well. There's room for hope."

McKnight stretched, trying to loosen the tight muscles between his shoulders.

After a moment, he spoke. "I'm not sure I have any hope. I only have fear." He stared at his hands in his lap.

"That's where I was, too, but I think there is cause for some optimism."

McKnight was on the verge of breaking down. He blinked away the tears that tried to overcome him.

He looked up at Tyler. "Whatever it is, please share it with me. I'm all out of optimism."

"Listen to me, Marc. I know you… better than you know yourself. If anyone is strong enough, or innovative enough, or even bold enough to pull this off, it's you."

McKnight stared at him.

"I mean it," Tyler said. "If anyone can get her through this and back home, it's you. You're well trained, you have the desire, and you'd be willing to die to bring her home. That's got to count for something."

"With all my heart," McKnight said, "I want to believe that."

"And you know Megan believes it. She would be more comfortable with you coming for her than anyone else."

He's right. I'm just not sure I have what it takes.

"Marc, we've been friends for a long time. We've been in school and in battle together. Dozens of missions. There's one thing I know about you that you don't."

"Yeah? What's that?"

"Your biggest enemy is self-doubt. Before every mission, you get like... *this*." He spread his arms to encompass the room. "You torture yourself with what could go wrong. But don't you see? It's preparation for you. Once the mission starts, all your doubts evaporate and you get the job done. Always."

McKnight hadn't noticed this about himself.

Could it be true?

He tried to think back, to experience it in his mind, but couldn't. Still, it brought him a sense of encouragement. Not much, but maybe just enough.

"Jeez, Winnie, I hope you're right," he said.

"I *am* right, dammit. You always pull it out. I agree this will be one of our biggest challenges, but you can do it."

"I want to believe that."

Tyler paused. He looked thoughtful, but McKnight couldn't imagine what might have distracted him.

"What?" McKnight said. "What else?"

Tyler smiled. "When I was in 2086," he said. "I met someone you'd like to meet."

"Who?"

"A U.S. Senator. Her name is Colleen Myers. She's in her early forties. She's fighting against Rachel and Number Four. While I was there, the Devotees attacked her home. That's how I got shot. To save her life, I brought her back with me. She was wounded, too... more than me. But she's alive and here in our time."

McKnight waited for Tyler to say more, but he didn't.

"And?" McKnight asked. "What else?"

"When I was in her home, I saw a picture of her parents. They looked familiar."

McKnight groaned with exasperation. "Winnie, if you don't get to the point, I'll toss you out the window. Who is she?"

"You and Megan are her parents." Tyler let the information sink in.

"We are? And she's here in *this* time?"

"Yes, and I'll take you to see her, but not until after the mission."

McKnight looked at his watch.

Tyler's correct — I don't have enough time before Tyler and Wheeler shove off.

"If I don't bring Megan back, she... Colleen?... won't exist. You're saying that, right?"

"More specifically, I'm saying she *exists*, which implies you'll get Megan back." He held up his hand. "Granted, we don't really know everything about time modification, because of the folds, and the immediate and gradual effects... But we have to pull hope from this. If the mission fails, then she would never exist and I wouldn't remember her. But I do."

"I see. This helps. Thanks."

"Good, but there's more."

"What else are you thinking?"

"We can't let those thoughts make us complacent and sit back and wait for all the dominoes to fall in place. You and me and the rest of the team *are* the dominoes. I just wanted to give you a clearer picture of the stakes, both the hope and the danger. You still have to be on the top of your game. Me, too. And Wheeler and Hatcher. We can do it, and now you have more to hope for."

"And you'll take us to meet her when we get back?"

"Megan's already met her. Remember, I came back before you."

McKnight's temper flared. "You asshole, why didn't you tell me before?"

"I planned to. At our briefing this morning. But things changed. Now we have stuff to fix first. But we'll meet her after this is all over. We don't have time before the mission, and you don't need your emotions ratcheted up any higher."

McKnight considered this, and his anger drained off. Tyler was right. As usual, his instinctive actions were on target and effective.

"Okay, we'll see her when the mission is complete."

Tyler looked at his watch and rose. "Speaking of which, Wheeler and I need to talk and then get going. I'll see you in the Lab for launch."

He saluted and left the room.

McKnight turned back to the window and the credenza. He put his feet up and looked out the window.

"A daughter," he said. "Me and Megan."

He smiled for the first time that day.

CHAPTER 48

Saturday, December 6th, 2036 — 2:36pm — HERO Team Lab, Telegraph Road, Alexandria, Virginia

The support team for the 2061 mission was Kathy, Trevor and Doctor Astalos. Tyler covered the overall battle plan with them and Wheeler.

"Okay," Tyler said. "I think we have it all laid out."

He turned to the others and said, "Are there any questions?"

Always the eternal planner, Kathy repeated the plan to the team.

"Okay, first we send you guys back to Hill 34... call it Watchful Hill... as far before the event as possible. Considering the limitations of the machine, that's about eight days before. We're sending you to Watchful Hill because Hill 23... call it Target Hill... is where the rendezvous will take place. We don't want you to run into the FTS troops, if any, who will arrive to set the trap for Major McKnight. Correct, so far?"

"Yep. Keep going," Tyler said.

"You and Lieutenant Wheeler will observe Target Hill from Watchful Hill. You'll create your attack plan, based on what you find on site. You'll send us a status through your beacon whenever you see something significant."

"Good," Tyler said. "What next?"

"At rendezvous time, we'll send Major McKnight, Lieutenant Hatcher, Freddie, and Rachel to 2086. As soon as they jump out, we'll bring our ten battle drones out and start sending them by twos through to your position. They'll already be in battle mode and will start shooting when they land there. We'll keep sending them through until we run out of drones or you tell us to stop."

"Correct. One more thing. We need to stage the drones elsewhere so that Rachel and Freddie don't see them. We don't want them to have any information about our plans. So we won't bring those two here to the Lab until the last minute before traveling." To the group he asked, "Any more questions?"

Doctor Astalos spoke. "Just one comment. When the battle drones land, they'll arrive in a time bubble with brilliant light. They won't be able to see as well. Until the first drones' bubble dissipates, I suggest you don't look like a target to them. Once the bubble goes out, they'll recognize you. And each additional pair will come with a new bubble. So, if I were you, I'd do my best to stay out of sight during their arrival."

"Excellent point, Doctor," Tyler said, and jotted down a note. "Anything else?"

"Yes," Trevor said. "What happens after the battle is over? Assuming you guys are still alive and we've won?"

"We jump back here and check on status from the other team," Tyler said. "If things are bad or we have no status, we send Wheeler and me and a battle drone to the FTS Lab. Once there, we'll assess the situation and disrupt, interrupt or otherwise force the enemy to adapt to a new situation."

"And what happens if one or both of you don't make it back?"

"Well, that's when we'll find out about your battle skills, Trevor." He smiled.

Trevor chuckled. "You guys are too funny. I'll be ready. Let's just hope you're in good shape."

"That's our plan," Tyler said. "Mr. Wheeler, do you have anything to add?"

"Yes, sir. When this is over, we need to send a team back to Target Hill to clean up. That should do it. Let's get going. I'm eager to put an end to these people."

There was agreement around the room.

Tyler looked at his watch. "Okay, we go in twenty minutes."

The team busied themselves with preparations.

Tyler and Wheeler intended to travel light. Minimal comfort for sleeping. Standard MREs for food. Sleep bulbs, just in case. They took as much ammunition and grenades as they could carry. When it came time to attack, they'd have to hike from Watchful Hill to Target Hill in a hurry and still have enough energy to fight.

Kathy programmed the beacons for the troops and the drones for both jumps. She and Trevor manned the Engine console, while Tyler and Wheeler dragged their packs to the platform.

Tyler checked the time. He and Wheeler were leaving two hours before the Major's jump. Assuming they arrived on Watchful Hill safely, they'd have eight days and two hours to prepare and plan. They would need that time.

Kathy and Trevor executed the checklist for the jump. It was Trevor's first time working on the console, but he was a quick study.

Kathy called out the countdown and pulled the trigger on the Engine remote.

The static electricity in the air spiked and the time globe formed around the two officers.

Tyler patted his breast pocket for the anti-nausea meds he always needed after time travel. He was already feeling a little queasy.

The bubble bulged, and they were off.

CHAPTER 49

<u>Monday, November 28th, 2061 — 2:36pm — Watchful Hill, New</u>
<u>Mexico</u>

The HERO Team examined and cataloged the hills in the Sandia
Mountains region of New Mexico in 2034 during their search for the
best place to test the Time Engine. Watchful Hill is one of the smaller
hills. Its crest was only forty-five feet across, so it was too small for
the Engine testing. But it was perfect for observing the crest of Target
Hill.

Static electricity spiked, and a time bubble formed. The two
officers crouched in travel position to avoid the normal backward
pressure felt in every trip.

The bubble bulged and went out, leaving Tyler and Wheeler and
their gear on the mountaintop.

Wheeler stood and oriented himself to directions, then turned to the
west, where he expected to find Target Hill.

Tyler pulled the anti-nausea medication from his breast pocket and
poured it on his tongue.

Wheeler pulled out his field glasses and focused them on Target
Hill.

No sign of activity yet.

"See anything?" Tyler asked.

"No, sir, nothing yet. I…" He adjusted the glasses to sharpen the
image. "Crap."

"What?"

"Stay low, sir."

Wheeler kneeled next to a yucca plant. "Looks like they are coming in. Any second now, they'll start looking around, just like us."

Tyler crawled over next to Wheeler and pulled out his own field glasses. He focused them on the large hill a mile away.

"See what I see?" Tyler said.

"I think so, sir. I count nine soldiers and one big-assed battle drone. Looks like an ELF-100."

"Roger on the count. They don't mess around, do they?"

"No, sir, they don't. We're outgunned. Do we go back for more firepower?"

"Nope," Tyler said. "They'd see us leave and guess our tactic. For now, we know something they don't and we'll keep that advantage. What do you see as the options?"

"We could ask them to surrender, sir, but I don't think that's a high probability of success."

Tyler smiled without mirth. "Agreed. What else?"

"Do you suppose we could go find a gun store?"

"We could do that, but unlikely we'd be able to buy what we need. And I suspect there would be a background check and a cooling-off period."

"Yes, sir. Then I guess we'll just have to do some kick-ass planning."

"I think that's the ticket, Lieutenant. First order of business is to take out that drone. I'm glad we have grenades, but we have to be close enough to toss one underneath it to have any effect."

"Yes, sir."

"Ah, but we're getting the cart before the horse. Let's send a status through the beacon. Tell them about the armaments and that we'll send the details on their setup on the hill as soon as we have it. Then we can tell them which direction to point the drones when they land and have them fire for best effect. With luck, we can attack as a diversion just as the jump begins and catch them off guard. Know what my main worry is?"

"No, sir. What?"

"Those guys look like Rangers. They might not be as well trained as we are, but that feels like a stupid assumption. It'll be hard to get close enough to take out the drone. They'll set a watch, so we'll have to be mighty sneaky to get close."

For the next six days, Tyler and Wheeler watched Target Hill. The FTS soldiers built foxholes with sandbags in front for cover.

More soldiers jumped in, along with a few officers, but they didn't stay. Apparently, they were inspecting the engagement plan.

Wheeler assumed they planned to capture the people who jumped in at the rendezvous time. Later, he and Tyler discussed the possibility that the troops intended to kill whoever jumped in.

There were clues to support that theory — the superior firepower, the troop positioning, and the large drone. With their strength, they could take on a good-sized force with little trouble.

On the other hand, Number Four wanted Rachel back and wasn't likely to blast away at whoever arrived. The force might simply be preparing for the worst. If the HERO Team came in with two squads of Rangers, their troop placement and battle drone would create an efficient killing field on top of Target Hill.

The FTS troops on Target Hill kept watch and ran patrols. At one point, Wheeler and Tyler had to abandon Watchful Hill and hide in the valley beyond when an FTS patrol ventured to its summit.

It would be hard to get close enough to damage the drone.

The night before the rendezvous, Tyler composed his engagement plan report for the beacon status message.

<*The enemy positions are on the edge of Target Hill, stretched out in an arc from 325 degrees to 45 degrees from the hill's center, with an ELF-100 combat drone sitting at the 5 degree mark. There are four resources on either side of the drone, equally spaced across the arc. We recommend all ten drones be programmed to target the drone first, then search for alternate targets. We will position ourselves at*

approx 100 feet down the hill at the 5 degree mark. Our priority will be to attack and destroy the drone, then split up to draw fire away from the jump landing site. With luck, we can disable it and allow the LF-50 drones to engage and destroy the enemy. ACK PLS.>

The local date/time stamp on the message allowed the Engine to respond in real time. After conveying the plan to Trevor and Kathy, they would make their way down Watchful Hill and partway up the slope of Target Hill in the dark.

Tyler transmitted the message, and they waited for a response.

When no answer came for three minutes, Tyler checked his phone. There was a message there on the beacon.

"Crap! There's already a message here. I didn't expect the response time to be compressed."

He retrieved the message and frowned.

"What the hell? Listen to this, Lieutenant. 'Negative. Position at 125 degrees and 245 degrees 100 feet downhill to provide supporting fire. Attack as soon as you feel the static electricity surge. ACK PLS.'"

"Trevor's trying to tell us how to do this," Wheeler said. "No. *We* do the battle tactics."

Tyler typed in a follow-up message.

<No, Trevor. Please follow my directions. We got this. ACK PLS.>

Tyler's phone chirped instantly. He retrieved the message from the beacon and read it to himself.

<Captain Tyler, this is Drake. No, I have this. Pls ACK my orders.>

He read it to Wheeler.

Wheeler rolled his eyes. "Well, then," he said. "Now that you've explained it to me. Hell, yes. Let's do it, sir."

Tyler laughed. "Yup," he said as he typed in his response to the General.

<Understood. Wilco.>

"I wonder what he has up his sleeve?" Wheeler said.

"I don't know, but he's the General and I'm not. Ready to take a little stroll in the moonlight?" He looked up. "I mean, on a cold and moonless night?"

"Yes, sir. By the way, after spending time here testing the Engine, I know from experience there are rattlesnakes out here."

"But they should be asleep, right?"

"Yes, sir, but even at night they don't appreciate being stepped on."

"But don't they go down in a hole or something?"

"Yes, sir," Wheeler said. "I'd look out for snakes, sir."

Tyler suppressed a laugh. "Point taken, Mr. Wheeler. I'll be careful. Are you ready?"

"Yes, sir."

They hoisted their ammunition belts and weapons over their shoulders and started down the unexposed side of Watchful Hill.

Wheeler chose the 245 degree position on the far side of Target Hill.

It took five hours to make the one mile trek across to Target Hill. Walking was one thing. Walking in stealth was much harder. He took a detour once to give wide berth to a mountain lion.

When he reached the bottom of the valley between the two hills, he took the time to give the hill a good hard look for sentries. He saw a few near the top of the hill.

Got to be very careful from here on in or we lose the element of surprise.

There were trees in the valley between the hills, and cover was plentiful there. But there wasn't as much cover as they split up and climbed the long slopes of Target Hill. They stayed low and even crawled in places.

He approached to within a hundred feet of the summit and saw the silhouette of a trooper on patrol thirty feet away. He withdrew a sleep bulb from his pocket and his knife from its sheath. The trooper stood still for a few minutes.

He's listening.

Wheeler switched to shallow and quiet breathing. He couldn't be silent, but he could get close. He checked his watch, shielding its dim glow from uphill. The time was oh-five-hundred. The rendezvous was over nine hours away. He hoped he didn't have to kill a sentry to avoid being discovered.

If someone goes missing, they'll come looking.

The sentry raised his field glasses.

They have the night vision attachment. If he looks at me, he'll see me.

Wheeler remained motionless. He was low in the vegetation, but any motion would attract the soldier's attention.

The sentry stood motionless for a long minute. Then he lowered his glasses and continued his patrol.

Whew!

Wheeler looked down the hill and considered his options. Where he was, he was close to the patrol path and would be easier to spot. He could retreat a few dozen feet and mitigate that danger, but then he'd have to crawl back up here in daylight at attack time.

He spotted a large bush forty feet down the hill.

That's my place.

He gathered his gear and cautiously crept back to the bush. There, he could rest and be less alert for the next nine hours.

It was a suitable compromise.

CHAPTER 50

Saturday, December 6th, 2036 — 3:55pm — HERO Team Lab, Telegraph Road, Alexandria, Virginia

Kathy and Trevor walked over to the Engine console where Doctor Astalos stood, making final adjustments for the mission.

Trevor was amazed at how fast the aged scientist could move as he made program changes.

"Are we almost there, Doctor Astalos?" Kathy asked. "It's 3:55. Just about time to go."

"Yes, we are there. Are our other guests ready?"

"Yes, sir. They're champing at the bit to get moving."

"Excellent. Okay, remember that Rachel and Freddie can't know about the drone deployment. Trevor? Would you fetch Major McKnight and the others so we can start?"

"Sure thing, Doc," Trevor said. He turned and dashed over to the double doors that led from the Lab to the office area.

Past the doors, he found McKnight and Hatcher, both armed and ready. Rachel and Freddie were across the hall from them, sitting in chairs with their hands bound behind their backs.

Rachel was smiling, but Freddie looked worried.

"He's ready for you now," Trevor said.

Rachel smiled at Trevor.

"And where are we going today?" she asked.

McKnight looked at Hatcher, then at Rachel. "I guess it's okay to share this... we're trading you for one of our resources. We're meeting Number Four and our resource in your lab."

"Oh," she said.

She turned to Freddie.

"Isn't that nice, Freddie? We're going back to explain to Number Four about how Major McKnight escaped. And how *you* got captured. What *were* you doing there on Telegraph Road anyway, Freddie?"

Freddie looked ill.

"You don't need me for this, do you?" he asked McKnight. "I'm a government contractor. I don't make policy or any decisions. I'd rather stay here in the past and share what I know."

"Oh, but he needs to come, too," Rachel said. "Number Four will want his report."

"I don't see why, I—"

"He asked for both of you," McKnight said. "So you're coming along."

"I have information," Freddie said. "I know more about their plans than they know, and more than you might think. I can be of help—"

"I'm sure you could. And you'll be of help today," McKnight said. "You'll see when we get there. It's time to go."

McKnight took Rachel by the arm and helped her out of her seat. Hatcher did the same for Freddie. Trevor turned on his heel and preceded them into the Lab. He heard Rachel speak to McKnight.

"He has your little girlfriend, doesn't he?" she whispered.

McKnight said nothing.

She's quick. He probably shouldn't have shared anything.

"I was serious about choosing you over Joey and Number Four, you know. That option is still open. Won't you reconsider?"

McKnight glanced at Rachel, then looked straight ahead.

She's really turning on the charm.

"Think of what we could do together. We'd make an impressive team in whatever year we settled. Your little girlfriend isn't the right match for you. You need someone strong like me."

Trevor thought McKnight wanted to respond, but didn't. He shuddered.

Damn. Just like she acted with me before. What an actress!

"You're making a colossal mistake, blowing me off like this," Rachel said. "You might not realize it now, but you don't know what I know, and one day you'll need my help, and you'll be sorry you treated me so badly."

McKnight chuckled. "Thanks for the laugh."

Astalos intercepted McKnight on the way to the Engine platform and handed him a small satchel.

"Marc," he said. "Here's the other equipment you asked for."

McKnight nodded, then slung it over his shoulder without a word.

They lined up on the Engine platform. McKnight and Hatcher helped Rachel and Freddie kneel, then knelt behind them.

"Ready, Doctor Astalos?" Kathy asked.

"Yes. Our time jump will defeat the TEI at the destination as they arrive in 2086. The console is yours, Kathy."

He stepped away, allowing her to take his place there. "Good luck, Major. And you, too, Lieutenant Hatcher."

Kathy sat at the console and picked up the travel checklist.

"Do you have your beacons, Travelers?" Trevor asked.

McKnight and Hatcher nodded.

"Travelers show they have their beacons," he said, and Kathy made a mark on the checklist.

"Check," she said. "We go in 5... 4... 3... 2... 1... *ZERO*."

The hum from the Engine rose in pitch and volume, and the time bubble formed. Rachel's hair and Hatcher's ponytail floated as the internal windstorm buffeted them. Tiny dust particles in the air inside the light globe lit up and spun. The light grew so bright it was difficult to see the people inside.

The bubble bulged to twice its earlier size and went out with a bang.

"They're off," Kathy said.

Across the Lab, the storage room door banged open and out came General Drake, followed by a dozen enlisted men carrying joysticks and laptops.

Drake looked over his shoulder at them and pointed to the break room tables. "Set up over there," he commanded.

The drone controllers split off and hurried to the tables and set up their workstations. The other two enlisted men ran to the loading dock doors in the back of the Lab.

Drake strode over to the console.

To Kathy, he said, "Did you set it up to switch to that second destination when we're ready?"

"Yes, sir. I have separate programs queued up for each destination."

"Okay, and in the second position, the orientation of the drones when they land will be 180 degrees from the original position, pivoted around the ELF-100?"

"Yes, sir."

"Excellent," Drake said. "Let's get started."

To the men at the tables, he shouted, "Let's get those damned drones in here."

The soldiers opened the loading dock doors, and ten LF-50 drones flew in with a deafening buzz. The men lined them up in front of the Time Engines in pairs. Once in place, the drones hovered without motion, the sound of their propellers reduced to a whisper.

"Kathy, how fast can we send them out?" Drake asked.

"No faster than ten seconds, sir, it takes a little time for the Engine to cycle back up."

"Not optimal," he said. "But it'll have to do."

He walked over to the drone controllers and stood before them.

"Gentlemen, it's critical we execute perfectly or we lose all drones *and* the battle. After you position over the platform, engage hover mode with sensors up. As soon as they detect weapons, they should engage battle mode and destroy the enemy. Am I understood?"

"Yes, sir!"

"Make me proud. Move the first pair into travel position."

The first two men used their joysticks to position their drones over the Engine platform, then furiously typed on their laptops to set up their programs.

"Go now, Kathy!" Drake commanded.

A time bubble formed almost at once. The Engine hum increased until it rumbled. The bubble bulged, and the drones disappeared with a loud bang.

"Drones away," Trevor called.

"Next pair!" Drake shouted, and the drone controllers moved the second pair of drones into place.

The bubble formed, the Engine roared, and the bubble distended.

BANG!

"Drones away," Trevor called.

"Next pair," Drake shouted. "Switch the deployment location to the secondary position."

"Done, sir," Kathy said, as she executed the second program.

The Engine hum slid up in pitch to near-deafening volume. The time bubble formed and surged, and the drones vanished with a loud crack.

"Drones away," Trevor shouted.

Drake and the team deployed the rest of the drones ten seconds apart.

Trevor saw Drake check his watch.

He's wondering how long it took.

He looked at his own watch.

Three minutes, give or take a few seconds.

He made his way over to General Drake.

"Did we get them there fast enough, sir?"

Drake shrugged.

"I hope so. These LF-50 drones are fast and smart, but they need three or four solid hits on the ELF-100 to bring it down. The ELF-100 only needs one direct hit to kill an LF-50, and it's nearly as fast as they are. We have to flood the zone with LF-50s to kill it. With any luck, Captain Tyler and Lieutenant Wheeler will keep the troops busy until we get all ten drones there. We'll see."

Drake looked at his watch again. "The battle's probably already over. We'll know what happened in a few minutes."

CHAPTER 51

Tuesday, December 6th, 2061 — 1:45pm — Target Hill, Sandia
Mountains, New Mexico

Wheeler checked the time again.

1:45 pm. Time to move.

He peeked around the edge of the bush. He didn't see anyone on patrol.

I hope the General knows what he is doing.

When the LF-50 drones appeared on the hill, that big-assed ELF-100 drone would have an easy time popping them out of the sky. Coming out of the time bubble, there would be a tiny delay before they could attack, but the ELF-100 would open fire as soon as the bubble appeared.

And what help are we bringing?

While the LF-50 drones appeared in front of the troops and got destroyed, he and Tyler were attacking from both sides, but not far enough back.

We should flank them, not attack their front.

It felt like suicide, but he resolved to follow orders, even if they made little sense. The General was counting on him.

He screwed the silencer onto the barrel of his weapon. Once the battle started, he wouldn't need it, but he didn't want to give himself away in the meantime.

Wheeler crawled back to the position he reached during the night. It took him ten minutes to crawl up those thirty feet without attracting attention.

He looked up the hill. When the battle started, he would run up the slope and start shooting.

He thought of Tyler.

By the time I reach the top of the hill, I'll be sweating like a pig. What about Tyler? He's just recovering from being shot.

A sentry appeared, not forty feet from him. The man was likely on his last patrol before joining the others for the ambush.

Gunfire! It's started.

Tyler aimed his weapon and shot the sentry.

One down.

He stood and sprinted for the top of the hill.

The last hundred feet were steep, and Wheeler's lungs were burning like fire long before he reached the top.

The gunfire sounded distant. When he crested the hill, he understood why.

Drake was a genius. Instead of jumping the drones onto the center of the hilltop, he jumped them into the air, a hundred feet above and behind the troop emplacement.

Of course. Drones fly. They didn't need to jump onto the hill.

The FTS troopers compensated for the rear attack by abandoning their foxholes and dashing to the other side of the sandbags.

Energized by Drake's tactic, Wheeler broke into a run toward what was now the enemy's rear.

He watched as the massive ELF-100 drone lifted off and turned to face the two LF-50s. The LF-50s split left and right, forcing the ELF-100 to choose one to engage. It moved after the LF-50 on the right, and the other immediately navigated in behind, firing away at its backside.

Out of the corner of his eye, he saw a trooper go down. He glanced to his right and saw Tyler running toward the enemy's rear.

Two.

The fallen trooper's foxhole mate whipped around and saw Tyler. Before he could get his weapon up, Wheeler killed him.

Three.

An explosion pulled his attention away from the troops. The ELF-100 had killed the LF-50 on the right.

At the same time, two more drones materialized in the air where the first two appeared. They fired several bursts at the troops, then disengaged and swarmed around the ELF-100.

The three LF-50s were outmatched, but they were holding their own with the big ELF-100.

Wheeler felt a heavy surge of static electricity.

Two more drones appeared, but this time they materialized in the middle of the hilltop and opened fire on the troops before the bubble dissipated.

One drone turned toward Wheeler and trained its gun on him. Wheeler stopped running, whipped off his helmet, and turned to face it.

God, I hope the Doc is right about their facial recognition.

It was only a second, but it seemed like an eternity. The drone redirected its gun at the troops and sped off.

Another explosion. The ELF-100 killed another LF-50. The remaining two LF-50s swarmed around the big drone. They scored hits, but its armor was too thick. Within seconds, it killed another LF-50.

Only one drone was still engaged, but then two new LF-50s materialized and killed two more troopers.

Down to three, the ELF-100 controller and two others.

Tyler killed the ELF-100 controller, but the drone was on automatic and kept fighting. The two new LF-50s rushed to engage the ELF-100 as it killed the last of the first four drones.

The remaining troopers turned their fire on Tyler, but Wheeler pinned them down with covering fire.

Tyler dropped a grenade underneath the ELF-100 console and dove out of the foxhole. He curled up into a ball behind a small mound of dirt.

Two more LF-50 drones materialized on the hilltop. They immediately veered off to engage the ELF-100.

Tyler's grenade blew the ELF-100 console to scrap metal. One of the LF-50s got caught in the blast, careened over the side of the hill, and crashed.

With its console smashed, the ELF-100 got a spike of signals it couldn't process and became erratic. It slowed to a hover as it struggled to interpret the garbled signals from the destroyed console.

All three remaining LF-100s swung around behind and below it to focus their fire on the underside.

The ELF-100 wobbled, then its two left fans stopped. Deprived of enough lift to keep it stationary, it listed to the left, slid past the edge of the hill and lost altitude. The LF-50s followed it down the slope until it crashed.

Tyler leapt up and swung his weapon around, looking for another target.

One of the remaining troopers rose behind him and fired. He missed, and Wheeler shot him. The last trooper surrendered to them. Tyler disarmed the prisoner and pulled him toward Wheeler.

The surviving LF-50 drones returned to the top of the hill and formed up. Wheeler and Tyler watched as the drones disappeared — recalled by Kathy.

Wheeler glanced at Tyler and smiled. Without a word, Tyler and Wheeler engaged their return beacons.

Against overwhelming odds, they prevailed. Target Hill was taken.

CHAPTER 52

Friday, December 6th, 2086 — 4:00pm — FTS Time Engine Lab, Alexandria, Virginia

McKnight felt the windstorm inside the bubble as they landed. With any luck, they'd achieve surprise.

He hoped Number Four would be there to supervise the operation to get Rachel and Freddie back.

McKnight tried to see through the brilliant light of the time globe. There were several figures near the Engine, one of which looked like he might be Number Four.

When the bubble dissipated, he saw he was right.

We surprised them!

Number Four was the first to realize the travelers were not his people. He ran for the door.

Hatcher fired a burst at the ceiling, and Number Four dived to the floor. She dashed over and dragged him to his feet as the Engine support team ran for the door.

McKnight glanced around the room.

I count two time Engines.

Hatcher poked Number Four hard in the back with her weapon and glanced at McKnight. "More will be coming," she said.

McKnight made eye contact with the man she held. "Number Four, I presume?"

The man tried unsuccessfully to shrug off Hatcher's grasp.

"I don't know what you're talking about," he said. "I'm Oliver Stagne, special advisor to the President of the United States."

"Have it your way," McKnight said. He ordered Freddie down on the floor and pulled Rachel in front of him.

The door burst open and a dozen troopers flooded the room, weapons up and ready.

Hatcher wrapped her arm around Stagne's neck and held her weapon in the small of his back.

"Out of the room!" she shouted. "Out or he's dead!"

The troopers didn't move.

Hatcher thrust her weapon into Stagne's spine.

"Do what she says," Stagne said. "Now!"

Slowly, the troopers lowered their weapons, then retreated through the door.

Keeping Stagne between her and the door, Hatcher dragged him back to stand with Rachel and McKnight.

McKnight drew his sidearm and pressed up against Rachel's temple. She squirmed, and he tightened his grip on her.

"Be still and live," he whispered in her ear.

To Stagne, he said, "Anyone else comes through that door, Rachel is dead. Got that?" he said.

Stagne nodded. He managed a small smile and said, "Okay, okay. Stay calm. We can work out a deal."

"Only if you can produce Megan," McKnight said. "Can you do that? Otherwise, I might get angry."

"Don't panic and don't be hasty. She's here, just down the hall."

"I hope you're right," Hatcher whispered. "We didn't come here to play games. I'd prefer to kill you."

A trace of fear crossed Stagne's face, but he managed another smile. "We can avoid bloodshed. Nobody has to die here."

"Here's the deal," McKnight said. "If any more troops come through that door, you and Rachel die. If anything happens to Megan, you both die."

"Let's be reasonable—"

"This is as reasonable as I get. I'm losing my patience, and that's about all I have left. Get Megan in here."

"Okay," Stagne said. "Would you release me, please? Where would I run to?"

McKnight nodded at Hatcher, and she loosened her grip on Stagne. Before she let go, she said, "Don't get creative. I can blow your head off at twenty yards without even trying."

She released him, and he pulled away from her.

He straightened his tie and his jacket. "It might take a few minutes to get her in here."

"I hope not, for your sake," McKnight said. "If I decide you're stringing us along and Megan is dead, I'll kill you both and be done with it. I have nothing else to lose."

"Nor have I," Hatcher said. "Let's get to it."

Stagne held up his arm and pointed at his watch. "Careful what you say. My staff can hear everything that happens in here, and if they think I'm in danger, they'll come in shooting."

"I hope they heard what I said. Just in case, I'll repeat it." He raised his voice. "Any attempt to stop or hinder us will get Mr. Stagne killed."

He looked back at Stagne. "I hope we now understand each other. Call them and have them send Megan in."

"Okay."

Stagne raised his wrist to his mouth and put in the order to release Megan and bring her to the lab.

"Do not let her into the room unless I am standing at least twenty feet from our guests," he shouted. He smiled at McKnight. "You'll forgive me as I take precautions to ensure I do not become your prisoner. If we can't do that, I'm afraid there's no deal."

"I have no use for you," McKnight said, and nodded to Hatcher.

Hatcher moved her weapon so it no longer pointed at Stagne.

"Send her in as quickly as you can," Stagne said to his watch. He raised both of his hands over his head and walked twenty feet away. Then he turned and faced McKnight.

"When Megan is here, I'll send her over and you can send Rachel at the same time."

Hatcher pointed her weapon at Stagne again, and tapped it with her forefinger. "Anything goes bad, mister…You're my first target."

Stagne's smile faded slightly.

The door opened, and Megan stepped through it. She walked tentatively toward them. When she saw McKnight, she broke into a run, but Stagne grabbed her as she passed him and pulled her close. She cried out.

"Calm down, Miss," Stagne said. "You'll be with your man in a moment."

Relief flooded McKnight's mind.

She looks okay. At least they haven't hurt her.

He reminded himself she wasn't free yet.

"Here she is, Major," Stagne said. "Are you ready to trade?"

McKnight pushed Rachel forward. She turned toward McKnight and sighed.

What's she thinking? Is she sorry to go back?

Rachel frowned and then shrugged. She turned back to Stagne.

"Release her from her bonds," Stagne said.

"Not likely," McKnight responded.

"No deal, then," he said and pulled Megan tightly to him. She struggled, but he drew her closer.

"Marc," Megan said, and sobbed. Her face showed utter despair and fear.

"Wait," he said. He drew his knife and cut the nylon restraints from Rachel's wrists.

"Walk slowly, my dear," Stagne said, and released Megan as she pushed away from him.

The two women walked toward each other in silence.

McKnight couldn't see Rachel's face, but Megan could. McKnight saw surprise on Megan's face, and guessed Rachel wasn't giving up so easily. He started forward, but it was too late.

When Megan and Rachel met in the middle, Rachel grabbed Megan, pinned her arms and gripped her throat. Megan struggled, but Rachel swung her between herself and their guns.

"Lieutenant Hatcher," Rachel commanded. "Disarm Major McKnight."

Hatcher spun and pointed her weapon at McKnight's head.

Rachel smiled.

Hatcher stepped behind McKnight and pressed her weapon against the back of his neck. She drew his sidearm from its holster and slung it aside. Then she removed the gun from the back of his waistband. Stepping aside, she tossed it to Rachel.

Rachel released Megan and caught the weapon. She pointed it at McKnight.

Megan ran to his arms.

"I'm so sorry," she said.

"You have nothing to be sorry for, honey."

Freddie got up from the floor and walked over, but Rachel pointed the gun at him and he paused.

"Wait right there," she said.

Hatcher came around to McKnight's side and stared at him. She was looking directly into his eyes and hers looked dead.

They didn't get rid of the programming. She's still under Rachel's control. She's lost to us.

"Number Four, what about me?" Freddie asked, and ventured a step forward.

"What *about* you?" Stagne responded.

Still pointing her pistol at Freddie, Rachel glanced at Stagne. "You don't need him for anything?"

Stagne shook his head. "Nothing I can think of."

"Okay," Rachel said, and shot Freddie in the chest. The impact drove him backward ten feet and he collapsed in a heap. He didn't move again.

Megan screamed and McKnight pulled her tighter.

"Good riddance," Rachel said.

I've got to distract them or we're dead.

"Mr. Stagne? You know Rachel plans to betray you, right?"

Stagne looked at Rachel and said, "Rachel belongs to me. I'd trust her with my life."

Rachel gestured at McKnight with the pistol.

"That's right. I take my orders from Oliver," she said.

"That's not what she told me," McKnight said. "She said she'd use her influence with Joey... that's what she called him... *Joey* Kosar. She plans to have you killed and take your place as his advisor. Didn't she tell you I was already dead? She's proved she can't be trusted."

Stagne jerked his head to Rachel.

"It's not true," she said. "He's just trying to save his own skin."

"If it's not true, how does he know about the Kosar brothers and your relationship to them? What did you tell him?"

Rachel turned toward Hatcher and said, "Lieutenant Hatcher, kill Major McKnight."

Hatcher stiffened and turned back to McKnight. He looked at her.

"Wait," Stagne said. "I'd like to hear what else he has to say."

Hatcher still hesitated. McKnight saw what looked like confusion in her eyes.

"Karen," he said. "No one controls you. You're a Ranger officer."

"Hatcher! I ordered you to *kill* Major McKnight," Rachel said. "You are a soldier of the Movement, a devotee of the Baron Kosar."

Hatcher pointed her weapon at McKnight again, and moved to stand with Rachel.

"I am a soldier of the Movement," she said.

McKnight pushed Megan away from himself.

"Do it!" Rachel shouted.

The hair on McKnight's arm stood up.

Static Electricity!

Hatcher whirled and struck Rachel in the face with her weapon. Rachel went down. Hatcher pulled the pistol from her hand and stood over her.

"I'm an officer in the Army Rangers," she said. "Nobody but my command tells me what to do."

A time bubble appeared. Inside it were two kneeling figures and an LF-50 drone.

Stagne began to back-peddle, but Hatcher beckoned him forward.

"Come here or I'll kill you where you stand."

Stagne stopped and went to her, and she took him by the arm.

The bubble bulged and dissipated. Tyler and Wheeler stood and approached McKnight.

"Sorry we're late, sir," Tyler said. "It took a little longer than we thought."

"No problem, Captain. But let's get the hell out of here. Hatcher, take Rachel and Megan back with you. Captain Tyler, Lieutenant Wheeler and I'll bring up the rear with Number Four. I don't think they'll attack as long as he's alive."

"Wilco, sir," she said.

Noises came from behind the door. Someone cracked it open.

Hatcher fired another burst at the wall over the door. It clicked shut.

"That won't keep them out long," she said. "I'm sure we're outgunned."

"Right," McKnight said. "Get moving, Lieutenant."

"What about you guys, sir?"

"We'll be along in a minute," he said. "Get her safe and take Rachel with you."

Hatcher lifted Rachel and carried her to an open area. Megan knelt beside them and Hatcher triggered her beacon. A bubble formed around them and started spinning.

"What's next, sir?" Wheeler asked. "Now that we have Rachel and the big dog?"

"What's your count, Lieutenant?" McKnight said.

Wheeler glanced around. "I count two, sir."

McKnight pulled the satchel off his shoulder and tossed it to Wheeler. "Me, too. Okay. Get them ready."

The bubble behind them surged, and the women were on their way back to 2036.

Wheeler drew two beacons and a roll of duct tape from the satchel, then slung it over his shoulder. He ran to each time Engine in turn and taped a beacon underneath the console.

"Ready, sir," Wheeler said, and returned to stand with McKnight.

"Captain Tyler, please message Doctor Astalos to recall all beacons."

Tyler touched a button on his phone. "Done, sir."

"Good," McKnight said. "With luck, we'll stop their interference and murdering innocent girls during our time. I hope so, anyway. Right now, I'm more worried about the troops here. They don't want to shoot because of Stagne, but they also don't want to explain why they did nothing to stop us. It's only a matter of time before they realize it, if they haven't already."

The door opened, and troopers flooded in with weapons trained on the four men.

"Let's stay calm, gentlemen," McKnight said. "I know you'd hate to explain how you killed your President's special advisor."

He saw the hesitation in their eyes as three time bubbles formed and started spinning.

"We won't harm him. He's our safe passage insurance. We'll be in touch."

The troopers became more agitated. Two of them started forward with their guns trained on McKnight and Stagne.

One of them spoke. "We can't let them take him. We'll all be court-martialed."

"Are you crazy?" the second trooper shouted.

The first trooper fired at Stagne, but they were gone before the bullet left the barrel.

They fell through the field of stars and found themselves back in the HERO Lab.

Two MPs approached and pulled Stagne away from them. They pulled his arms back behind his back and secured his hands with nylon restraints.

McKnight looked around for Doctor Astalos. After a moment, he found the ancient scientist hovering over Rachel's two time Engines.

He smiled.

I'll bet he can't wait to dive into the new technology. And they can't launch a rescue mission. At least, not right away.

Megan rushed to McKnight's arms.

I got her back. She's safe.

He smiled at Megan through the tears that threatened to flow.

"I'm so sorry," she said. "How could I have been so stupid? They met me at the hospital and told me you were back, but you were injured. When we got in the car, they grabbed me and threw a sack over my head."

"Don't be sorry," he said, as he pulled her closer. "It wasn't your fault. If I had shared more with you, you'd have known better. My fault, my responsibility. I'm sorry, and I promise to keep you in the loop as much as possible, going forward."

She stood on her tiptoes and kissed his cheek.

"I knew you would come for me, no matter what."

"I'm just glad you're okay. I couldn't forgive myself if they'd hurt you because of me."

She buried her face in his chest, and he wrapped his arms around her and closed his eyes.

Rachel was still unconscious. Hatcher knelt beside her as Kathy sprayed antiseptic on the long cut across her nose.

The rest of the team gathered around them.

McKnight heard General Drake's voice and opened his eyes.

Drake was talking to a conference call monitor. He saw that President Taylor was on the conference.

Drake looked unhappy.

What's that about?

CHAPTER 53

Saturday, December 6th, 2036 — 4:48pm — HERO Team Lab, Telegraph Road, Alexandria, Virginia

General Drake got a text invitation to join a web conference with President Wanda Taylor. When he got on the call, she introduced him to the participants. All the other attendees were in the Oval Office with her.

President Taylor, President-elect Wade Harrison, and one other person were on the call — Avery Detweiler, the President's Chief of Staff.

Drake had never met Detweiler, but by all accounts, he was a shrewd political advisor and an excellent manager for the President. The President picked him for those reasons, but also for his background in economics and finance.

Detweiler was short, balding, and wore glasses for reading. He was a stocky man, but moved like an athlete. He stayed fit by getting his exercise along with the President during her daily workout.

"Can you give us a report, General Drake?" President Taylor asked.

"Yes, ma'am. I'm happy to report that we have in custody the individuals who used time travel to murder innocent people and influence the political direction of the country. Unfortunately, they are officials in a future administration of the United States. There's no doubt about their guilt, but we're covering new ground here. There's no precedent for arresting someone from another time and trying them in the present day."

Taylor frowned. "What do you want to do? Take them back?"

"No, ma'am. I want them out of action. I'm just pointing out the issues as I see them."

"Understood. For the record, I didn't ask for your opinion. I just wanted your report."

"Yes, Madam President. I apologize."

"No reason to apologize, Mike. I *do* appreciate your thoughts. But not right now."

She gestured to Harrison. "Wade, what do you think we should do with them?"

President-Elect Harrison shrugged. "I appreciate your predicament, Wanda. It's a sticky wicket. The media will have a field day if we put them on trial—"

"Right," Detweiler interrupted. "I can hear it now, Madam President. 'President Taylor prosecutes politicians for influencing the political direction of the country.' Never mind that they killed a bunch of people. Your popularity numbers would bottom out—"

"Excuse me, Avery," Harrison said. "I was going to say I'd like to confer with my advisors before deciding. But to your point, I'd like them to disappear. They deserve death, but locked up for life seems appropriate. I can't speak to the legality, but it's unprecedented and I'm sure someone would challenge it in court. If anyone ever finds out about it."

Drake shifted in his chair. *I don't think I want to know much about this discussion.*

"Madam President," Detweiler said. "If I may jump in before we say too much. This is not something you should be pondering. Whatever is done with these people, you as President need plausible deniability. Unless you want to prosecute them."

"That would be a lot of uncharted territory, and anything could happen," President Taylor said. "As General Drake and President-Elect Harrison here pointed out. I'm ruling that option out."

"Speaking of me," Drake said. "This conversation may be over my pay grade. Perhaps I should log off?"

"Not yet, Mike," the President said. "There's a method behind my madness."

"Madam President," Detweiler said. "I must insist that you be a little less straightforward about this. You don't want to give a direct order here."

"Yes, of course, Avery. Thanks," she said. "And let's switch subjects for a second. Let's talk about George Kosar."

Drake was very much aware of the threat posed by George Kosar. Most senior military officers understood that Kosar worked for years to undermine the U.S. government. Evidence of his support for radical groups with insurrection goals was irrefutable.

But Kosar was smart enough to separate himself from violations of federal or state law. Nonetheless, he was a thorn in the side of every President for the last thirty years.

"I've asked my Attorney General to look into his activities," Taylor said. "Kosar supports a myriad of subversive causes, but there's no evidence he controls or directs their agendas. There's lots of smoke, but no fire the DOJ can find. But we're convinced he's at the root of much of our country's troubles." She looked at Harrison. "We've had that discussion before, haven't we, Wade?"

"Yes, ma'am, we have," he said. "It's a tough problem. We see a growing threat, but we can't address it until someone breaks a law. But then, the person who gets prosecuted is the fall guy Kosar pushes forward to do the dirty work."

Taylor nodded. "Exactly. It's time to address this." She leaned back in her seat. "It's too bad we didn't know about him fifty years ago when he was just getting started on this path." She smiled at Drake.

Uh-oh. That's not a good idea. She's not thinking this through.

"Madam President," Detweiler said, "you should be cautious here not to say something that you'll regret."

"Yes, I will," she said. "So, let me be clear—"

"Madam President?" Drake said. "May I add a consideration before you go forward?"

Taylor hesitated for a moment. Drake sensed she had already decided and was ready to take action.

"Yes, Mike, but be brief. I want to get ahead of this."

"Yes, ma'am, I will. We know that these people — Rachel Patterson and Oliver Stagne — have done horrible things, but we don't know what else they've done and we might need that information one day."

"Are you kidding?" she said.

"No ma'am, I'm serious. In my opinion, these people deserve the maximum penalty for what they've done, illegal or not. But there may come a time when we'll need their input to figure out how and why something happened. Going forward, I'd hate to lose the option of interviewing them at length about their operations."

Taylor laughed. "Mike, that's exactly why you're still on this call. I want you to be aware of the disposition of these people so you can take appropriate action if or when the need arises."

"Madam President?" Drake said. "There's more. Regarding George Kosar... No one hates what he has done more than me. He's a danger to our freedom and our way of life. But if you're considering grabbing the man fifty years ago—"

"I didn't say that, Mike."

"Yes, ma'am, I know you didn't. But it's my duty to point out the repercussions of that particular option. Mr. Kosar is an oligarch who has built a financial empire that employs thousands and affects tens of thousands. A good percentage of those lives are here in the U.S. If that empire is never built, all those lives will be affected. Some positively, some negatively. The point is, there's no way we can predict the impact of this separate timeline. A huge divergence from the current timeline might be created. Not to mention the fact that the HERO Team is charged with preserving history, not with manipulating it."

"I understand that," she said. "What would you suggest?"

"Thanks for asking, Madam President." Drake said. "There are at least two options that are less impactful on history. You can avoid impacting history by taking Kosar out today. Grab him. Fake a heart attack and spirit him off someplace. At least we avoid impacting all the people in his empire. Someone might pick up the reins and follow him, but they wouldn't have his knowledge and goals."

"That person might be worse than Kosar, General," Harrison said. "We might be worse off."

Drake nodded. "That's a possibility."

"Mike, what about the other option?" Taylor asked.

"The other option might be to go back fifty years and warn Kosar of the consequences. Scare the bastard. You know, something like 'We're here to let you know we can reach out and touch you at any time. Behave yourself or we'll be back to get you.' It might not scare him off completely, but maybe he'll think twice and the threat will be reduced. Now that I think about it, there's another option."

"What's that?" she asked.

"A combination of the two. Disappear Kosar today and warn his successor that we can touch him, too. Maybe that successor will divert the empire's resources in a more productive direction."

"Interesting. Don't you think so, Wade?"

"Yes, Madam President. I'd like to hear more," Harrison said.

"Okay," Taylor said. "We don't have to decide on our course of action yet. Here's what I have to say."

She straightened in her chair and pointed at Detweiler. "Avery, write this down."

"The actions of certain individuals, including George Kosar, Rachel Patterson, and Oliver Stagne, present a clear and present danger to the security of the United States. The United States should take decisive action to mitigate and/or prevent the impact of their actions and take appropriate steps to remove their ability to perform those activities."

She glanced at Harrison.

"I make this statement without consulting with or getting advice from President-Elect Harrison. This action is mine and issued on my sole authority as the President of these United States. End of Statement."

Detweiler jotted down the last few words and smiled. "Nicely done, Madam President."

She smiled back at him. "Thanks, Avery."

"Madam President," Harrison said. "It would have been okay to leave off that last part."

"Yes, Wade. But this way, when you take over the Presidency in a few days, nobody can pin this action on you. If anyone asks, you can just shrug and point out that the previous administration made the decision. I'm good with that. There's no need for you to come into office with baggage like this dragging you down. I've done my eight years and I'm looking forward to relaxing at home and watching the media roast someone else for a change."

She laughed and patted Harrison on the shoulder.

President Taylor turned to the conference call. "Mike?"

"Yes, ma'am?" Drake said.

"Now you have what you need, just in case. I won't know where they are and Wade won't either, but he'll be able to point you in the right direction if something comes up and you need access to them. Fair enough?"

"Yes, ma'am. And may I say I'll miss you when your term is over?"

"Thanks, Mike. Nice to hear. Don't forget to tell your team how grateful their country is for their service, and also me personally."

"I will, Madam President."

"Oh, and one more thing, Mike?"

"Yes, ma'am?"

"In a few weeks, we'll need someone from your team to go back to 2086 and verify the success of our endeavors."

"Yes, ma'am."

"It's nice to have the option to act and look forward to seeing the impact you've made."

"Yes, ma'am, though I'm not sure it's good to know too much about the future."

"I agree, Mike. That's the downside. I may be out of office by then, in which case it'll be Wade who calls you, but we'll want your team to carry out a short mission to assess the result of our actions."

"Thank you, Madam President," Drake said. "We're ready when you need us."

The President smiled and disconnected the call.

Drake sighed.

The HERO Team just moved into the business of changing history to save the future. And we have no idea about how far reaching those changes will be.

CHAPTER 54

Friday, December 19th, 1986 — 4:00pm - Lake Balaton, Hungary

Tyler stood among the vehicles in the parking lot next to Lake Balaton. He had never been to Hungary before. In the distance, out on the lake, he saw the sailboat they were waiting for. It appeared to be coming toward the shore.

This mission was completely outside the HERO Team charter and scope, but they needed a trained time traveler to accompany the U.S. Navy SEALS. With no training, the mission might go south.

Tyler studied the three SEALS with him.

Not likely.

He only knew them by their nicknames — X-Ray, Roscoe, and Bowie. Roscoe was the leader, Tyler decided. He took the lead and the others followed his requests.

They all looked pretty much alike to him. Hair trimmed rather short, full beards, large and strong. Their demeanor was calm. Beneath the relaxed veneer, he knew these were among America's finest and fiercest warriors. Even as an Army Ranger officer, he felt like a 'B' player next to their 'A' game.

They were friendly and respectful of his rank, but they didn't allow themselves to be too familiar with him.

They brought little gear with them to this place in 1986, just a stretcher and concealed sidearms. Roscoe wore a small pouch on his belt. Tyler wasn't sure what their plan was. His own orders were to manage the time travel part — to make sure the SEALS jumped to the right time and returned with their prize.

Tyler glanced back at the lake.

No doubt about it.

The boat was moving toward the shore.

The SEALS were aware. They stopped their idle chatter and prepared to work. They glanced at the boat a few times, but Tyler was convinced they knew exactly where it was and where they needed to be.

The sailboat pulled up to the shoreline. First the man, then the two boys leapt from the boat and began pulling it onto the beach.

Roscoe stood.

"Showtime," he said.

He left the parking lot and walked toward the man and the boys.

X-Ray and Bowie stood and leaned against a car with their backs to the water. Bowie handed Tyler a smartphone.

"What's this?" he asked.

"Check the translate app. I downloaded the Hungarian dictionary to the phone so it'll work in this time."

"You can do that?" Tyler said.

"Sure, anyone can. Here, try this." Bowie produced a distance mic and an earbud on a split cable.

Tyler plugged it into the phone, put the earbud in his ear, and pointed the mic at Roscoe and the man.

The man noticed Roscoe and stepped forward to meet him.

"Helló," he said.

"Helló," Roscoe said. "Are you György Kosar?"

The man seemed wary, but not afraid.

"Yes," he said.

"Come with me, please," Roscoe said. "Now."

"Why?" the man said, holding up his hands in a defensive position.

"Your presence is required." Roscoe said.

X-Ray and Bowie left the parking lot from opposite sides of the car they had been leaning against. They walked toward the water, but there was no doubt they were coming to assist Roscoe. From his vantage point forty feet away, Tyler saw the fear in the man's eyes.

"Who are you?" the man asked.

Roscoe said nothing.

"Are you KGB?" the man asked.

"No," Roscoe said.

Bowie and X-Ray took a position on each side of Kosar. He glanced at both of them, and Tyler saw resignation on his face. He glanced back over his shoulder at the two boys.

"Please don't hurt my children," Kosar said.

"Do not worry. It is only you we require."

Kosar nodded. He turned to the boys. They clung to the sailboat, but their eyes never left their father.

"Stay with the boat," Kosar said to the boys. "I'll be back soon."

He turned back to Roscoe.

"Are you Americans?" he said in English.

"Yes," Roscoe said.

Tyler pulled out the earbud and put the phone in his pocket.

Roscoe beckoned Kosar forward and turned to walk away. The man trembled as he followed Roscoe. X-Ray and Bowie brought up the rear as they walked together back toward Tyler.

"Are you going to kill me?" Kosar asked in English.

"Those are not my orders," Roscoe said.

When they reached the cars, Roscoe directed Kosar to sit on the stretcher.

"You cannot see where we're going," Roscoe said.

He unzipped the pouch on his hip and pulled out a syringe. "This will make you sleep. I promise I will not hurt you or your children."

Fear showed in Kosar's eyes now, but he nodded as Roscoe inserted the needle in his wrist and pushed the plunger. Kosar blinked, then his eyes closed, and they laid him back on the stretcher.

X-Ray secured him with some straps, then he and Bowie picked up the stretcher. They walked away from the shore to a stand of woods.

"Nice country," Roscoe said to Tyler, looking around at their surroundings.

"Yeah," Tyler said.

"That went well," Roscoe said. "We got the job done and didn't have to kill anyone. It could have been lots worse."

"Do you do this kind of thing a lot?" Tyler asked.

Roscoe smiled at him and said, "Hey, what do you say we get the hell out of here?"

I can take a hint.

"You're ready? Okay, let's kneel, lean forward and squeeze that little beacon Kathy gave you. Let's all do it together. Everybody got their beacon out?"

Nods all the way around.

"Okay, on the count of three, we'll squeeze them together. Ready?... Three... Two... one... go!"

The time bubble formed around them. In a few seconds, the bubble bulged, and they disappeared.

CHAPTER 55

Monday, December 22nd, 2036 —2:30pm — The Oval Office, The White House, Washington, DC

Drake sat in the Oval Office with President Taylor, President-Elect Harrison, and Avery Detweiler.

They had an open video link in progress with the HERO Lab at Telegraph Road. In the video, they could see Kathy Wu standing at the Engine console with Trevor George.

"Doctor Wu?" Drake said. "What are we hearing from Major McKnight in 2086?"

"Nothing yet, sir," she said. "We're waiting for him to send a status message."

"Mike, who's on the mission with Major McKnight?" President Taylor asked.

"He took along Captain Tyler, Lieutenant Wheeler and Lieutenant Hatcher. All of them were key players in this whole thing, so he wanted to allow them some closure on it. They were very much eager to go as well."

"That's good, I think," she said. "How long have they been gone?"

Drake looked at his watch.

They're running long. I thought they'd be back by now.

"Six hours. But they have a lot to do if they intend to be thorough. They'll check the news feeds, get online and look up the Movement, and see what conspiracy theory stuff is being talked about on the Net. Kosar started out in Hungary, near Csopak. Later he moved his family to Cuenca, in Ecuador, up in the Andes Mountains. They'll want to run some checks to see if there is any sign of history heading in the same direction Kosar was taking it."

"I see," Taylor said.

Drake said, "Oh, I think something's happening."

"Doctor Wu?" he said to the video link. "What's going on there?"

Kathy stood still — frozen in place.

Drake saw Trevor touch her shoulder. She looked up at him, then at Drake on the video link.

"No, sir," she said. "Their status message asked me to invoke Andromeda protocol."

"Doctor Wu?" he said, his voice rising in volume. "Did you say Andromeda protocol?"

"What's that?" President Taylor asked.

Drake ignored the question. "Doctor Wu, did I hear that correctly? Andromeda Protocol?"

"Yes, sir," she said.

"Okay, acknowledge the status message and start the protocol. We'll stay online here."

"Yes, sir, I'll be right back," Kathy said, and left the Engine console.

"What's going on?" the President asked.

Drake turned toward her. "Can we get a direct line to CDC in Atlanta?"

Taylor paused, looked at Harrison and said, "Yes, of course we can. Avery?"

Detweiler ran to the door and left the office.

"Tell me what's happening," the President said.

Drake leaned forward on the Oval Office couch.

"Andromeda Protocol is what we use when our time travelers venture into an area that they determine to be contaminated. If the team thinks they might bring something back to the Lab, they invoke this protocol and instead they jump to a special chamber in the CDC.

That chamber is hermetically sealed, so everything in the chamber stays in the chamber."

"You mean like they brought back a plague or something?"

Drake shook his head. "We don't know anything except Major McKnight wants the travel team isolated when they return."

The video screen to Telegraph Road beeped.

"General Drake, sir?" Kathy's face appeared on the video link. Drake recognized the background as her office.

"Yes, we're here, Kathy. What's going on?" Drake asked.

"Sir, I can confirm the travel team has jumped from 2086 to the CDC isolation room."

"Are you in contact with them?"

"Yes, sir. But it isn't a strong connection. It's pretty spotty."

"I'll bet my connection is better," Taylor said. "Let's switch." She pressed a button on the table by the sofa.

A voice came through the intercom. "Yes, Madam President?"

"Where's that connection to the CDC I asked for?"

"Just getting it completed, ma'am. Hold on... There! You should be online with Major McKnight, but there's no video link yet. It will appear when it's operational."

"Okay, thanks... Major McKnight, this is Wanda Taylor. Are you there? Can you hear me?"

McKnight's voice sounded hollow through the speaker. "Yes, Madam President. I can hear you."

The video came alive and they saw McKnight and the rest of the team standing in a big room, surrounded by jars and boxes.

"General?" President Taylor said. "Want to take it from here?"

"Yes, Ma'am. Major McKnight, please report," Drake said. "I'm here with the President. What did you find and why are we on Andromeda Protocol?"

McKnight's image on the screen looked haggard and he shook his head.

"Things aren't right, sir. We jumped to Manassas Virginia in 2086 and worked our way into downtown DC…"

"And?"

"We gathered some air samples and some soil samples. We even brought back some plant samples."

"What about the people? Who did you talk to? How did they act?"

"Sir, we didn't find anyone. No one at all."

"No one would talk to you?" the General asked. "Is that what you're saying?"

"No, sir. I mean there's nobody here. We found some human bones here and there. But we haven't found anyone alive. Not one person. We can't detect any radio or TEV broadcasts. No drivers on the roads, nothing. We're afraid some biological agent got out of containment or maybe was released on purpose. That's why I invoked Andromeda, sir. I didn't want to bring something back with us. It might be all gone by now, but we'd rather be safe than sorry."

"Thank you, Major," Drake said. "Stand by for orders."

"Yes, sir."

Drake turned to look at the President. Her face was as pale as her dark skin would allow.

"Something we did?" she said, her voice little more than a croak. "Did I cause this?"

"I don't know, Madam President," Drake said. "But we'll find out."

THE END

A Note from The Author

Thanks for reading this book.

Scan the QR code below for a short note from me.

Cheers and Regards,

Kim

The Marc McKnight Time Travel Adventures
Book 1 – TIME LIMITS
Book 2 – THE TIME TWISTERS
Book 3 – TIME REVOLUTION
Book 4 – TIME PLAGUE

Coming Soon
A new series for Marc McKnight and the HERO Team:

THE TIME PATRIOT

ABOUT THE AUTHOR

Kim Megahee is a writer, musician, and retired computer consultant. He has a degree from the University of Georgia in Mathematics Education. His background includes playing in rock bands, teaching high school, and much experience in computer programming, security, and consulting.

In addition to writing, he enjoys hanging out with his wife, reading, boating on Lake Lanier, playing live music, and socializing with friends. Kim lives in Gainesville, Georgia with his soulmate wife Martha and Leo, the brilliant and stubborn red-headed toy poodle.

www.AuthorKimMegahee.com
Facebook: author.kmega

Made in the USA
Columbia, SC
22 June 2023

18413305R00228